PRAISE I

"I'll read anything Uzma Jalaluddin writes."
—Kate Quinn, *New York Times* bestselling author

"I am such a fan."
—Emily Henry, *New York Times* bestselling author

"A writer who has mastered the art of blending romance with laughter."
—Marissa Stapley, bestselling author

YOURS
FOR
THE
SEASON

OTHER TITLES BY UZMA JALALUDDIN

Ayesha at Last

Hana Khan Carries On

Much Ado About Nada

Three Holidays and a Wedding

Detective Aunty

YOURS FOR THE SEASON

A Novel

UZMA JALALUDDIN

MINDY'S BOOK STUDIO

This is a work of fiction. Names, characters, organizations, places, events, and incidents are either products of the author's imagination or are used fictitiously. Otherwise, any resemblance to actual persons, living or dead, is purely coincidental.

Text copyright © 2025 by Uzma Jalaluddin
All rights reserved.

No part of this book may be reproduced, or stored in a retrieval system, or transmitted in any form or by any means, electronic, mechanical, photocopying, recording, or otherwise, without express written permission of the publisher.

Published by Mindy's Book Studio, New York
www.apub.com

Amazon, the Amazon logo, and Mindy's Book Studio are trademarks of Amazon.com, Inc., or its affiliates.

EU product safety contact:
Amazon Media EU S. à r.l.
38, avenue John F. Kennedy, L-1855 Luxembourg
amazonpublishing-gpsr@amazon.com

ISBN-13: 9781662533044 (hardcover)
ISBN-13: 9781662533037 (paperback)
ISBN-13: 9781662528576 (digital)

Cover design by Kimberly Glyder
Cover image: © AspctStyle, © Ievgenii Meyer,
© NAVINBHAI BABUBHAI PA / Shutterstock

Printed in the United States of America

First edition

*To the ones who accept and love, who learn and grow,
even when it makes them
uncomfortable—this is for you.*

A NOTE FROM MINDY KALING

If you're the kind of person who gets way too emotionally invested in holiday rom-coms, then *Yours for the Season* is the next book for you! It has everything: fake dating, meddling families, cozy small-town vibes, and two people who are clearly into each other but refuse to realize it! Ah, my favorite!

The story follows Sameera and Tom, who accidentally become the subject of a romantic rumor, and instead of shutting it down like normal adults, they're like, "Sure, let's fake a relationship to get everyone off our backs." One thing leads to another, and suddenly they're spending the holidays together in Tom's hometown in Alaska. This kick-starts a chaotic culture clash between Sameera's Muslim family and Tom's Christmas-obsessed one—and of course (and more importantly), lots of kick-your-feet chemistry between our two protagonists. Basically, prepare to grin like an idiot.

Chapter One

Sameera Malik did not hate workplace Christmas parties. They were fun, theoretically, and contained the potential for bonhomie, good cheer, festive joy—all intrinsic to the holiday season. Admittedly, she didn't have much firsthand experience, having grown up in a practicing Muslim household, and though she no longer considered herself observant, Christmas wasn't her thing, either. Still, even she recognized that this particular holiday party was a dud.

This was her third year at Greaves, Hargrave & Bury, a.k.a. the Undertakers, the boutique commercial litigation firm in Atlanta where Sameera worked as an associate lawyer. At twenty-eight, she had been at the midsize firm long enough to know the holiday-party drill: chat, drink (sparkling water with a wedge of lime for her), wander around the spacious foyer that had been converted to a party venue, and try not to think about the pile of work waiting in her office.

Or worry about the rumors circulating faster than this year's signature cranberry-basil cocktail: *Layoffs are coming. Brace yourself.*

There had been rumblings of financial trouble at the firm for the past few months, the result of a stagnating economy, client attrition, fewer big settlements, and shrinking market share. It was the reason this year's party was being held in the office foyer instead of a restaurant or party hall. It was also the reason that instead of a sit-down dinner, they were having a reception with passed appetizers, and why the firm's gift was a fifty-dollar Amazon gift certificate. Last year, even lower-level associates like her had received iPads. Still, the firm had made the most of its stripped-down budget: The spacious foyer had been transformed with twinkle lights and potted poinsettias, while discreet black-clad servers circulated with trays of delicious-looking snacks and drinks. She hadn't eaten anything since breakfast, and accepted a wonton-wrapped samosa with mint-jalapeño chutney. She raised her eyebrows at the burst of flavor before smiling at the cute server. He had warm blue eyes, curly dark-blond hair, and a close fade.

"Having a good night?" Cute Server asked, his voice a deep drawl she felt down to her toes.

"Not really," she admitted, then looked around to make sure none of her colleagues had overheard. "This appetizer is the best part so far."

"I'll let the chef know," he said, smiling warmly. "Can I get you anything else?"

Sameera shook her head, holding up her glass of soda water. "Not unless you have cranberry ginger ale."

Cute Server moved on, and Sameera passed a trio of first-year associates whispering: *Layoffs start in the new year. I heard they're chopping the bottom ten percent of billable hours.*

Sameera gripped her drink tightly and tried to breathe. Lawyers lived and died by their billable hours. Hers had been excellent . . . up until this past year, when her life imploded.

Her friend Bee Whitlock, a paralegal at the firm, sidled up to her. As usual, her oversize glasses dwarfed her small oval face. Paired with her tiny nose, rosebud lips, and petite figure, her glasses helped complete the look of an adorable praying mantis.

In contrast, Sameera was dressed in her uniform of a black skirt and black blazer, a red blouse—her one nod to the season—and her favorite kitten heels. Her straight black hair was pulled back in its usual chignon, her large dark-brown eyes touched with the barest hint of liner, the shimmery glow on her high cheekbones a result of blush and not excitement, her full lips shiny with gloss. Presentable, approachable, pretty—according to the reflection in the brass fixtures surrounding them.

"I saw you flirting with the waitstaff," Bee said out the side of her mouth. "It's nice to see you relax."

"I'm always relaxed," Sameera joked.

"You have the worst poker face. That line on your forehead gives you away every time."

Sameera attempted to smooth her brow, and Bee laughed, linking arms with her. "Did you start your timer yet?"

Bee was a good friend to Sameera. She fed her the latest office gossip, warned her who was throwing a tantrum that day, and advised her on who was the most approachable partner. There was usually distance between associates and paralegals, but the two had become friendly, then started socializing outside of work hours. When Bee had recently become engaged to her longtime boyfriend, Lorenzo, a pediatric nurse, Sameera knew before the rest of the office. Sameera wasn't sure what she would have done without Bee—or her older sister, Nadiya—this past year.

Sameera showed her friend her cell phone, where she had set a timer for sixty minutes, the amount of time she intended to stay at the party. She had a system: An hour was more than enough time to show her face and greet partners and the few clients invited before she slipped back to her office to work.

Bee shook her head. "You're so predictable," she teased.

"I have several hundred hours to make up in the next week," Sameera said. "Blake said—"

"Blake couldn't keep a story straight if he used a ruler," Bee said. "Forget about him. Let's track down that cute cater-waiter you were flirting with and see if he'll show us his snacks." She waggled her eyebrows, and Sameera laughed, her shoulders loosening. Unfortunately, they were up by her ears again a moment later when Blake joined them.

Blake "Chip" Latham II was a fellow third-year associate but acted as if he were already a senior partner. Blake—she refused to call him

Chip—was her workplace nemesis, a self-satisfied walking bag of entitlement who acted as if he were her boss, even though they had started working for the firm at the same time. He was always coming around her office to offer friendly "suggestions": She should wear skirts more often. Had she thought about a brighter shade of lipstick? Could she set him up with one of her "hot Brown" friends? Blake was the worst. He was also the grandson of one of the late named partners—she couldn't remember which one, though he brought it up often enough.

"Samantha and Bertha, what are you gossiping about in the corner, and why is it me?" Blake asked, putting an arm around each woman.

Sameera and Bee immediately wiggled out from his embrace, grimacing. Blake had clearly imbibed more than a few of the signature cocktails. He always made up names for them when he was half drunk.

"It's Sameera, not Samantha. And you know that's not Bee's name," Sameera said primly. Blake grinned at her; she bet he thought he looked adorable. He was wrong.

"That's right, *Belinda*," he said. "Don't worry, your little paralegal job is safe in the new year. Can't say the same for you, Sameera. Remind me, what were your billable hours last quarter?"

Half of what they should have been, just like last quarter, and Blake knew it. Just then, Cute Server tapped Sameera on the shoulder, and she blinked at him in surprise, her retort forgotten. "Pardon me, *Blake*," he said, the barest hint of condemnation in his tone. He turned to Sameera with a smile. "Cranberry ginger ale, and a few more wonton samosas for you and your friend to share," he said, offering her a drink and the snacks to Bee, the ghost of a smile on his handsome face.

Sameera accepted gladly, and Bee whistled as he walked away. "He likes you. You should get his number."

Sameera shook her head and turned back to Blake. "My billable hours are just fine—or they *will* be in the new year. Maybe you should worry about your own."

Blake leaned close, and his breath was sour in her face. "We both know I don't have to worry, *Samantha*."

When he walked away to make nice with one of the named partners, Bee had to remind her not to grind her teeth. Sameera sipped on her cranberry ginger ale instead, the one festive drink she looked forward to every year. But not even the sugary soda could put her in a good mood now.

Blake was right. Not only was he guaranteed a job by the power of nepotism, but he was also considered a future rainmaker because of his many finance-bro friends, who seemed to be in constant need of legal representation. If there was one thing law firms coveted more than billable hours, it was a stream of well-heeled clients with plenty of legal trouble.

Sameera's superpower had always been her work ethic. She had been at the top of the leaderboard in billable hours for the past ten quarters. But for the past six months, she had trailed the pack.

"Are you sure you don't know any obscenely wealthy people in need of commercial litigation advice?" Bee asked.

Sameera shook her head. She had grown up squarely middle class. Her family circle was upwardly mobile, but the only lawyerly services they ever needed were when they were buying a house or making a will—sadly, neither one her specialty.

"What about that Andy Shaikh guy? He's rich as God. If you wrangled that whale, they'd make you a partner," Bee said, and Sameera nearly choked on her drink.

"Not every Brown or Muslim person in Atlanta knows each other," Sameera said. While she did not know Andy Shaikh personally, she definitely knew *of* him. Sometimes described as the Warren Buffett of the trendy-food industry, Andy was a local legend for a chain of bubble tea stores that could now be found in every major city in the country.

"My nonna definitely knows every Italian family in Georgia. These appetizers are *amazing*. Do you think your cater-waiter will bring us more?"

Sameera's phone started to buzz, interrupting Bee's ramble. Somehow, Sameera knew it was her mother before she glanced at the screen. She considered her options: If she sent the call to voicemail, Tahsin would hit redial until her daughter picked up. If she did answer, Sameera would have to sit through a lecture about still being at work—and yes, holiday parties counted as work, in her mother's estimation. Just last week, Tahsin had suggested Sameera give up the mortgage on her one-bedroom condo in Alpharetta and invest in a pull-out couch for her office instead.

It was true that she often didn't return home until after midnight, but that was the life of an associate. Besides, the criticism was ironic coming from her mother. Tahsin had spent the bulk of her career in education—first as an elementary school teacher, then as a principal—and had worked all the time. However, Tahsin had retired last year, and now spent her time alternately bemoaning her lack of grandchildren and dropping unsubtle hints about at least one of her children completing their desi duty by getting married.

"Nadiya should get married first. She's the eldest," Sameera had countered more than once. Studious, serious Nadiya, two years older at thirty, was the golden child who never put a foot wrong. She was currently finishing up her PhD at Oxford, which she had decided to pursue after working at a nonprofit in Pakistan after undergrad. Every time they talked about Nadiya, her parents practically inflated with pride.

Sameera had a feeling their shoulders drooped a little when they spoke of her. But she would not dwell on what she had taken to calling "the lost years" in her mind: the three years in her life when she hadn't spoken to her family at all. Things were better now. Her parents tried hard to mend the breach, and so did Sameera . . . when she could find the time.

By the time this had all gone through her mind, her phone had stopped ringing. After a moment, it started buzzing again, and with a roll of her eyes at Bee, Sameera answered.

"Hi, Mom. I'm at the office. I can't talk now."

"Assalamu alaikum, Sameera. I thought we agreed you would start to leave work early. It's nearly seven. Have you eaten dinner?"

Sameera looked at the wonton samosa in her hand, which definitely counted. "Yup."

"What is that music? Are you at a party? I can barely hear you." Her mother sounded suspicious. Ever since their uneasy reconciliation a few months ago, Tahsin couldn't seem to stop probing Sameera for details about her life. As happy as she was to be back in touch with her family, she had not missed these intrusive questions.

Bee didn't really get it; she had a great relationship with her mother and told her everything, including details about her sex life. If Sameera admitted to even *having* a sex life to her Muslim mother, she was pretty sure they would both spontaneously combust from embarrassment.

Not that she would have much to report lately. She hadn't felt any desire or interest in dating in over a year—not since Hunter had left. She hoped he was lying in a ditch somewhere.

"I'm at the office Christmas party," Sameera said, but her mother again repeated that she couldn't hear her, before telling her to call back once she found a quieter spot. Sameera looked around the crowded foyer, and briefly contemplated taking the elevator to her office on the sixteenth floor before deciding to duck into the kitchen instead.

The abrupt silence as the kitchen door closed behind her felt like a jolt of cold water, and Sameera breathed deeply, staring at her phone. How mad would Tahsin be, on a scale of one to pissed-off-aunty, if she "forgot" to call her back?

"Did you need a refill?"

The question caused Sameera to glance up guiltily. Cute Server stood by a long table, hovering over half a dozen trays of appetizers. He held a piping bag expertly, squeezing a bright-green garnish on the tops of delectable morsels. Her stomach rumbled, betraying her hunger.

"I was going to bring you some more samosas as soon as I was done with this. You and your friend are the only ones who seem to appreciate the spicy stuff," he said.

"Firstly, those aren't real samosas. And if you consider this spicy, you need to try my mother's recipe," Sameera teased.

"I'm always on the hunt for new recipes," Cute Server said. "If you don't need a refill, why did you follow me into the kitchen?"

"I wasn't following you," Sameera said, flushing.

He flashed her another smile, and her stomach gave a traitorous lurch. She was not here to flirt with handsome "cater-waiters," she reminded herself. Still, at his beckoning look, she approached the table and admired his quick, efficient movements.

"What is all this?" she asked.

"Wonton-wrapped faux-samosas," he said with a wink, pointing at the individual trays. "Pickled-shrimp ceviche, vegan-chili shots, and mini sushi burrito bites." His big hands were steady as he plated and sprinkled garnish. He had fine gold hairs on his muscled forearms, Sameera noticed. "That tray is for the staff, if you want to try," he said, pointing, and Sameera was too hungry to refuse. Each appetizer was delicious, an instant burst of unique and familiar flavors.

"Are you helping the chef?" she asked.

"Something like that," he said, concentrating on adorning the mini cakes on a dessert tray with tiny edible flowers. Yet when her phone rang, he clocked her grimace when she glanced down at the screen. "Boyfriend?" he asked.

She shook her head. "Moms always pick the worst time to call."

Cute Server shrugged. "I wouldn't know. My mom died when I was ten, before I got a cell phone."

Sameera stilled. "I'm so sorry."

He nodded toward the phone. "I shouldn't have said anything. My stepmom nags me plenty. Are you going to get that?"

Sameera answered. "Salams. I just found a quiet spot. You'll be happy to hear I'm eating something."

Tahsin's voice sounded aggrieved. "I hope it's not more fried food, *beta*. A growing girl like you needs her vegetables."

She was twenty-eight, but sure. "What did you want to ask me?" she asked, hoping to hurry the conversation along. Her mom always had a question, or a comment, or a passing thought to justify her frequent phone calls. In some ways, it was nice—there had been a time when her mother had stopped calling, and though Sameera had sometimes missed the lack of regular phone harassment, she was also grateful to be back in touch with her family. Whom she loved very much, she reminded herself.

"You're always so busy, *beta*. I wanted to make sure you're still coming to the Eid party this weekend," Tahsin said.

Sameera sighed. She had already confirmed her attendance for the annual Eid al-Adha celebration. Tahsin was calling to double-check, and part of her understood why: Their reconciliation sometimes felt shaky. A flicker of guilt made its way into her voice as she responded. "I said I would be there. You don't need to remind me."

"Which Eid is this?" Cute Server asked. He grinned at Sameera. "You know you're on speaker, right?" His smile was a little crooked at the edges, drawing her attention to his full lips, and the faint suggestion of a dimple. She flushed; her mother was a diligent user of FaceTime.

"Who is that?" Tahsin asked. "I thought you were at a work party."

"The kitchen was the only quiet spot. I'm with my new friend . . ." She raised her eyebrows.

"Tom Cooke, ma'am," he said with perfect Southern manners.

"Your name is Cooke, and you're a server?" Sameera asked.

"My name is Cooke, and I'm the chef, beautiful," he drawled.

Through the screen, Sameera watched her mother inhale sharply. With one careless endearment, Tom Cooke had activated Tahsin's finely tuned and hyperactive relationship radar.

"When did you and Tom meet?" Tahsin asked.

Sameera made a valiant effort not to roll her eyes. "About five minutes ago," she said. Somehow, Tahsin did not seem convinced, and a small ball of tension tightened in her stomach at the sight of her mother's pinched, suspicious face. Would Tahsin ever give her the benefit of the doubt, or had she lost her trust forever?

Not that you deserve to be trusted, an insidious voice mocked. *Not after you spent most of the last ten years lying to them.*

Thankfully, Tom wasn't tuned into her dark thoughts. "So, which Eid is it?" Tom asked again, friendly blue eyes fixed on Sameera. "The hungry one or the other one?"

She laughed; clearly, he had a Muslim friend in his life. "The other one."

"And they're both called 'Eid' because . . ."

"To confuse white people, of course," Sameera said, grinning impishly.

Tom's soft chuckle was silk over her skin, and Sameera felt again the flicker of something, an unexpected fizzle of attraction. She focused on her screen, where her mother had moved from suspicion to worry. Damn FaceTime.

"*Beta*, you said you would be honest with us. How long have you and Tom been dating?" Tahsin's voice was tinny on the phone, and Sameera tried not to sigh. Of course her mother would think any flirtatious male within a mile of her daughter was her secret boyfriend. Not that she could blame her.

"I should get back to the party," Sameera said, not even bothering to reply. She felt her face prickle with embarrassment and couldn't look at Tom.

"Come early to the party, *beta*," Tahsin said. "Very nice to meet you, Tom Cooke, caterer. And Sameera, you should go home. You work too much."

"I can't leave. They'll notice," Sameera protested.

"Your boss doesn't even know your name," her mother countered.

"The partners don't remember anyone's name; it's an intimidation tactic," Sameera said.

"What do you think, Tom Cooke?" Tahsin asked.

Tom's voice was an amused drawl. "In my experience, ma'am, lawyers never much care what the caterer thinks."

Sameera smiled, and on the phone, her mother's expression softened. They quickly exchanged salams, and she turned to leave before turning back.

"I'm sorry about that. My mom gets suspicious every time a man looks twice at me. Brown girl problems."

Tom shrugged. "Then she must be constantly on high alert. I know I couldn't stop staring." He winked, and Sameera shook her head, amused.

"You're a terrible flirt," she said.

"It must be working, because you're still here," he shot back, crossing his arms to show off those impressive forearms. He flexed, and her eyes lingered before making their way back to his face. He was smirking.

"You should add green chili to your fake samosas," she said.

"That's a quick way to get fired. Not everyone can handle the heat," he replied.

"I can," she said. Tom's eyes darkened, and suddenly, she didn't think they were talking about fried snacks anymore. She really shouldn't be here, trading suggestive remarks with this cute, witty stranger.

The kitchen door flung open, and a trio of black-clad waitstaff entered, their cheerful chatter shattering the moment. Tom straightened, professional mask smoothly slotting into place.

"If there's nothing else, miss?" he asked. Sameera shook her head and left the kitchen.

Despite her protestations to her mother, Sameera returned to the party but with little enthusiasm. She was tired, and exceptional food notwithstanding, Sameera longed to change into her flannel pajamas and crawl into bed. The thought of returning to her office to complete more work in—she checked the timer on her phone—twenty-three minutes made her feel tired. Maybe her mom was right, and she should just call it a night.

Except she needed to keep working. She had a plan—if she could put in twelve to fourteen hours every day until January 1, she might keep her job, inshallah. She tacked on the Muslim exhortation automatically. As the sole nonobservant member of a practicing Muslim family, she found that the term still felt natural. She had always appreciated the versatility of "inshallah," which translated to "God willing" but could also be applied to any number of situations: *Inshallah, we'll meet for lunch one day*, as in *We probably never will*, all the way to *Inshallah, I'll win the lottery, so I can finally finish paying off the thousands of dollars of debt my loser ex-boyfriend saddled me with before skipping town*. To use a random example. See? Versatile.

Bee sidled up to her and reached for the appetizers in her hands. "What took you so long? Blake just invited me to a private after-party." She shuddered.

"Tahsin thinks I'm hiding another secret boyfriend from the family," she said.

"Ooh, who's the lucky guy?" Bee asked.

"Tom Cooke. You might know him as the cute server, but he is actually the caterer."

Bee's eyes widened as she examined the appetizer in her hand. "*Yes, Chef.*" She snapped her fingers. "Wait a minute. I know that name. I thought he looked familiar." She fumbled for her phone, pulling up Instagram and scrolling until she found his account. "*Cooke with Tom*! Look, he's got nearly two million followers, and he's even bigger on TikTok. His fusion cooking series went viral recently."

Sameera watched a video as Bee talked, and her heart lurched when she recognized the familiar warm blue eyes, those forearms and capable hands rinsing lentils for soup, then dressing a fattoush salad. She started another video. His guest host looked familiar, too.

"That's why I was thinking of Andy Shaikh!" Bee said. "He's Tom's best friend or something. I just watched this video in the bathroom before the party. Lor thinks I have a crush," she said, referring to Lorenzo, her fiancé. "Which I totally do." Bee giggled.

"How nice for Tom to have rich friends," Sameera muttered. A quick glance at her phone let her know that though she still had another fifteen minutes on her timer, it was definitely time to leave. She had several more files to look over tonight, and likely wouldn't get to bed until well into the early-morning hours. But what other choice did she have? Sameera couldn't afford to lose this job, not if she wanted to pay off the debt Hunter had left her with, and not if she wanted to continue to live on her own. Moving back home was not an option, no matter how much she loved her family. Too much had happened between them.

With a final lingering glance at Tom's face on Bee's phone, Sameera left.

Chapter Two

Sameera ended up working a few hours at the office before taking her work home. She got to bed close to 3:00 a.m. The next few nights were the same, which was not unusual. Long days in the office and a few hurried take-out meals, followed by long nights at home catching up on her pile of never-ending work, felt routine now. Her mother's criticism about her workaholism was justified, but Sameera wouldn't know what to do without the familiar grind. When Saturday rolled around, she barely had enough time to change into a navy-blue salwar kameez with silver embroidery around the neck and sleeves, fluffing her hair loose and applying a rose-pink lipstick before popping into the grocery store for a box of sad-looking macarons and rushing to her parents' home in Brookhaven, nearly an hour late.

Unlike most desi families, her parents started their parties exactly on time—in this case, at noon—which was why Sameera had to park the next street over and pick her way through double-parked cars in front of her parents' two-story home on a quiet cul-de-sac. The white clapboard Colonial was set back from the street, and her parents had decorated for Eid with twinkly green and red fairy lights around the windows. Their neighbors must have wondered why the Malik family had put up Christmas lights, not realizing the second Eid festival fell in December this year, too. A cheery wood cutout spray-painted gold greeted Sameera: *Eid Mubarak!*

She knocked and waited. After a few minutes, she knocked again, then decided to try the door. It was unlocked, and she made a note to talk to her little brother, Esa, who routinely forgot to flip the dead bolt.

Inside, the party had already begun, and delicious smells emanated from the kitchen, her favorite room in the house. Sameera had skipped breakfast and lunch in her hurry to finish a brief before leaving for the party, and her stomach rumbled.

"Salams, Mom. The door was unlocked again. I brought macarons. Did you make samosas . . ." She trailed off.

A stranger was in her kitchen. Correction: not a stranger.

Tom Cooke stood sentry before her mother's Wolf range, wearing Tahsin's favorite pink apron, the one her sister Nadiya and Sameera had bought her as a joke years ago: *Desis do it better.*

"Do *what?*" Tahsin had asked upon unwrapping her gift, whereupon both Sameera and Nadiya had descended into uncontrollable giggles.

It looked good on Tom, Sameera thought wildly. The apron emphasized his slim waist and broad shoulders, though it did nothing to explain his presence. Tom half waved, looking a little self-conscious.

"What are you doing here?" she asked. Was she dreaming? It was embarrassing how many times her work-addled mind had drifted toward Tom Cooke in the days since they had met, usually as she tried to fall asleep. Despite Bee's needling, she had yet to follow him online; she had *some* pride.

"Learning how to make authentic samosas," Tom said. "You look pretty in that outfit. I have something similar at home. A gift from my buddy when his cousin got married. Though I think I was only included in the wedding party because they wanted a discount on catering." He grinned at her.

She was officially hallucinating; that was the only explanation. She discreetly pinched herself. *Ow!*

"Are you okay? I brought you some cranberry ginger ale in case you needed a pick-me-up." Tom twinkled at her, and she wanted to yell at him to stop being so *charming* and explain why he had moved from her guilty daydreams and straight into her mother's kitchen. Then a thought stopped her cold: This was Tahsin's doing. She didn't know how or why, but Tom's presence here today had her mother's machinations written all over it.

"What did my mother tell you? Did she talk to you about Hunter?" Sameera demanded, and his eyes widened.

Tahsin bustled into the kitchen. "You're late, *beta*," she said. Her mother was a diminutive woman, just like Sameera, standing barely five foot two, but unlike her daughter, she didn't try to hide the fact by wearing heels. She was dressed in a bright-turquoise salwar kameez with red embroidery around the neck and sleeves, paired with a discreet gold necklace and matching earrings embedded with semiprecious gemstones. Her makeup had been applied with a light touch, highlighting her smooth brown skin, and her hair was tied up in its habitual bun.

"It's your fault for starting your parties on time," Sameera said, hugging her mother and inhaling Tahsin's signature scent, a mixture of Clinique Happy and garam masala. "It's unnatural."

"Everyone knows our rule: 'Come early, come hungry,'" Tahsin said, smiling at her daughter. "Tom beat you here. How lucky for us that he had a last-minute cancellation and agreed to help with catering. Though I assumed you would drive down together." The look Tahsin threw Tom made the back of Sameera's neck prickle. Surely she didn't believe they were actually an item?

"The pleasure is all mine," Tom said. "I've already learned so much. Your mom is an amazing cook, Sameera."

Sameera reached for the samosas beside the stove. The explosion of flavors and heat as she crunched into the flaky pastry made her moan a little. "Perfect as usual, Mom," she said.

"Tom made that batch," Tahsin said with a fond smile. "He's a quick study. For a gora," she added before disappearing into the dining room with a stack of napkins.

"Let me guess: 'Gora' means 'white guy,'" Tom said.

"You never answered my question. Why are you here?" she countered.

"I needed your mom's samosa recipe." Off her skeptical glance, Tom shrugged. "Tahsin called me a few days ago and asked me to cater her Eid party."

"You can't call her Tahsin," Sameera said, appalled. "She's a Brown aunty. It's Tahsin Aunty, or Mrs. Malik. How did she get your number?"

"I'm online. That's how people book me," Tom said, watching her carefully. "Are you okay? I can leave if my presence is making you uncomfortable."

"No, it's fine. I'm fine. I'm just a little thrown, that's all." Sameera passed a hand over her head, where a dull headache was starting. She could really use a coffee—or better yet, a gallon of chai, the extra-sweet kind her mother made. "My parents . . . my mom has a tendency to jump to conclusions and interfere in my life."

"I think Mrs. Malik just needed a caterer," Tom said calmly.

"Or maybe she thought I was hiding another boyfriend from the family and wanted to check you out," Sameera countered. "For instance," she added weakly.

Tom's eyebrows were at his hairline now; she should probably stop talking.

"Never mind. Pretend I didn't say anything," Sameera said, blushing bright red. "These samosas really are amazing." She reached for two more and stuffed them in her mouth, more to stop herself from speaking further. Bee was going to laugh so hard when she shared this story with her later.

"I tried out a few different fillings," Tom said, watching her eat with appreciation. "There's Hakka chili chicken, Korean barbecue, and jalapeño paneer." He pointed to three trays.

Esa, dressed in a brown salwar with embroidery around the starched collar, wandered into the kitchen and nodded at his older sister. As usual, Sameera greeted him with a forced heartiness that made her inwardly cringe. "Hey, kiddo, nice suit," she said too loudly. "Are you hungry? There are samosas. And, um, macarons."

Esa only stared at her, and she tried to fight against a wave of guilt. Esa was fifteen years old now, a sophomore in high school, and only a few years older than she had been when he was born. She remembered how five-year-old Esa had cried for days when she left for college, his excitement whenever she came home to visit, how eager he had been for her attention, how he used to talk to her nonstop.

Then she had stopped coming home, and when she finally saw him again, after three years of tense silence, she barely recognized her baby brother—the carefree twelve-year-old boy he had been the last time they'd met replaced by an intense teenager who towered over her, a coolness in his eyes, as if he didn't quite trust her not to disappear on him again.

"I ate already," Esa said now. He turned to Tom and was about to nod politely when he did a double take. "*Cooke with Tom!*" her brother said in a different voice. "I follow you!"

The men dapped, Esa nearly levitating with excitement, while Sameera looked on enviously.

"I've got a channel on YouTube, too, but only have, like, fifty subscribers. How did you grow your audience? What's the 'secret sauce' to going viral?" Esa grinned at his joke.

"I didn't know you had a YouTube channel," Sameera said. "What is it? I want to subscribe, too."

"You wouldn't like it. It's fun," Esa said, not even looking at her.

Tom threw her a sympathetic glance before answering Esa. "Honestly, I got lucky. A few of my chef friends shared my stuff, and the audience grew steadily." He glanced over at Sameera. "Your sister is the real superstar. She's a cool lawyer."

Esa barely glanced at his sister. "How often do you do paid partnerships? Are you going to retire from catering and create content full-time? You have to tell me what Andy Shaikh is really like."

"Andy is an acquired taste, but I consider him my brother," Tom said with a smile. "I've known the guy since undergrad. We were roommates at Georgia Tech."

"Say wallahi," Esa said, eyes shining with excitement.

"It's true. I knew Andy before he became *the* Andy Shaikh. Though, unlike him, I never finished college. I dropped out during my third year," Tom said.

Esa held out his hand for a high five, which Tom returned reluctantly. "Not sure I'd recommend that path," he added. "My dad cut me off. Didn't talk to me for a whole year."

Esa looked from Sameera to Tom. "You two have so much in common. Though Sameera was the one who cut us off."

"It wasn't like that," Sameera said, embarrassed.

Her brother shrugged. "That's what it felt like to me."

There was an awkward beat of silence, and Tom cleared his throat. "I've got a bit of time. If you like, we can film a video together now," he offered Esa, and her little brother's eyes lit up.

"Really? That would be awesome! Afterward, can you introduce me to Andy?"

"Not a chance," Tom said, laughing.

Within minutes they were ready: Tom propped his phone up using a few books, and Esa's oversize ring light provided flattering illumination. She watched, bemused, as Tom and Esa immediately started to riff, joking and teasing, and then Tom pulled her into the conversation.

"We're making my friend Sameera's favorite snack: samosas. I think it's my new favorite, too."

"I'm surprised. The first time I met you, Tom, you were making samosas all wrong," she joked. Surprise and delight flared in Tom's eyes at her banter, warming her. Had he assumed she would freeze in front of the camera or play the silent sidekick? If so, it was fun to surprise him.

"I don't know about that. No one else complained," he said, playing along.

She pretended to think. "I wonder why. Maybe because I was the only desi girl in that crowd?"

Tom laughed, accepting her point. "In my defense, wonton wrappings make a great samosa shell, and they're easy to find in the grocery store."

Sameera put a hand on her heart and faked a look of outrage. "Tom Cooke, nobody gets into the samosa game because it's *easy*. Real desi cooking is not for the faint of heart."

Tom grinned at her. "What do you think of my second attempt?"

She considered, then shot a sly smile at the camera. "From a rating of one to ten, with ten being aunty level, and one being those faux-samosas you made last time, I'd give these . . ." She reached out and took a bite of the jalapeño-paneer samosa, chewing thoughtfully. "A seven."

Tom made a face at the camera. "You're supposed to help me get more customers, Sameera. Not damn me with faint praise."

"Seventy percent is passable," she corrected. "And that's only because your pastry is on point. Flaky and homemade, just like Mom intended."

Tom laughed and turned to face the camera. "While I go work on my recipe, Esa, why don't you share your handle with our viewers so they can give you a follow?"

Her brother happily took over, and Sameera made a mental note to check out Esa's channel when she got home that night.

Off-screen, Tom sidled closer to Sameera and murmured, "You said my samosas were amazing."

"Which is why I want to keep them to myself," Sameera shot back, smiling.

Tom chuckled. "You're a natural on camera. Have you considered making content?"

Sameera shook her head. "I've got my hands full with my job. Besides, I don't have any particular talent. Not like you."

Tom seemed about to say something, but Esa had finished recording and was nearly vibrating with excitement. Tom took the phone from him and posted the video without editing, calling it a "candid," while Sameera polished off a few more samosas—she was stealing all the Hakka ones—just as Tahsin bustled inside the kitchen.

"Come say salam to Ali Uncle and Khurshid Aunty. They brought their son to meet you. Amin is in wealth management, thirty-five years old, and recently divorced." Tahsin looked meaningfully between Sameera and Tom. "Unless there is some reason you would rather not?"

Sameera thought quickly. "Let me go check on Dad first." She fled.

Naveed Malik was exactly where Sameera knew he would be—hiding in the basement. Her mother was an extrovert who thrived on the energy of others, her father, an introvert who enjoyed his wife's energy but also needed quiet time to recharge, which he usually did in their basement. Here, he read, listened to his extensive collection of old movie scores, and puttered about with his latest hobby. After retiring two years ago as head of neurosurgery at Emory, Naveed had proceeded to try out a succession of retirement hobbies, from learning how to crochet and volunteering at the mosque to trying his hand at carpentry. He had most recently become obsessed with assembling intricate Japanese Gundam models. Sameera wasn't sure how long this hobby would last; she and Nadiya had a bet going, and her money was on three months.

After hugging her father, she admired his latest purchase, a Bandai Spirits model, and made small talk about their holiday plans. Tahsin wanted to declutter the basement (which they both understood as code for clearing out Naveed's abandoned projects), and they might have a few friends over on Christmas Day. Though her family didn't celebrate, they took advantage of the time off to visit family, travel, and catch up with friends; it was a much-needed reset for everyone.

"Your mother was very impressed by your new friend's cooking," Naveed said, clearing his throat and not meeting her eyes. Not him, too, Sameera thought.

"It's not what you think, Dad," she said firmly.

"Even if it were, I hope you can be open with us. We want to be part of your life, *beta*. Leave the past in the past. I know Hunter hurt you deeply, but we *learn* from our mistakes; we don't repeat them."

Her father's words, more than her mother's obvious actions, filled her eyes with tears, which she discreetly brushed away. The reminder of those lonely years without her family was painful, complicated by feelings of shame, fear, and panic, which she definitely did not want to sift through right now. She changed the subject. "Mom invited Khurshid Aunty's son. She wants to introduce me."

Naveed snorted. "Everybody knows that boy has a girlfriend. Ali and Khurshid need to grow up and accept it."

Sameera laughed and, feeling braver, went upstairs. Her phone rang, and she answered the FaceTime request with a sigh.

"Mom says you're hiding," her older sister started with no preamble. Nadiya Malik was everything Sameera wasn't—outgoing, dutiful, the life of every party. After distinguishing herself at Cornell University with a brilliant academic and activist record, she had moved to Pakistan to work with an NGO that helped widows and orphans in rural communities, before being admitted to a doctorate program in human rights at Oxford. She wanted to work for the United Nations. Sameera wouldn't be surprised if she ended up being an ambassador or a US senator someday.

The sisters also looked nothing alike. While Sameera was most often described as "cute," with her large dark eyes, warm brown skin, heart-shaped face, and curvy figure, Nadiya was a regulation hottie. Tall and willowy, with large eyes framed by sooty, thick lashes and a creamy, blemish-free complexion paired with full pouting lips in a permanent expression of indifference, she could have had a career as a model. She was also fiercely loyal, blunt to the point of tactless, and the only family member Sameera had stayed in touch with during her "lost years." Sameera adored her.

Nadiya was clearly not at home; her beautiful curly, dark hair was covered by a hijab securely tied around her head. She had started wearing hijab during her time in Pakistan, another testament to her independent spirit, as none of the women in their family wore the head covering.

"I hear you brought an inappropriate dessert to the party," Nadiya said now.

"Macarons?" Sameera asked, just as her sister said, "Tom."

Sameera groaned. "Mom overheard me talking to him at the firm Christmas party and jumped to the usual wrong conclusions. He was the caterer. *Nothing* else."

"She's worried about you," Nadiya said. "Mom and Dad can't stop worrying about any of us. It's only gotten worse since they retired. They need to find a hobby. Or, in Dad's case, a hobby that actually sticks."

"You're pretty judgmental for someone with two body piercings you're hiding from your mother," Sameera said.

Her sister made a face. "It's three body piercings, and stop changing the subject. No one is forcing you to marry Wealth Management Guy," Nadiya said, her tone turning brisk. "You know the drill."

"Don't smile. Avoid eye contact. Tell wildly eccentric stories," Sameera said.

"'How exciting to meet Future Husband Number Five!'" Nadiya said in a falsetto, batting her eyes on the screen. "'You'll look great in my basement with the others.'"

Sameera giggled. "'I hope you're okay with living in Antarctica on a research vessel.'"

"Nice one," Nadiya said. "How about: 'Hope you're comfortable living with a reformed cannibal who can't get the taste for human flesh out of their mind.'"

"That's a little dark," Sameera said, laughing. "I miss you. Are you coming home over the holidays?"

"As soon as I crack my thesis, I'll be back," Nadiya said. "But you'll have to face this latest guy on your own. I have total faith you can make him run in the opposite direction."

"I appreciate your confidence in my ability to repulse men," Sameera returned.

"Not all men. About Tom . . ." Nadiya started. "Is there something going on?"

"Not even a little bit," Sameera said solemnly. "This is Mom, up to her usual tricks."

"Well, don't freak out and stop talking to them again. I'm not there to drag you back from the brink," Nadiya said. She was joking, but also not. Sameera knew how much she owed her sister. She only wished she could be honest about what had really happened.

They hung up, and Sameera knew she couldn't delay the inevitable. It was time to meet her parents' guests and their various eligible sons, then stuff her face with her mother's and Tom's delicious food before returning home to work until the wee morning hours. Just another Eid holiday, back in the warm embrace of her family, she thought, smiling to herself.

The truth was, despite the impending awkwardness, she wouldn't trade the experience for anything. Sameera had lived through the opposite—coldness, distance, holidays spent alone and lonely—for too long not to appreciate what she had now. She was back in her family circle and determined to stay, no matter what.

Chapter Three

Wealth Management Guy—Amin—turned out to be very nice. They chatted about the food, the unexpected cold snap in Atlanta, their respective jobs. It was abundantly clear he had zero interest in Sameera and had only shown up to make his parents happy. She could appreciate an obedient desi boy, especially one who posed no threat to her happily single status, and she let her thoughts wander as they talked.

Was she happily single? It had been over a year since Hunter had walked out on her, ending their tumultuous five-year relationship: eleven months and two weeks since she realized the extent of the financial disaster her ex-boyfriend had left her in, and how long it would take to pay back the debt he had accumulated in her name.

The shame of being duped by her intimate partner had been almost worse than the debt. She'd had no idea about any of it—not the credit cards he had opened in her name, not the line of credit he had opened up for both of them, not the secondary lines of credit and predatory payday loans he had resorted to by the end. He had an addiction, he finally confessed after he couldn't hide the truth from her anymore. Online gambling had him in its grasp, and he was sure the next payout was just around the corner. They had shared one last tearful night, with promises on his side to do better, and on hers to stand by him while he got the help he needed.

In the morning, he was gone, leaving only a few items of clothing, and his debt, behind.

Maybe "happily single" wasn't the right term. Perhaps "warily single and emotionally shattered" was more accurate. As she chatted with the amiable Amin, she wondered if he knew about her past. Who was she kidding? Of course he did—everyone knew about the Malik family's wayward daughter.

"So?" Tahsin asked when the two separated after their chat. "Amin is very successful, and his mother said that he is ready to settle down. He had a few lost years, too, just like . . ." She trailed off.

Just like you, Sameera finished silently. "He's not interested, and neither am I," she said firmly.

"Lubna Aunty brought her son, too, but he had to take a call from his second ex-wife. When he comes back, I'll introduce you," Tahsin said.

"Hard pass," Sameera said.

"*Beta*, what's the harm in talking? You've known some of these boys all your life," Tahsin said, trying to keep her voice low, though a few of the guests were already looking their way.

"And if anything was going to happen, it would have already," Sameera said.

Lubna Aunty sidled up to her, dark eyes inquisitive. A skinny woman, her hair covered by a dopatta and dressed in a flashy salwar kameez with matching jewels, she had always reminded Sameera of a heron, with the matching vicious beak.

"So nice to see you again, Sameera," Lubna Aunty started, reaching for a deep-fried pakora and chewing thoughtfully. "Tahsin says you are working very hard at your little job. Don't forget, you need balance in your life for other things, too. My Nabiha just had her third child. I went to visit, and she was so happy. The body just snaps back to normal at that age." Lubna eyed Sameera's waistline. "It will be much harder for you."

Sameera sighed. She had long ago decided not to bother arguing with her mother's friends. They weren't all like Lubna Aunty, thankfully. She excused herself and retreated to the kitchen, deciding she would rather inflame her mother's suspicions by hanging out with Tom than spend more time being passive-aggressively interrogated by mean aunties.

Inside the kitchen, Tom was loading the dishwasher, a pot of water slowly coming to a boil on the stove.

"Are you making chai?" she asked, impressed.

"I was informed there would be a riot if the aunties and uncles didn't get their caffeine fix," he said solemnly. "I googled a recipe."

"Blasphemy. Every family has their own chai recipe. It's the one thing I know how to cook," Sameera said, reaching for a tin with whole cardamom.

"If you think boiling water for tea is cooking, I have some terrible news," he offered. She smiled back, shoving him playfully so she could reach the cinnamon sticks and cloves, plus the special loose-leaf black tea they used for serious chai-brewing. Her hand tingled from where it had come in contact with his firm, rather muscular shoulder. *Is working out a requirement for chefs?* she wondered. They were quiet as she stared into the water and Tom started clearing the food from the kitchen island.

"Does your mom really think we're dating?" Tom asked, breaking the silence.

Sameera stiffened. "Who knows what she thinks."

"That explains a few things," he said thoughtfully. "She asked me what my suit size was, and if there was a family history of diabetes and high blood pressure. Also if I had dated a Muslim girl before."

Sameera was horrified. "She didn't!"

Tom started laughing. "You should see your face!"

She punched his arm—a deceptively firm bicep, she noted—and he rubbed it, pretending it hurt. Again, her hand tingled from the contact, and from the change in his expression, she could tell he felt it, too. There was an immediate attraction that seemed to flare to life anytime they were in the same room.

Which was terrifying.

Maybe she should have taken her chances with Lubna Aunty and her twice-divorced son.

"Can I ask you something?" Tom asked, and Sameera nodded. "You said your mom assumed you were hiding me from them. Have you . . . done that before?"

An image of Hunter flashed through her mind from the first day they met, at a campus party her senior year. He had been kind then, funny and charming and completely into her. Sort of like Tom was now.

"It's a long, boring story, and it doesn't end well," she said.

Tom nodded, and though he seemed intrigued, she appreciated that he didn't push. "Your family is pretty great," he said instead, urging a reluctant smile to her lips. "I cater a lot of events, and I've seen it all. I knew I would like your mom when she shared her samosa recipe, and when your dad tried to convince me to assemble Japanese Gundam robots with him in the basement instead of cooking."

"If you like random eccentricity and vigilante-level competence, you should meet my sister," Sameera said.

"I'd like that," Tom said, smiling. He was so nice, and his eyes were so friendly, and she wanted to run her hands through his short fade. Her heart was doing that strange somersault thing in her chest; she really didn't need this distraction right now. Not until she was out of debt, and sure she wasn't about to be fired from her job. And had figured out how to thaw her reckless, frozen heart.

Her phone pinged with a text from Bee. **Are you and Yes Chef hooking up???**

Sameera immediately flushed and turned away from Tom to reply. **What are you talking about?**

Her friend responded by posting a screenshot of the video Tom had uploaded to his Instagram account, followed by comments below.

Who is that? They have a VIBE. 😳

Tom Cooke has a girlfriend! 🔥

He's dating a brown girl? Tom, I'm available! You can make me samosas any time!

She's not that pretty. He could do better.

Sameera felt faint. Looking over her shoulder, Tom snorted.

"Don't worry about those messages. A by-product of having so many followers. My agent says I should interact more with the commenters, but they seem really happy arguing among themselves."

He seemed unconcerned about the allegations. "This doesn't bother you?" she asked him.

Tom shrugged. "I know it's not true. Are you worried your mom will see the video online and assume we're a couple?"

The idea hadn't even occurred to her until he'd said it, and she tried to dial down her panic. She texted Bee. My mom hired Tom to cater our Eid party. He made a quick video in our kitchen, with me and my brother. Nothing is going on.

Her friend responded instantly: Booo. Stop being a coward and kiss him already!

Sameera quickly flipped her phone over on the counter and turned back to the chai, which was now boiling vigorously. She turned the heat down and poured milk without measuring, more to keep her hands occupied while her brain scrambled.

Her mom didn't spend a lot of time on Instagram, but her friends probably did. What if they came across Tom's video and the comments, and sent them to her mother? She would never hear the end of it. She peeked at Tom, who had finished filling take-out containers for the guests and was now wiping down the counters, his forearms flexing. She forced herself to look away.

"Did you really cut your family off for years, like Esa said?" Tom asked, startling her out of her reverie. She flushed, wishing her little brother had kept his mouth shut.

"Sort of. Did your dad really cut you off because you dropped out of school?" she asked.

"I asked first," Tom said, flashing a smile.

"It's a long, complicated story—" she started.

"With an unhappy ending?" he guessed, finishing her sentence. "You're not much of a talker. I thought that was practically a job requirement for a lawyer."

"Attention to detail and no social life are the only requirements, as far as I can tell," she joked. "Though that might not help me in the new year." Off Tom's questioning look, she explained. "My firm is having some financial difficulties. The rumor is that layoffs are coming, and they're starting with associates who have the lowest billable hours."

He pointed at her, and she nodded. "I had . . . a rough year," she said.

"Is there anything you can do about it now?" he asked, and she was touched by his concern.

"I plan to work through the holidays to catch up on billable hours and make a Hail Mary attempt not to get fired. Not that it will help much," she said.

"Any other options?" he asked.

She shook her head. Then, thinking it over, added, "I could hook a whale."

Tom blinked. "What does that mean?"

"A whale is an important, powerful client, preferably someone with deep pockets and an efficient Business Affairs department that pays promptly. If I could bring one of those clients to the firm, it would stop the axe. I might even get a promotion. The only problem is, I don't know anyone with resources significant enough to save my job. So, if you have need of a commercial litigator in January, give me a call. I have a feeling I'll have a lot of time," she finished glumly.

Tom was giving her a curious look. "I'll keep you in mind," he said. "I have to ask—do you even like working for the Undertakers?"

Sameera nodded. "In my field, they're the best. And I always want to work with the best."

Tahsin walked back inside the kitchen, her eyes narrowed. "Sameera, have you been hiding here the entire time? Lubna Aunty's son is waiting."

"I'm making chai," Sameera said quickly, and her mother sighed.

"*Beta*, I only want to help you settle down. You're working at a prestigious firm. The next step is to find a good partner." Her gaze moved speculatively between Sameera and Tom, but thankfully, she didn't say anything. "Your father and I only want what's best for you."

Sameera exhaled in relief once Tahsin left the kitchen, and traded a weak smile with Tom. She hoped he wouldn't judge her, or worse, pity her. "I bet your parents aren't breathing down your neck, trying to convince you to get married because it's the right time," she said, then remembered he'd told her his mother had died when he was a child. "Your dad and stepmom, I mean."

"Families are complicated. I don't think my dad cares about my love life at all. Or anything else about me, actually. Even before he cut me off, we didn't have the best relationship," Tom said, but his voice grew wistful as he added, "I think about him the most during the holidays. He starts decorating as soon as the Thanksgiving leftovers are put away. My stepmother bakes treats and freezes them, and we used to spend hours picking out our tree. Every year, my dad experiments with a new eggnog recipe. Last time I was home, he tried lime mojito." He made a face. "Not his finest, but we drank it anyway."

"It sounds magical," Sameera said, sighing. She had never celebrated Christmas before, but her family went all out for the two Eid celebrations, especially for the feast after the month of Ramadan. Her father would make delicious snacks for the evening iftar meal throughout the month, while her mother made sure to buy everyone special Eid outfits, new salwar kameez with matching accessories. During those lost years, when she had stopped coming home for Eid and observing Ramadan entirely, she missed the little daily rituals most of all. The memory of that time still felt like an open wound; she had taken to working through both Eids, just to keep her mind occupied, yet the feeling of loss never abated. "Will you be spending Christmas with them this year?"

Tom shook his head, and she was about to ask why not when one of her favorite aunties, Fazila, walked into the kitchen.

"*Beta*, can I have some water?" she asked, holding out a cup. She stared at Tom in frank appraisal while Sameera filled her glass. "You're much more handsome than her last boyfriend," Fazila Aunty remarked, and Sameera wanted to sink into the floor.

"Thank you, ma'am," Tom said, shooting her a grin.

Fazila Aunty accepted the glass from Sameera and patted her arm. "I know we're supposed to pretend Hunter never existed, but at least this time, you found a man who can cook."

"It was at the top of my list," Sameera said. "Right after a good sense of humor and no white-collar financial crimes."

Tom looked at her strangely once Fazila had left. "Have you considered leaning in?"

Sameera was sorting through the pile of take-out containers, wondering if she could take half without getting busted. "Huh?"

"Tell your family we're together, and maybe they'll lay off trying to find you a boyfriend," Tom said. "At least over the holidays."

Sameera straightened, shooting him an incredulous look. "They don't want me to have a boyfriend. My family are observant Muslims—they want me to get married."

To her shock, Tom jokingly got down on one knee. "Will you pretend to marry me?"

Sameera laughed. "Sure thing, weirdo."

He took a selfie of the two of them smiling into the camera and shared the picture with her.

"Just so you know it's an option," he said, and she shook her head. Tom was a shameless flirt—but she was enjoying the attention. It felt nice, and easy. Not much had felt easy, lately.

Sameera left her parents' Eid party with a stack of food, and maybe a new friend. Not a bad haul for one afternoon.

Chapter Four

Sameera had her office door firmly closed to dissuade visitors on Monday, but she shouldn't have bothered. Blake bounded inside first thing to regale her with stories about his weekend exploits, and then slyly rub in the fact that yet another of his friends would be sending business to the firm. He ended by once again needling her about her billable hours before offering to put in a good word with the partners when the time came for her exit interview.

"I'll write you a stellar reference, don't worry," he offered. She deserved a cookie for not throwing something at his big dumb head.

Which was why when someone knocked on the door fifteen minutes later, she growled at them to go away.

"But I have coffee!" Bee said, and Sameera opened the door.

"I thought you were Blake," she said, and her friend wrinkled her nose.

"Yuck. I'm here to talk about you, not our office nemesis." Bee handed her a coffee and settled down on the padded white chair in front of Sameera's desk. "I know you have a lot of work, so quickly, tell me what happened at your parents' house."

Sameera had already filled Bee in somewhat, and now shared the remaining details. Her friend gasped in all the appropriate places, and when they got to Tom's fake marriage proposal, she clasped a hand to her mouth.

"I knew it! He wants you," Bee squealed. "Please tell me you went home with him."

Sameera threw her friend a withering look. "I went home *by myself* and worked for six hours straight."

Bee blew a raspberry and gave her a thumbs-down. "No fun."

"I'll have fun if I still have a job in the new year. Or if I lose my job and have nothing to live for. Whatever happens first." Sameera leaned back in her desk and sipped on her too-sweet vanilla latte. She hoped the caffeine and sugar boost would keep her awake.

"Would it be the worst thing if you had to leave the Undertakers?" Bee asked. "You'd never have to talk to Blake again."

"Happy days," Sameera said. "Except that it took me months to find this job. I still owe thousands of dollars on various credit cards, and my mortgage broker made it clear I have no flexibility if I miss a payment. I'll have to sell the condo, and move in with *you*."

Sameera kept her other reason to herself—that sometimes, it felt like her tenacity, persistence, and work ethic was a double-edged sword. Her job and career was so demanding, had required so much effort, sweat, and tears over the years, that losing it now was unthinkable. If she wasn't an associate at the Undertakers, who was she? Nobody.

"You're welcome anytime, babe," Bee said staunchly. "Stop changing the subject. You should have gone home with Tom. You deserve to enjoy mutual orgasms with a talented hottie. I bet he knows his way around . . . the kitchen." Bee waggled her eyebrows.

"Please stop," Sameera said, laughing.

But when her phone pinged later that afternoon with a message from Tom, she couldn't ignore the swoop of happiness at the distraction.

Are you free for dinner tonight? he wrote.

She stared at the text. Had Bee somehow manifested this message with her joke about mutual orgasms? Her friend would claim this was a clear indication of his interest. Or was this more of a "let's be friends" sort of invitation? Not that it mattered—she didn't have the time or space in her life for a romantic entanglement, even if Tom was a particularly attractive prospect. She responded, careful to keep her tone light.

> I have to work, remember? Billable hours, job in trouble, imminent ruin ahead.

His response surprised her. *I've been thinking about your situation. I think I can help.*

Sameera's eyes lingered over that last sentence. *I think I can help.* She couldn't imagine how he could. But she had been working nonstop for weeks, and nothing seemed to make a dent in her situation. Sometimes she felt like a cartoon character sticking her fingers and toes into the wall of a dam, trying to stop the river from overwhelming her, but knowing it was too little, too late.

What if he really could help, in some way? After all, she had met Tom twice now, and each time he had made things better—first by taking care of her at the firm's holiday party, and then by supporting her at her parents' house. As if in a dream, her fingers typed back: I can meet for an hour.

Tom replied with a thumbs-up, and she instantly started to panic. What had she done? She couldn't afford an hour to meet Tom, which would turn into two hours including transit. She was already so deep underwater, any time away from her files would feel wasted. She quickly drafted a message to get out of their meeting: Something just came up, I have so much work to do, I have no life and nothing to look forward to and I wish I could but I really shouldn't . . .

As she stared at the rambling message on her phone, finger hovering over the send button, her thoughts drifted to annoying Lubna Aunty's words from the Eid party: *Don't forget, you need balance in your life for other things, too.*

Her mother's friend was a judgmental old bat, but that didn't make her wrong about everything. Something had made Tom reach out. Something had made her accept his random invitation. Maybe instead of pushing whatever this was away, it was time to "lean in," as he had suggested in her mother's kitchen.

She could spare one or two hours to satisfy her curiosity. With any luck, Tom would try to sell her on an MLM scheme, which would dissipate any lingering attraction. She turned back to her files.

When she parked near the address he had texted, Sameera stared at herself in the rearview mirror. She looked pale, her hair limp, dark shadows below her eyes, lips tight with fatigue and worry. She started to reach for a lipstick but stopped herself just in time; this wasn't a date, and she didn't want to give Tom—or herself—any ideas. It wasn't until she locked her car and started walking toward a large white building that she realized he had invited her to dinner inside . . . an industrial unit? A side door opened, and Tom motioned for her to join him. He must have been watching for her from the window. She took a deep breath and set a timer on her phone for fifty minutes. After that, she would leave. Maybe earlier if possible.

"Did you invite me here to murder me?" she asked, only half joking.

"To cook for you, actually," he said, lips quirking. "I rent out a commercial kitchen."

Sameera followed Tom into a large, airy space that contained a massive range, a walk-in freezer, a line of deep sinks, and two of the biggest refrigerators she had ever seen. The place smelled delicious, and she perched on a barstool by the center island.

"I followed the Malik family chai recipe," he said, handing her a small cup with a frothy, perfectly golden-brown liquid. She sipped cautiously. It was heavenly.

"I hope you like biryani. The Eid party really inspired me to work on my South Asian cooking skills," Tom said, reaching into a large oven to withdraw a black aluminum roaster.

He lifted the lid, and Sameera inhaled the aroma of saffron and ghee and spices. Her mother had tried to teach her to make biryani, but it never turned out like this, a fragrant mixture of baked marinated meat and delicately seasoned basmati rice.

"If my mom saw this, she would marry us off immediately," Sameera blurted, instantly regretting her words. She wasn't here to flirt with Tom. She glanced at her phone—forty-three minutes left on her timer. Her nervousness mounted.

"It's funny you should say that," Tom said, and when she looked up at him, she noticed he had a faint flush across his cheekbones.

"Is this . . . bribery biryani?" she asked, mock-affronted.

"How long have you been holding on to that zinger?" Tom asked.

"Ever since you told me you made biryani," Sameera admitted, her light tone masking another spike in anxiety. Seriously, what was she doing flirting with Tom and accepting his excellent food? She had billable hours to make up, and a complicated life to manage. And yet, here she was, on what felt a lot like a first date. The thought made her palms sweat.

Sameera hadn't been on a first date since law school. After Hunter left, she couldn't bring herself to "get out there," as Bee put it (and as her friend had encouraged more than once). It felt too vulnerable, and she wasn't sure how she could trust anyone—or her own judgment—again.

Once her plate was clean, and there was less than thirty minutes on the timer, she lay her palms flat on the table. "Are you going to tell me the real reason I'm here?"

The flush returned to Tom's cheeks, and he rubbed the back of his head, a gesture she recognized from when they had hung out at her parents' home. Why was he nervous?

"I want to start off by saying, I would have asked you to dinner no matter what."

Something softened at these words, but then her mind caught up with her ears. What did Tom mean by "no matter what"? She nodded at him to continue.

"My agent, Lauren, called me today. I started working with her after my cooking videos went viral last year. She told me I had more attention from that candid video I shot at your house than any others in the past six months," Tom said. There was a pleading look in his eyes she didn't quite understand.

"Do you want to ask my mom if you could use her kitchen again?" Sameera asked. Tahsin would definitely think they were an item if her supposed not-boyfriend wanted to come over again. Another secret, shameful part of her deflated at the request; he wasn't interested in her after all.

"Nothing like that," Tom said, reassuring. "I started the online thing as a hobby, mostly. It's taken off in a way I didn't anticipate. Half of my gigs are a result of those videos, including the one from your firm. Apparently, the Undertakers' managing partner is a fan." He smiled faintly.

Now Sameera was confused. If he didn't want to use her mother's kitchen again, what did he want? She had no idea where he was going with this. "Congratulations," she said, careful to keep her voice neutral.

The red tinge was back on his cheekbones, serving to highlight how defined they were, damn him. "I'm sure you didn't read the rest of the comments on our video. I know how busy you are with your work."

Actually, she had read all the comments. She had even creeped on his account following the Eid lunch and watched the video they had shot in Tahsin's kitchen a dozen times, sometimes focusing on how happy her brother looked, and other times pausing to stare at Tom's friendly, handsome face.

She had also noted that while Tom posted videos regularly, their video was the first one he had made with a woman. No wonder his followers had inundated him with questions about his personal life. Sameera felt a prickling at the back of her neck.

Tom took a deep breath. "You said you were worried about being shown the door in the new year. That the only thing that could save your job was if you hooked a whale."

Her heart started beating fast, as if her body knew somehow that something momentous was about to happen. "Is this the part where you reveal that you're a secret billionaire?" she joked.

Tom threw her a faint smile. "Not me, no. But I could introduce you to my friend Andy Shaikh. I happen to know he's looking for new legal representation. If I recommend you, he'll listen."

Sameera stilled. People like Andy Shaikh were hard to meet. She imagined a lot of people asked Tom to introduce them to his very wealthy friend; her brother had done it just the other day, and had been turned down immediately. Yet here Tom was, dangling his connection to Andy in front of her like bait.

She had googled Andy Shaikh after the Eid party, of course, and now knew more than she wanted about the wealthy tycoon and local legend. She knew from a profile in *Business Insider*, for example, that while Andy was a born-and-raised Atlantan, his father was born in Pakistan, while his mother's roots were Scottish and English. She also knew that after graduating from Georgia Tech, he had founded a chain of boba and chai tea shops, which had proved to be so wildly popular they were now a feature in every major city across the country. But sweet drinks were just a starting point—Andy had quickly started buying up commercial real estate, dabbling in rezoning construction, and building scalable communities. He was considered a local Muslim success story—the profile had mentioned he accompanied his father to Friday jumah prayers weekly. If she could convince someone like Andy to hire her firm, her job would be saved for sure. Every lawyer knew there was nothing more enticing than the prospect of an untapped market, which was exactly what Andy Shaikh represented.

If she could just get in front of Andy, if she could pitch him on her firm, there might be a chance . . . She narrowed her eyes at Tom. "What do you want in return?"

He took a deep breath. "How would you feel about filming cooking videos with me?"

Caution made her hesitate. "That's it?"

Tom closed his eyes. "I also want to pretend that we're in a relationship. For the camera only, of course," he hurried to reassure her. "I'll introduce you to Andy no matter what your answer."

The expression in his blue eyes was pleading, and part of her wanted to sign on the dotted line, while another part of her, the same part that had been hurt so badly by Hunter, hit the emergency brake.

"I don't understand," Sameera said. "Do you want to be an influencer that badly? Why do you need a showmance to entice your viewers?" She couldn't bring herself to ask the other question: *Why me?* Tom Cooke was cute and kind and he cooked like a dream. If he wanted some arm candy to help him film videos, she was sure thousands of women would be happy to oblige.

As if reading her mind, Tom answered, "On-camera chemistry is a hard thing to find, believe me. I've always been a bit of a lone wolf. That's why I'm a caterer, not a restaurateur. I like to do things on my own. To be in control."

He met her gaze, and a frisson of something that felt a lot like desire bolted through Sameera, taking her by surprise. She liked being in control, too. He went on.

"But when we were filming, it all felt . . . effortless," he said softly.

He was right—their banter had felt real, because it *was* real. She had enjoyed poking fun at Tom, teasing and flirting. It felt so natural in the moment, she had almost forgotten they were on camera. The commenters had picked up on their effortless vibe right away. It was what had so captivated his audience. The internet loved a good ship.

She refocused on the conversation. "What do you get out of this?" she asked bluntly.

"I don't want to open a restaurant. I don't want to be an influencer. However, my agent has been talking to a few television producers . . ." He trailed off. "I'm in the running to lead a new cooking show on the Food Network. Or rather, I was, until my viewership numbers started dropping."

Sameera sat back. She felt on firmer ground, now that she had all the facts. "Your agent thinks I can help get those numbers up and land you that television gig," she said, and he nodded, looking hopeful for the first time since they'd started this conversation. She tried not to notice the adorable way his hair curled by his brow, or the warm heat of his gaze . . . and its effect on her. She swallowed and tried to think through his proposal logically, like a lawyer. Which she was. A very, very tired, overworked, and worried lawyer. If Tom could get her in front of Andy, that might solve one of her problems. And what he was asking in exchange was a small price to pay. Filming a few videos with him, giving into the flirty banter she so enjoyed, would be no hardship. In fact, it might be . . . fun. Something she hadn't had a lot of recently.

"If we're going to do this, we need some ground rules," she said, trying for a businesslike tone. She ticked off the rules on her fingers. "We fake date for a month, maybe two. In that time, we can film three videos together."

"Ten videos," Tom countered. Something in his posture had relaxed once she started talking about rules. "I upload twice a week."

She scoffed. "I already have a demanding job. I can't add another. Five videos," she said firmly.

"Six," he said, eyes glinting with playful energy.

"Deal." They smiled at each other, and Sameera continued, "We need an end date. I should know if I still have a job by the end of January, and the novelty of seeing us together should have worn off by then for your viewers. Can you pretend to be madly in love with me for that long?"

"I think I can manage," Tom said, eyes steady on hers. She tamped down her immediate reaction to these words, the flare of awareness low in her belly. *This is business, not pleasure,* she reminded herself.

"Great. You can dump me at the start of February," she continued. "I'll be heartbroken, naturally. There will be pictures of you in my apartment with devil horns and scratched-out eyes."

Tom shook his head. "Beautiful, no one is going to believe that *I* dumped *you*."

She wanted to ask him why, but knew that would make it seem like she was fishing for compliments. Which she definitely was. "Fine. I'll break up with you; feel free to use pictures of me as target practice."

"Never," Tom said gallantly. "I'm a gentleman. I'll take my heartbreak like a man—by shitposting and crying into my perfect samosas."

This time, Sameera didn't hold back her grin. She stuck out her hand. "It's a deal."

He took her hand in his, carefully. His hand was warm and large, completely enveloping her own. She was the first to let go, and her hand felt different than it had a moment ago. She looked up to find Tom's eyes soft and warm on her face.

"Sameera middle name unknown Malik, will you be my fake girlfriend?" he asked softly.

"My middle name is Ayla, and yes," she said, suddenly feeling shy.

"Tom Tipper Cooke," he said.

They shot their first video that night. Tom had already taken footage from cooking the biryani, but he wanted to include Sameera's reaction to the food. True to form, she mocked him for a few minutes, questioning his technique, ridiculing his spice cabinet, then declared her mother's biryani to be much better than his dish, and that furthermore, Hyderabadi biryani was the best, just to cause a ruckus on the comments thread. Nothing got desi people going quite like an argument about which country, region, or state made the best biryani.

After he pressed post, he texted Andy and showed her his response:

Andy, I found your new favorite lawyer. Her name is Sameera Malik, and she's a commercial litigator at Greaves, Hargrave & Bury.

Three dots, and then Andy Shaikh—*the* Andy Shaikh—wrote back. Sure thing. Is she coming to Alaska, too?

Sameera looked at Tom. "Alaska?"

Chapter Five

Despite his Southern charm and manners, Sameera was shocked to learn that Tom Cooke wasn't a native of Georgia. Rather, he hailed from a small town in Alaska, where he had spent his formative years before moving south for college, he explained while serving dessert—a delicate French vanilla ice cream. Sameera was so intrigued, she turned off her timer and listened as Tom explained that he didn't return home after dropping out of college. But after catering her family's Eid party, he realized how much he missed home—and decided to accept his family's invitation to visit over the holidays.

As an added bonus, his agent was excited by the idea of Tom making content in a new locale; his viewers would love a glimpse inside the small town where he had grown up, and where his family had lived for generations. He would be gone for only a few days, and when he returned, they would start filming. Tom promised to put in a good word with Andy while in Alaska, and Sameera could pitch him right after Christmas.

They shook on it, and Sameera felt more hopeful than she had in months. Maybe there was hope for her after all.

The next day she went to work, a lightness to her steps and a big smile for everyone—even Blake. She had a plan, and it was a good one. With any luck, Sameera would return to work in the new year hauling a whale behind her. It made the long hours in her office fly by, and her good mood lasted until she returned to her condo late that night to find her parents waiting in the lobby, tension and worry clear on their faces.

Her heart sank, even as she pasted a big smile on her face and welcomed them to her unit. The one thing she had forgotten to account for was her parents' suspicious nature. Her family never visited, not without calling ahead. They weren't back to the casual drop-in phase of their relationship yet. She had a feeling she was well and truly cooked.

As if anticipating her worry, Naveed hastened to reassure her. "Everyone is fine, *beta*." He turned to his wife. "I told you we would only worry her by showing up like this."

They settled on the cream leather couch in front of the television. Her condo was small but homey; she was grateful she had been able to keep it after Hunter left. For a few weeks following his abrupt departure, she was sure she would have to sell the condo to pay off the debts he had left behind, but she managed to cobble together a patchwork of loans and keep her home. Yet another reason why she needed to impress Andy Shaikh—she couldn't afford to get behind on her payments.

Her mother began with no preamble, and Sameera was relieved. She hated small talk almost as much as Tahsin did. "Lubna Aunty sent me the video you made with Tom," Tahsin said. "I *knew* you were dating. You never want to cook biryani with me."

Sameera exhaled slowly. Of course, she had known something like this was likely to happen. Her parents had a lot of friends, and many of those friends loved nothing more than to gossip. She wouldn't be surprised if Lubna Aunty had a Google Alert for all the black-sheep children of her closest friends.

But Sameera had a plan: She was going to tell her parents the truth. While she had agreed to fake date for the internet, as she'd explained to Tom last night, she was done lying about her relationships—or, in this case, the lack of—to her family. Tom had agreed, of course.

"Tom and I are not together, and we're not dating," Sameera said now. "I would have told you if we were."

There was a long, awkward moment of silence as her parents looked at each other; clearly, they didn't believe her. She inwardly cursed. Of course they didn't—she had kept Hunter a secret from them for years. He wasn't the first boyfriend she had hidden from them, either. It made sense that they would suspect Tom was merely the latest. Her parents' lack of trust hurt; she thought they had made progress in the months since their reconciliation.

Hunter had never liked her family. This had worked out in her favor, because she hadn't been eager to introduce them. By the time he had shown up in her life, she was used to code-switching between dutiful, Brown Muslim daughter in front of her family to the nonobservant person who just wanted to fit in with everyone else. It felt normal to keep the two parts of her life separate.

He hadn't understood why she needed to visit home so frequently or why her parents called so often. Hunter's family did not figure into his future plans at all, while she knew she would return to Georgia to settle after law school. He had followed her after finishing his MBA, and at first, Sameera was flattered by this loyalty. She later realized he had become used to having her do things for him, from finding them an apartment to doing all the grocery shopping, organizing their social plans, and making sure their bills were paid once they'd moved in together. All while she had kept their relationship a secret from her family.

"He's acting like he's your bored husband already," Nadiya had once complained. Her sister was the only one in her family who knew about Hunter from the start. Sameera always confided in her older sister, and though Nadiya didn't always approve of her secret relationships, she had never betrayed her trust.

Hunter's influence had been subtle. Every time she made plans to visit her parents, he would make comments. *That outfit doesn't look comfortable,* he would say when she reached for the new salwar kameez her mother had bought for her. Or: *You never return from your parents' place in a good mood.* He would complain the food she brought home was too spicy or made him sick. He would point out that his parents never expected him to call or visit as often as hers did, that they were content their son was living his life. One time, after a minor argument over yet another invitation to a family party, he called her parents "controlling." *Why are you the only one who makes an effort, Sameera?*

She would push back, argue that he didn't understand the dynamics of a first-generation South Asian immigrant family, that he preferred to view everything from his own perspective.

But over time, his words were a slow poison.

She started visiting her parents less often, which became easier as she grew busier with work. She returned their calls after longer and longer intervals. When her parents finally found out about Hunter and confronted her about her deception, the blowup that followed was the worst ever. They hurled accusations and cruel remarks at one another, the eruption of emotions that had been bottled up for years. They questioned her judgment, her competency, even her sanity in choosing a man like Hunter. Both Tahsin and Naveed said Hunter was clearly using her. She shot back that they had never trusted or supported her, that their lack of faith had messed with her sense of self, and she was tired of living according to their impossible expectations.

The fight echoed long after she stormed out of the house, vowing never to return; the estrangement that followed had lasted more than three years. If she were being honest, her father's long silence had rankled the most. In the past, he had played peacemaker, but not this time.

Their frosty cold war ended only when Hunter was no longer in the picture, and after Nadiya forced the issue with an intervention organized at a local café. By then, Sameera missed her family so much, she was ready to swallow her pride and pretend their fight had never happened. Tahsin and Naveed had done the same. But here they were again, immediately jumping into the role of accuser and defense, all because of a harmless social media video.

"*Beta*, we're worried about you," her father said now, and his words brought her back to the present, and the excruciating conversation in her living room. "You're always working. You showed up late to our party, you never seem happy, and you're stressed all the time."

"I'm a lawyer. That's just how we are!" Sameera protested. She didn't want to alarm them by sharing what was really happening at work. That would only add to their worry.

"I understand work is stressful. But you don't need to hide your boyfriend from us as well," Tahsin said. There was a pinch of disapproval around her lips that made Sameera want to shrivel up.

Sameera took a deep breath. It was time for the truth. "Tom and I are not together. We're not dating. We're . . . faking it."

This made her parents blink. "What?"

"It's a fake relationship. Like a showmance?" Off their confused expressions, she explained, "Tom and I are only pretending to be in a relationship. He got a lot of views and comments for the video we filmed at your house over the weekend. He asked me to help him out by filming more videos, and by pretending to be his girlfriend, in return for . . . some help with my job."

"But he's a chef, and you're a lawyer. How could he possibly help you?" Naveed asked.

"I'd rather not say," Sameera said, grasping for straws. If her parents knew about Andy, they would know that she was in danger of losing her job. The last thing she wanted was for them to think her incapable of getting any part of her life right. It was bad enough that they knew she had terrible taste in men. Her only saving grace was she had always been a good student and had landed a prestigious job, as far as they knew. She had some pride.

"Um . . . attorney-client privilege," she added lamely.

Again, her parents exchanged another, longer glance, this time conducting an entire silent conversation. She hated when her parents did that. Finally, her father sighed, and her mother nodded.

The prickling sensation at the back of her neck was the first indication that whatever her parents had just decided wouldn't be good news.

"Then it's settled. We are all going to Alaska to spend the holidays with Tom and his family," Tahsin said.

Chapter Six

"*What?*" Sameera said.

"We bought tickets for everyone," Tahsin explained breezily, as if that were the problem. "Well, not Nadiya." Again, her parents exchanged a loaded look, and Sameera wanted to scream.

"What is happening?" she said. How did her parents know Tom was traveling to Alaska? She had found out only last night.

"We simply wish to meet the man you are seeing," Tahsin said.

"I told you, Tom and I are *not together*," Sameera said.

"We want to be part of your life, *beta*. Even the parts you are ashamed of," Naveed said. Perhaps because the words came from her calm, anxious father instead of her suspicious, prickly mother, Sameera stayed silent. "We can't lose you again, Sameera. I don't think we could stand that."

"When we first found out you were seeing Hunter, it was a shock to learn you had a long-term boyfriend we knew nothing about. We allowed our shock and hurt feelings to ruin our relationship with you," Tahsin said.

Sameera was stunned by her parents' admission. She had no idea they felt this way. So much had been left unsaid during their emotional reconciliation earlier this year. Sameera could recall every moment—her sister's coaxing and nagging over weeks; walking into the café where her parents waited, huddled over two lukewarm black teas; bursting into tears and falling into her mother's arms while her father hovered, wiping his eyes, patting her back. Their mutual apologies and professions of love followed, and it had all felt beautiful, touching, a balm to her soul.

It wasn't until much later, when she was alone in her condo, that Sameera realized that while both she and her parents had resolved to do better, to be better, they hadn't actually discussed what had led to their huge fight in the first place. Hunter, her feelings, their sense of betrayal . . . It was all swept under the rug in the name of family togetherness and solidarity—an unspoken agreement that she now realized had left gaping cracks in their relationship.

Clearly, her parents still didn't trust her judgment—or lack thereof. They still wanted to control her, to insert themselves into her decision-making, to demand that she live according to their expectations. Their lack of trust felt like a slap to the face, sudden and stinging. And here they all were, again.

"When I saw the biryani cooking video, I knew you were hiding something from us," Tahsin continued, the *again* clearly implied. "I knew I had to do something about it this time. I looked up Tom online and discovered he was from Alaska. I checked his social media and sifted through his followers until I found his parents. Then I messaged them."

Sameera stared open-mouthed at her mother. "You *stalked* my fake boyfriend and looked through his millions of followers?"

"I got in touch with my daughter's new boyfriend's family because I was concerned she was in over her head or being taken advantage of," Tahsin corrected. "After all, it has happened before."

Sameera's stomach tightened in response to her mother's allusion to Hunter. Sensing her immediate defensiveness, Tahsin added, "I would do anything for you, *beta*."

Sameera closed her mouth with an audible snap. This was insane. She was in the middle of a bizarro nightmare and would soon wake up, surely.

"Tom's stepmother, Barb, is a lovely woman," Tahsin went on. "When I introduced myself, she immediately recognized you from Tom's video. She agreed that you two seemed to be hiding your relationship, though we couldn't figure out why. We got to talking, and I suspect that your new boyfriend also does not visit his parents as often as they would like. In fact, we seemed to have a lot in common."

"I'll bet. What happened next?" Sameera asked. It was like watching a car crash, yet she couldn't look away.

"I mentioned how much we wanted to visit the beautiful state of Alaska. Barb generously invited us to visit her and Tom's father, Rob. They live in a charming little village called—what was the name, Naveed?" Tahsin said, turning to her husband.

"Bear Paw?" Naveed asked, wrinkling his forehead.

"Wolf Run," Tahsin said, snapping her fingers. "Population: less than two thousand."

Sameera stared at her parents. "You invited yourself over to Tom's family's home? For Christmas? In *Alaska*?" This last came out as a shriek, and her parents winced in unison.

"I would never invite myself where I'm not wanted. Barb extended the invitation, Sameera. Do keep up," Tahsin said. "And you know your father has always wanted to take a cruise to Alaska to see the icebergs."

"This will save me the trouble of planning a trip," Naveed said, as if he could sense his daughter's head was about to explode.

"No," Sameera said flatly. "I'm not flying across the country because you refuse to believe me or trust me. No way."

Naveed placed a gentle hand on his daughter's arm, and the gesture was grounding. "*Beta*, we haven't taken a family trip together in so long. When we told Esa, he was so excited to spend time with your boyfr— with Tom," he amended. "And with you, of course."

She sincerely doubted that, but she also recognized what her father was doing. Frankly, she was amazed he was capable of such a low blow. Naveed and Tahsin knew she was desperate to mend her relationship with Esa. A flare of resentment ignited, and she put her head in her hands. "I have so much work to do," she moaned.

"Your work is unending, and you need a break," Tahsin said in a soothing voice. "Besides, Alaska has the internet. You can work there. We've emailed you the flight information and will see you at the airport."

"This is impossible. I can't leave, not now. I'm in so much trouble at work. You have no idea . . ." Sameera trailed off as her parents stared at her, even more worry and questions clear on their faces. More confirmation that she was keeping secrets, she realized, and quickly changed the subject.

"Does Nadiya know you're kidnapping me and taking me hostage in Alaska?" she asked, hoping to distract them. *I'm in the worst timeline. Wake up, Sameera!*

"It was Nadiya's idea," Tahsin said. "I called her last night. You know she keeps odd hours these days, all that studying for her dissertation. She was happy to take my call," she added pointedly.

This made Sameera pause. What was her sister thinking?

"By the way, did Tom mention whether he was willing to convert to Islam? I don't think his family is religious, anyway," Tahsin said.

"Mom!" Sameera yelled, and her mother shrugged.

"I can ask him when we get to Alaska," Tahsin said, standing up. Sameera was immediately consumed with panic. This trip couldn't happen. Tom would think she was nuts, and her parents complete weirdos. Not to mention *they weren't together.* How could she make Tahsin and Naveed understand?

"Please, it's not too late. Don't do this," Sameera ground out.

Her father paused in tying a scarf around his neck. "Don't shut us out again, Samu," he said. It was the childhood nickname as much as the plea behind his words that silenced her.

That didn't stop Sameera from immediately reaching for her phone the minute the door shut behind her parents. She should call Tom, but he was mid-flight. She dialed her sister instead. Like her mother noted, Nadiya would most likely be awake, even though it was early in the morning in the UK. Surely Nadiya would have some answers for her, or at the very least some sympathy.

Except it turned out she had neither. "You *lied* to me," Nadiya hissed. She was home this time, inside her tiny apartment near Oxford. On FaceTime, her curls streamed down her back while her eyes flashed with anger.

"No, wait, what are you—" Sameera started, but Nadiya cut her off.

"I asked if you and that Tom Cooke person were together. I specifically *asked*, Sameera. You lied to my face! I had to find out from

Mom and Dad about your new boyfriend. After everything you put us through with Hunter, the minute your situation stabilizes, you're back to hiding things from the family again."

"That's not what happened!" Sameera cried. Nadiya was her rock. If she abandoned her now, Sameera wasn't sure what she would do. She had to make her understand. "Tom needed a favor, and he offered to introduce me to—"

"I don't want to hear it," Nadiya said, and the expression on her face made Sameera cold. It went beyond disappointment and dove straight into despair. "I can't do this again. You need to take responsibility for your actions. For once."

"That's not fair," Sameera said.

"What's 'not fair' is trying to console my hysterical mother from thousands of miles away, when she calls me sobbing that my little sister is keeping secrets again!"

Sameera inhaled sharply. This was a gross mischaracterization. Hadn't she tried to mend the breach between her and her parents and Esa? Hadn't she shown up, answered her mother's many phone calls, brought macarons to the Eid party, even sat through Tahsin's inept matchmaking attempts?

Or would they consider her the untrustworthy family screwup forever, no matter what she did? She felt like the girl who cried wolf. Or in her case, the stereotypical desi girl hiding things from her family forever.

"Fix your shit, Sameera," Nadiya said, and then her phone screen went dark. She stared at it for a second, shocked. Her sister had hung up on her.

She texted Bee, knowing her friend typically stayed up late. **I need you.**

Her friend responded immediately. **Leaving now.**

Sameera dropped her phone to the carpet and let herself cry.

Bee came over an hour later, armed with cookie dough—which Sameera hated—and a bar of hazelnut chocolate, which she reached for immediately. By the time Sameera had finished sharing the story, Bee was a quarter of the way through her cookie dough, and there was a thoughtful expression on her face.

"Okay, so, what your mom did was completely manipulative, but it's also sort of . . . sweet?" Bee said. Noticing Sameera's outraged expression, she backpedaled. "You should definitely not get on that plane to Alaska. Who even buys their daughter a ticket to visit her fake boyfriend in . . . Where did you say Tom's family lived?"

"Some place called Wolf Run," Sameera said. Her parents had informed her of the details via email, along with a link to her boarding pass. The flight left in three days. Not that she was going.

Bee nodded. "What are you afraid of here, babe? No one can force you on a plane. Also, 'never turn down a free vacation' is my personal mantra. From what you've shared about your mom, this seems pretty on-brand behavior. Didn't she ground you for an entire summer because you snuck out one night when you were eighteen years old?"

Sameera flushed. She had forgotten she had shared that story with Bee. Her parents had always been strict about things like curfew and had never let her attend parties. These rules never seemed to bother Nadiya, the dutiful, studious daughter, and for the most part, Sameera had toed the line all throughout high school. Then, the weekend before senior prom, one of her friends arranged a small party at her family cabin and begged Sameera to join the overnight trip. Sameera knew her parents would never agree—boys and girls were invited, and she knew there would be plenty of alcohol as well. But she was tired of always missing out, and soon she and her friends would be scattered across the country when they went to their respective colleges. She made arrangements with a friend to cover for her and went on the trip anyway. One night of high school freedom for four years of mostly dutiful obedience felt like a fair trade-off, she had reasoned at the time.

Of course, she got caught—her friend slipped up, and to Sameera's complete mortification, her father had shown up at the cabin in the middle of the night. She would never forget the haunted look on

Naveed's face as he walked through a pile of passed-out teenagers, empty cans of beer and pizza boxes littering the floor, to wake her up. Her father hadn't said a word the entire two-hour car ride home.

Her mother, on the other hand, had ripped into her the moment she'd stepped over the threshold.

It was one of her most painful memories. In addition to Tahsin revoking her driving privileges, her mother had grounded her for the entire summer before college. It had been a relief to leave home for school that fall. Things hadn't really felt the same since. "I guess I'm hurt they don't believe me. I thought we were further along in our reconciliation?"

"I don't think it works like that," Bee said carefully. "From what you told me, you only recently got back in touch with your family. It isn't a straight line from no contact to open communication, you know? I kind of get why they would freak out about this whole Tom thing if you never told them about Hunter. Maybe they thought history was repeating again."

Sameera was quiet, thinking. Bee was right. Her mother was reacting rather than communicating, as usual. The truth was, her family wasn't very good at talking things out.

Perhaps her mother's meltdown and purchase of four plane tickets to Alaska was understandable when viewed through a certain light. The one that painted her as the screwup, the black sheep, the villain.

"I can see you've already decided this is all your fault," Bee said. "Do you want me to agree with whatever you say, or do you want me to tell you the truth?"

"Is there a third option?" Sameera asked, taking another morose bite of her chocolate. It wasn't making her feel better, but at least it had nuts in it.

"There's always a third option, and it's always chocolate, so we've got that covered. Which one, babe? Lorenzo finally agreed to watch that new Prime rom-com, so I've got a small window tonight before he gets sucked into another moody HBO drama tomorrow."

Sameera considered. "Brutal honesty, please," she said.

"Go to Alaska. Maybe you'll find some time, in between staring at icebergs or getting lost in the woods or flirting with Tom, to actually talk to your parents. It's easier sometimes to have the hard conversations when you're outside your comfort zone." Bee smirked. "As an added bonus, once your parents realize there is nothing going on with you and Tom, they will feel so bad, I'll bet they won't even question you the next time you agree to fake date a random hot man." Bee was laughing now, and Sameera threw a pillow at her.

"I hope the movie sucks," she said, but she was smiling.

Bee was already dancing toward the door. "Who cares, so long as the leads get together in the end!"

The friends embraced. "What about work? This is the worst possible time," Sameera said, gripped with a sudden panic.

"It's only four days," Bee said, serious for once. "I'll cover for you, if needed. But you know, the office is a ghost town at this time of year. Plus, you'll have internet, and you can work on the plane." Bee paused, thinking. "Didn't Tom mention that Andy would be in Alaska for the holidays, too?"

The women stared at each other, their minds perfectly in sync. Slowly, a smile blossomed on Sameera's face. This dire situation suddenly had a very large, very wealthy upside. "I'll work on my pitch before I get to Alaska. With any luck, Santa will bring me a whale for Christmas."

Bee cheered, raising her arms in the air. "This will be good for you. Plus, you'll be happy your parents are there if this turns into a *Get Out* situation."

Sameera shook her head. "I'm so glad I called you."

"Don't forget to send a picture when you convince Tom to take his shirt off!"

"I will not be doing that," Sameera said, but her heart felt lighter once her friend left. Maybe this trip wouldn't be the absolute worst. A girl could dream.

Chapter Seven

The trip to Wolf Run now inevitable, Sameera prepared for it like she would a court case: with precision and deliberation. She picked out her warmest clothes, unearthed her small carry-on suitcase, and refused to respond to Tahsin's text messages reminding her to buy winter boots and a hostess gift. She was still angry at her mom, even if Bee had made a lot of sense.

Nadiya still wasn't answering her calls or messages, which was concerning. Sameera and her sister argued and bickered all the time, but this felt different. She composed three different versions of the same long message explaining her situation but couldn't bring herself to press send. The truth was, her showmance agreement with Tom felt silly. A case of stranger than fiction, one her suspicious sister would assume was made up. No, she needed to have this conversation with Nadiya face-to-FaceTime. In the meantime, Nadiya was right about one thing—Sameera had to fix her shit.

At least Tom was on her side. She had called him the day he landed, though his stepmother, Barb, had already informed him about the plan. He was just as annoyed as Sameera, but he also took full responsibility.

"I promise to make this up to you," he said on the phone, concern and worry laced in his voice. "There will be chai on tap, and I promise an unlimited supply of homemade samosas and biryani."

"If you want my family to leave after four days, I suggest you rethink that plan," Sameera joked.

He was silent on the phone. "I nearly passed out when Barb told me what she had done," he admitted. "I think she got excited when your mom reached out. You're not the only one with a complicated relationship with their parents."

"I figured," Sameera said dryly. Another thought occurred to her—had Tom told his family that they weren't actually dating? Maybe they hadn't believed him, either. She was about to ask when his next words distracted her.

"At least you'll be able to pitch Andy sooner, and in person," Tom said. "He's eager to meet you, Sameera."

She had to impress Andy from their very first meeting. Everything was riding on this. "When will he be there?" she asked. She had already started pulling files, drafting a preliminary contract for her firm's services, and preparing a slide deck. Andy wouldn't know what hit him.

Tom made a noncommittal sound. "Hard to say. The superrich really are different from the rest of us. But he said he would be there by Christmas Eve at the latest. He'll hear you out, I promise."

Sameera would have to be satisfied with that, for now. Her focus would be on trying to land Andy as a client for her firm. If she could manage that, this entire trip would be worth it, and her financial problems would disappear. She had already informed her direct supervisor—a senior lawyer in her late forties named Helen—that she would be out of town for a few days for the holidays. She hadn't been able to resist adding that she had a lead on a VIP client. Helen's interest had been piqued. A good sign that her plan would work, because Helen was rarely impressed. This had to go well.

More surprises waited for her at the airport. For one, her parents had not packed light: Four large suitcases and a carry-on each were piled on two luggage carts, in stark contrast with her small carry-on and laptop bag. Tahsin didn't hide her disapproval, and Sameera didn't hide her reaction to her parents' and Esa's travel outfits.

"Why are you wearing Christmas sweaters?" she asked. Her family didn't even celebrate the holidays. When she was seven, she had begged to have a Christmas tree in their living room, with a pile of presents. Instead, she had gotten a long lecture on Muslim holidays.

Her mother was still fixated on Sameera's lack of luggage. "Alaska has *bears*," Tahsin tut-tutted. "And *snow*. How can you be prepared for both with one little bag?"

"I'm sure you'll have enough supplies for all of us, and for Tom's family, too," Sameera shot back. "About your sweaters . . ."

Esa rolled his eyes. "You should be more worried about what they packed in their bags," he said.

Well, that was ominous. She figured her parents' bags, in addition to parkas, hats, mittens, and snow boots, also contained Christmas gifts. Or what her parents considered Christmas gifts. The thought stopped her cold.

It wasn't as if her parents were unfamiliar with the holidays. They had lived in the United States for nearly forty years, and their children had been born here. But for Tahsin and Naveed, the Christmas holidays had always been something that others celebrated. They never sent out holiday cards or hosted Christmas parties; they never decorated the house or bought gifts for their neighbors. Any festive cheer they had was reserved for the two Eid holidays, which had led to more than a few confused neighbors wondering why the Malik family distributed boxes of Indian mithai sweets during random times of the year. Sameera and her siblings had never sat on Santa's knee and told him what they wanted for Christmas; in fact, her parents had told her Santa did not exist, and that furthermore, every gift she received was a result of their hard work and diligent savings.

Which made the holiday sweaters Tahsin and Naveed were wearing seem even stranger now. Her father and mother sported matching red sweaters with one half of a reindeer on each—Naveed had snagged Rudolph's red nose and antlers, while Tahsin got Rudolph's rump and the words *Merry Merry Christmas!* Her brother, meanwhile, had opted for a bright-green-and-yellow sweater with a light-up Christmas tree and a matching Santa hat.

"What do you think?" Naveed asked now.

"Is this a joke? Are you making fun of the holidays?" she demanded.

Disappointment crossed her father's face, and she immediately felt bad. "We thought you would like it, Sameera. Remember how you begged us for a Christmas tree when you were younger?" he said.

She did, and the memory of that, contrasted with her father's silly sweater, felt confusing and infuriating. What could they mean by it? She wasn't a child, distracted by bright lights and tinsel. Then she felt badly for dismissing this attempt to make her happy, however clumsy it was.

Digging inside his carry-on, he pulled out a bright-green abomination. "We even got you one."

She stared distastefully at the itchy-looking sweater, which had a picture of a rosy-cheeked elf holding a giant candy cane. "Thank you," she said slowly. "I'll put it on later."

"If I have to wear this, so do you," Esa grumbled.

Sameera dutifully put the sweater on over her clothes. It was just as itchy and unflattering as she suspected.

"We want to make sure we fit in with Tom and his family," Tahsin said as they walked to the checked luggage drop-off. People passing by stared, though they also gathered more than a few amused smiles. Sameera wanted to disappear. Her family had a tendency to make a spectacle everywhere they went, or that was how it felt to her. Her brother must have felt the same, because his hat was pulled low over his face, and his headphones were cranked so loud, she could hear his angry blasting music from where she walked beside him.

Once seated at their gate, Tahsin squeezed her hand. "You don't need to be nervous. We are looking forward to meeting Tom's family. We even brought them the perfect Christmas gifts. You will see—everything will go smoothly, inshallah."

"Inshallah," Sameera echoed, and tried not to notice how her mother's face brightened at her use of the word.

Their flight was long, nearly ten hours, and she pulled out her laptop as soon as they were in the air. She didn't look up for anything other than to request another cup of coffee from the flight attendant, despite Tahsin urging her to eat. But she was too busy perfecting her pitch to Andy and trying to catch up on work. She also read through the notes she had made on Tom and his family. Research soothed her, and she wanted to know more about her hosts.

Tom's family lived a few miles outside Anchorage. Wolf Run, population 1,786, was a small hamlet, and Tom's father, Robert Cooke, seemed to be a prominent local figure, judging from how often he appeared in the weekly newspaper.

After an interminably long flight, they finally arrived in Anchorage. When they emerged in the arrivals lounge, she spotted Tom immediately. Despite her exhaustion and jet lag, she felt her heart gave a traitorous leap when he smiled at her, quirking an eyebrow at her sweater. She flushed at his amusement. Dressed in faded jeans and a navy-blue cable-knit sweater that emphasized his broad shoulders and bright-blue eyes, he fixed his gaze on hers, though she noticed more than a few passersby throw him appreciative glances. She felt a blush starting, and to distract herself, she took in the trio beside him, who were holding a large banner that read **WELCOME, MALIK FAMILY!!!** Her heart sank.

"Mom, I thought you ordered a car. Or an Uber," Sameera muttered. She needed a shower and a latte, in that order. The last thing she wanted was to make small talk with strangers.

Her mother waved as Tom and his family approached, as if she were greeting family or old friends and not virtual strangers. "Don't be silly, Sameera. Barb offered to pick us up, and I accepted. It was the least they could do, after we came all this way."

"You mean, after you invited yourself to a stranger's house in another state for the holidays?" Sameera said before turning to examine their welcome party.

The tall, bulky white man with thinning blond hair and a handsome, friendly face was clearly Tom's father, Rob Cooke. Beside him stood a petite Black woman who looked to be her mother's age: Tom's stepmother, Barb. Beside them was a boy in his mid-teens, his curly hair left natural, with light-brown skin and dark, curious eyes. With a jolt, she realized she hadn't even asked Tom whether he had siblings.

Luckily, Rob was already performing the introductions. "My lovely wife, Barbara, and our son, Calvin," Rob said before turning to hug Sameera, nearly lifting her off her feet.

"Nice to meet you, Mr. Cooke," Sameera said, suddenly feeling shy.

"Call me Rob," the older man said. He was clearly delighted that Sameera and her family were here, and she relaxed.

"Thank you for picking us up. It's been a long trip," she said now.

"We brought our trucks. Plenty of space for you and . . . your luggage," Barb said.

"Are you moving in?" Rob joked. "Tom won't be happy to hear it."

Sameera caught Tom's wince at his father's words. He caught her looking, and after giving her a quick hug and muttering "I'll explain later," he reached for her bag, as well as Tahsin's large suitcase, before leading the way to the covered parking lot and the promised trucks.

Tom, Sameera, Tahsin, and Barb piled into a white Ford F-150 while Rob, Calvin, Esa, and Naveed climbed into a matching black truck, their luggage piled in the beds. Sameera sat next to Tom in the back seat of the extended cab while her mother and Barb took the front.

"Now, Sameera, you must tell me how you and Tom met. My son keeps insisting you tell the story better. I'll bet it was love at first sight," Barb said in a cheery voice. The look she threw Tom, which Sameera caught in the rearview mirror, was one of exasperated fondness.

"Let's let Sameera settle in before we start the interrogation, Barb," Tom said. "Plenty of time to share that story once we get home."

Sameera startled. "Home?" she asked. She leaned forward to glare at Tahsin. "Mom, you said you made reservations at a hotel." She hoped she didn't sound as desperate as she felt.

Barb laughed, a musical sound. "Nonsense. You'll be staying with us, dear. It's no problem at all."

"But . . . but . . ." Sameera stumbled over her words. Her dream of a single room with a sturdy lock, and a warm shower where she could enjoy a tiny little breakdown, was the only thing that had kept her going. "We wouldn't want to impose," she finished weakly.

"You're our guests. I insist," Barb said firmly.

"Yes, ma'am," Sameera said meekly. "If it's okay with my parents."

"Oh, your mom and I have the details all squared away. We just want the young people to enjoy yourselves while us older folk get to know one another. Isn't that right, Tahsin?" Barb pronounced her mother's name perfectly, and from the beaming smile her mother threw Tom's stepmother, it was clear that they were on their way to becoming fast friends.

Not an alarming development at all.

Sameera threw Tom a panicked look, and he cleared his throat. "I think Sameera might be more comfortable in a hotel, Barb," he said meaningfully.

She nodded eagerly at his words. All she wanted right now was a quiet room of her own, where she could nap, shower, and then do five hours of work on her laptop without being interrupted. Knowing her luck, if they stayed with the Cooke family, she would be stuck sharing a tiny bedroom and bathroom with her parents and Esa.

"There aren't any hotels in Wolf Run, and I'm sure all the bed-and-breakfasts are already full for the holidays. But of course, we want Sameera to be comfortable," Barb started.

Tahsin interjected before Sameera could chime in.

"Nonsense. We're grateful you offered to have us stay in your home," Tahsin said, shooting her daughter a stern look. "Sameera is thrilled, aren't you, *beta*?"

"'Thrilled' doesn't begin to do justice to my feelings," Sameera said, and Tom covered his laugh with a cough. When she caught his eye, he winked at her, reminding her that they were in this together. Strangely, the thought made her feel better, even as she wondered whether Tom had shared that their romance was only for the camera. Surely he had? She resolved to ask him soon. Well, as soon as she dealt with the plastic container full of samosas he now passed her.

"As promised," he said before handing her a thermos filled with chai, still steaming hot.

"I could kiss you," Sameera said, and Barb caught her eye in the rearview mirror, a fond smile playing about her lips.

She shared the fried snack, though her mother waved away the tea, and settled in her seat, admiring the view as she ate. The scenery was stunning. The pictures she had looked up on Google Images hadn't done it justice. Bright-blue clouds and dramatic, snow-capped mountains in the distance entranced her immediately. She could spot small bodies of water, ponds, and tributaries, all frozen over as they drove. The thick forest of evergreens on either side of the near-empty road were blanketed by snow, the contrast stark and beautiful.

They made casual conversation about the flight, and Barb shared her plans for their visit. Sameera half listened to something about Christmas trees, a local market, and Christmas morning brunch. It didn't really matter, as she would opt out of the group activities. She had too much work to do, and her pitch for Andy wasn't quite complete. She was determined to have it ready and memorized before he showed up. If she was very lucky, she might be able to email her boss with good news before Christmas.

Maybe it was good that Barb had so many plans; that way, her family would stay busy, and she wouldn't feel guilty about ditching them after they'd had their much-needed talk.

The conversation soon turned to Tom and his job. "Tom loved to cook when he was younger," Barb said. "Rob can't even manage toast. Which means I'm stuck doing all the holiday baking every year. I hope you'll lend me a hand while you're in town, Tom."

Tom stiffened beside Sameera, but his voice was casual as he answered Barb. "I'm sure you've got everything covered. No pie left unbaked, if I know you."

Barb laughed heartily at this joke, though it wasn't especially funny. Sameera wondered what was really going on.

"Tom and I will be filming a few videos for his social media while we're here," Sameera said brightly. "I'm sure he'll make something delicious to share."

The conversation moved on, but Tom remained strangely quiet. They turned off the main road and Sameera spotted the white pickup truck with Rob, her dad, Esa, and Calvin as they entered what looked like the outer limits of a township. Sure enough, a cheerful, hand-painted sign proclaimed they were about to enter the village of Wolf Run.

Beside her, Tom shifted in his seat, and when she glanced over, she saw that he had a death grip on the door handle. She impulsively reached over and took his hand in hers. A jolt of electricity passed through her at the contact, and she nearly gasped. A static shock? He smiled at her, and her heart started to beat fast. *Maybe a different sort of shock,* she thought. His expression was uncertain; she was sure she looked the same. They were both in uncharted territory, and with a full audience watching their every move. A wave of frustration crawled over her skin, and part of her wanted to demand Barb drive her to the nearest bed-and-breakfast after all. She had been in Alaska for only a few hours and already felt as if she had lost control.

She remembered this feeling from when she was younger and still lived at home. It was strange how quickly she was reduced to that state of mind when she was around her parents: annoyed and impatient, her own needs and desires disregarded as her parents made plans without bothering to consult with her. She hated feeling powerless and backed into a corner.

Barb had slowed down to navigate Wolf Run's small main street, and Sameera noticed that many of the businesses were named after the family: Cooke's Grocery, Cooke Convenience, and Cooke Gas. Tom's surname was everywhere.

"Do you have a lot of family in town?" Sameera asked.

Beside her, Tom shifted in his seat, and she noticed an embarrassed flush stain his chiseled cheekbones. "Dad's an only child," he said.

"Then why—" she started, but Barb cut in, bemused.

"Didn't Tom tell you? The Cookes are the founding family in the village. Rob runs many of the businesses here. In fact, he's served as the mayor of Wolf Run for nearly two decades!"

"That's because no one else wants the job," Tom muttered.

"He's been talking of stepping down," Barb said, not taking the bait. "If you're interested in the position." She laughed as if this were a joke, but no one else joined in.

Clearly, Sameera was missing something. She added it to the mental list she was compiling of questions to ask Tom. She decided to start with the most obvious one and leaned over to whisper, "Why didn't you tell me you were Alaskan royalty?"

"Heavy is the head that wears the crown." He winked at her, and Sameera realized she might be in serious trouble—she was starting to genuinely like Tom.

They left the outer limits of the town, and Barb turned onto a private drive, the truck climbing a steep hill easily. At the very top, a sprawling estate came into view, and Sameera tried not to gape. Her joke about Alaskan royalty felt even more accurate.

"Welcome to Cooke Place," Barb said, pride and delight evident in her voice. "Better than any hotel around, I can promise you that."

The house was enormous, a sprawling three-story building that could have easily doubled as a conference center or spa, and surrounded on three sides by lush pine forests. The house faced the village of Wolf Run, like a medieval lord surveying his fiefdom, Sameera thought. A large veranda wrapped around the house, and brightly painted Muskoka chairs dotted the white wooden structure. A gravel-strewn path led from an oversize custom double-door entrance to a circular driveway that could accommodate a fleet of cars. They parked and piled out, Barb leading the way inside, where the tiled stone floor gave way to a massive sitting room with soaring thirty-foot ceilings and floor-length windows that looked out at a sprawling snow-covered patio. A creek bisected the property, and Sameera sighed at the beauty surrounding her. The picture before her belonged on a postcard, or maybe a screen saver.

"You grew up here?" she asked Tom, and he nodded, his body tense.

"Lucky me," he said softly, looking around with a strange expression on his face.

"What do you think of our little shack?" Rob asked with a smile, entering the sitting room behind them and throwing his hands wide.

While Naveed and Tahsin managed to keep their composure, Esa was less discreet. "Dude, you live in a palace," he said to Calvin, who shrugged, a tiny smile tugging at the corner of his mouth.

"One time a moose wandered onto the back patio," he offered. "He stared through the window of the kitchen, and Mom freaked out."

"Awesome!" Esa said.

Sameera tried to catch Tom's eye, but he looked away. A change had come over him since they had pulled up to Cooke Place—*more like Cooke Mansion*, Sameera thought wryly. In Atlanta, Tom seemed at home no matter the venue, from a stuffy law firm holiday party to the Maliks' raucous Eid celebration to his own stainless steel commercial kitchen. Yet two minutes inside his childhood home, and he already radiated restless unhappiness. There was tension between Tom and his father, too. Sameera could see it in the way he held himself, in the careful way he stayed silent while his father boasted about the house and property.

"My great-grandfather built the original log cabin. He was a prospector, but he recognized an opportunity here. He decided to stay, found himself a wife, and built the town from the ground up. That's why his name is everywhere. Tom is named after him—Thomas Tipper Cooke. My grandfather built this house after his businesses took off, and every generation has added to it. Someday, this will all belong to Tom and Cal," Rob boasted.

With his hands on his hips, Rob looked like a contented king, and Tom his reluctant heir apparent. "If he ever returns home, that is," he added.

"I'm here now," Tom muttered. Then, as if coming out of a trance, he threw Sameera a wry half smile. "Ready to see the guesthouse where you'll be staying?"

"Guest*house*?" Esa said, eyes wide.

"Three bedrooms, two baths," Rob confirmed, looking smug. "Set near the woods, so it's nice and private."

The Malik family followed Rob, Barb, and Tom out the sliding glass doors and through the grounds, toward a small bungalow on the edge of the property. It looked different from the main house, and Rob explained that he'd had it built around the time Tom was supposed to graduate from college. "Still waiting for that diploma," Rob said genially. "He's only got one year left, and he knows I'll pay his tuition when he goes back."

"Not going to happen, Dad," Tom said tightly. "Sameera and her family are tired. We should let them rest."

But Rob wasn't finished boasting about the guesthouse. "There's a gourmet kitchen, too, top-of-the-line appliances. I know how Tommy likes to fiddle around with his recipes, just like his mom used to do."

"I never asked you to build me a house," Tom muttered. His father ignored him, and Sameera caught the strained smile Barb exchanged with her mother.

Inside, the house was airy and bright, and obviously well maintained. A large wood-burning fireplace took center stage, and though the ceilings were not as impressive as in the main house, the sofas looked comfortable and the colorful wool rug inviting. The walls were adorned with framed photographs of the Alaskan sky, regal mountains and crystal blue and green lakes, but the real showstopper was the entire back wall, which consisted of floor-to-ceiling windows overlooking forest and a frozen-over creek. Her family exclaimed over the view, but Sameera noticed that Tom's eyes lingered on the appliances in the kitchen before firmly looking away.

Once the house tour came to an end, Sameera hoped her hosts would take the hint and leave them to settle in. She had spotted an espresso machine in the kitchen. Instead, Barb and Rob stood in front of the fireplace, grinning. "We wanted to make y'all comfortable," Rob announced in an exaggerated Southern twang before reverting to his normal voice. He gestured to the stained oak mantel, and Sameera focused on the three figurines neatly arranged across the top. Frowning, she stepped closer to take a better look. *Was that . . . surely it can't be . . .*

"Lord Ganesha; Kali, the destroyer and creator; and the god Vishnu!" Barb said proudly. "I know how important it is to have your deities with you, so we made you a shrine, right here!"

Sameera wanted to face-palm. Behind her, Esa stifled a laugh while their parents looked at the idols in shock.

"Dad," Tom started, and she was relieved that he had taken the initiative. For her part, she wasn't sure what would come out of her mouth—hysterical laughter or a groan. "Sameera and her family are Muslim, not Hindu." He waited expectantly, but Rob and Barb only looked at him. With a sigh, he continued, "Those aren't their gods. I mean, it's all one god, really, but their worship is more . . . reincarnation-free."

Understanding seemed to dawn on Rob's and Barb's faces simultaneously, followed by embarrassment.

"You said they were Indian," Rob muttered while Barb carefully removed the statues from the mantel.

"India is a country with many different religions. Sameera's family are Muslim Indians," Tom said, his face flushing further, and this time Sameera really did want to laugh. She stepped forward with smiling reassurance.

"This was very kind of you," she said. "My parents grew up in Hyderabad, India, and many of their close friends are Hindu, Parsee, even Christian."

"I'm so sorry for the confusion," Barb said, flustered. "I'll find these beautiful statues a good home. There must be a temple somewhere in town, right?"

"Maybe in Anchorage," Rob said doubtfully.

Behind them, Tahsin was rummaging through their largest suitcase. "Since we're exchanging gifts, I had this custom-made for your family."

She pulled out a large navy-blue box tied with a red ribbon, so wide it nearly engulfed her small form. Intrigued, Sameera helped her place it on the wide-plank oak coffee table with a live edge. Both Rob and Barb made appreciative noises, no doubt eager to move on from their gaffe. Tahsin pulled off the lid with a flourish, and the group gaped.

Inside, nestled in white tissue wrap, was an enormous chocolate crucifix. The Cookes turned to Tahsin, confusion writ large on their faces, and Sameera felt a foreboding fill her. Behind her, Esa raised his cell phone to film their hosts' reaction.

"It's filled with cherry cordial," Tahsin said, beaming at them. When they didn't respond, she continued, "Because Christians eat the blood of Christ!"

There was another shocked silence, broken only by Cal's muttered, "So awesome."

"Okay, I think we've had enough of the welcome gifts," Sameera said, hastily putting the lid back on the chocolate box. "Rob, Barb, thank you so much for the warm . . . um . . . welcome. I'm sure you have a lot to do, and we wouldn't want to keep you . . ." She ushered the elder Cookes outside, Cal and Tom following a few steps behind. Tom turned to her at the door.

"I think it's going really well," he whispered, eyes twinkling.

"Our parents get an *A* for effort and an *F* for research," Sameera agreed.

He grinned at her, and a thousand butterflies took flight in her belly. "Why don't you come find me after you've had a chance to relax? We should talk."

Sameera watched him return to the main house, and tried to fight the urge to follow.

First, she had to talk to her family.

Chapter Eight

"Esa said it was Christmas tradition to give a gag gift to your host!" Naveed said, eyes wide. Sameera's parents and her unrepentant little brother were arranged on the couch like recalcitrant children, facing the fireplace, where Lord Ganesha had so recently blessed them.

"It's probably not a good idea to take holiday gift advice from your teenage son," Sameera said severely, though she was relieved to hear the chocolate and cherry cordial crucifix had been a joke, however ill-advised. They would have needed a longer conversation if her parents had thought the chocolate a genuinely tasteful gift for the holidays. She fixed her gaze on her mother. "You know what kids are like, Mom. You were a school principal!"

Tahsin hung her head. "I like chocolate with cherry cordial filling," she admitted. "I might have been having a craving."

Sameera threw up her hands in frustration before wheeling on her brother, who seemed completely unmoved.

"I'm going through your bags to vet the other Christmas gifts," she said.

Despite Esa's protests, she started with his bag first, but she couldn't find anything. From his innocent expression, she was sure she must be missing something and vowed to keep a closer eye on him.

She pulled an oversize box from her parents' bag. "Karaoke Santa? Really?" Sameera said, gesturing to the front of the box, where a joyfully gyrating Santa promised fun times for all.

"Esa said karaoke was a Christmas tradition," Naveed said. "They're always singing in holiday concerts and church, and everyone always knows the words."

She shook her head. "I will remind you once again not to take gift-giving advice from your teenage son," she said.

The family retired to their separate rooms, and after Sameera had taken a long shower, making liberal use of the organic, locally sourced shampoo and body wash, she dressed in her warmest sweater and fleece-lined leggings before making her way to the main house. She and Tom definitely needed to talk. They had to come up with a game plan, and she also needed an update on Andy's whereabouts. Once she secured him as a client, she might finally be able to calm down.

She had texted before making the short walk across the yard to Cooke Place, her new boots making a satisfying crunching sound as she walked through the snow. But when she got to the front door, it was Barb and not Tom at the door.

"Are you settling in? I hope you're not going to leave on account of the . . . mantel incident," Barb said, lowering her voice.

Sameera schooled her face into a polite smile. "I'm here to see Tom."

Barb smiled nervously. "Of course!" She called up to Tom, who yelled that he would be right down. Barb led her to the enormous sitting room, indicating for Sameera to take a seat on the couch. "I'm glad you came by. I hope you don't mind that we didn't put you and Tom in the same room together."

Sameera's eyes widened, alarmed at the idea. If Barb had tried, her mother would have immediately summoned an imam. "I like having my own space," she said carefully. "How much has Tom told you about . . . our relationship?" She winced at the word, but it was probably better to find out what Barb knew first.

"You know how he is," Barb said, smiling.

Not really, Sameera thought. "I was surprised when my mom said she had reached out to you online. I'm sorry for intruding during your holidays," she started, but Barb waved her words away.

"No, dear, I'm the one who should be apologizing to you. We were both so excited," Barb said.

"About what?" Sameera asked.

"I saw that video Tom posted from your mom's house, and of course, I noticed the way he looked at *you*. Completely smitten, and who can blame him?" Barb continued, "When I called to invite him home for the holidays as usual, he told me how much he enjoyed catering for your family, and how it made him miss home. Then when he posted a second video with you by his side, I knew I had you to thank."

"I don't understand," Sameera said. "Why would you thank me?"

"For bringing our son home," Barb said simply, and Sameera tried not to flinch. Before she could ask any more questions, Tom joined them in the sitting room, his gaze moving from his stepmother to his fake girlfriend.

"I hope you haven't been telling Sameera embarrassing stories," he said, his tone wary.

"Only how happy we are to have you home at last," Barb said, rising. "Why don't you take your girlfriend"—this time, Sameera definitely flinched—"on a tour of the property? It's so pretty this time of year."

When they were outside, breathing in the fresh wintry air, Tom tried to explain. "I'm not sure what Barb told you . . ." he started.

"Does she know this is all a ruse?" Sameera asked, gesturing between the two of them.

"A 'ruse'? I don't think I've ever heard anyone actually use that word in a sentence," he said, but she would not be distracted.

"I told my parents we're not really dating." At least, she had *tried* to tell them. Whether they believed her was their problem. "Have you been honest with your parents, too?" she demanded.

Tom looked at the ground, and Sameera stopped in the middle of the clearing to stare. "Your family knows we're not actually together. Right?"

"It's complicated," he said to his feet.

Sameera wanted to scream. "I promise it's not. It's bad enough my mom thinks I'm lying, but if you haven't come clean with your parents—"

"Tahsin thinks we're really together?" Tom asked. "Is that why she cold-called my mom and invited herself to Alaska? I don't understand why she would think you'd lie about that."

"She assumes I'm hiding another relationship," Sameera said, and his eyes widened. Even admitting this to someone outside of her family was humiliating. "I don't have time for this. I have work to do, and a pitch to prepare. Which reminds me—when will Andy Shaikh be here?"

Tom smiled at her, and despite her annoyance, it was hard to remain unmoved. He was ridiculously good-looking, and she was starting to resent it. "Sick of me already?" he asked. She would *not* allow him to charm his way through another conversation. The look she gave him was stony, and he relented. "Okay, okay, you're right. You deserve answers. Go ahead."

"Why does Barb think we're dating? Why did she respond to my mother's message with an invitation to visit instead of blocking her, like a normal person? What is going on between you and your dad? Do you have any other siblings besides Cal? Seems like basic information a *girlfriend*, even a fake one, would know."

They had walked to the outer periphery of the property now, and entered a densely wooded lot, the snow higher here. Sameera was glad she had listened to her mother and bought a pair of well-lined winter boots for this trip. She inhaled deeply after all those questions, the sharp hint of pine needles and crisp cold hitting her. As much as she loved her life in Atlanta, she couldn't remember the last time she had just . . . breathed.

Beside her, Tom was deep in thought. "Barb thinks we're dating because I didn't tell her we're not," he said. He raised his hands in mock surrender at her outraged expression. "To be clear, I never called you my girlfriend. She just assumed, and I didn't correct her. The reason for that is a bit more complicated." Tom sighed and looked around the wooded area. Cooke Place appeared smaller behind them, though his eyes lingered on the guesthouse—his house, if he wanted it, Sameera thought.

"It sort of ties back to your other question about my dad. You're right; there's tension between us, and has been for a long time. Rob has made it clear over the years that he wanted a different type of son than the one he got." The smile that accompanied this devastating remark was wry, and Sameera had to fight the urge to give him a hug. So, he had daddy issues—didn't everyone? Well, not her, but that was because Naveed was amazing. Her mother, on the other hand . . .

"Everyone has issues with their parents; it's a cliché for a reason. I don't get how pretending to have a girlfriend helps with that. Is Rob not happy to have us here?" she asked, a sudden thought occurring to her. "Does he not like Indians, Muslims, or immigrants, and you're trying to make him mad—"

Tom shook his head, alarmed. "Nothing like that! I promise. It's more like this relationship is a bit of an escape hatch for me." Off her inquiring look, he explained. "My dad wants me to move back to Alaska and pick up the family mantle." He winced at his choice of words. "I mean, family legacy means a lot to him, and he has this idea that his eldest son should live in Wolf Run, become the next mayor, run the family empire, and basically step into his shoes and do the same thing he's been doing all his life. I don't want any of that."

"What about Cal?" Sameera asked.

"Cal is Barb's son. As much as Rob loves him, he's not a Cooke. Not really. Or at least, that's how my dad sees things. Besides, Cal's just a kid, and my dad is not a patient guy."

"When my mom got in touch with Barb and invited herself over, your stepmother thought what, exactly?" Sameera asked.

Tom shrugged. "I'm not entirely sure, but I can guess. When I told her I wanted to visit this year, she thought it was due to your influence, that maybe I was ready to settle down at last, and she got excited and invited your entire family here."

"Barb sounds like a total aunty," Sameera said, sighing, thinking of her own mother.

"She wants everyone to get along and isn't above emotional manipulation," Tom allowed. "She hates that I don't visit more often. As for your last question, I don't have any other siblings. My mom died when I was ten, but she was sick for a long time before that, and my dad wasn't in the right headspace to think about getting married again for a long time."

"I'm sorry," Sameera said automatically. They had walked to a sort of clearing with a large hill to the right, with a slope cleared of trees.

"I used to go tobogganing here when I was a kid," Tom said, indicating the hill. "Cal uses it now, or at least he used to. It's been a long time since we hung out, and that's my fault entirely. I'm sorry about all of this, about dragging you into my family issues."

Something inside Sameera softened at Tom's ready confession, at his willingness to be honest and vulnerable. Impulsively, she told him about her own brother. "Esa was a surprise baby. My mom was forty-two when she had him. He used to follow me and Nadiya around when he was a baby. When things got . . . tough between me and my parents, I didn't see Esa for over three years," Sameera said. "When I got back in touch, it was like he was an entirely different person—more than a foot taller, his voice deeper, and he was really quiet, especially around me. I didn't know him at all. And now he wants nothing to do with me."

They stood in silence for a minute, and she thought about time—how quickly it ran, and how slowly it crawled, depending on where you stood in its current. "I won't lie to your family about us," she said quietly. "I've lied in the past to the people I care about, and it's led only to trouble."

"I wouldn't ask you to," he said. "This is my mess to sort out."

She put a hand on his arm, and even through the layers of his heavy jacket and the warm sweater he had underneath, she could feel the firmness of his bicep, the warmth and strength of the real man beneath. "You came back here for a reason. Maybe you should spend some time thinking about why."

They turned back to the house and made the journey back in silence. It was late, and Tom invited her inside. There was a new shyness between them now, an extra level of vulnerability. Sameera needed some time to examine her feelings and the information Tom had confided, and she demurred, explaining that she had to check on her family. She had been gone for nearly an hour. Who knew what mischief her parents and Esa had gotten into by now?

Besides, the samosas had not been entirely filling. She wondered if they could order a pizza delivered to Cooke Place.

Inside the guesthouse, she discovered that Barb had anticipated their hunger and delivered a picnic basket filled with snacks, along with a note: *Enjoy and rest up, Malik family! We are so happy to have you here. Breakfast at the main house once it's light out, before we start our holiday adventures!*

The basket also included a few movies on DVD, and, looking at the flat-screen television, Sameera noticed a DVD player. Esa held up the discs and wrinkled his nose.

"Did we travel back in time to 2006?" he asked, and Sameera laughed.

"You haven't lived until you've watched a film on disc," she said.

"When Sameera and Nadiya were little, they would pile all their favorite movies on the floor and go through them one by one. Remember how much you liked those princess movies, meri jaan?" Naveed asked, using the Urdu endearment for "my life."

Esa hooted. "Is Tom the Prince Charming you always dreamed of?"

Sameera rolled her eyes at her little brother. "You were obsessed with *Dora the Explorer* and *Cars*, brat," she said, and he laughed. This felt good, joking around with her little brother, chatting with her parents. Maybe it wouldn't be the worst, being stuck in the same space for a few days.

She pulled out the cheese, fruit, crackers, and bread from the basket, and Tahsin set about making a snack—grilled cheese sandwiches, grapes, and sparkling water to wash it all down. Barb had even included a few packets of microwave popcorn.

Naveed set the small table, and the four of them settled around with plates and glasses. Sameera had a vivid memory of eating dinner with her family when she was a teenager, Esa in his high chair, of shared meals and quiet conversation, of laughter, and later, tears. She blinked the memory back and took a bite of the grilled cheese. Her mom always knew how to make it the way she liked.

Afterward, Sameera retreated to her room with her laptop to work on some files, and her pitch for Andy, determined to make a dent. As she worked, she realized Tom hadn't answered her question about Andy Shaikh's ETA. She texted, asking once more, before turning back to her laptop. There was no guarantee that Andy would even agree to work with her firm, of course. All Tom had promised was access; she would have to impress him with her pitch, but right now, the best way to ensure she wouldn't be freshening up her résumé in the new year was to keep working.

Tom texted her back: I hope things weren't too weird this afternoon. Andy got back to me about his plans.

He had attached a video, and Sameera stared at a face that felt familiar to her by now, after all her hours of online research. The business tycoon was a handsome man, his skin a deep brown, eyes sparkling with energy and good humor. He was dressed in a hoodie and track pants, thick dark hair flopping as he jogged. "Tom, I've got a meeting in Hong Kong, but I'll be at Cooke Place for Christmas! Love you, brother. Try not to get married before I land in Wolf Run. Can't wait to meet your new friend and tell her every one of your embarrassing secrets, starting with how long it's been since you last had a girlfriend!"

Tom ended his message with a big-eyed emoji, and Sameera couldn't resist replying.

So how long HAS it been?

His reply was immediate: I'd rather not answer questions that will incriminate me. Would you like to know how many different types of souffles I can make?

Sameera smiled to herself. *Nope. How long, Romeo?*

Don't you have people to sue?

Sameera stuck her tongue out at the screen. While it was frustrating not knowing exactly when the great Andy Shaikh would grace them with his presence, she would do her best to use this extra time to prepare. Besides, Tom had warned her: The rich could be unpredictable. She flipped the phone over and tried to concentrate, for about thirty minutes. Until her family's conversation filtered through her door.

"Let's watch *Home Alone*," Esa said. "It's a classic for a reason."

"*Elf* is the obvious choice," Naveed argued.

"What about *A Christmas Carol*?" Tahsin put in. "I like the black-and-white classics."

"Let's ask Sameera," Naveed said, and seconds later, her door opened and her dad poked his head inside. "Which movie should we watch tonight, Samu? Come out, the popcorn will be done soon. You know your mother cannot resist."

"I have a lot of work to catch up on. Why are you watching Christmas movies, anyway?" she asked, trying to soften the rejection. She stood up and wandered into the sitting room, where her family had gathered on the couch. "Are you all in desperate need of a Christmas tutorial?"

"Clearly," Esa said, cackling. "Unless we want another chocolate crucifix episode."

"It was a joke!" Tahsin protested. Her tone turned sober. "We want to make a good impression on Tom and his family. For your sake, Sameera."

Despite herself, she was touched by her mother's words, however misguided. "Tom and I are only friends," she repeated.

"Friends with benefits?" her mother asked, and both Sameera and Esa stared at her, appalled.

"Mom, *ew*," Esa said.

"Do you know what that means?" Sameera asked.

"It means you are friends, with the possibility of it turning into a real relationship," Tahsin said indignantly. "I know things."

Sameera closed her eyes. "I have work to do. Have fun. And you should definitely start with *Home Alone*. It's a classic."

It was hard to concentrate with her family laughing in the sitting room, and she needed more coffee to counteract the jet lag. She ventured outside in search of caffeine and took her time preparing a cup, peeking at the television while the espresso maker puttered. On screen, Macaulay Culkin, a.k.a. Kevin McCallister, was telling his mother that he didn't want his family, that families sucked. She felt a pang at this and hurried back to her room.

"You're working so hard, *beta*. Why don't you join us?" her father called twenty minutes later, and Sameera hesitated.

"We saved you some popcorn," Tahsin wheedled.

A few minutes might make her feel more refreshed, Sameera thought. She settled between her parents on the sofa, reaching for the popcorn. Soon, she was laughing alongside her parents and Esa at Kevin's antics, and she couldn't force herself to get up once the bowl was empty.

"I don't understand how this is a Christmas movie," Tahsin said. "A white, upper-middle-class child is left alone in his house by accident and thwarts robbers by mutilating them. It doesn't seem very festive."

"It's funny. Humor is very Christmas," Sameera said.

"Kevin has every advantage—youth, intelligence, the privilege of a large home with plenty of resources, not to mention familiarity with the terrain. No serious scholar who watched this movie would assume those clueless 'robbers' had the upper hand," Tahsin argued. "*Home Alone* seems anti-Christmas, if you ask me."

"Firstly, it's a children's movie," Sameera said. "Secondly, it made a gazillion dollars and spawned an entire franchise. There's snow, Santa, and twinkly lights. Ergo, Christmas movie."

This started a lively debate over what was considered a Christmas movie versus a movie only set during the holidays. Sameera grabbed her yellow legal pad to list the essential ingredients for a holiday movie, according to the Maliks.

"We're agreed, then," she said. "It's a Christmas movie if there is a scene in a church, a holiday song, culturally specific accoutrements like Santa or an elf, and most importantly if it includes . . ." She checked her notes. "The central Christmas themes of love, charity, and forgiveness."

"Instantaneous redemption appears to be another common theme," Naveed mused. "Think about Ebenezer Scrooge. He wakes after a night of being terrorized by ghosts with a sudden change of heart and a complete personality transplant. In reality, change is difficult, and redemption only possible after much effort and time." He looked thoughtful, then added, "Most modern Scrooges, our modern billionaire industrialists, are so far removed from their lower-level employees, this level of empathy would be nearly impossible."

Sameera and Esa threw popcorn at Naveed, always the academic.

"I've never understood elves," Tahsin admitted. "Are they like jinn?" She referred to the beings made of smokeless fire known as the Unseen, which were part of the Muslim belief system.

"No, jaan, they're more like angels. Santa is their imam, and they help him," Naveed said.

"Okay, but have you ever seen one of those Elf on a Shelf things? Those guys are definitely jinn," Esa said. "One time when we were kids, Tyler invited me to his house around Christmas, and he told me the elf moved in the night and spied on the kids to make sure they behaved."

"Not a jinni," Sameera said firmly. Most Westerners had no concept of the Unseen beyond the "genie" in Aladdin's lamp; the opposite seemed to be the case for her Muslim family, who suspected the presence of jinn everywhere.

"I never understood why they decorate pine trees instead of palm trees," her little brother said now. "Prophet Esa was born in the Middle East. Not a conifer in sight."

"The pine trees are tradition, not religion, like breaking your fast with samosas or haleem," Sameera said absently.

"Prophet Esa was born in the spring, in any case," Tahsin added. "I read that somewhere. But December is a convenient time to celebrate, nah? Not much else to do in the middle of winter. It's like with your Yaqub Nana—no one knew when his birthday really was, so we just celebrated every Fourth of July. Easy to remember."

Usually, Sameera became impatient with her family's random musings, but tonight she felt buoyed by a sense of contentment. When the movie finished, Tahsin waited until both men had cleared out before turning to Sameera.

"It's been so long since I've seen you laugh like that," Tahsin said, reaching out to smooth Sameera's hair. The gesture was automatic and affectionate. Sameera wondered if her mother was thinking about the scene halfway through the movie, when Kevin spoke with his scary neighbor at church about his fears, and the neighbor confided that he was estranged from his adult son, and had been for years. The scene had hit Sameera especially hard.

They had never really talked about Sameera's love life before her situation with Hunter blew up. Her parents had been raised in traditional South Asian families in India, and hadn't learned how to talk to their children about relationships, romantic and otherwise. That was part of the problem, Sameera knew. She had internalized their silence until it had grown toxic.

"I like Tom a lot," Tahsin said.

"I'm aware I don't have the best track record when it comes to men," Sameera started. She knew she should try to convince her mother that she and Tom weren't together, but she was tired, and the evening had been so peaceful that she didn't want to get into another argument about this tonight.

"What Hunter did was *not your fault*," Tahsin said, her voice so severe it made Sameera blink. She patted her daughter on her shoulder.

"In any case, you have learned from your mistakes and have chosen better, this time. Alhamdulillah."

A feeling rose in Sameera's throat: love, helplessness, despair, all mixed together. Even though Tom wasn't her boyfriend, it soothed something in her heart to hear that her mother approved, or at least didn't immediately jump to judgment. Perhaps if she had been more open about Hunter all those years ago, things might have turned out differently.

Or maybe the pain that Hunter had caused her and her family was the price for this new understanding. A scary thought.

"We are always on your side," Tahsin said.

Naveed had finished tidying the kitchen, and he came to join them, taking his wife's arm. With a hushed "shabba khair"—"good night"—they made their way to their bedroom, leaving Sameera in the dark.

Chapter Nine

"Is that a wolf?" Esa said, and Sameera's eyes flew open.

She had fallen asleep on the couch last night, relocating there after tossing and turning in her bed for hours, her mother's words ringing in her ears. Despite her justification and rationalization during the day, when she closed her eyes and tried to sleep, all the worry, guilt, and fear she'd tamped down rose in a panicky wave.

What was she doing in Alaska when she needed to be in Atlanta, trying as hard as she could to catch up on her billable hours this quarter? Instead, she had spent last night watching a holiday classic and arguing about what made a good Christmas movie, then sleeping in until—she peered at her phone—nearly 9:00 a.m.

"I think there's a wolf in our backyard. Sameera, come see!" The delight and wonder in Esa's voice had her throwing off the blanket she had dragged to the couch from her bed.

Esa stood in front of the big bay window. The sun hadn't risen yet, but a lamp was lit and she followed his pointing finger toward . . .

A wolf. Or maybe a snow leopard. Sameera wasn't sure. Either way, a white furry ball of fluff, almost as tall as their mother, with icy blue eyes and a lolling tongue, stared straight through the window at them. And it looked hungry.

"Get down!" Sameera said, pulling her brother to a crouch beside her.

"Why?" Esa said.

"It thinks you're breakfast!" she said, panicking.

"Can we keep it?" Esa asked.

They popped up their heads to take a look, and the wolf or snow leopard yawned widely, showing off razor-sharp teeth. Sameera whimpered. Beside her, Esa snapped a picture.

Just as Sameera was starting to regret every decision that had led her to this moment, including her decision to apply to law school, Tom appeared in their backyard. Instinct took over, and she jumped to her feet and ran out the door, pausing only long enough to put on her boots.

Cold. It was freezing outside, and she wasn't even wearing a sweater. She frantically waved at Tom.

"There's a wild animal!" she yelled. "A snow leopard slash werewolf hybrid! Save yourself!"

Both Tom and the predatory fluff ball looked at her as if she had lost her mind. The creature yawned again, already bored, before butting Tom with its big head. Tom scratched the animal fondly behind its neck. "This is Atlas. She was at a neighbor's house yesterday while y'all settled in. She's an Alaskan malamute—her great-great-grandmother used to haul sleds around town. But Atlas doesn't work for a living, right, girl? You're a lady of leisure, aren't you?"

Esa emerged from the house in snow boots and a warm parka and, approaching Atlas, proceeded to pet the big animal with enthusiasm.

Tom smirked at Sameera. "Are you afraid of dogs?"

"I'm afraid of mythical predators wandering the forest looking for bloodthirsty revenge. That thing looked like it was in the mood for breakfast, and I am not on the menu," she said.

Tom's gaze slid down Sameera's outfit—a flimsy long-sleeve shirt and flannel pajamas. "You're going to get sick dressed in that," he said gruffly, and he was right: She was shivering. "I came to remind you all about breakfast at the big house."

Sameera promised they would be there soon, once she had roused her parents, taken a scalding-hot shower, and put on several dozen layers of clothes.

"Come on, sweetheart, time to go," Tom cooed, and Sameera's stomach clenched in response before she realized he was talking to Atlas. Her hands were half frozen now. With a nervous smile at Tom, she retreated to the house to get ready for the day.

By the time she had finished taking a shower and straightening her hair, her parents and Esa were waiting for her in the sitting room, her brother regaling them with a highly exaggerated account of their morning brush with the local wildlife.

"And then Sameera *ran outside* to protect her man, except the big cuddly beast turned out to be a family pet. Her name is Atlas, and I hope she has a sister because I know what I want for Christmas," Esa finished.

"We're not bringing an Alaskan sled dog home to Atlanta," Tahsin said severely. "Come along, Sameera; we're late for breakfast."

Inside the main house, a feast waited on the kitchen island: eggs, roasted vegetables and potatoes, three different types of juices, mini quiches, a tray with pastries, and a carafe of coffee. The Malik family were assured that the meal was vegetarian—the Cookes hadn't been sure of their dietary preferences. Touched by this consideration, Sameera loaded her plate with a croissant and some eggs before pouring herself a large cup of coffee with a generous dollop of cream and three sugars. She needed sustenance following her near-death experience. She didn't care what Tom said—Atlas had definitely seemed hungry when she'd looked at Sameera.

Hovering by the stove, Tom gave her a small smile, as if he could read her mind. He was dressed in a rumpled blue shirt that brought out the blue of his eyes, hair tousled in a way that made her want to run her fingers through the short curls. Instead, she curled her hands around her mug and took a sip of her coffee.

The family made small talk about the Cooke estate, and her parents complimented the guesthouse's many amenities. "There's been a Cooke living in this town for over two hundred years," Rob said proudly.

"Once Tom returns, he'll take up the tradition." Sameera remembered what Tom had told her last night, about being his escape hatch.

"I have a life in Atlanta," Tom said. "A business. Other . . . relationships." He looked at her. Not lying, exactly.

Rob snorted. "Cooking for other people, as if you were a domestic," he said. "Nothing wrong with making meals. I'm a modern man. I just don't understand why you would rather work around the clock for others, or post those silly videos, instead of staying where your people have lived for generations, and where everyone knows you. What's so great about Atlanta? No seasons. Nonstop traffic. No mountains, no ocean. What kind of life is that?"

There was silence after he had spoken, and Sameera could sense something else beneath his words: a sadness and confusion she remembered from when she had been estranged from her own family.

"I guess you think being the king of nowhere is a better alternative," Tom said tightly, arms crossed.

Barb hurried to interrupt the brewing confrontation. "We're so happy you all could make it! Especially you, Tom, honey. We've missed you terribly, right, Rob?" Her cheerful smile was still fixed on her face, though it had tightened at the edges. Tom looked away, while Rob didn't bother to respond.

Sameera's father broke in. "Sometimes, it does not matter if you live across the country, or across the street. The pain of separation cuts deep either way. My family knows something of this."

The silence stretched, and Sameera wanted to sink into the ground. Barb turned to her, obviously eager to change the subject. "Sameera, I hear you're a lawyer. What sort of law do you practice? I used to work in marketing for retail companies before I moved to Wolf Run."

The conversation continued in a different direction, Naveed and Tahsin chiming in between sips of coffee and tea, but the atmosphere remained tense. At the end of the meal, her parents rose to help clear the dishes, but both Rob and Barb waved them away.

"Our compliments to the chef," Naveed said, making a little bow to Tom.

"This meal is all Barb," Rob cut in. "Tom doesn't cook for us."

After breakfast was cleared away, Barb laid out her plans for the remaining days they would spend in Wolf Run. As she spoke enthusiastically, Sameera's heart sank. Tom glanced at her once and immediately spoke up.

"Sameera and I have our own plans, but y'all go right ahead. We'll join in when we can," he said firmly, and Sameera felt a burst of gratitude for him.

Her parents and Barb protested, but she noticed Rob only scoffed and rolled his eyes. It made her mad. Tom had flown all this way to visit his father and stepmother, and so far, Rob had done nothing to warrant the effort. She reached across and grabbed Tom's hand. "I promised I'd film a few videos for Tom's social media," she said, smiling at him. Esa perked up at this.

"I can help," he said, and Cal chimed in that he was free, too.

Despite Tahsin's protests, Barb quickly agreed to the plan—the parents would head into town, while the younger set stayed behind.

"Have fun messing around in the kitchen," Rob said, his parting shot.

Sameera flung a sickly-sweet smile his way. "Thank you, Rob. We sure will."

Tom shook his head at her after the parents had left soon afterward. "You didn't have to do that. I was trying to buy you time. I know you're buried under work."

"So what else is new," Esa muttered.

"Your sister works really hard," Tom said, but Esa rolled his eyes. "We get it, you love your girlfriend. You don't have to perform for us."

"We're not together," Tom said.

"'Situationship,' 'dating,' whatever you want to call it. I really don't care," Esa said. "I'm here to film. What are we making today? I'm hungry."

"You just ate your weight in eggs, toast, and fruit," Sameera said, smiling at her always-hungry teenage brother.

"What's your point? Less talking; more cooking and filming."

In the end, Tom convinced Sameera she should get some work done while he talked over ideas with Esa and Cal. She didn't need much convincing—after the movie night with her family and then sleeping late, the familiar panicky feelings were creeping up.

She returned to her room in the guesthouse and settled in to answer emails. She'd managed to concentrate for almost an hour when Bee texted her.

Helllooo? Are you alive? Do I need to send a hot rescue SEAL team? Blink once for yes, twice for YES, PLEASE.

Sameera stretched first. Her legs were cramping. She answered quickly. Sorry, things have been busy.

Bee's response was immediate: In bed with Tom busy?

Sameera smiled. Trying to catch up on work busy, you perv.

There's been no video uploaded in the past two days. Inquiring minds want to know.

Sameera imagined her friend drinking coffee, Lorenzo lounging by her side. Sameera changed the subject. Have you heard anything from work?

I'm on vacation. What's work?

Just then, her laptop pinged with a notification, and Sameera's heart sped up. It was from HR. She skimmed the email quickly and tried not to pass out. She typed a message to Bee.

HR wants a meeting the first day I'm back to review my work. This is it. I'm getting fired.

Bee added an exclamation point to her message. What? Are you serious?

Sameera's heart was pounding as she typed. I should be grateful they kept me around this long.

Bee's indignation was clear from her text: The Undertakers are lucky to have you. Listen to me: Do NOT panic. Do NOT spiral. You're going to hook a whale, and if that doesn't work, I promise you can move in with me. I'll kick Lorenzo out to make room, don't worry.

But it was too late. Sameera was already spiraling, sinking under a cloud of shame. She remembered the last time she had felt this way—after she'd failed the bar exam on her first attempt. When she'd received the results, four months after she had written the two-day exam, she couldn't believe it. She was an excellent student. There must have been some mistake.

Except there wasn't. Despite extensive preparation, she had failed. And Georgia had a near 70 percent pass rate! The humiliation she had felt then was debilitating.

She was still with Hunter at the time, and his reaction didn't help. *I hope you can still pay your half of the rent,* was his only comment. His cold response had stung, but Hunter had always been brutally honest—it was one of the things she had admired about him, when they'd first gotten together. It took her years to realize that he often used his so-called honesty to justify his cruelty.

No other words of encouragement? she had thrown back, jokingly.

Study harder next time.

But she had studied hard the first time. She had been nervous, but she thought she'd done well. It didn't make any sense. Even worse, the bar exam was offered only twice a year, and she had to scramble to get ready for the next one. Though she passed on her second try, her confidence was shot. The boutique law firm where she had been interning didn't ask her back, and she was soon on the hunt for a job. She polished up her résumé and sent it out to dozens of firms, with no response. By the time she was offered a job at Greaves, Hargrave &

Bury, she was desperate. Hunter was happy for her, and they went out to celebrate that night, but all she could think about was how badly she wanted to call her parents and share this news.

Except when she called her mother, Tahsin's "Mubarak" was muted. She said she had never heard of the firm, and when Sameera told her it was one of the best-known midsize firms in the state, her mother asked why she hadn't tried to find a job with a bigger firm instead. They hadn't talked for months after that call. Nadiya had been happy for her, at least—she had sent flowers, all the way from Oxford.

Things were better now, she reminded herself. Her parents were putting in the work, and so was she. Hunter was gone, and good riddance. Once she finished paying off the last of his debts, and the money she owed her father, she could think about what she really wanted to do. In the meantime, she needed this job. The idea of being set adrift on the job market again was terrifying.

Her thoughts were interrupted by a large *bang!* from the patio, followed by the sound of her brother screaming. Sameera grabbed her parka, pulled on her boots, and started to run.

Chapter Ten

"Whoooooo!" Esa yelled. "Let's light another one!"

Sameera arrived breathless at the edge of the patio and had to bend at the waist, hands on her knees, until her heart stopped pounding. When she looked up, Tom, Esa, Cal, and even Atlas were staring at her.

"Relax, Sameera, they're just fireworks," Esa said.

For the first time since they had arrived—the first time in even longer than that, she thought—her brother was unabashedly grinning at her. His cheeks were flushed, both from the cold and from the excitement, and his dark hair sprouted from under his woolen hat in wild curls. He looked happy. It was a shame she would have to shut it all down.

"Absolutely not," Sameera said firmly. "We can't set Tom's house on fire."

"He doesn't even like it here. He won't mind," Esa whined, and beside him, Cal laughed.

Her eyes were fixed on Tom. "You're supposed to be filming a *cooking* video," she said.

Tom lifted an eyebrow. "There was fire involved." The boys muffled their laughter while Sameera sighed. "Besides, you heard my dad," Tom continued. "In Alaska, I'm useless in the kitchen."

So, that was the real problem, she realized. What was it about their respective families? Every word they said had the potential to burrow deep underground and sprout entire ecosystems of hurt. Tom had millions of views on his cooking series, more bookings than he could handle, and yet Rob said one word, and Tom was convinced he was useless. It was the same with her.

"Will you make me chai?" she asked, and Tom started to shake his head, but she pressed on.

"You promised chai on tap, and unlimited biryani," she said. "And I saw the way you were eyeing the guesthouse kitchen. Admit it: You cooked there recently."

Tom shrugged, noncommittal.

"I understand. The appliances are really pretty," she said, and he snorted his amusement, relenting.

"Where do you think I made your snack for the ride home from the airport?" he asked, and her heart lurched at the word *home*. "But I promised your brother I'd help him first." His hand reached up to scratch his head in that nervous gesture Sameera recognized.

"Help with setting off firecrackers?" she asked, unimpressed.

"Not exactly," Tom said. Behind them, Esa's smile turned mischievous.

Ten minutes later they stood in front of Toboggan Hill, as Cal called it, with a row of bright-red firecrackers.

"Is this safe?" Sameera asked, looking at the very flammable trees surrounding them. A part of her knew she should make her excuses and return to the work waiting for her in the guesthouse. But another part didn't want to spoil Esa's fun—or Tom's. And maybe she was enjoying this interlude, too. Just a little bit.

"There's snow everywhere, the trees are far away, and these aren't those kinds of fireworks. They just make a loud bang," Tom reassured her.

Sameera frowned. "And we're igniting incendiaries in the woods because . . ."

"It's fun?" Esa said, and the boys exchanged high fives.

"Your brother asked for my help in growing his audience," Tom explained. "Have you checked out his videos?"

Sameera had, actually. She had found them amusing, but Esa didn't seem to have a theme or niche. The videos spanned topics as disparate as sports commentary, jokes, skits, and even unboxing and product reviews. Nothing that really stood out, to her mind.

"It's okay. I know they suck," Esa called. "I'm trying to figure out my style. When Tom asked me what I like to do, I told him I like to play jokes."

"Jokes?" Sameera repeated. This was news to her. When he was younger, Esa had enjoyed eating junk food and watching anime. Now that he was a teen, she had no idea what he was into.

"He likes to pull pranks," Cal said, a delighted smile on his lips. "Now, Esa!"

And suddenly, there was a loud bang as the firecrackers ignited, causing Sameera to jump what felt like a foot in the air. "Eek!" she screeched.

Another one went off, and she waved her hands in the air. The boys were falling over themselves laughing at her reaction, and she realized they had the camera aimed right at her. "Why are you filming *meeeeeee*," she said, the final word combined with a shriek when the last one went off.

"They thought it might be funnier to watch someone react to the firecrackers rather than filming them explode," Tom said with a smile.

"I disagree," Sameera said, her heart pounding.

"Wait until you see the edited version set to music," Esa said. "You look hilarious!"

Once her heart had calmed down, Sameera could see the humor. And watching her brother enjoy himself was almost worth her humiliation. She met his grin with her own. Scratch that—it was definitely worth it.

But then Esa's smile slowly faded, and he took a step back, his usual cool reserve slotting into place. "I'm sure you're busy with work,

Sameera. Cal, let's go look at the footage." He took off for the main house without waiting for her to reply, his new friend following close behind.

She wasn't sure how long she stood there staring at her brother's retreating form, but when Tom placed a hand on her shoulder, she jumped.

"That was fun," she said brightly. "Thanks for helping Esa. He's got plenty of enthusiasm, and I think your suggestion that he focus on his strengths is a good one." Her voice sounded brittle even to her own ears, and from the gentle expression on Tom's face, he knew she was masking her pain at Esa's dismissal.

She couldn't stand to be an object of pity, and she rushed to change the subject. "Esa's right. I have a lot of work to do," she said, though the thought of heading back to the guesthouse to lock herself away for the rest of the day now made her feel sad.

After another careful glance at her face, Tom said, "I could use a walk. Want to check out Main Street instead?"

The email from HR, written in the carefully terrifying language that only a department responsible for discipline and firings could achieve, flashed in front of her eyes, and a feeling of despair flooded her senses. If she didn't clear her head first, she knew she would sit at the small desk in her room and catastrophize for hours. She would work all evening to make up for this little break, she decided, trying to tamp down her guilt. All night, if necessary.

"A walk sounds nice," she said quietly. "Thank you, Tom."

Fifteen minutes later, Tom eased the black pickup truck into a parking spot off the main road and cut the engine. The tiny village of Wolf Run looked even more charming this afternoon, with picturesque storefronts, the streetlamps decorated with red ribbons and green ferns. Evidence of the Cooke family's legacy, as Rob had boasted, were everywhere: an old-fashioned post office, with brass-laid windows and a curlicued sign that read **Cooke Copy and Ship**, while Cooke Convenience and Cooke's Best Gifts rubbed shoulders across the street. Even the local bank was owned by the Cooke family. The main strip had other stores as well: an ice cream shop, now closed for the season, a beautiful apothecary that sold locally made natural supplements . . . Sameera ogled the window display of Hilda's Bakery, with its mouthwatering selection of breads, pastries, and cakes.

"Let's start here," Sameera said, and Tom followed her inside after only a slight hesitation. She frowned at him, wondering what was wrong, before mentally shaking her head. Tom's mood wasn't her problem, because he wasn't her boyfriend. She was just feeling sensitive after her interaction with Esa; that was all. Luckily, the delicious pastry on display served to be a wonderful distraction, and she perked up at the sight of the walnut brioche bread, Danish, and homemade pies. At the register, she ordered a nutmeg latte and three pastries to go. She turned to ask Tom what he wanted. He had his head lowered and his hat pulled low over his eyes. Almost as if he were trying to hide.

She was about to ask what he was doing when the older woman behind the register, dressed in jeans, a wool sweater, and an apron, made a squawk of outrage. Emerging from behind the counter, she stalked over to Tom, and Sameera noted that her forearms were as big as his. "Tom Cooke, you damn fool. Were you really going to walk by without saying hello?"

Sameera was certain the older woman was seconds away from grasping Tom by the ear, when he sheepishly introduced her as Hilda, the owner of the bakery. The woman examined Sameera thoroughly. "Aren't you a beauty," she remarked before poking Tom with enough force to drive him back a step. "You back in town for good this time?"

Tom reached for Sameera's hand and gave it a squeeze, taking her by surprise, the contact sparking a burst of electricity that left her fingers tingling. "We're only here for a few days. We plan to head back home in the new year." Sameera tried not to glare at Tom. It was one thing to pretend to be together for a hypothetical social media audience, another entirely to keep their showmance going in person. She kept silent when Tom squeezed her hand once more before letting go. She instantly missed his touch, which only made her more annoyed.

Hilda frowned at Tom. "This is home, honey, whether you like it or not." She turned to Sameera and smiled in welcome. "I keep trying to get this one to take over my business. He worked part-time for me when he was a boy. Best pastry chef I ever had. With your vision and work ethic, you could take Hilda's global, Tom."

Tom's smile was strained. "Did my dad put you up to this?"

Hilda laughed at that. "Honey, you know your daddy and I don't see eye to eye on much." A sly expression crossed her face. "I bet it would piss him off plenty if you took over the bakery and not one of his businesses." She leaned over to Sameera, voice lowered conspiratorially. "Rob likes to boast about how long his family has been settled in Wolf Run. He forgets there were people here way before his kind. I like to remind him about that every chance I get."

"Hilda is Dena'ina Athabascan on her mother's side," Tom explained, referencing one of the many Indigenous tribes native to Alaska. "As much as I would love to annoy Dad, I'm settled in Atlanta. Now that I've met Sameera, I have another reason to stay."

His words made Sameera's face heat with embarrassment and confusion. This wasn't part of their agreement, and resentment flared. She had told Tom she wouldn't lie for him. She had spent too many years of her life deceiving those closest to her, with catastrophic results.

The look Hilda threw Tom now was speculative, but she said nothing, only hugging Tom once more. "I'm happy for the both of you. Hope you'll stop by for a proper visit before you leave again." She waved away Sameera's payment and added a few more walnut brioches, complaining that Tom was too skinny. As they were about to leave, she called Tom back. "Emily is in town, visiting her ma. Thought you'd like to know."

Sameera waited until they were on the sidewalk to confront Tom. She shoved the bag of pastry at him and glared. "You can keep your guilt pastries. I want nothing to do with them."

Tom stared at her as if she had lost her mind. "What did I do?" he asked, and she wanted to take the white pastry bag back, just so she could pelt him with the contents. Though that would be a waste of Hilda's efforts.

She snatched the bag back and savagely bit into a walnut brioche; her eyes nearly rolled back in her head. Hilda was a genius and didn't deserve to have a lying liar like Tom in her life. She resolved to immediately replace him in Hilda's affections.

"Our fake romance is for your social media audience only. I didn't consent to fake dating you IRL. You're reneging on the terms of our agreement, Thomas Tipper Cooke," she said.

Understanding, followed by embarrassment, instantly flooded into his eyes, and Tom stopped in the middle of the sidewalk, inviting more than a few stares. She had noticed how much attention they had gathered since they'd arrived on Main Street. It was hard to ignore the lingering looks and whispers as they walked: *Is that Tom? Is the Cooke boy finally home?*

Another uneasy feeling landed in her stomach. What had she gotten herself into? The feeling quickly morphed into anger. "Are you going to introduce me as your girlfriend to everyone we meet, or just the people who have known you since you were a child?" Another thought occurred to her. "And who's Emily?"

"Emily is a friend," Tom said.

"Ex-girlfriend, got it," Sameera said. They stared at each other. "You've been holding out on me with a few key details. Such as the fact that your family is famous and owns an entire town."

Tom wasn't looking at her, but there was a mulishness to his lips that hadn't been there a minute before. "Wolf Run is a tiny hamlet in the middle of nowhere. My family is not the House of Windsor."

"Why do you talk about your home like that?" she snapped. She wasn't sure why she was digging into him like this. Perhaps on some level, he reminded her of herself—running from her family, from anything that made her feel rejected and unsure.

Tom was wielding their fake relationship like a "get out of jail free" card, and she didn't like it. She didn't want to be anyone's excuse for not dealing with their life. She wasn't sure she even recognized this version of Tom: The laid-back man she had known in Atlanta was being slowly swallowed up by this moody, unhappy ice prince.

"Like what?" he asked, leaning close, and a whiff of his scent—cinnamon, sugar, and something else that was distinctly *Tom*—hit her, and she nearly took off running. This wasn't why she was here. She couldn't allow herself to be caught up in Tom's life, his problems, his dysfunction. She had enough of her own.

She shook her head. "You know what? Never mind. I don't care. This isn't real, and I'm not going to pretend for you. I won't play that game. When will Andy arrive?" Ignoring the vulnerability that flashed across his face, Sameera waited for an answer.

Except they were interrupted by a familiar voice. "Sameera! What took you so long?" Tahsin asked.

Chapter Eleven

Her parents and Barb were gathered in front of what looked like a parcel of forest tucked into the end of the main street. Sameera and Tom joined the trio, and Naveed immediately reached for the white paper pastry bag in her hands. His sweet tooth was infamous. When she was younger, he had instituted a "dad tax" on all dessert, which he still enforced to this day.

"Where's Rob?" Barb asked Tom.

She could feel Tom standing behind her, the rumble of his deep voice as he answered. "He's not with us," he said. She tried to ignore him.

"He returned back home to pick you all up. Jan said we can do the scavenger hunt today. Except none of you were picking up your phones," Barb said. Sameera checked her cell. There were no missed calls, and with a bolt of panic, she realized she had zero bars. What if Bee, or one of the partners, or even a client, wanted to get in touch? Even remembering that it was December 23, and this was unlikely, didn't calm her. What if Nadiya had tried calling? She would be even more angry that Sameera wasn't picking up. She needed to return to the guesthouse, where she had cell reception.

Sensing her tension, Tom laid a warm hand on her arm, making her feel even more jittery than she already did.

"Do you need to leave?" he whispered, and though she was still annoyed at him for the scene in the bakery, she was grateful for this moment of care. She nodded, and Tom turned to make their excuses.

Just then, Rob pulled up in the black pickup truck, and Esa and Cal emerged. Her brother was beaming with excitement and even seemed happy—or at least, not annoyed—to see her.

"We have to go," Tom said abruptly. "Sameera has a lot of work to catch up on, and I've already taken up enough of her time by dragging her on a tour of Wolf Run. You all have fun with the Christmas tree scavenger hunt."

Instantly, Esa's smile dimmed. She could feel her brother's disappointment radiate off him in waves, and her heart clenched. She put her phone away.

"It's okay. We're already here. A scavenger hunt sounds . . . fun," she added weakly. Esa's expression immediately brightened, and Sameera breathed a sigh of relief. Staying here was the right call, even if she had no wish to spend more time with Tom. She mentally resigned herself to the prospect of working all night to make up for this sojourn. Even if it might be too little, too late at this point.

"Do we . . . hunt the trees?" Esa asked, jumping to the ground from the truck. He turned to Sameera and stage-whispered, "They know conifers can't fight back, right?"

She smiled at him, grateful he was joking with her, and Esa gave her a small smile back.

"It's a Cooke family tradition, a scavenger hunt to find the perfect Christmas tree," Rob said, waving behind him at what was clearly a Christmas tree lot. "Tom's mother, Pamela, ran the game every year, until she passed. We looked forward to it every year."

"Even though Mom mostly just made up the rules," Tom said. He cast Sameera a quick glance, as if to reassure himself that she was still on board. "We had to find every item on her list in the tree lot. The list changed every year, of course. It made picking out a tree feel like an adventure."

"What do you win?" Esa asked. Sameera recognized the glint in her little brother's eyes. Her entire family—herself definitely included—was a tiny bit competitive, even her mild-tempered father. As in, they would mow each other down if there was a plastic trophy on the line.

Tom seemed at a loss. "I mean, the person who won got to pick out the tree," he said.

"Which means there's a winner and seven losers, right?" Esa said, eyeing their group of eight. When Tom nodded, he yelled "First tree choice is mine!" and ran into the tree lot without looking back.

"We already have a tree set up at home. This is just for fun," Rob said, puzzled.

"I should have warned you not to mention the c-word in front of my family," Sameera said to Rob. She leaned forward and whispered, "'Competition.'"

Tahsin, ever the teacher, took charge and suggested they break off into pairs: herself with Barb, Rob with Naveed, Calvin with Esa, and the happy couple would of course want to work together. Sameera tried to hide her wince.

Barb handed out sealed envelopes, each containing a paper with the names of random items chosen for the scavenger hunt this year. With a smirk, Sameera realized that Esa's head start wouldn't do him any good. He must have realized the same thing, because he sheepishly returned and stood peering at the paper beside Calvin, the two young men already talking strategy.

"This is a *friendly* competition," Barb reminded the group, eyes lingering on Esa. "We're going based on the honor system." Her tone implied her misgivings about this particular group's honor, but she soldiered through. "Whoever finds the items has to ring a bell." She handed out red-ribboned cowbells to each couple. "Our volunteer judge will decide which team gets the point, and any arguing with the judge will get you immediately disqualified. And this year, the prize isn't only the honor of picking out the tree. There will also be a special treat from Hilda's Bakery."

Esa fist-pumped, and everyone laughed.

"Who's the judge?" Sameera asked.

"That would be me," a voice called behind the group. Sameera turned around and came face-to-face with a beautiful blond woman, eyes crinkled in a welcoming smile, windswept hair loose around her shoulders. With her sharp features and blue eyes that shone turquoise in the weak afternoon light, she looked like she belonged on a holiday movie set. She was dressed in soft-pink fleece leggings that hugged her shapely legs, a white parka, and an oversize woolen scarf snug around her neck. Sameera had to stop herself from looking around for the camera crew following Margot Robbie's doppelgänger. Next to her, Esa's mouth hung slightly open.

"Hi, Tom," the vision said shyly.

"Hello, Emily," Tom answered.

"We're searching for a diamond, a star, something golden, a familiar tune, good luck, and Santa's helper," Sameera said, squinting down at the list. "Are you sure your stepmom doesn't have a side hustle making cryptic puzzles? I have no idea what any of these clues mean, or where to find them."

Sameera and Tom were walking around the large tree lot, their steps muffled by a dense undergrowth of snow and pine needles, and it felt like they were all alone in a forest. So far, Sameera had managed to stay focused on the task at hand. She could hear Esa's whoops faintly to the left, but no one had rung the bell to summon the goddess Emily.

Knowing that Tom had an ex-girlfriend in Wolf Run and coming face-to-face with the stunning reality were two different things. Not that Sameera was jealous. You had to care to feel jealous, and she was entirely without care. Completely careless. She flipped her heavy wool scarf over her shoulder to demonstrate her carefree attitude, and ended up stumbling.

"All right?" Tom asked, helping her up.

"I'm perfect," she said, hoping the red on her cheeks would be attributed to the chilly temperature, and not embarrassment. "I was just . . . thinking really hard. About the scavenger hunt. I think we're looking for a piece of coal. Coal makes diamonds, right?" She checked beneath a tree for a bag of coal, because why not? She looked up to see that Tom had stopped following her, and was standing still in the middle of the path. "Did you find something?"

"I'm sorry," Tom said.

She stood up, uncertain. "About Barb's cryptic clues?"

"For behaving like an ass," he said. "You were right to call me out. I had no right to introduce you as my girlfriend to Hilda. And I should have talked to Barb about our real arrangement. I've been acting like a spoiled toddler ever since you got here. No, I've been behaving like Blake."

She gasped. "Not Blake!"

"I'm really sorry, Sameera," Tom said. "Can you forgive me?"

Sameera wasn't used to people apologizing to her. Blake constantly took jabs at her, and Hunter had never said sorry for committing credit fraud and ruining her life, and Sameera had been too brokenhearted to legally do anything about it. At work, her entire job revolved around neither admitting nor accepting culpability. Even her parents had never acknowledged the role they had played in their estrangement, how their inability to adjust their strict expectations, combined with an overall lack of communication, had contributed to her yearslong deception. "Never apologize" was practically a mantra in her life. It was strange to have Tom, a near stranger, admit he was wrong, to take responsibility for his mistake, and to ask for her forgiveness. She wasn't quite sure what to do, actually.

Tom took a step closer, then another, and then that intense gaze was examining her as if she was the most interesting thing in the tree lot, and possibly the entire town. Which couldn't be true, because Miss Alaska was nearby, keeping a well-shaped ear out for any ringing cowbells while presumably dodging a barrage of marriage proposals from passersby.

Which made her wonder if Tom had ever proposed to Emily.

Focus, Sameera, she told herself. A gorgeous man was apologizing to her. Also, of course, he had proposed to Emily. Hell, Sameera had just met the woman, and she wanted to get down on one knee, too. Or at least, get some skin care tips because Emily's skin *glowed.*

"Thank you for admitting you were acting like a big dumb toddler," she said, and his lips twitched in that half smile she was starting to get addicted to. "You're so different here." She shouldn't invite his confidence, but despite her firm reminder to herself to remain impartial, she couldn't help but wonder about Tom Cooke.

He rocked back on his heels, hands buried in his pockets. "It's this place. Every time I return to Wolf Run, it all comes back. The same frustration that chased me away. My dad, going on and on about family legacy, and what he expects from me. I start to feel . . . trapped." His eyes were an intense blue now, glowing with their own light. "None of which is your fault. I apologize for making you feel uncomfortable. My family baggage is my issue to deal with, not yours. Especially since you're doing me this massive favor. I'll tell Barb and Rob the truth about us." He quirked a smile at her. "And you were right earlier. Barb doesn't just solve cryptic crosswords; she also makes them for the local paper."

An answering smile tugged at Sameera's mouth. "Game recognizes game."

Tom ducked his head. "I've been a terrible fake boyfriend."

"You really have," Sameera agreed. "While I've been setting the gold standard. You'll have to make it up to me."

"Deal." He held out his hand to shake, and she grasped it. His hand tightened in hers, and even through the layers of mittens and gloves, she could feel how warm he was. His eyes darkened as he met hers, and suddenly, his gaze turned hot, and hungry. Sameera shivered, wetting her lip, and his eyes followed the movement.

The sound of a cowbell made them jump apart, and they laughed awkwardly.

"I bet that's my dad," she said. "He's the most low-key Malik, but don't be deceived. He manages to win most of our games. We're convinced he cheats."

"It's always the quiet ones," Tom said. He let go of her hand, and his expression returned to its usual geniality. "I think you had the right idea with the coal. I know where we can find something golden, and I'm pretty sure 'good luck' is the old horseshoe Emily's mom nailed over the entrance to the storage shed. Come on."

In the end, Naveed and Rob scored the first point by finding a bag of coal beneath a tree, and Barb and Tahsin identified a familiar tune as the sound of sleigh bells. Esa and Calvin had worked out that a word scramble clue was "tinsel" and found a pile of the glittery gold decoration on one of the smallest trees on the lot, but Tom was right about the horseshoe. That left the final clue, a star. Now that each team was tied, the search took on a new energy, with each couple yelling distractions to their competition and engaging in some friendly trash-talking.

"Are you sure you don't need a stepladder to look for the star?" Naveed asked his petite wife with fake sincerity.

"I hope Hilda sells supersize chocolate bars, because I plan to win *big*," Esa said loudly when they passed him and Calvin down one aisle, and she responded with her own cheerful ribbing. It felt good to tease her little brother, and be mocked in turn.

Sameera was goading her father about stars when Tom tugged on her arm.

"Emily and I had a spot on the lot where we used to hide as kids," he whispered to her, and Sameera tried to ignore the sudden stab of jealousy at his words. Of course he and Emily had a special spot; they had grown up together in Wolf Run. It didn't mean anything.

Except Hilda had warned Tom that Emily was back in town, which implied they had a relationship that went beyond simply old childhood friends.

Not that it mattered. So what if Tom's ex-girlfriend (ex-fiancée? *Ex-wife?*) looked like a blond Hollywood bombshell and had eyes only for him? As soon as she got that intro to Andy Shaikh and this trip was over, she and Tom would go their separate ways.

Which was . . . fine. Exactly the plan. Perfect, really.

Tom led her to a secluded spot in the middle of the grove. It was quiet here, and the trees grew in an almost perfect circle, taller than the other conifers surrounding them. "This is the oldest part of the tree lot," Tom whispered to her. "Emily's mom never let anyone buy these trees for some reason. Said they were special. When we were younger, we thought maybe she was a witch, and this was where her coven met up. Now I think she just knew we liked to play here. It was one of the only places in Wolf Run that felt like it belonged only to us." He reached up to one of the trees, gently pushing aside the needles, and plucked something shiny hidden at the top.

"This feels like a setup," Sameera teased. "Insider trading."

"All is fair in love and hot chocolate," Tom quipped. He passed her the golden star, which was actually made from dented brass. She grinned at him and rang the cowbell. A minute later, an older woman—definitely not the ethereal Emily—appeared at the edge of the tree circle. The look she shot Tom was as cold as the snow surrounding them, and his smile instantly vanished.

"I told that girl not to hide the star here. Knew you'd find it right away. Come on, golden boy." The older woman turned abruptly without waiting to see that they were following.

"Who is that?" she whispered to him.

"Jan Michaels. Emily's mom," Tom said, keeping his voice low as they retraced their steps.

Sameera contemplated Jan's tense shoulders, her angry stride through the trees toward the main clearing. "I don't think she likes you," Sameera said, and beside her, Tom huffed out a laugh.

"She's the president of my fan club, actually," he said.

Jan turned around and eyed them suspiciously. "Bit tacky, isn't it? Bringing your new girl here to meet the woman you abandoned when you went down south."

This stopped Tom short. "Sameera is a friend, Jan. Nothing more."

Sameera flashed him a grateful smile. He had listened to her.

Jan snorted. "That's not what you told Hilda. Afraid to hurt my feelings? I always knew you were a snake."

Tom didn't take the bait. "Emily and I broke up a long time ago. It was mutual."

Jan snorted again. "Whatever you need to tell yourself, pretty boy." Her eyes wandered to Sameera. "Be careful with this one. He knows how to say all the right things. Too bad he's not as great at backing up those words with action."

"Tom has integrity. He would never attack someone in public and try to drag their character down in front of others," Sameera snapped back, clocking Tom's surprise at her immediate defense. She was surprised, too. But something about Jan's words bothered her. Tom had accepted his mistake the minute it was pointed out, and had just tried to do better. Besides, anyone who could brew chai like he did couldn't be all bad.

Jan wasn't impressed with her words, and scoffed. "Golden boy has you under his spell, too. Don't say I didn't warn you."

They approached the store, where their respective families waited, alongside the beautiful Emily, whose face fell when she caught sight of her mother.

"Look who I found showing his new girlfriend your special spot," Jan said, her tone derisive.

"We're not—" Sameera started, but Emily put a placating hand on her arm.

"Did you find the star?" she asked Tom, and he handed it over wordlessly.

While Emily mediated Esa's accusations of cheating, Sameera took the opportunity to examine Tom. Despite Jan's needling, he didn't appear upset at the situation. In fact, his reaction to Emily had been one of distant friendliness, without a hint of heartbreak. Jan seemed more upset than either Tom or Emily.

"Tom and Sameera found the last clue, which means they win!" Emily announced. She offered to buy Esa a hot chocolate as consolation, which silenced his complaints immediately.

Sameera excused herself to wash her hands before they set off. She needed a moment alone to collect her thoughts. She wasn't a confrontational person by nature, but she wouldn't let anyone attack her friends. She paused, thinking. Were they friends? At the very least, she and Tom were in this thing together. Even though they both had something to gain from their arrangement, he was her partner in crime, and Sameera had always been loyal. Despite the people she was loyal to not always deserving it, she thought, thinking of Hunter. Somehow, she knew Tom was different.

In the bathroom, she stared at her reflection and fixed her hair. The cold brought a rosy blush to her cheeks and a brightness to her eyes. In Atlanta, she spent so much time indoors, her light-brown skin usually looked dull by this time of the year. Her dark-brown hair was in its usual style, but she pulled off the elastic and fluffed it around her shoulders, then fished a tinted lip gloss from her bag. After a minute, she wiped off the gloss and retied her hair. Impressing people wasn't why she was here. She was here to meet Andy Shaikh, save her job, and maybe talk with her parents—in that order. Everything else was a distraction.

When she returned to the wood lot, everyone else had left, but Jan stood uncomfortably close to Tom, her finger poking into his chest. Sameera didn't feel bad about eavesdropping, because the older woman hadn't tried to lower her voice.

"You broke my girl's heart, and now you're back to rub it in her face. I won't stand for it."

Tom gently pushed Jan's hand away. "Emily doesn't want me anymore, Jan. I wish things had ended differently, but we've both moved on, and we're both happy. You have to find some way to accept that. It's the only way forward with your daughter."

The older woman took a step back, shaking her head. "All you do is take, Tom Cooke. Your entire family is the same."

Sameera cleared her throat loudly, startling them both. She pointedly asked Tom if he was ready to go and pulled him toward the door without waiting for an answer.

"Aren't you forgetting something?" Jan called after them.

Sameera turned around, hoping this wouldn't turn into another scene. But Jan was pointing at a Christmas tree, neatly tied and ready for transport. "Your parents said they wanted a souvenir. Hope you paid for extra luggage on your flight back home, Atlanta girl."

Chapter Twelve

"Hold your end straight. Now it's too high; lower it a bit. No, wait, watch where you're going!" Sameera said. Faced with the enormous tree, she and Tom had decided to carry it to the truck themselves. Not that they had a choice, as Jan was clearly not about to offer any help. Though Tom insisted he could carry it himself, Sameera had insisted right back that she would help. The neatly wrapped conifer was her parents' souvenir, after all. What Tahsin and Naveed had been thinking, she had no idea. There was no way they could bring a tree back to Atlanta.

"How do you usually decorate your Christmas tree?" Sameera asked.

"In Atlanta, it's just me, so I don't bother. What about your family?"

She thought fast. "With whatever we have lying around. Stickers. Paint. Streamers. Potato chips?"

"Not cheese balls? What about doughnuts on a string? Maybe some of those Ringolos, or Bugles," Tom teased.

"Doritos are good, too," she agreed.

"So, you've never decorated a Christmas tree," Tom said.

"What gave me away?"

The grin he threw her was warm and genuine. As if he saw her silliness, and liked her all the better for it.

Hunter's voice floated in her head then, always inconvenient and never welcome. *Really, Sameera, why would you say such a ridiculous thing? Sometimes I wonder where your head is at.*

Her despicable ex had routinely made little demeaning comments whenever she'd said something silly. She sometimes wondered if Hunter had recognized something broken in her that he could burrow inside—or had he done the breaking, so that she would never be open to love again?

"About Jan . . ." Sameera started.

"I'm sorry for what she said back there. She's known me since I was a little kid, which means she doesn't hold back. I haven't been her favorite person for the past few years."

"Because you broke up with Emily?" Sameera asked, hating herself. At least she hadn't added, *your drop-dead-gorgeous ex-girlfriend/fiancée/wife.*

"Something like that," Tom said, evasive. "Also, because I left town and made it clear I didn't intend to move back. That's considered treason in some Wolf Run households, including my own."

Sameera tilted her head, thinking. "It's a small town. I get why you might have wanted to explore the world a bit more."

Tom stopped abruptly. "I loved living here when I was a kid. It felt like the town belonged to me. My dad certainly talked about Wolf Run as if it did. I felt special. Except as I got older, it started to feel wrong. Like I had been given something I never earned. Then my mom got sick. For a long time after she died, it was hard to reconcile the part of me that belonged in Wolf Run and the part that wanted to leave, that needed to leave. When I got accepted to Georgia Tech, I took it. Rob didn't even know I had applied."

Sameera gripped the end of her tree tightly—it was tempting to drop it and embrace Tom instead. "You didn't do anything wrong," she said, and a flash of gratitude passed over his face, but then he shrugged.

"When I told my dad I was moving away, he predicted I would never come back," he said.

Sameera made a big show of looking around. "You're here now. It's never too late to come home." After Hunter left, Nadiya had encouraged Sameera to get back in touch with her parents. It had taken a long time for her to work up her courage, to swallow her fear and pride, and agree to talk. She was grateful every day that she had, and that her parents had welcomed her back in their lives.

Tom's smile was wary, clearly not convinced. "All this to say, when you see people staring—it's me they're wondering about, not you. I'm the traitor who left."

They had reached the truck now, and Tom lifted the tree into the bed without any help. Sameera tried not to stare as his muscles flexed, but it was difficult. He grinned when he caught her, and she schooled her features back to neutral.

"Or maybe they're wondering how Tom Cooke, Wolf Run's prodigal son, managed to ensnare all of this," she said, pointing at herself. She was joking, of course, but his gaze heated as it traveled up her body and came to rest on her lips.

"Me, too," he said softly.

They stared at each other for a moment, Sameera caught off guard by his admission. *Not what I'm here for,* she reminded herself. Tom was a flirt, and she was lonely. She couldn't do anything about the former, but once she had signed Andy as a client and her job was no longer in danger and she had—politely—told HR where to take their passive-aggressive threats, she could do something about the latter. But nothing could happen here, in the middle of all this confusing drama, with her future unknown and shaky.

Wordlessly, they got back in the truck and set off back home. In the cab, Sameera decided it would be in both their interests if she moved the conversation away from dangerous topics and back to Tom's issues with his family.

"I don't really buy your story," she said.

This surprised a laugh out of him. "Excuse me?"

Sameera dropped her end of the tree and put hands on her hips. "Your 'poor me' act. I don't think you believe it, either. Not really."

"May I remind you that we met a week ago? You don't know me very well." Tom's lips were set in a firm line, and his body language told her he didn't want to continue with this conversation. But she was a litigator, used to coaxing testimony from unwilling witnesses.

"I'm not basing my conclusions on any intimate knowledge of your character," Sameera said calmly. "I'm basing it on facts." She began to tally her points on her fingers. "You think no one wants you here. Well, Barb is thrilled to see you, and Calvin clearly wants to hang out. Hilda practically offered you a job on the spot, no questions asked. Not to mention Emily seemed excited to have you back," she couldn't help but add.

Tom was having trouble meeting her gaze now. "That's true, I suppose."

She gave him an extra second to see if he had anything to add about Emily. He didn't. She continued, "Secondly, there's an easy solution if you want to stay away from home." She took a deep breath. "You simply *stay away*. Ergo, you are exactly where you want to be." Atlas would have approved of her sharp smile. "Does the defense have anything to add?"

Tom shook his head ruefully. "No, ma'am."

"That's what I thought," she said.

He mulled over her words. "What about you?" he asked. "Alaska is a long way to travel to meet your daughter's alleged boyfriend's family. Your mom could have just FaceTimed—I know Tahsin Aunty loves her video calls. What's really going on there?"

Sameera looked out the window, even as she smiled at the honorific Tom had added to her mother's name. She wanted to tell Tom the truth about her complicated family relationships but found she couldn't. "My parents are retired, bored, and have a lot of disposable income," she said instead.

Tom was a good man; he didn't call her on her lie. They drove back home in companionable silence, each lost in thought.

Back at Cooke Place, everyone was gathered in the guesthouse. Rob and Barb had picked up on the Malik family's enthusiasm, and they had decided to set the new tree up in the guesthouse sitting room. Barb hurried to the main house to grab extra ornaments from the attic, and they considered their options. Esa held up one made of Popsicle sticks.

"Your handiwork?" he asked Calvin, eyebrows quirking.

Cal laughed and shook his head, nodding at Tom.

"I made it in preschool," Tom said, reaching for the ornament, which had clearly been glued together by a toddler with more enthusiasm than eye-hand coordination.

Rob stood beside his son. "You were so proud to hang it on our tree that year." He reached out and turned it over to reveal a framed picture on the other side, featuring toddler Tom, his blond hair a halo of soft curls and an adorable pout on his face, cradled in a younger woman's arms—his mother, Pamela. Behind them, Cinderella's castle was visible. He placed the ornament on the tree and stared at it.

Rob cleared his throat. "I'm afraid we don't have enough decorations for a second tree. Barb went on a bit of a decluttering spree last month."

"You always need the thing you just threw away." Barb laughed.

"Do you have any potato chips?" Tom murmured, glancing at Sameera. "How about cheese balls?" Sameera smothered her smile. Despite the strangeness of their interaction in town, she enjoyed Tom's teasing.

Tahsin jumped up and disappeared into her bedroom. Tom leaned close to Sameera. "She knows I was joking, right?"

"Never joke about food with a desi aunty," Sameera said. "Mom considers it her personal mission to feed everyone."

Tahsin returned with an armload of gauzy material and a few jewelry boxes. Catching on, Sameera reached out to hold up one of her mother's elaborate, colorful dopatta shawls for everyone to admire.

"Good thing I always travel with some of my favorite earrings," Tahsin said, holding open the boxes to display large jhumka earrings, an elaborate necklace, and a dozen bangles with filigree and crystal work.

The Malik family got to work, and a short while later stood back to admire their handiwork. Their very first Christmas tree was swathed in three shawls that ran the gamut of red, yellow, and purple in chiffon, satin, and wool. Interspersed between were shiny flashes of costume jewelry, each individual earring, necklace, and bracelet catching the light. On Esa's suggestion, they decided to top the tree with a bright-red wool hat with a jaunty pom-pom, in honor of the Alaskan chill.

"It's beautiful," Sameera said, standing back to admire their tree.

"I've never seen anything like it," Tom said, looking at her. Beside them, Esa mimed sticking a finger down his throat, but Sameera didn't mind. She would take her brother's jokes and teasing over his chilly silence any day.

"It looks a little bare underneath," Barb said. "We'll bring over the presents Santa got for you all from the big house later."

Tahsin, who had been smiling in satisfaction at the tree, now frowned. "Oh yes, presents. We have some for you as well. Santa just had some trouble with the local customs officer." She shot Sameera an annoyed look; clearly, her mother had not forgiven her for the luggage check their first night.

Barb waved her hand away. "Oh, you didn't have to get us anything! Just being here with us over the holidays is a gift." She tugged on Rob's hand, but her husband's eyes were still lingering on the small Popsicle-stick ornament. "We'll let you rest after all the excitement today. Come along, Cal, Tom."

Once the Cookes had left, Tahsin whirled on Sameera. "We must return to town immediately."

"Why?" Sameera asked.

"You would have me show up empty-handed to a Christmas celebration? I would never recover from the shame," Tahsin said, reaching for her jacket and pulling on her boots. "Naveed, we have a lot of shopping to do."

"But Barb said it was fine . . ." Sameera started. Tahsin held up her hand.

"Since you threw out the thoughtful gifts I *did* pack, you can come with me to pick out new ones."

"Anything is better than a chocolate crucifix and karaoke Santa," Sameera muttered, but she took her mother's point.

"I have to pick up a few things, too," Esa said, careful to keep his voice casual. Sameera was immediately suspicious, but Tahsin beamed at her youngest child.

"You want to buy a nice gift for our hosts? Such a generous boy," she said.

"I certainly am," Esa agreed. "Can I borrow a couple hundred dollars? You can't put a price on good manners."

That settled it. If Esa was going shopping with their parents, she would have no excuse not to join. Someone had to make sure they stayed out of trouble. She thought of the work waiting for her, and her half-finished pitch for Andy. It was Christmas Eve tomorrow, and she would buckle down and finish it all later, she promised herself. Andy wasn't expected until Christmas Day, anyway, according to that video message to Tom. Tonight she would make herself a double—no, triple—shot of espresso, stay up late finishing her pitch, and put a dent in her billable hours. It would be fine. There was plenty of time.

Besides, it had been nice, trimming the Christmas tree with her mother's trinkets and dopattas. Watching *Home Alone* last night with her family had been nice, too. Same with the holiday scavenger hunt, though perhaps not the confrontation with Jan.

"Coming, Sameera?" Esa asked, pausing by the door. There was a challenge in his gaze, and the tiniest tinge of hope in the question.

"Wouldn't miss it," she said. Sameera reached for her boots and followed her family outside.

Chapter Thirteen

Rob offered her father the keys to the truck for their trip back to town, which Naveed promptly passed to Sameera.

"She's the designated driver," he explained.

"That doesn't mean what you think it means, Dad," Sameera said, leading the way outside. Part of her was relieved Tom hadn't offered to accompany them. She needed a break from his relentlessly charming, handsome presence. Their last conversation had been laced with an intimacy she didn't have the energy or space for in her life. *Andy, my job, my family,* she reminded herself. Those were her priorities over the holidays. Definitely not enjoying Tom's smile, hands, words, or attention.

The drive was lively as everyone discussed the scavenger hunt and their first impressions of the village. Sameera also learned that Nadiya had been in touch with their parents and that her sister had asked for regular updates on how events were transpiring in Alaska, even though she couldn't be bothered to respond to Sameera's texts. Which was fine.

Esa asked her to stop the car in the middle of the intersection and jumped out before they could ask where he was headed, promising he would find them when he was done.

"Should he be allowed to go off on his own like that?" Sameera asked. "He's just a kid."

Tahsin and Naveed exchanged a bemused glance. "He's almost sixteen, and it's a small village. We're happy he's enjoying himself," Naveed soothed.

Her father was right. Esa probably needed a bit of space, in any case. She certainly had, at his age, though she hadn't gotten much of it. Maybe her parents had changed their parenting approach in the years since she was a teenager.

"How has he been?" she asked awkwardly as she pulled into a small parking lot and neatly maneuvered the truck into a spot at the back.

"Alhamdulillah," Naveed said, and her ears perked up. Though the phrase translated to "praise be to God," "Alhamdulillah" was actually the Muslim equivalent of "I'm fine, we're fine, everything is fine."

"Is something wrong with Esa?" she asked, trying to keep the alarm from her voice.

Again, her parents exchanged a glance. "He's a teenage boy, *beta*," Tahsin soothed. "It's hard to tell what is going on in his mind. And we have learned not to push too hard. It didn't work with you, after all."

Stung by the backhanded comment, Sameera lapsed into silence, though it was hard not to pepper her parents with more questions.

As if sensing her disquiet, Naveed added, "Esa is quieter lately, that's all. It happens as children grow. But he appears fine otherwise, Sameera. Perhaps a bit lost in the clouds sometimes. I think it has been good for him, this trip. He misses you."

"I miss him, too," Sameera said, her voice thick. The trio had walked to the main street by now, and silence descended between them, filled with unasked questions.

She should broach the subject now, while they were alone. Invite her parents to Hilda's for hot tea and snacks, and then start their long-delayed serious conversation about their estrangement, about why she'd kept Hunter a secret from them for so long, why she had cut them off after their big fight—and why they had let her, especially why Naveed had stayed silent and distant for so long. She opened her mouth to say something, but what came out was, "I have a lot of work to do back at the guesthouse, so don't take too long, okay?"

Naveed and Tahsin nodded their agreement, but she thought she spotted a fleeting expression of hurt at the words. Sameera cursed herself—she was a coward after all.

Their first stop was Cooke's Best Gifts, where Tahsin examined glass figurines, clocks, art, and collectibles. Sameera had to talk her father out of buying Rob and Barb a three-foot-tall resin King Kong statue dyed a bright festive green.

They perused a few more stores, and Tahsin picked up a pretty flannel throw with matching cushions, crystal glasses, and a cake tin in the shape of a Christmas tree, while Naveed coaxed Sameera and Tahsin into letting him buy a set of inflatable antlers that could double as a ring toss game.

The whole shopping expedition didn't take as long as Sameera feared, and she was mentally planning what file she would tackle first once they returned to the guesthouse when her parents suddenly bolted across the street.

Mystified, she checked for traffic (there was none—the term "sleepy village" had been coined for Wolf Run) and crossed. Her parents were already deep in conversation with someone when she joined them, though her eyes were trained on the storefront. What was a Middle Eastern restaurant doing all the way out here, and who could possibly run it?

The answer to at least one of the questions became clear when she noticed the man engaged in earnest conversation with her parents. He was tall and broad through the shoulders and belly, dressed in a black-and-red-flannel shirt with red suspenders, with a long, fluffy white beard, silver hair curled to his shoulders. His cheeks were rounded and red from the cold, and his generous mouth was fixed in a wide smile, eyes a bright, twinkling blue. The man's entire face was wreathed in smiles.

"Sameera, guess who this is!" Naveed said, excited.

Saint Nick? she nearly asked, but stopped herself.

Naveed gestured toward the restaurant, which had a tiny placard below.

"'Masjidul-Emaan,'" she sounded out. Like most Muslim children, she had been taught the Arabic alphabet and could phonetically pronounce some words.

"A mosque in Wolf Run!" Naveed crowed.

The man at their side seemed delighted by her father's excitement, and his smile widened, increasing his resemblance to a beloved holiday figure who belonged on the side of a cola can. "It's a restaurant, actually, but we host jumah prayer every week, and have some events in the basement, too. We are busiest in the summer months and during Ramadan, of course," the man said, his voice marked by a strong Middle Eastern accent.

"This is Abu Isra," Tahsin interjected, gesturing at the silver-haired man. "The imam of the mosque. He also owns the restaurant."

Abu Isra nodded at her in a friendly manner, explaining that he had moved to Wolf Run with his family from Syria a few years ago. *Syrian Santa,* a mischievous voice that sounded a lot like Esa whispered in her mind. She wondered where her brother had disappeared to; he would love this.

Her parents were fascinated to learn about the tiny Muslim community in Wolf Run, which numbered about a dozen people in the off-season and swelled to nearly twice that during the warmer months. Abu Isra—the name meant "father of Isra," by which Sameera understood that his eldest child's name was Isra, an honorary naming convention many Muslim and Arab men adopted after becoming fathers—was happy to chat, and clearly overjoyed to meet the Malik family.

"You must come over for dinner!" Tahsin said. "Please, allow us to cook for you."

Syrian Santa . . . *Abu Isra,* Sameera corrected herself, made a mild protest, but her mother insisted.

"Mom, we can't invite Mr. Abu Isra over for dinner," she murmured, sending an embarrassed smile at their new friend. "I'm not sure Rob or Barb would like company this close to Christmas. We're their guests, remember?"

But Tahsin only waved away her objections. "Nonsense, *beta*. The Cooke family won't mind. Rob is all about family. And Abu Isra, his wife, and their six children are our new Muslim family!"

Sameera wanted to sink into the ground. Her parents' enthusiasm for new acquaintances was legendary. Tahsin loved entertaining, and Naveed enjoyed finding new audiences for his stories, especially those featuring how things used to be when they had first immigrated to the United States. She was sure her parents' present excitement was largely the result of spotting another Muslim in Wolf Run. The town was nearly uniformly white, present company excluded.

Sameera tried again. "We're guests at Rob and Barb's home," she said in a discreet aside to her mother. "Please don't do this."

But Tahsin only ignored her concerns and doubled down, badgering poor Abu Isra until he promised to show up that night for dinner. By the time her parents waved goodbye to their new friend, Sameera was furious.

As soon as Abu Isra returned to his restaurant, she wheeled on her mother. "Why did you do that?" she demanded.

Tahsin blinked at her. "What do you mean?"

She appealed to her father, but Naveed shared her mother's confusion. "What is the issue, Sameera *beta*?" he asked.

Sameera tried to take a deep breath and calm down, but suddenly, she wanted to throw something. Her fingers itched to smash her mother's newly purchased crystal glasses, but she settled for kicking at a pile of snow. Her parents stared at her.

"You always do this," Sameera said. "You never listen to me. You assume you know best. You barge into my life and then try to take over."

Tahsin and Naveed looked at each other. "*Beta*, you need to calm down. You're making a scene."

"Stop calling me '*beta*.' I'm not a little kid, and I am *not* making a scene!" Sameera yelled, and a handful of pedestrians looked over. Okay, maybe she was making a scene, but they had started it. Her parents reached for her arm, tried to pat her on the shoulder, but she took a step away from them.

"Do you want us to tell Abu Isra not to come over?" Tahsin asked. "I can tell him right now that my daughter is not comfortable with his presence. Of course, his children will be so disappointed."

Sameera closed her eyes. This entire trip was spiraling out of control. She should have stayed in the guesthouse and worked. No, she should never have gotten on the plane in the first place. Her presence here had not stopped her parents from their usual kooky behavior. It never did.

"I wish you would listen to me," she repeated, suddenly feeling defeated and tired. "I don't understand why you're even here."

"I think you do," Tahsin answered, and her tone was hard now. Beside her, Naveed tried to defuse the situation, but both women ignored him. "If you had been honest with us from the start, we would all be in Atlanta right now."

"I was honest! There is nothing going on between me and Tom!" Sameera said.

"Just as there was nothing going on between you and Hunter? Or you and Colin? Or you and Umar? You have lied to us again and again."

Sameera flinched at the names of her high school and college boyfriends—all fleeting relationships. She hadn't realized her parents had known about them. But of course they had—her mother was not above snooping in her room or even on her phone. She closed her eyes, willing herself to calm down.

"Remember what you did when you were eighteen?" Tahsin said, referring to the infamous overnight cabin trip. Her mother's voice was goading, as if she, too, was tired of skirting around the issue. She sounded furious now, too. "You've proven again and again that we can't trust you, Sameera. That you are incapable of thinking clearly when a man is involved. That you still need us to save you from yourself. Look at what happened with Hunter—if you had only been honest with us about your relationship, we would have been able to stop what he did to you. We could have guided you. Instead, you messed up your life."

Ice entered Sameera's veins as she stared at her mother, before her gaze traveled to Naveed, who couldn't meet her eyes. This was what they really thought of her, she thought: that she was naive, weak, her judgment innately flawed. They thought she deserved every single setback. That she had deserved Hunter's cruelties, small and large.

She was so sick of it.

"I'm sorry I've been such a disappointment. I know I'm not the daughter you wanted. But you're not the parents I wished for, either," she said flatly. With a sick sense of satisfaction, she watched as her words landed, watched as Naveed's face grew pale, watched her mother's sharp inhalation. Good. She wanted them to hurt, too.

She handed her father the car keys and walked away before she started to cry.

Somehow, she found herself at Hilda's Bakery, nursing a chili hot chocolate. The temperature and the spice level of the drink both fit her dark mood. She had regretted the words the minute they were out of her mouth, and she hated her momentary happiness at seeing them land even more.

If Nadiya were here, she would know what to do. She would have forced Sameera to be brave, to talk to her parents. Their argument was even more proof that they had things they still needed to say to one another, but she had messed it all up. Instead, she sat and sipped and seethed quietly.

Hilda had left her alone, but when Tom showed up twenty minutes later, she knew the baker must have called him, and part of her was grateful. He settled into the seat across from her, and she stared out the window at the people walking by.

"Want to tell me what happened?" he asked gently.

She shrugged. "My family is crazy."

Tom's laugh was soft, and kind. "You'll never believe this, but same."

"I'm the little girl who cried wolf, and now no one will ever believe me again," she said. She felt ridiculous even trying to explain the situation to Tom. "They still haven't forgiven me for the way I kept things from them. For lying to them about Hunter. They think I deserve what happened."

She waited for Tom to ask for details, to press for the whole, sorry story. Instead, he put his forearms on the table, leaning forward. "When I was in middle school, my dad thought it would be a good idea to sponsor the local hockey league. Not a team: the entire organization."

"That sounds . . . generous?" Sameera said, wondering where he was going with this.

"He had only one condition—I had to be a starter on the twelve-and-up boys' team."

"Sounds like a nice opportunity," Sameera said cautiously.

"It would have been nice, if I knew how to skate. Or liked hockey. Or was friends with anyone else on the team," Tom said.

"Oh no," Sameera said, covering her mouth with her hands to stifle a horrified laugh.

"Rob showed up to every game and sat front and center, just to watch me fall on my face on the ice. He sat there while my teammates, who had been playing hockey from the age of three, made fun of me," he said. "I think he thought I'd magically get better, through the power of his money and childhood bullying." There was a wry smile on his face, but Sameera wasn't fooled. Tom had unearthed a painful childhood memory and presented it to her as if it were a talisman. It made it easier to share her thoughts, the ones she wished she didn't have.

"Sometimes, I feel embarrassed by my parents," she said in a low voice, hating herself. "I don't want to feel this way. I hate that I do, and I know I should have grown out of this by now. But they will be walking down the street and say something outrageous, or wear something silly, like those Christmas sweaters, and I'm thirteen years old again and mortified, and I want to disappear."

They looked at each other in silence, and for the first time, Sameera didn't feel the usual self-disgust mixed with toe-curling anxiety when she thought about what she had shared.

"It will be okay," Tom said solemnly. "Whatever they did, I promise it will be all right."

"They invited a random stranger over for dinner at Cooke Place. Tonight," Sameera blurted.

Tom paused. "That's fine. My dad loves company."

"Abu Isra plans to bring his wife and six kids," she added.

Tom broke out in a smile. "Abu Isra is coming over? Then there's no trouble at all. My parents eat at his restaurant all the time."

This startled a laugh from Sameera. "Does everyone just know each other here?"

"Pretty much, yes," Tom said. "It used to drive my mom crazy. She was an introvert."

Sameera raised a brow. "That must have been difficult, in a place like Wolf Run."

"I think she understood what was expected of her when she married my dad. There's always give and pull in any relationship."

"That hasn't been my experience," Sameera said wryly, thinking of Hunter. She returned to people-watching, but this time she could feel Tom's gaze on her.

"Why are you single?" he asked, something more than curiosity in his voice.

"How do you know I'm single? Maybe I have a boyfriend in Atlanta. Or a fiancé," she teased, and his eyes went wide. "Relax, I'm single. I have been, ever since my boyfriend and I broke up last year."

"That's a long time," he said.

"When you work sixty- to eighty-hour weeks, what's impossible is keeping anyone around," she countered. That wasn't the only reason, of course. Bee had installed a few apps on her phone several months after Hunter left, had even offered to set her up with her cute next-door neighbor, Diego, a visual artist. She had rebuffed every encouragement. The scars Hunter had left by his betrayal ran too deep to be quickly forgotten.

Sometimes she wondered if she would ever be able to let someone into her heart again. No matter how amazing their samosas.

"I understand what it's like, being too busy for a relationship. I'm just wondering how you walk anywhere without tripping." Off her questioning look, he added, "Because of all the people dropping at your feet." She threw her balled-up napkin at him, and he smiled at her before ducking his head, suddenly shy. "Andy wasn't lying in his message. It's been a while for me, too," he admitted.

"Now that I can believe," she said, and he made a face at her.

"We both work crazy hours. We're both ambitious and driven. *Some of us are more charming than others*," he added, waggling his brows.

"You mean *some of us* have to try harder," she teased, and he grinned, accepting her parry.

"Plus, there's the online hellscape of dating apps." He shrugged his shoulders in a *who is even dating amid the trash fire that is modern life* sort of way. Except, in her case, it wasn't the whole story, and for the first time in a long time, she found herself wanting to talk about Hunter.

"My last relationship didn't end well. When Hunter left me—"

"Your ex was named Hunter?" Tom asked, unimpressed. "His name is a red flag."

Sameera started laughing. "That's what my sister Nadiya said!"

"Nadiya has good instincts. You should listen to her."

"She's currently not talking to me, because she thinks I'm dating *you*."

Tom leaned back. "Give me your phone. I'll text her right now and tell her you're smarter than that."

Sameera laughed and shook her head.

"What happened with the Walking Red Flag?" Tom asked.

"We met while I was in law school," Sameera started. "He was finishing up an MBA."

"Second red flag," Tom murmured. "Never trust a finance bro."

"He's an engineer. And weren't you in business school?" she asked.

"Which is why I know what I'm talking about. I bet he couldn't cook, either," Tom said darkly.

Sameera shrugged—Tom wasn't wrong—before continuing. "I fell for him, hard. I thought I was in love, but he wasn't Muslim, and I knew my parents wouldn't understand. Not that I ever told them about any of my relationships. Only Nadiya knew how much I liked him. He wasn't terrible, not at the start."

Tom snorted. "Neither is arsenic." He put his hands up at her expression. "I'll be good. Please, continue, and make sure to include this guy's full name and last known address. I'd like to pay him a visit when we return home."

Home. Tom thought of Atlanta as home, but the way he had said it, it almost sounded as if he meant *their* home. Sameera took a deep breath. "I wish I could tell you where Hunter is right now. Last year, five years into our relationship, I came back to the apartment we shared to find it cleared out. His belongings were gone. But he did leave behind about seventy-five thousand dollars' worth of debt, on credit cards and lines of credit he had taken out in my name."

The shocked expression on Tom's face nearly turned her brittle smile into a genuine one. "I guess I'm not so smart after all," she said, and her voice shook. Tom instantly reached for her hand, clasping it tightly in his own warm grip.

"I promise you, Sameera," he said, his eyes steady on her face. "I will name my garbage disposal after that turd."

She laughed, but it sounded like a sob, and she realized her cheeks were wet. She hadn't thought she had any tears left for Hunter. She wiped them away, embarrassed. "I'm sorry. I didn't mean to tell you the story of my greatest mistake. I should come with caution tape." She knew she sounded pitiful, but the gentle look Tom gave her now somehow made her feel lighter, like less of a disaster. "Do you have any sad stories you want to share?"

Tom leaned back. "How about this? One night, I was catering yet another holiday party. The people who hired me wanted classy, upmarket, bland food that looked expensive. The party was full of the usual type, boasting about their yachts or whatever, and I was incredibly bored. Then suddenly, a spotlight shone down on the most beautiful woman I'd ever seen, right in the middle of the party."

Sameera raised her eyebrows. What was he talking about?

Tom continued, "Except there wasn't a spotlight. It just felt like it, because all I could see was *her*. Beautiful, sure. But there was something about her. She carried herself with this aloof vitality. She handled her idiot colleagues without breaking a sweat. She told me my samosas weren't spicy enough, and she was right."

Sameera's heart started to pound.

Tom's smile was almost sad. "She didn't notice me, of course. Goddesses usually don't notice mortals, not until they make themselves into a nuisance, but still, I tried to capture her attention. I got the special drink she requested, even though I had to run to the corner store, but she barely looked my way. When she walked into my kitchen to take a call, I knew I was in trouble. Because in addition to being the most beautiful woman I'd ever seen, she was funny and kind and smart, and she told me her mom made the best samosas and . . ." He trailed off, eyes coming to land on hers, which were wide and staring. Was he serious? Were any of these words true?

"And that's when I knew that even if nothing ever came of it, even if we never met again, I had met someone special," Tom said simply. They stared at each other, the moment lengthening, stretching, gaining heat in an impossible way.

"That's some story," Sameera said, her voice faint. She swallowed and tried again. "Not sure it's believable, actually."

But Tom wasn't done. "The next day, her mother invited me to cater an Eid party. And even though I was double-booked and had a wait list of clients, I canceled everything and accepted. Just so I could see her again."

Her words had dried up now, and Tom's eyes were steady on hers, warm and sincere. She felt a rising panic.

"Tom, I—" she started before stumbling to a stop. He stood and held out a hand to her.

"It's okay, Sameera. You don't have to say anything. I just wanted you to know that I think you're spectacular," he said softly.

Her mind was reeling. Did Tom mean any of it? He had been nothing if not honest since they met, attentive and generous, eager to please and capable of accepting when he was wrong. If she wasn't so damaged, she might be in real trouble. But she was too messed up, mixed up, and confused to accept the hand he was metaphorically holding out to her. Instead, she reached for her signature move and deflected.

"We should head back to Cooke Place and break the news to Rob and Barb about our last-minute dinner guests," Sameera said. After an infinitesimal pause, Tom tucked his hand in his pocket. She walked out of the store, her heart twinging only a little, but not so anyone would notice, least of all Tom.

It was better this way. For both of them.

Chapter Fourteen

"He said *what?*" Bee screeched on the phone early that afternoon, and Sameera had to hold it away from her ear or risk injury.

She had immediately returned to her room upon their return to the Cooke property, and though she felt bad for leaving Tom to break the news of the impromptu dinner party to his parents alone, she really couldn't face them right now. Or him.

After losing the battle to concentrate on her files, she called Bee. *Just for five minutes,* she promised herself. *Just to get that conversation with Tom out of my head. Then I'll be able to finally sit down and work!*

"I *knew* he was gone for you. He kept staring during the party and hovering and bringing you snacks! That boy is in deep. Maybe he lured you to Alaska because he *loooooves* you," Bee said, cackling with glee.

"That was all my mom and Barb's doing," Sameera reminded her friend.

"That's what they want you to believe!" Bee said. "Just don't get married and move there. It's too far to visit, and I don't handle the cold well. But wait, what are you doing talking to me? Shouldn't you be smooching your not-so-fake boyfriend?"

"This doesn't change anything," Sameera said, and on the other line, Bee grew dangerously quiet.

"Wait a second. What did you say when he told you he liked you?" her friend asked.

"Nothing," Sameera said. Bee's shriek nearly ruptured her eardrum. "Stop screaming. I didn't know what to say. Things are so strange. I got into a huge fight with my parents. Nadiya has been ignoring me. I don't even know where my little brother *is*. And let's not forget I have a meeting with HR next week, whereupon I will officially be out of a job, unless I can convince a random billionaire to hire me. I can't add whatever *this* is with Tom to the chaotic mix. I just can't."

Bee's voice was gentle when she spoke again. "Is this about Hunter?"

As usual, her friend knew to get to the heart of the matter. Sameera exhaled. "No. Maybe. I told Tom what he did. He promised to name his garbage disposal after him."

"Good man," Bee said with approval. "All joking aside, you don't have to do anything but take care of yourself, Sam. And maybe talk to your parents. But other than that, you don't owe anyone your peace of mind, or your happiness. Okay?"

"Okay," Sameera said, and then she was crying again. What was up with all these tears? She thought Christmas was supposed to be a festive, joyous holiday.

Once she'd settled down and assured Bee that she was fine, and promised to call if she needed anything, Sameera got to work. She even made some headway, but it was hard to concentrate. Her parents still had not returned, and she resisted the urge to text her brother to find out what was going on. Not that the message would go through, she recalled, with the spotty cell reception in town. She forced herself to concentrate for another fifteen minutes before pulling out her phone and texting Nadiya. Hopefully her sister would still be up, despite the time difference.

Her fingers hovered over the keys and she typed: **Nadiya, we need to talk. It's not what you think. I miss you. Please, call me back. I love you.**

She pressed send before she could overthink it. A moment later, the message appeared as read, but as much as she willed those three little dots to appear on her screen, Nadiya didn't respond. Her sister had told her to sort her shit out. But how?

A knock on the patio door brought her out of her reverie, and she wasn't surprised to see Tom at the sliding glass door, holding a grocery bag.

"I know you have work to do, but I thought maybe we could film a video, as per our legally binding contract," he said, leaning against the doorjamb. From his forced-casual posture, she knew that he was trying to play it cool, trying not to make things strange between them, and her heart warmed, despite her protests to Bee.

She liked Tom; more than that, she knew that if she begged off, he wouldn't judge her, or say she was working too much, or try to make her feel guilty. It made the decision easy, really. She stepped aside, and Tom made his way to the brand-new kitchen as if he were approaching a holy temple. Feeling shy after his recent admission, Sameera followed him, even as another part of her was eager to spend time with him; it was a better alternative to brooding over her fight with her parents, or her silent sister, or whether Esa had returned to the house. She realized with a jolt that out of everyone she knew in Wolf Run, he was the one she felt the most comfortable around right now. He demanded the least from her, even though he had the most to lose if she broke off their arrangement. In some ways, his future career path rested on her, the same way hers did on him.

He started putting groceries away and rummaging through the cabinets with familiarity, which confirmed her suspicion that Tom had cooked in this kitchen before.

"What did your dad mean when he said you never cooked when you were home?" she asked.

Tom shrugged. "I usually don't visit for long enough. I used to cook all the time when I lived here. It was something my mom and I used to do together, before she got sick. These days, not so much." His words were glib. This was clearly a subject he didn't want to talk about further. He had been so respectful of her boundaries; the least she could do was stay within his.

"What are we going to make, Chef?" Sameera asked brightly instead.

Tom placed a series of saucepans on the stove. "I thought we would dazzle our audience with a simple chai tutorial. We can make karak chai, Kashmiri chai, and maybe attempt Irani chai, too. What do you say?"

Sameera raised an eyebrow. He had clearly done a thorough investigation on three popular tea varieties from the subcontinent; the third one was a deep cut—Irani chai was a specialty from Hyderabad, the city where her parents were born.

"I'm impressed," she conceded. "Most people can just about figure out that chai is tea. But you also have no idea what you've gotten yourself into if you think you can make Kashmiri chai on the first try," she teased. The drink, made by brewing green tea in milk, then garnishing with pistachios, almonds, cashews, and candied rose leaves, was a favorite, but the brewing process was notoriously finicky, as was achieving its famous pink hue. Unless he planned to cheat and add food coloring.

"Certainly not," he said indignantly when she asked. "I've got some baking soda. I can do this. If you don't believe me, how about a friendly wager?" He raised his chin in challenge, and she laughed.

"You're on," she agreed. "I bet you won't be able to make real, pink-colored Kashmiri chai."

"And I'm confident I can nail it on my first try. What do I get if I win?" he asked. There was a wicked glint in his eyes. He was flirting with her again, but after what he had said at the bakery, she wasn't sure she should encourage him.

On the other hand, she was a Malik, and no one in her family could resist a challenge.

"If *I* win, you have to make me your three favorite meals when we get back to Atlanta," Sameera said.

Tom instantly agreed. "Deal. And if I win, I don't tell Barb and Rob our relationship is fake until after Christmas."

She frowned at him. "What?"

His gaze took on a pleading expression. "I won't ask you to lie to them if they come out and ask. I won't introduce you as my girlfriend to anyone else. It's just . . . my dad keeps dropping hints, trying to make me feel guilty for not moving home. If he knew that I didn't have any real ties to Atlanta—"

"What about your business? Your friends, your life, it's all in Atlanta," Sameera said.

Tom shook his head. "I know it doesn't make any sense, but none of that matters to him, not the way a serious relationship does. It's complicated, and I know I'm asking a lot of you, but I don't think I have it in me to have that conversation with them. At least, not right now. Please, Sameera?"

She wanted to refuse. To tell Tom that he was being a coward and that he needed to have the hard conversation with his father, instead of reaching for the easy lie. But wouldn't she be a hypocrite? She couldn't talk to her parents, either. So she just nodded. There was no way he could make the Kashmiri chai anyway.

Tom set up the camera, and they started filming. He gathered the ingredients for the three types of chai—whole milk, cream, condensed milk, black tea, green tea, nuts, and baking soda—while she explained the techniques for the three different tea varieties, how they differed, and the unique properties of each tea. She even shared anecdotes about the role chai played in her life. Once they started brewing, they bantered and joked for the camera, and it all felt so easy, their chemistry palpable. If anything, their connection had grown stronger over the past few days, a result of all the time they had spent together.

It was all so fun and such a good distraction that when Tom's careful brewing and steady hand managed to coax the first telltale pink bloom in the Kashmiri chai, even Sameera cheered.

Afterward, as comments and heart emojis piled up on his feed, and they sampled the trio of chai and joked about not being able to sleep that night from all the caffeine, Tom slung an arm around her shoulder and pulled her close in a friendly hug. Sameera had to school her features to make sure she didn't melt into a warm puddle.

"Thank you," he whispered in her ear, his breath hot and sweet against her skin.

"Anytime," she said. "This was good for me, too." She felt calmer, somehow, after brewing the chai and spending time with Tom. He had that effect on her, she realized.

She started to tidy up the countertop. Only an hour had passed, but it felt like no time at all, and as she worked, whatever spell they had woven while they cooked together—though Tom would never refer to making tea as "cooking," she recalled with a smile—broke, and all her worries rushed back: her work, her parents, Esa, Nadiya. Tom.

"I hope my parents aren't terrorizing Rob and Barb," Sameera said.

"They just got back. I heard the truck in the driveway a few minutes ago. I can finish cleaning up here, if you wanted to check on them."

She didn't, actually, but she probably should. Tom stopped her with a hand on her arm. His casual touches were becoming more frequent, but the electrical jolts didn't seem to be going away. Maybe it was the Alaskan chill.

"I mean it, Sameera. Thank you for agreeing to go along with our ruse"—he quirked a brow—"in front of Rob and Barb. I'll make you my three favorite meals anyway. I'm grateful."

"I lost the bet," Sameera said. "Though I still think you cheated. Admit it, you've got a bottle of red food coloring in your pocket."

"You're welcome to give me a pat-down, beautiful," he drawled, throwing his hands wide.

Sameera laughed and, after pulling on her boots and jacket, went to face her parents.

To no one's surprise, her mother had taken full command of the kitchen. The counter was lined with shopping bags full of groceries, and Tahsin was rooting inside the Cookes' large fridge while Naveed, Rob, and Barb watched.

"Where do you keep the ghee?" Tahsin asked, her voice muffled by the heavy fridge door.

"Do you mean butter?" Rob asked, googling the term on his phone.

"Certainly not," Tahsin said, affronted.

"I think I have some from when I tried to cook an Indian curry last year," Barb said, peering in the pantry. Naveed noticed Sameera hovering by the doorway and beckoned for her to join him at the kitchen table. Swallowing her resentment and embarrassment, she entered the kitchen and took a seat beside him. Her father was always the peacemaker, the first one who wanted to make up and sweep any unpleasantness under the rug. It used to annoy her, but right now, she appreciated his willingness to make space for her without admonishment. They had to keep up appearances, at least for the Cookes. It wouldn't be fair to drag Tom's family into their issues, especially not when Tahsin had sprung a last-minute dinner party on them all.

Naveed set up the Cookes' coffee grinder alongside packages of whole spices—cardamom, cumin, cloves, cinnamon, coriander, and fennel seeds—which Sameera knew he would use to prepare a fresh garam masala spice mix used in almost every dish. Sameera clocked Barb's wince as he started grinding and made a note to send her a brand-new coffee grinder once this was over.

"It looks like you have everything under control," Sameera said.

Tahsin, finished plundering the refrigerator, pierced her with a look.

"You can start chopping onions since you're here," her mother said gruffly. It was more of an order than an acknowledgment or apology, but at least Tahsin wasn't ignoring her. Wordlessly, Sameera moved to the ten-pound bag of onions on the counter and started sorting.

"I know inviting people over for dinner is a huge imposition," Sameera said, not looking at her mother, but Rob waved her protests away.

"Nonsense. I like Abu Isra. Makes the best hummus in the state. Should have had him and his family over for dinner years ago. The more the merrier, especially at this time of year." In that moment, Sameera could see Tom in his father: the same generous spirit and can-do attitude that made his son so much fun to be around, at least when he was acting like himself in Atlanta.

To Sameera's pleasant surprise, it didn't take long for both the Cookes and the Maliks to relax and let their guard down. They were soon laughing over potent spices, and then Rob offered to make a batch of his latest eggnog flavor, green tea and licorice—minus the alcohol, of course.

"I started the yearly eggnog experiment because of Tom," Rob explained after his second cup. Sameera suspected he had spiked his own drink. "He loved to mix up ingredients and experiment. I thought he was going to become a scientist when he got older." The older man seemed wistful. "We would make a batch and have his mother try it. She pretended to like all the flavors, of course, and Tom was so pleased."

"He still likes to experiment," Sameera said. "When my mom showed him how to make samosas, he made a whole batch with different fillings, each inspired by different cuisines, from Hakka to vegetarian options."

Rob finished his eggnog. "I'm glad to hear that, glad he's doing well for himself down south," he said.

"Tom would love to talk to you about his life in Atlanta, if you asked," Sameera said, and Rob seemed thoughtful. Maybe he would listen to her. Then again, habits were hard to change, as she knew all too well.

Sameera started chopping onions, wondering how she had wound up on sous-chef duty while Esa and Cal got off scot-free. Barb came over to help, and Sameera joked that the first step in Indian cooking was to open a bag of onions and keep dicing until Tahsin told them to stop, whereupon they would have roughly half the onions the recipe required.

"Don't listen to Sameera. She can't cook," Tahsin said, in full generalissimo mode. "Cut those very fine, *beta*, no one wants an onion wedge in their channa." Her mother was a whirlwind, simultaneously washing spinach, dicing tomatoes, and opening a giant can of chickpeas.

They had decided on karahi chicken, marinated in a flavorful blend of yogurt, green chilis, and coriander, plus garam masala; a savory vegetable biryani made with fresh produce; channa chickpea curry cooked in a rich brown gravy; and palak saag, a North Indian dish that was her mother's favorite and involved slowly simmering spinach and mustard greens with aromatic spices.

Sameera and Barb worked companionably, making their way through the onions before mashing garlic and ginger together into a paste. "Maybe Tom will join us," she said. Barb threw her husband a quick look before leaning close.

"Tom doesn't like to cook when Rob is around. I think he's out helping Emily with something."

Sameera nodded, keeping her face lowered so Barb wouldn't notice her consternation. Tom hadn't mentioned that the reason he didn't cook in Wolf Run was because of his father, but it made sense. He also hadn't said anything about helping Emily when they were filming in the guesthouse. Not that he owed her an explanation, of course.

Barb turned to her, expression earnest. "You don't have to worry about Emily, you know."

"Tom and Em go way back," Rob chimed in from the dining table, where he had clearly been eavesdropping. "Dated all through high school. I thought for sure they'd get married. They were good for each other. When he came home halfway through his sophomore year, we all expected him to pop the question. Instead, they broke up." Rob shook his head. "They even had one of those cutesy couple names. What was it, Barb?"

Barb must have noticed how quiet the kitchen had gotten. "Who can remember? It was years ago. Ancient history."

"'Tomily,'" Rob said, snapping his fingers. "Catchy, right? Don't know what happened there, but Tom likely screwed it up." He disappeared through a door, muttering something about looking for the linen napkins.

"I'm sorry about that," Barb said quietly. "Rob can be critical. He can't help but snipe whenever Tom comes back to visit, though I've told him again and again that he's pushing the boy away."

Sameera's eyes were on her parents now. Though their conversation was muffled by the hiss of mustard seeds popping in oil, her eyes were drawn to their faces, the lines on her mother's forehead, the gray that almost entirely edged out the brown in her father's hair. She remembered thinking the same thing. *If only Mom would stop criticizing me. If only Dad would stand up for me. If only they tried to understand me instead of condemning or trying to control me.*

"Believe me, I understand," she said, matching Barb's somber tone.

Barb smiled, and it transformed her face. "You and Tom are a much better match. I truly believe that when you're meant to be with someone, things have a way of working out. I wasn't born in Wolf Run; I came here to visit a friend. But then Rob and I found each other and decided to build a life together. That's the key, my dear—love isn't a magic bullet. It just opens a door, but you both have to do the hard work to walk through it together."

Sameera was touched by Barb's words, but also alarmed by how far away she was from the truth. "I don't know about that," she hedged. Mindful of the bet she had recently lost, she settled for a weak, "It's early days yet."

Which, naturally, her mother overheard, judging by her tightening lips. *Great.*

"You're being modest, my dear. Tom came home to us, all because of you. I have a feeling we'll be seeing a lot of each other from now on," Barb added happily. She looked up to see what Tahsin was up to, muttered something about turmeric on the counter, and hurried away, leaving Sameera alone with her thoughts.

As a desi girl, Sameera was no stranger to guilt. But what she felt now made her want to dig a hole in the backyard and let Atlas eat her for lunch. Quietly excusing herself, she made her way outside, wrapping her arms tightly around herself for warmth. Luckily, the sun was out, though not for much longer; she raised her face to the sky, closed her eyes, and breathed deeply.

She didn't want any of this. Not her mother's ill-advised interfering or her father's peacemaking. She definitely didn't want Barb to attribute Tom's reappearance in Wolf Run to their "relationship," as if she were the sort of good little woman who could inspire a family reunion. Sameera knew her role and who she was—the black-sheep daughter of a respectable desi family, the one who had cut her parents off for years. The one who had terrible, terrible taste in men.

Her pattern of avoiding conflict and keeping secrets hadn't started with Hunter. Her first boyfriend in middle school had told the entire student body that she was his girl, and she had been so flattered to be picked, to be wanted, that she had gone along with it for an entire week, until he showed up to school holding hands with another girl.

Then there was her high school crush, who had "let" her do his English homework for two semesters while publicly mocking her to his friends. A few others in high school and undergrad were more typical relationships, though they hadn't lasted long.

Each time, Nadiya had counseled her to guard her heart, to be less naive and willing to believe her boyfriends' lies. Hunter's betrayal was only the latest heartbreak in a long line of them. In the end, it hadn't even been that surprising, really. On some level, maybe she thought she had deserved it all because she hadn't been the daughter her family wanted.

Tom's estrangement from his family and her own situation as his faux-girlfriend were both bringing back a host of unwelcome memories she had no idea how to process—not without Nadiya. As supportive and kind as Bee was, she didn't know her like her sister. A sudden wave of fatigue hit her, and she cleared snow from a bench in the backyard and sat down.

She was tired. It wasn't just the jet lag, or the discomfort of being in a strange house far from home, or even the stress of keeping track of her family, or the realization that she would have to work all evening and maybe even all night to make a dent in her billable hours and to put the finishing touches on her pitch for Andy Shaikh.

All right, it was all of that, but also so much more. Bee was right: This had to do with Hunter. More than that, it had to do with what he represented.

Hunter's departure had blown down the house of straw that was her life. While it was true she hadn't seen the signs of his gambling addiction and the serious financial problems it caused, a truer assessment could be that she hadn't wanted to see them. Hadn't wondered why they never had any money left every month, despite their reasonably good jobs.

Even before he abandoned her, their relationship wasn't perfect. But there had been happy moments, too, when he would tease her and hold her close and make her laugh. He could be surprisingly generous, such as when he came home with concert tickets to a favorite band, or decided to splurge on a fancy dinner out or take her dancing. Hunter was her first love, her first long-term relationship, and she had thought the highs and unpredictability of being with him were all normal.

It wasn't until she and Bee had grown close and Sameera had a chance to observe the easy camaraderie and deep affection between her friend and Lorenzo that she started to suspect the anxious overthinking Hunter always seemed to inspire in her wasn't healthy. And yet she had stayed.

Over time, his comments about her family started to resonate with a small, resentful part of her that agreed with his words: Why didn't her parents try harder to understand her? Why hadn't they talked about things like relationships and dating when she was younger? Had they truly not realized she was struggling with her faith and identity? She started to agree with Hunter's assessment, even when she knew it was unfair: Her parents were old-fashioned, stuck in their ways; they were too stubborn to change; they would never understand her, so why bother trying?

As for her parents' part, they allowed her to drift away. They accepted her excuses. When they learned that she was in a long-term relationship, their hurt and anger and—yes, she could admit it—resentment over her absence had led to the sort of knock-down, drag-out fight that was difficult to forget.

She could recognize now that they had all made mistakes: her by avoiding confrontation and tamping down her resentment and hurt instead of dealing with it, and her parents by not making space for who their daughter truly was and how she lived her life.

Two weeks after Hunter disappeared, Sameera had realized the extent of his financial crimes. She had to take on an extra job, freelancing as a consultant, which was hard and unpredictable and sometimes meant she got only three or four hours of sleep at night. Soon, she was working seven days a week, canceling on dinners and brunch dates with friends, not picking up the phone when they called. She couldn't even call her parents for help, because they weren't talking at the time. Overlaying that nightmarish time was her bone-deep shame. Her intimate partner had taken advantage of her, betrayed her in devastating fashion, and then left her to pick up the pieces of her life. Worst of all, her parents had been right all along—Hunter had been using her. None of it was real after all.

If it weren't for her sister's encouragement, nagging, and arranging that first awkward meeting, Sameera knew she would not have Tahsin, Naveed, and Esa back in her life.

No wonder she was so tired.

A movement caught her eye in the fading light. Esa, dressed in his bright-green parka, slowly picked his way through the woods behind the creek, Calvin by his side. From the exaggerated way Esa looked around him before disappearing into a copse of trees, she could tell her brother was up to something. At least he was having fun.

She had some time until Abu Isra and his family arrived for dinner. Her parents had things under control in the kitchen. Tom would have cleared out of the guesthouse by now—he was spending time with his good friend Emily, according to Barb. And Esa was having fun with Cal.

It was time to stop daydreaming and focus on the important things. Maybe she wouldn't be able to have a heart-to-heart talk with her parents like she wanted, but at least she could be ready to pitch Andy the moment he arrived. For now, that would have to be enough.

Chapter Fifteen

When Sameera returned to the main house a few hours later, the dining room had been transformed. Rob had done a wonderful job: The long table was set with red linen napkins and gold charging plates, a lush green velvet runner, and candles in silver holders, with a large bouquet of poinsettias and pine boughs taking pride of place at the center.

From her perch on the couch, she watched as Tom brought the food to the table, and he caught her gaze and held it. Her stomach swooped, and she could feel an electrical tingling in her fingers. She was in real trouble if he could cause this reaction without even touching her. The doorbell rang, and, grateful for the distraction, Sameera hurried to greet her parents' guests, pasting a smile of welcome on her face as she reached the door.

On the Cookes' porch, Syrian Santa—*Abu Isra*, she reminded herself—and his family stood, beaming and holding gifts. His wife, a petite woman wearing a navy-blue hijab and woolen overcoat, thrust a tray of kunafe dessert at Sameera before introducing herself as Hiba, which was Arabic for "gift." She presented her six children: Isra, twelve; Daniyal, ten; twins Akbar and Ali, eight; Batul, five; and little Ikhlas, who held up three fingers when Sameera asked her age.

Syrian Santa—*Abu Isra*, Sameera reminded herself again—carried a large tray of honey-glazed crispy baklava, and her mouth was already watering at the thought of biting into the nutty, buttery dessert. She was so distracted by greetings and taking everyone's coats that she didn't notice a tall figure standing by the porch.

Not until the figure suddenly let loose an earth-shattering *roar*!

Sameera stared in horror as an eight-foot-tall Tyrannosaurus rex charged straight toward their group.

Hiba shrieked, her children scattering like bowling pins, as the dinosaur lumbered toward the crowd. Abu Isra bravely stepped in front of the beast's path, and Tom pushed Sameera behind him at the same moment her brain caught up with what she was seeing.

Sameera wriggled between the bodies cowering on the porch and marched up to the T. rex—or rather, the person inside the inflated dinosaur costume. She peered through the clear plastic at the dinosaur's neck and recognized her brother.

"Esa!" Sameera said sternly. "What are you doing?"

Esa launched into a complicated dance sequence that finished with him moonwalking toward the door. Abu Isra's children squealed—in glee or terror, Sameera wasn't sure—at his approach. Behind them, Calvin filmed the entire thing, a delighted smile stretched across his face.

"Kevin McCallister would approve," Cal said cheerfully, and her lips twitched with reluctant amusement. She wondered what else her brother had planned.

Inside, Esa deflated the costume and chased Abu Isra and Hiba's kids around the foyer, much to their delight, while Naveed and Tahsin apologized for their son's prank. Now that the dinosaur had been unmasked as a friendly nuisance and not a rampaging monster, Hiba and Abu Isra—whose name was actually Younus—shared a good laugh.

"Our children were afraid they would be bored in a house full of adults," Hiba said, shooting an apologetic glance at Rob and Barb. "That was a good joke the young man played." Like her husband, Hiba had a Middle Eastern accent. She explained that her family had moved to the United States five years ago from Syria; little Ikhlas was born in Texas, where they had lived before moving to Alaska. Hiba herself had grown up in the United Arab Emirates, though she was born in the United States and had settled in Syria, where she had gone to school. When civil war broke out, they had fled, leaving behind family members, including their parents. With the recent news, they were considering their options, and had even talked about returning to help rebuild their home country.

The members of the dinner party took their seats at the dining table and soon were busy chatting about life in Alaska, Abu Isra's restaurant, and his work as the volunteer imam for the small Muslim community in the area, while Rob shared his experiences growing up in Wolf Run. Even Tom offered a few stories of his childhood in the village, and chatted easily with Abu Isra about recipes, comparing notes on the difficulty of sourcing sumac and other ingredients up north. Sameera watched as his face came alive when he talked about food and cooking, and she remembered their easy camaraderie when they'd filmed their latest video. She had peeked at her social media earlier that afternoon and was pleased to see their video was already racking up likes and comments, even more than the biryani video. Surely the television executives would take note and put him back on the short list. Tom was exactly the sort of TV chef she would happily watch for hours—on- or off-screen.

All seemed to be going well until an air siren went off when Barb opened the pantry door, making the entire party jump. Calvin and Esa laughed themselves silly, and even Tom had to lift a hand to cover his smile.

When Tahsin yelled "Esa!" in an uncanny imitation of Catherine O'Hara yelling *"Kevin!"* Sameera snorted a laugh. Esa met her gaze, and something in her chest eased at his mischievous grin. Luckily, her little brother also realized he had gone too far with the air siren, and apologized profusely to Barb.

"Sameera told me pranks are part of the holidays," he explained, blithely throwing his sister under the bus. "And Tom encouraged me to make the most of my time here, to work on content that spoke to me."

"It's true," she said, playing along. "Though *Home Alone* has to share some of the blame." Esa seemed surprised by her support, and she couldn't help adding, "I don't think Tom meant you should play pranks on his family, though."

Esa shrugged. "I'm only trying to spread some holiday cheer."

Thankfully, everyone had a good sense of humor, and Esa promised to hold off while they all enjoyed the meal their parents had spent all afternoon preparing.

The dinner party gorged on channa curry, biryani, palak saag, and karahi chicken. Tahsin made a point to assure Rob that none of the dishes were too spicy.

"I like a bit of spice," Rob protested. "I bet I could go toe to toe with you, Naveed. Pass me the Frank's RedHot."

Naveed gave Rob a lazy smile, and Sameera's grip tightened on her fork. Her father was a mild-mannered man, but living with his competitive wife and even more competitive children had taught him to never back down from a challenge.

"My dear Robert, I would not wish to embarrass you in front of our guests," Naveed said. "Especially if that vinegary red water you call 'Frank's RedHot' is your idea of *spicy*."

"*Oooooh,*" Esa catcalled.

"Are you going to take that, Dad?" Calvin asked, leaning forward in his seat. From the delight on his face, the young man was enjoying the chaos the Malik family had brought with them from Atlanta.

Rob stood up and disappeared into the kitchen, returning with a jar of bright-red paste. "Buddy of mine mixed this up for me. Mixture of scotch bonnet, cayenne, and Thai chili peppers. Calls it his 'good morning mix.' I put it on my scrambled eggs." His eyes fixed on Naveed, he plopped a generous tablespoon onto his filled plate and took a large bite.

Naveed grabbed the jar and added two tablespoons to his own plate before digging in. His brown skin took on a slightly red cast, but he shrugged his shoulders insouciantly. "A bit sweet, actually. I might use this as a topping for my baklava later."

Puzzled, Tahsin reached out and tried the hot sauce, nearly sputtering. "What are you talking about, Naveed? My tongue is on fire!"

Tom and Sameera exchanged an amused glance. Beside them, Esa and Cal were slapping the table and laughing, while Abu Isra's children took in the spectacle, their eyes wide.

Rob took up Naveed's challenge and made another trip to the kitchen, returning with a bright-green bottle, this one with a cartoon picture of a skull and crossbones wearing a sombrero. "Maybe this ghost chili pepper will add some taste to that bland chickpea curry, then," he said, offering it to Naveed with an evil grin. "This hot sauce is illegal in forty-eight states."

"Shots fired!" Esa crowed, and even Tahsin's brows narrowed at the shade thrown at her cooking.

"I put plenty of spice in the channa, I assure you," Tahsin said, but Naveed had already reached for the green bottle and was dousing his chickpeas. Calvin and Esa both whooped as Naveed took a large bite, his gaze pinned on Rob, one eyebrow raised in challenge.

Rob reached for the bottle and doctored his own meal. Both men then proceeded to eat, visibly sweating and in clear discomfort but neither willing to back down. Esa happily recorded the entire exchange.

"Spicy Uncle Throw-Down!" her brother crowed. "This content practically writes itself!"

After their plates were cleared—and both Rob and Naveed had each hurriedly excused themselves from the table, presumably to run to the bathroom—Abu Isra asked Sameera what she thought about Wolf Run.

"I don't think I've ever visited a more beautiful place," Sameera answered honestly. "The mountains, the woods, even the main street—it all feels magical. I find myself wondering whether I've stumbled into Santa's village."

The eldest of Abu Isra's children piped up, her voice scornful. "There's no such thing as Santa. *Everyone* knows that."

Isra's younger siblings started to argue. "If there's no such thing as Santa, who was that man at the store?" one of the twins demanded while his brother nodded. "Jacob from my school saw Santa in his house last year, when he snuck downstairs at night. He even ate the cookies they laid out for him!"

Daniyal snorted. "That was just his dad in a costume, and I bet he enjoyed those cookies, too. We're Muslim; we don't believe in Santa Claus."

The children started to bicker, and Esa, with a mischievous grin at Calvin, waded into the discussion. "You believe in jinn, though, right?" he asked, and the children nodded eagerly. Sameera shot her brother a warning look, which he ignored.

"What's a jinn?" Barb asked. She had placed two tall glasses of milk at both Rob's and Naveed's place settings for when the men returned with the air of someone resigned to such impulsive actions.

"Jinn are the Unseen, beings made of smokeless fire," Sameera explained. "They are a part of Muslim mythology. Muslim believe jinn live in our world, but we can't see them. They have their own civilization and culture, and mostly stay away from humans."

"Except when humans bother them, or if they're mischievous and want to cause trouble," Tahsin added. "There are stories of jinn possessing humans, helping them, sometimes even falling in love and marrying them. They can be good or bad, just like people."

"Have you ever met one?" Tom asked, eyes twinkling at Sameera.

"They're mostly stories told to scare kids," Sameera said.

"Jinn are real," Esa insisted. Next to him, Abu Isra's kids nodded in agreement. Every Muslim child was taught about the Unseen as part of their faith, deliciously creepy stories about the beings playing tricks on humans, or humans trying to get the better of jinn, shared like ghost stories.

"My dad said he used to see lots of jinn in Syria," Daniyal offered. "There were a few who even attended his mosque."

"It's true," Abu Isra said. "My father was friends with a jinni when he was younger—at least, that's what he told me."

"There's a jinni living in this house, too," Esa said solemnly. Around him, the children's eyes grew wide. Sameera watched her brother's masterful performance with amusement and a growing realization. Esa was so different from the rest of her family, from her. He was a fun, playful young man, always willing to be silly and do anything for a laugh. She wondered if sometimes he felt as if he didn't fit into their mostly serious, mostly professional and academic-focused family. She felt another pang at all the years she had missed watching him grow up, and she resolved to try even harder to make up for lost time.

"I don't believe you. Where is the jinn?" Isra demanded. She was clearly skeptical.

"We don't have any of those things in our house; don't worry, kids," Rob said, retaking his seat beside Naveed. His voice was hoarse from the hot sauce standoff, but he and Naveed had clearly trauma-bonded over their ordeal. Both Rob and her father drained their milk, Sameera noted. "If there were, I'd get rid of it right quick, little lady," he assured Isra.

"This is a big house. An old house. And you know how much jinn love a nice dark forest, not to mention moving water, both of which surround Cooke Place," Esa improvised.

"Esa," Tahsin warned, but he ignored her.

"It's true," Calvin added. "Sometimes, late at night, I'll hear people talking in a language I've never heard before."

Wide-eyed, the children were starting to get scared. "Where do the jinn stay?" Daniyal asked.

"When it's cold outside, they like to find a nice warm, cozy little nook," Esa said. "Like a little shelf, where they can watch us, especially in the weeks leading up to Christmas."

"You can tell it's a jinni if it's dressed in striped pants and a pointy hat," Calvin added. "And it moves around the house, so you never know where it will turn up next. It likes to spy on little kids, in particular."

Sameera's parents looked confused, while Tom shook his head in amusement. "Are you talking about the Elf on a Shelf?" He tried to reassure the children. "That's a holiday toy."

"That's what *they* think," Esa said to Isra, indicating Tom and the rest of the Cooke family. "But we know better, don't we?"

Isra nodded, eyes wide.

"Just watch out for the jinn," Esa said, right as Tahsin, who had had enough of her son's shenanigans, put him and Calvin to work clearing the table.

"He's only kidding," Sameera assured Abu Isra's children, but she wasn't sure they believed her. She wondered if her parents were regretting their impromptu dinner party. Maybe they would think twice next time before issuing a hasty invitation, or perhaps even listen to her.

"Never a dull moment with the Malik family," Tom whispered beside her.

Esa and Cal set up dessert in the large sitting room. While the young men distributed plates and cutlery and arranged the fruit, kunafe, and baklava, joking and laughing like old friends, the rest of the dinner party claimed chairs and sofas. Sameera settled on a love seat, Tom beside her, and his warmth and smell instantly invaded her senses; it felt so familiar to her now, after only a few days. She realized she was leaning over to smell him, and forced herself to stop.

Which was when Isra jumped out of her chair, screaming and pointing at the bookshelf. *"Jiiiiiinnnnnn!"* she yelled, backing away.

The other children leaped to their feet and started screaming, too, until Esa heroically lunged at the bookshelf and grabbed the Elf on a Shelf, dressed in the usual striped pants and pointy hat, just as Cal had described at the dining table.

"I told you to leave my friends alone!" Esa yelled at the toy. "They're well behaved all year around." He leaned in close, pretending to listen to what the toy said. "You're not sure about the little one?" He turned to three-year-old Ikhlas, his expression severe. "Do you promise to behave?"

Ikhlas nodded, eyes wide, before reaching for the toy. Esa held it away with a severe shake of his head.

"Okay, me and my little friend are going to take a little walk. I'll make sure he doesn't bother you again, okay?" Esa left the sitting room to applause from the kids, who were now convinced he was their hero.

Beside her on the couch, Tom was laughing into his hand. He leaned over to whisper, "Your brother is hilarious. If he wanted, he could rule the internet."

A warm feeling suffused her. Esa had turned what might have been an awkward and dull dinner into a fun time, and had succeeded in charming everyone in the room. Tom was right—her brother had a gift, and she was proud of him for throwing himself wholeheartedly into whatever he did. A lot of that new confidence was due to Tom.

Tom had been so kind to her, to her family and Esa. He had encouraged her brother to run after his passion, and had helped him grow his audience using his own channel. Tom had also cheered her up twice today, first at the bakery and then at the guesthouse. It was growing more and more difficult to ignore her feelings for him. She gave his hand a quick squeeze. "Who wants more kunafe?" she asked brightly, and started refilling everyone's plates.

Chapter Sixteen

Sameera stared at her phone. It was nearly 1:00 a.m., and she had been working steadily for the past few hours, ever since dinner concluded. She had finished the slide deck for her pitch with Andy. Now she was picking away at her files. *Another two billable hours down, five million to go,* she thought glumly.

Dinner had been . . . nice. For the first time in as long as she could remember, she hadn't felt embarrassed by her family's antics. Almost as if admitting her feelings to Tom had somehow banished them. In a strange way, she felt more comfortable here in Wolf Run now, at ease with who she was, and it was easier to find her family's foibles and quirks endearing instead of mortifying, if only because the Cookes had quirks of their own.

Tom found Esa's jokes funny, and Rob had gotten into the spirit of things with the hot sauce throw-down, acting just as silly, playful, and competitive as her father. Even Barb seemed to appreciate her mother's masterful kitchen takeover and had vowed to put more onions in everything.

It all felt . . . easy. Lovely. Completely baffling. Was this what it would have been like if she hadn't allowed Hunter into her life? If she hadn't let his jokes and comments about her family, his constant criticism, interfere with the way she thought about everything? Except she knew it went deeper than that, to her own feelings of self-worth.

Even before Hunter had slithered into her life, she had felt a nagging, enveloping sense of her own difference, one that found little respite in her own family and community, or in the outside world. Her mother wanted her to be a perfectly poised success machine who was a credit not just to their family but to all Muslims in the country. The outside world required her only to be a producer and consumer, then to fade into the background, which was much easier to accomplish. Slowly, she stopped practicing her faith regularly. It was easier to exist as a lapsed Muslim rather than a struggling one.

With Tom, she felt like she could put her guard down, and simply exist as her confused, mixed-up, ever-striving self.

She opened the next file and tried to sink back into her work, to ride the wave of productivity she had been surfing all night, but her brain was fried. Her thoughts kept drifting to Tom in a loop.

His smell had infiltrated her brain and snagged into every crevice of her anxious, worked-up mind. It was like she had imprinted on him, which was ridiculous. Even if he was sincere in his admiration for Sameera, Tom clearly had his own issues. It wouldn't be smart to complicate things, especially not while they were in Alaska. They both had work to do on themselves before they could enter into a healthy relationship.

What about a hot, unhealthy, no-strings-attached relationship instead? a voice whispered in her mind. She tried to tell it to shut up, but as a counterargument, it brought up Tom's eyes, his hair, his arms, his laugh. Sameera stood up and started to pace. She was developing a tiny crush on Tom, that was all. Crushes passed.

She needed fresh air and a change of scenery. She put on her coat, eased into boots, and grabbed a blanket from the living room couch before sliding the glass patio doors open and tiptoeing outside.

She stood in the dark for a moment, appreciating the silence. As much as she loved her hometown, Atlanta was never really quiet, and never this dark. Walking to the edge of the backyard patio, which had been cleared of the latest snowfall but was still covered with a dusting of snow, she looked up at the sky. It was a cloudless night, the stars so bright, they looked like diamonds a giant hand had spilled on a rich velvet cloth. The air felt refreshing, cold but clean, and she inhaled deeply.

"Can't sleep?" a voice called from the gloom, and Sameera stifled a scream. As if she had conjured him, a familiar figure sat on a bench tucked into a copse of trees. The glow of an outdoor heat lamp flickered to life, casting long shadows over Tom's handsome face.

"What are you doing here?" she asked, and she could just make out his shrug in the soft dark as she drifted closer.

"I shouldn't have had that coffee after dinner, not to mention all the chai we drank," he said. "Sorry if I disturbed your nighttime stroll. Watch out for bears." He stood to leave, stretching as he rose, and Sameera caught a tantalizing flash of flat belly. And was that the bottom half of a six-pack? Her mouth immediately went dry.

"You don't have to go," she blurted. He was kidding about the bears, right?

"Are you sure?" he asked, but he had already settled back on the padded bench seat, and she cautiously took a seat beside him, arranging the blanket to cover them both.

The silence stretched, and once again, it was a comfortable sort of quiet, the sort that didn't ask much of her. She leaned back, and her shoulder brushed against Tom's. The heater was clearly effective.

"You're so warm," she said absently.

"I think you mean, I'm so hot," he said, and she laughed quietly. Flirting was as natural as breathing to him. It didn't come with any expectations, either; he just enjoyed teasing her, and being teased in turn.

"It's like you can read my mind," she said, and his smile flashed bright in the dark. They settled back into silence, and feeling brave, she leaned her head on his shoulder. A purely friendly gesture, of course.

He shifted so that his arm lay on the back of the bench, and she cuddled closer. The darkness made everything feel more intimate, and Sameera could feel her inhibitions evaporate into the night sky, as if nothing that happened here, while the rest of their family slept, would really count. Sameera felt her body relax as the steady churn of her mind finally calmed, like a boat stumbling into a sheltered harbor.

"Esa is funny," Tom said, his voice a soft rumble above her cheek. "Cal likes him a lot. It usually takes him a while to open up to strangers." Tom shifted again, and his arm lightly curled around her shoulder.

"Are you close with Cal?" she asked. Her lids were getting heavy. He was so warm, and the air was fresh and crisp on her face, the contrast delicious.

Tom was quiet, thinking. "I wish we were closer. But that's not his fault. I had moved out by the time he arrived. He was seven years old when Barb married Rob. I'm not sure he's ever felt like he truly belonged in Wolf Run, either."

That answered a question Sameera had been wondering. As much as Rob clearly loved Cal, she had wondered why the older man's fixation on family and legacy had settled on the son who didn't live in his beloved hometown rather than the son who did. "I did notice that Wolf Run is a bit . . . homogenous," Sameera said tentatively, and Tom laughed.

"That's one way to put it. Barb gets on with everyone, and it's nice to see that things are changing slowly and growing more diverse. Abu Isra and his family have been a welcome addition. But yes, some people can be set in their ways and wary of newcomers, which in their world means anyone who can't trace their family in Wolf Run back four generations. They're also not happy when one of us leaves."

"Like you did," Sameera said. He had mentioned this to her before; she suspected it was foremost on his mind now he was back.

"Those Christmas pranks," Tom said, changing the subject. "Is it customary to play jokes on Eid?"

Sameera laughed. "The Christmas pranks are entirely Esa's and Kevin McCallister's fault," she said. "Plus, he took your advice about making content and has decided to specialize."

"I wonder how many pranks that movie is responsible for," Tom mused. "Maybe an entire industry."

"Just another Christmas mystery we will never solve," she agreed. In the soft glow of the patio lights, Tom's face was wreathed in shadows, which did interesting things to the planes of his cheekbones and the sharp line of his jaw, his nose just a touch too big for his face, eyes that looked almost hooded in the dark, eyebrows thick and dark. He raised one at her, smiling quizzically, and she wondered if he knew how attractive he was, or whether he'd had a glow-up as an adult. Nobody really told men they were beautiful. Hot, maybe, but not that they were pretty.

"I'm really glad you're here," Tom said. His voice felt like a delicious rasp against her skin, and Sameera shivered.

"Did you enjoy watching our fathers give themselves ulcers from eating too much hot sauce? Or when that air siren went off in Barb's pantry, and she jumped a mile? Or the terrified screams of Abu Isra's children when they spotted your resident jinn, a.k.a. an ordinary Elf on a Shelf?" Her tone was teasing, but a part of her worried.

When he turned to face her fully, she could see the sincerity on his face as he replied. "I loved it all," he said. "Christmas in Wolf Run usually means silent family dinners and stilted conversations where no one says what they really mean. Barb always tries to draw everyone out, but it's hard when you can cut the tension with a knife. No jokes, no laughter. Not even an inflatable T. rex. I love the energy and unpredictability the Maliks bring everywhere they go."

"What's Christmas without a battery-operated Halloween costume?" Sameera said.

"Joyless. With plenty of guilt for dessert, and land mines waiting in every conversation, until the only safe subject is the weather, or hockey. And as you now know, I don't watch hockey."

"Nobody watches hockey; you breathe it into your veins," Sameera said. "We need to get the Thrashers back from Winnipeg is all I'm saying."

But Tom was not easily distracted. "I still can't believe someone like you is here with me."

Sameera snorted. "Okay, this is starting to feel like an act. You're hot, Tom, and you know it."

His lips widened in a slow smile. "You think I'm hot?"

"You are objectively attractive. If you like that sort of thing," she grumbled.

An expression of delight suffused his face. "You like that sort of thing," he said.

"'Like' is a strong word," she started, and then he kissed her.

It was a good kiss. Aside from Hunter, there had been her few boyfriends in high school and college, and the most she could say about them was that whatever their technique lacked in finesse, it more than made up for in enthusiasm. Hunter's kisses had been better in comparison, but now she realized they had merely been adequate, always a prequel to the main event, not something to be enjoyed and savored on their own.

Tom's kiss wasn't like that. His kiss made it clear he had nowhere to go, and nothing in the world that he would rather be doing than to cradle her jaw in his large, rough hands and devour her. When a whimper escaped her mouth, he pulled back to look into her eyes. She pulled him closer, giving him permission to continue, and the kiss became less and so much more—his tongue a little less gentle against hers, his grip on her waist firmer, and then it was messy, their teeth clashing, breathing erratic. When he lifted her onto his lap in one fluid motion, she could feel how badly he wanted her. She made a sound low in her throat that made Tom pull her harder against him, and she nearly cried out from the pure, frustrating bliss of pleasure left unsatisfied.

Her parents and brother were asleep not thirty feet away, and there might be bears in the woods behind them, but none of that mattered because this was the greatest kiss in the history of kisses, and she was pretty sure she would die if he stopped now.

Except he did, pulling back and resting his forehead against hers, his breathing rasping and erratic. His arms were tense around her body.

She readjusted on his lap, and a spasm of pain and pleasure crossed Tom's face.

"What if you regret this? I couldn't stand it." His words were an ice bath dousing the raging fire within, and she took a deep, shaky breath, grateful for the pause, for the chance to think. Because, of course, he was right.

She carefully disentangled their limbs and climbed off his lap, her legs jelly. As soon as she put distance between them, her anxieties, temporarily muted by his touch, by his presence, roared back to life. She had ventured into the yard to clear her head and stop thinking about Tom and how much she wanted him. Instead, she had nearly ravished him on the bench by the heat lamp. She couldn't afford this added complication to her life—no matter how badly her body wanted it. She tried to steady her breathing.

Beside her, Tom leaned forward and put his head in his hands, breath rasping in the cold. "I'm going to regret this in the morning," he said, voice muffled.

Instantly, her heart bottomed. He didn't really want her; he had simply been carried away. "I'm sorry. I know kissing me was a mistake—" she started.

He turned to her, and the expression on his face held such longing and hunger, it shut her up immediately. "Not that," he growled. "Kissing you wasn't the mistake, Sameera. I'm going to regret stopping." His look was hot on her face now, lingering on her lips, her throat, before dragging up to her eyes, and she felt heat flood her body, pooling low in her belly. He made a slight, almost involuntary motion toward her, and then stood up abruptly.

"It's cold," she said, eyes helplessly drawn to his body and lingering on a few choice parts. The cold was clearly not affecting all of him.

"I feel like I'm on fire," he said, not looking at her. "Can we talk about something else?"

Sameera's mind blanked, fixated on his chest, his arms, and how it felt to have his strong hands around her waist, inching higher . . . "Tell me how you met Andy," she blurted. It was the first thing she could think of, and the words had the required effect. He stilled, not quite looking at her.

"Andy. Right. Of course you're curious about him. Everyone always is," Tom said, and there was something in his voice, a kernel of resentment, that made Sameera pause. "I already told you Andy was my roommate in college. It was chance and luck that brought us together, though we couldn't be more different. I went to Georgia to escape my family. He was there to prove something, to himself and to everyone else. While I went to parties and skipped class, he was busy charming profs, making connections, and kicking everyone's ass in class."

"It's so strange that you're friends," Sameera said.

"Because he's so successful, and I'm just the caterer?" Tom asked, and now she could see it—a thread of vulnerability in the question. She should rush to reassure him, to tell him the truth—that what she felt for him now wasn't because of his proximity to Andy, or because her job was on the line, but because she was falling for him.

But the words wouldn't come. She was too damaged, and things were too complicated, and the longer she stayed here with her family without the daily grind to distract her, the more she realized that Hunter had messed her up in a fundamental way. She wasn't sure she would ever recover from those wounds, and it wouldn't be fair to Tom to deny those hurts existed. She felt cold and shivered, rubbing her arms to stimulate some warmth.

After a loaded pause, Tom continued, though his tone had shifted. "It was weird—my father ran a bunch of businesses in Wolf Run, but Andy's the one who was born to lead a boardroom. Maybe it's because he has more to prove. His dad was a high school science teacher, his mom a homemaker, and he was there on scholarship. He wanted to be taken seriously so badly. Actually, I think he just wanted it more than anyone else in our program."

"Wanted what?" she asked. She felt a bit unsteady. If she tried to stand now, she was sure to stumble. Her mind was a tumble of thoughts, fears, worries, and most of all, *hunger.* She wanted Tom, desperately. She couldn't trust it, or herself, especially not right now.

"Everything," he said, and risked meeting her gaze. They stared at each other for a single, breathless moment before he looked away again, swallowing hard, and continued with some effort. "I don't think you can achieve the kind of success he has, at the speed he did, without an insatiable appetite. Plus, he has more luck in his pinkie finger than our entire class put together. Everything he touched made money. Including my catering business. I started off just cooking for me and him, and then a few of our friends, and pretty soon our dorm. I was good at it. The kitchen was where I felt like I belonged. He was my first investor."

"He has great taste," she said, and he groaned at the pun. She wanted more than his appreciation of her humor, though, and had to wrap her arms more firmly around herself to keep from dragging him back down on the bench. Or climbing him like a tree. *Stop,* she told herself. This feeling for Tom was nothing but lust, multiplied by time and circumstance. It wasn't real. It couldn't be. There was too much at stake.

"Andy said I was his good luck charm. He had started a few businesses before, but none as popular as mine. I made snacks and meals for busy undergrad and graduate students. I grew so busy, I had to rent out a commercial kitchen a few times a week." He frowned, remembering a less happy memory. "When I tried to tell my dad about what I had done, he asked me why I was wasting my time cooking when I should be concentrating on my program. As if starting a successful business wasn't the entire point of going to business school."

"I'm sorry Rob couldn't see what you were building. That has more to do with him than you. He probably worried that once you were gone, you wouldn't come back," Sameera said softly. "Anything that took you away was a betrayal."

Tom jerked his head in an affirmative. "Andy lent me my first ten thousand dollars at the end of our sophomore year. He had saved it over the summer, working three jobs and living on ramen. He said it would be better used on my culinary talents than on paying back his student loan." Tom's smile was grim. "I doubled the money by the end of the year. I dropped out of school six months later. Dad demanded I return home. I chose door number two instead. I slept on Andy's couch and grew my business. So, you see, we're more than roommates or friends. Andy is my brother."

Tom took a seat beside her, and even now, the chemistry between them pulsed like a live current. The confidences they shared in the dark felt just as delicious.

"Why do I imagine you with a hacky sack?" she asked.

"Ultimate Frisbee," Tom said. "Andy called me a college stereotype."

"It sounds like Andy had your back," Sameera said, and after a moment, Tom nodded.

"What about you? Is Bee your bestie?" Tom asked, nudging her shoulder. He had sat down and somehow shifted closer; his friendly gesture sent a shower of sparks through her body. She put some more space between them—for his protection as much as hers.

"Bee is awesome. But to be honest, for a long time I never felt I needed a best friend because I had Nadiya," Sameera said. "I told her everything. She knew about Hunter from the very start. She didn't like him, but she doesn't like most people. We're so different. I floated through school, but Nadiya always knew what she wanted to do."

"What's that?" Tom asked. His fingers caressed the edges of the blanket she had drawn up, and she couldn't look away.

"To save the world." Sameera smiled wryly. "Her faith is strong, too. She used to call me Kafir. It means 'unbeliever.' She meant it as a joke. I think."

"That's kind of mean," Tom said. "Did that bother you?"

Did her sister's teasing, however threaded with love, bother her? "Yes," she said, surprising herself. "It's not that I don't have faith, exactly. It's just that the volume is turned way down in my heart. But for Nadiya and my parents, it's turned way up. She even wears a hijab, the head covering. She started when she was sixteen. My mom tried to talk her out of it. No one in my family wears it, but Nadiya has always been stubborn." She smiled at the memory of that conversation, her mother's careful arguments against wearing the hijab and Nadiya's crossed arms and raised brow, her repeated *This is what I have decided to do, and I accept the consequences. Stop worrying, Mom. I promise I'll give you something real to worry about soon enough.*

And she had. As soon as she graduated high school, she had taken a gap year and spent it as an aid worker in Pakistan. She had then returned to the United States and attended college, where she majored in political science and international relations, then promptly signed up for the Peace Corps. The sisters remained close throughout, keeping in touch through texts and WhatsApp phone calls. When Hunter left, and Sameera realized the extent of the debt he had left behind like soiled underpants, Nadiya had flown home to be with her. She sat with Sameera while she cried on the kitchen floor of the condo she wasn't sure she could afford anymore, then helped her come up with a plan to climb out of the mess that was her life.

Nadiya loved her, even when Sameera felt like she wasn't enough. Her love had been a tether during dark moments; it had helped give her the courage to get back in touch with her parents, and her steady encouragement had made their hard-fought reconciliation possible. Which was why her silence over Tom was so hurtful. She hoped her sister hadn't finally washed her hands of her. Sameera wasn't sure what she would do without Nadiya in her life.

Tom absorbed all of this in silence. "I'd love to meet her one day." He paused. "What does she think about us?"

Sameera shook her head, then shrugged. "She thinks you're my latest mistake."

Another beat, another charged moment of silence. "Am I?"

It was close to two in the morning at this point, but she felt more awake than ever. Maybe she should stop overthinking. "I don't know," she admitted, and Tom's face went carefully blank at her response.

If only Nadiya were here to talk her down from her spiral, and remind her that she was here for two reasons only: to charm a billionaire so she could save her job, and talk to her parents. Not to kiss Tom.

She blurted, "Any updates from Andy?" just as Tom said, "Thanks for sharing your story with me."

He paused, and a strange expression crossed his face. "Not yet. I'll text again in the morning, and let you know what he says." Tom paused. "It's late, and we have a long day ahead. We should get some sleep."

It was Christmas Eve; no doubt their parents had a full day planned. Still, his quick dismissal, after everything they had shared tonight, stung. Not that it should—she was the one who had yanked the emergency brake at the first sign of things getting complicated.

As she made her way back to the guesthouse, she could feel his gaze burning between her shoulder blades. But when she turned around, he was already gone.

Chapter Seventeen

Sameera was first in the kitchen later, and she stood staring morosely at the Cookes' fancy coffee machine when Barb joined her. A few moments later, Sameera gripped a fragrant-smelling latte like a life preserver.

"I hope you don't mind my saying so, dear, but you look as if you really needed that," Barb said with a smile. "Late night?" Sameera flushed.

"I couldn't fall asleep," she admitted. "Tom and I were up talking." Even after she'd left him on the patio, her thoughts kept doomscrolling between him, Hunter, her job, her parents . . . She wanted to text Nadiya again, but part of her knew she couldn't handle being ignored.

Barb laughed. "Goodness, child, you don't have to look so guilty. I was young once, too. I remember what it's like to lose track of time when you're with someone special. Not that you want to hear about any of that, of course! Why, when Rob and I first found each other, we were on the phone for hours. We were long-distance for the first few years."

Sameera smiled. "I'd love to hear that story," she said. She was curious about how Rob and Barb had met.

But Barb changed the subject. "Ancient history," she said. "What would you like for breakfast?"

Fifteen minutes later, she was seated at the large breakfast counter in Barb's kitchen, feasting on a pile of fluffy scrambled eggs and orange juice, reaching for toast and accepting a second latte. She looked around the kitchen—as usual for this time of year, the sun had not risen for the day yet, but the warm interior lighting made the house feel welcoming, despite its size. Cooke Place was enormous. Sameera had been in many large homes in her life; her parents' well-heeled friends had bought sprawling houses in gated communities all across Georgia and other states, but this house was something else. She could feel the history in the walls, and though it had a well-loved and lived-in look, she was pretty sure Cooke Place could host two dozen guests and still feel empty.

"How do you maintain a place like this?" she asked.

Barb laughed. "With a lot of help, and the understanding that you won't get to everything. I can't remember when the attic windows last had a good scrub."

Sameera flushed. "I didn't mean to criticize," she said, but Barb waved her words away.

"No offense taken, my dear. Would you believe me if I told you that I married Rob *despite* the large house and his stature in the community?"

Sameera could understand that. "It would intimidate anyone," she agreed gamely.

Barb fixed herself a cup of coffee and took the stool next to Sameera. "I wasn't intimidated, exactly," she started, looking around at her domain. "I just understood the sort of legacy Rob carries, the history and responsibility. I know the toll it can have on a person. My mother started her own business back in the seventies, supplying uniforms for schools in Philadelphia. By the time she retired, she had a mini empire, built from the ground up. She ended up employing half of her friends and most of the family, too. It can cause a lot of friction when everything rests on your shoulders. Rob and I had that in common." Barb sighed and, reaching for a cloth, wiped down the spotless counter.

"Is that why you don't want to talk about how you and Rob met?" Sameera ventured. Thinking about her encounter with Tom last night, and the way he'd seemed to shut down at the end, her curiosity was piqued. She wanted to know more about him, and Barb was far more approachable than the prickly Rob.

Barb smiled. "You don't miss a thing, do you? The truth is, Tom wasn't always my biggest fan. I used to think his relationship with Rob soured when I arrived in the picture, but I soon realized they had their own issues well before. Tom is more like Pamela, may she rest in peace. Rob just about fell apart when she passed. By the time he got his life back together, the damage to him and Tom's relationship was done. It doesn't help that Rob's a stubborn old ass, and refuses to accept Tom for who he really is. Don't think I haven't told him so a dozen times."

"And who is Tom?" Sameera asked, careful to keep her voice neutral, but Barb wasn't fooled.

"One of the most promising young chefs in the southern United States," she said. "But of course, you know that."

Sameera didn't try to hide her surprise. "You never talk about his career."

Barb's smile was sad. "I don't think Tom would like it, not when his father doesn't say a word. I loved that cooking series he did, and of course, the videos he's done with you. The one about chai you posted yesterday was fun. It's been obvious from the start that he is absolutely smitten, and no wonder."

Sameera ducked her head in acknowledgment of the compliment, and tried not to wince at their ongoing deception. Still, she had promised she wouldn't say anything to Tom's parents about the real status of their relationship, not unless they specifically asked. And things were getting more and more complicated between them, in any case. "You said he doesn't cook when he's here," she said.

Barb sighed. "Believe me, I've tried to encourage it. Before you, he hadn't come home in a long time. Last time he was here, he tried to talk to his dad about what he had built in Atlanta, but Rob wasn't ready to listen, and I think that really hurt him. I think Tom decided that if his father wasn't curious about his life and the things he was passionate about, then he wouldn't bother sharing. Which is why I'm grateful to you, Sameera." Barb's face was earnest, and Sameera's stomach dropped. *Not this again.*

"I've never seen Tom this relaxed, and it's all due to you. This family was broken, so badly I wasn't sure we would ever heal. But now that you're in his life, our son is coming back to us. Rob has never been happier."

Sameera didn't know what to say. Everything had felt so simple when she and Tom first struck their bargain. It was supposed to be a mutual arrangement that hurt no one. She hadn't signed up for this. Before she could respond, they heard the sound of a powerful engine, and they looked at each other.

"Is there a plane in your backyard?" Sameera joked, and Barb's face lit up. She pulled on her boots and disappeared outside. Mystified, Sameera followed her, then abruptly halted.

There was a plane in the Cooke backyard. A small two-seater propellor plane, neatly parked two dozen yards away from the guesthouse, as casual as the pickup trucks in the driveway. Esa, alerted by the racket, ran up to her, and Sameera watched Tom join his stepmother, along with Rob. Barb's face was wreathed in smiles.

"What's going on?" Esa asked, and she shrugged, though she was pretty sure she knew who had finally turned up at the Cooke residence in such spectacular fashion: *Andy Shaikh*.

This was it. The reason she had agreed to the bargain with Tom. Her entire future rested on Andy's response to her pitch. Her palms instantly felt clammy. Esa ran ahead to question his hosts, while Sameera took a moment to steel her nerves. This man held the key to her continued employment, and her future. She walked up to Tom.

"Did Andy tell you he would arrive this morning?" she asked him. What she really wanted to ask was if he had spent the rest of last night thinking about her the way she had about him. Part of her regretted not inviting him to join her in her room, while the more rational part applauded her caution. Not to mention that her parents would have been scandalized.

Still, it was hard to resist the temptation to lean against him and soak up his warmth.

"We expected Andy today or tomorrow," Tom said, and she noted the slight coolness to his tone. Was he not happy to see his friend? "He tends to come and go as he pleases." There was an amused exasperation in his voice now; she must have imagined the coolness. Tom had called Andy his brother, after all.

Though she was currently not on speaking terms with one of her siblings.

The man in question opened the door and popped out with a flourish. Andy Shaikh was a handsome man, Sameera considered, as he climbed down the stairs, already in animated conversation with a thrilled Esa. A few inches shorter than Tom, Andy had sharp features and thick, dark hair, a wiry build that reminded Sameera of a coiled spring. He held a small leather backpack in his arms, and after they watched Esa excitedly introduce himself, Andy motioned for her brother to follow him to the—trunk? Did planes have trunks? Esa's excitement was clear as he took in whatever Andy had just shown him.

"I hope he didn't go overboard again," Barb said, affection clear in her voice. "He always brings treats when he visits, though we keep insisting we don't need anything."

Grinning, Andy approached his welcome party with arms outstretched. Behind him, Esa was entirely dwarfed by a giant box that contained a one-hundred-inch flat-screen television. Sameera willed him not to trip.

"You must be Tom's mysterious new girlfriend," Andy said. Her gaze had been fixed on Esa, but now she focused on the man of the hour, and her sudden nerves made her breaths shallow.

Andy's eyes were so dark, they almost looked black, and fringed with thick eyelashes, eyebrows a bold slash across light-brown skin. Though his smile was easy, his gaze missed nothing. This was a man who wore his friendliness like a razor, using it to slice inside whoever had caught his interest. Which right now seemed to be her.

"Sameera Malik," she said, offering her hand to shake. She smiled in what she hoped was an open, friendly manner while inside she tried to tamp down a rising nervousness. What if she forgot her carefully prepared pitch? What if he didn't respond, or—a horrifying thought occurred to her—Andy thought she was taking advantage of Tom? Sameera tried to keep her rising panic from her features, but Nadiya had always said she had zero poker face.

His grin widened, and he came in for a hug. "I hope you're treating my boy like the prince he is," he said once he had let her go. "He's the best person I know."

Sameera tried not to flinch. Of course Andy didn't know about the truth behind their relationship. Would it help or hurt to tell him? She had promised to keep quiet in front of Tom's parents, who stood nearby. She settled on an awkward smile, and watched as Tom pulled Andy into one of those one-armed, back-slapping bro embraces. Tom whispered something in Andy's ear. Throwing her another swift glance, Andy nodded before turning to greet his hosts.

"Rob, Barb, how is it that neither of you seem to age? Tell me your secret, so I can bottle it and make us all rich," he said, hugging each in turn. Barb actually giggled, and even Rob seemed thrilled to see him. Sameera didn't remember him looking this happy to see his own son.

"You're already rich, Andy," Rob said, clearly delighted. Andy looked modest.

"Yet you're the one with this killer view," Andy said, looking around him with genuine admiration. Sameera felt a prickle on the back of her neck, what Nadiya would teasingly call her "lawyerly Spidey sense" hinting at something. "I've been all over the world, but you Cookes have something no amount of money can buy. My offer to take Cooke Place off your hands is still there, whenever you like—just name your price!"

What was he talking about? Sameera looked from Rob's and Barb's happy expressions to Tom's, noticing his sudden frown. But before she could ask, they moved inside, Andy regaling them with stories of his flight, of his business trip to Hong Kong, and shamelessly name-dropping his friends, all of whom seemed to be celebrities or tech moguls, or both.

Tom lingered back, and Sameera seized the chance to lean close to him. "What did Andy mean, about Cooke Place?" she asked.

"Just a joke he makes every time he visits," Tom said dismissively. "He offers to buy Cooke Place; my dad laughs. It's a bit."

Somehow, Sameera doubted Andy was joking. "Funny."

Tom shook his head. "You don't know him the way I do. Andy is brilliant, but he gets distracted easily. Unless something is right in front of him, he won't think about it. Which is why he needs someone like you working for him." The look he shot her now had no trace of humor or warmth. "You can pitch him on your firm soon, don't worry. I know that's the real reason you came to Alaska."

Stung by his words, Sameera stared at Tom. Was he . . . angry with her? After he had asked her to continue with their farce, after he had made her like him with his charming personality, clever hands, his jokes and flirting and kindness to her family? Confused, she followed him inside.

Esa had managed to put the television down in the sitting room without incident, and he and Cal were staring at the box and talking excitedly while Andy stared out the large floor-to-ceiling windows in the sitting room, peaked mountains in the distance.

"You're a lucky man," he said to Tom. "My childhood house looked over a busy intersection, and my bedroom had a great view of a dark alley."

A reluctant smile curled Tom's lips, and Sameera thought again of how handsome he was, his face a perfect combination of every feature she liked best. "I bet you like your view now. One for every season. How many houses do you own, again?"

"Four," Andy said promptly. He turned around and grinned at his friend. "Or is it six? I can't remember."

Tom shoved Andy. "Idiot business bro."

"Entitled diva chef," Andy threw back. He clapped his hands together. "I'm hungry. Tom?"

Tom shook his head. "Nice try."

Barb came forward. "Breakfast is ready in the kitchen. Help yourself, dear."

Andy quirked a brow at Sameera. "Would you care to join me? I want to hear all about the woman who captured my best buddy's heart. And I hear you have a question for me, too." He disappeared inside the kitchen, leaving Sameera to look uneasily at Tom. He smiled at her in encouragement.

"Go ahead," he urged.

"He doesn't expect me to pitch him while he eats scrambled eggs, does he?" she asked in a low voice, trying to keep her panic at bay.

"He's just hungry and looking for an audience while he eats. I'm sure he'll listen to your fancy pitch later." There was something about the way Tom described her pitch, as if it didn't matter, that made her instantly defensive.

"Is something wrong?" she demanded. "You know how important talking to Andy is to me, Tom. My job depends on how he responds."

Tom couldn't look at her. "I know," he said in a low voice. "Believe me, I'm well aware that talking to Andy is the only reason you're here."

He left her before she could respond. What was going on?

Andy had already made himself at home. He was seated at the kitchen island, within easy reach of the fluffy scrambled eggs, toast, and fruit that Barb had prepared that morning, and had already filled his plate.

"Do you want to warm that up?" she asked. Andy shook his head.

"Eating cold eggs reminds me of how far I've come in life," he said. "To know I could warm them up, or make more, or fly an entire chicken coop here, or buy this entire town if I wanted." He grinned to let her know he was joking, even though she suspected he wasn't. She returned his smile, feeling uneasy. Tom's strange comment had rattled her, and she forced herself to concentrate on the man before her.

Andy Shaikh was a good-looking man, and he knew it. From the half smile on his perfectly exfoliated face to his meticulously lined-up beard, expertly tousled hair, designer clothes, and custom sneakers, his image was clearly designed to impress. Now he ducked his head in a blatant show of fake modesty that made her eyes narrow in suspicion.

"Coffee?" she asked blandly, ignoring his previous comment.

"Tea, if you have it," he returned easily, and she filled the kettle. Andy's gaze was fixed on his food, but she wasn't fooled. He was paying attention to her, too.

"Barb was so excited when she heard your plane, and Rob is thrilled, too. I thought billionaires were too busy to make impromptu visits."

Andy's eyes crinkled at her. "Reports of my wealth are greatly exaggerated. My net worth is six hundred million at most, so I can spend my time as I please. Real billionaires are held to a different standard. Besides, Rob and Barb are like my adoptive parents."

Sameera furrowed her brows, thinking. Tom said his father had cut him off when he dropped out of college, and that Andy had saved him from being unhoused. Why would his best buddy be on visiting terms with his estranged father? *The math ain't math-ing,* as Bee would say. Andy's next words revealed that the suspicion clearly went both ways.

"I was surprised when Tom told me you agreed to come out to Alaska," he started. "He hasn't invited anyone except me to visit before. Definitely never a girlfriend."

That made her inexplicably happy, in a way she didn't want to examine too closely. "It's a long story," Sameera said, deflecting. "Do you often visit Rob and Barb, without Tom? He told me he hasn't been up to Wolf Run in a few years."

Andy didn't answer, shoveling eggs into his mouth. "I'd love to hear about how you and Tom met, Sameera. I have to keep an eye on my boy, you understand."

Sameera's stomach squeezed. She clearly hadn't thought this plan entirely through. She had told Tom she wouldn't lie about their relationship. If she pitched Andy now and got the job, a part of her would wonder if it was because he thought she was Tom's significant other. On the other hand, if she came clean and told Andy the truth— that she and Tom were not dating, that she had agreed to film a few videos for Tom's social media in exchange for an introduction to him—that wouldn't exactly paint her in a positive light.

The kettle clicked off, and she automatically made him chai, strong and hot, sweetened with honey, just the way her parents liked it. He accepted the cup and took a cautious sip.

"You can take the desi girl out of the boardroom and out to Alaska, but she will never forget how to brew a proper cuppa," he joked. Andy had cleared his plate, and she reached for it, but he shook his head, rising to put it neatly in the dishwasher.

"Tom's chai is actually better than mine," she said, and a fond expression crossed Andy's face.

"Did he tell you how we met?" Andy asked.

"He said you were roommates in business school. That you invested in his catering company. That everything you touch makes money," Sameera added.

Andy laughed, putting down his tea. "I was terrified when I went to that school. I felt completely out of my element. Most of my classmates came from upper-middle-class and wealthy families, people with money. I was the only Muslim kid in the entire cohort, and one of the only Brown guys, too. I'm sure you know what I'm talking about."

Sameera nodded. Of course she did. It had been the same for most of her classes, even on the East Coast, and definitely in her firm—exhibit A being Blake "Chip" Latham—though things were starting to change. It was strange that though she was a nonpracticing Muslim, and in some ways more comfortable around white and Black Americans than her parents' desi immigrant friends, she was also aware of the ways she was instantly judged and labeled when people first met her. How her last name—Malik—instantly put her on the outside, while her lack of community and faith adherence put her on the outside with her own people, too. It was a situation that often made her feel lonely and frustrated. Her estrangement with her own family only emphasized that Sameera didn't really fit in anywhere. It was a surprise to realize that Andy could empathize with these feelings.

"Tom made me feel like I was all right, just as I was. He's got this way about him. Like he's comfortable in his own body and has nothing to prove. I felt like I could relax and just breathe when he was around. That made it easier to plot strategy and figure out how to take over."

Sameera laughed. Behind the blustering, swaggering man who'd shown up at his friend's house in his own plane, there was a real person who had once been scared and uncertain and full of dreams he didn't know would ever come to fruition. Sort of like her. He was right about Tom, too. She felt instantly calm and accepted around Tom, no matter what she said or did. Forget cooking; that was his true superpower.

"Do you always plot strategy, or do you sometimes go with your gut?" Sameera asked.

Andy watched her over his tea, which had cooled down considerably. Maybe he liked everything just a little cold. He had made his fortune selling bubble tea and frozen drinks, after all. "It's funny you should say that, Sameera. Because I have a question I'd love to ask you."

But before he could elaborate, Barb joined them in the kitchen. "Tahsin wanted to check out the Christmas market, and today is the last day. Andy, you're welcome to join us, dear."

Andy swallowed the last of his tea and rubbed his hands together. "Stock market, Christmas market, I love them all. Lead the way."

Barb bustled out of the kitchen, and Andy caught her eye. "We'll talk more later," he said, heading for the foyer.

Chapter Eighteen

Andy noticed the changes on the grounds since his last visit, asking about the new porch light and repairs in the stonework as their party strolled outside. He was also attentive and polite to his hosts, which went over well with her parents. Tahsin and Naveed were thrilled to meet Andy in person. Not that she could blame them—he was a bona fide community success story.

After parking the trucks in a lot near Main Street, their group, which consisted of everyone except Cal and Esa, wandered toward the town square, where the Christmas market set up stalls every year. Barb explained that the local market was quite the draw; people drove in from all over the state to browse the selection of handicrafts, as well as homemade treats.

"I'm surprised your wife didn't accompany you to Alaska," Tahsin said as they strolled. Naveed and Sameera exchanged an amused glance—her mother wasn't even trying for subtle.

"No wife or girlfriend, Aunty. With my schedule and many commitments, I'm afraid I haven't made the time to find someone special," Andy answered with a smile. *He must get set up by people all the time,* Sameera thought. He was an attractive, single Muslim man with multiple homes and a fortune. Which meant that, in the eyes of every desi aunty, he must be in want of a wife.

"If you're too busy to find someone, you should ask your parents," Tahsin persisted.

"*Mom,*" Sameera hissed. "He's been here five minutes." She tried to tamp down her embarrassment.

"Andy doesn't mind. Your mom can set up a WhatsApp profile for you. That's how it's done these days. Why don't you give me her number, and I'll get the ball rolling?" Tahsin said, but luckily, Naveed distracted his wife by telling her that Barb was eager to learn her channa recipe.

"Sorry about that," Sameera said once her father had steered Tahsin away, leaving her, Tom, and Andy to walk leisurely behind.

"I'm used to it," Andy said. He nudged Tom in the ribs. "Watch out, brother, or Tahsin Aunty will arrange your entire wedding and mail you an invite."

Tom met Sameera's gaze, but his expression was impenetrable. Again, she wondered what he was thinking. "That doesn't sound too terrible," he said mildly.

Andy hooted. "You said you'd never marry! Now look—you can't keep your eyes off your woman."

"And you said you'd never step foot in Alaska, not without me. Yet Barb tells me you've been a regular visitor this year." Tom was joking, but also not. Sameera held her breath, but Andy only laughed and urged them to walk faster, since the parents had disappeared around the corner.

Her mother was already browsing the craft tables, her plan to set up Andy momentarily forgotten. "I can buy Eid gifts for everyone. Only ten months until Ramadan!" she said happily when Sameera joined her. She refrained from pointing out that Tahsin's mostly Muslim friends and family might not be the target market at Wolf Run's holiday market. Then again, if the cherry cordial chocolate crosses were anything to go by, her mother's eclectic taste was impossible to predict. Which might not be a bad thing, Sameera mused. Tom had found the crucifix hilarious, and so had Esa. Maybe it was time to meet her parents where they were, instead of constantly trying to police or manage their behavior to fit her standards. Wasn't that what she wanted from them in turn? Feeling thoughtful, she obediently followed her mother and managed to offer her opinion only when prompted.

The Christmas market was located at one end of Main Street near a gazebo and bandstand, which were both covered in fresh white snow and decorated with twinkling white fairy lights and Christmas trees festooned in red, white, and blue. Booths had been set up in neat rows, selling handmade ornaments, woolen handicrafts, cider, and hot chocolate. There was also a stage set up for live performances; Rob shared that Tom and even Calvin had participated in plays and concerts performed in the open air when they were younger.

"Do you think Razia will like this one, Sameera?" Tahsin asked, waving her over to a table. Their aunt Razia lived in Tennessee and was obsessed with porcelain figurines. Tahsin pointed to a delicately painted bear, and Sameera gave her a thumbs-up. Her mother was acting as if their argument yesterday had never happened. Which had been fine while they were cooking for Abu Isra and his family, but today, it didn't sit right with her. For the first time in years, Sameera didn't want to brush their issues under the rug.

Perhaps this was what Nadiya meant when she told Sameera to "fix your shit."

Their party stopped by the hot chocolate stall, run by one of Hilda's young employees. While Naveed broke out in a sweat at the sight of the cayenne pepper flavor, Barb and Tahsin both ordered salted caramel. Sameera couldn't decide between lavender rose or chai hot chocolate topped with Biscoff whipped cream.

"We could get both and share," Tom suggested.

Sameera was surprised by this suggestion. Ever since Andy had arrived, it felt as if Tom was reverting to his former moodiness, making snarky comments one minute and then trailing her through the market the next. Maybe he was trying to give her space, because he knew that his presence was a distraction? Except that his presence was also a soothing balm for her anxiety. In any case, she agreed to his suggestion readily. They purchased the hot chocolate and wandered deeper into the market, Sameera sipping her rose lavender. It was sweet, and the flowery taste reminded her of Rooh Afza, the popular rose-flavored syrup her mother used to make falooda during Ramadan. She much preferred the chai hot chocolate, and Tom let her finish the rest of the drink while he sipped on the flowery one.

They paused to admire a series of ice sculptures. Beside her, Tom closed his eyes and leaned his head back to soak up the weak sunshine, and she found she couldn't look away. When he opened his eyes again and caught her staring, he seemed to stiffen and look away, leaving her to wonder, again, what she had done wrong.

Nothing, she told herself. Whatever was going on was Tom's issue, not hers. This was exactly why she didn't want to muddy the waters of their friendly relationship with love drama. She ignored the voice in her head that wanted to push back, to point out the ways Tom had shown up for her, to their shared vulnerability. It didn't mean anything.

Beside them, Andy observed their interaction, and she flushed at his knowing glance. His attention reminded her of what she *should* be focusing on—winning him over. That was her first priority. She wondered if she could somehow convince the two men to head back to Cooke Place, where she could quickly practice her pitch, then find Andy and . . .

Looking around, her gaze was drawn to a clearing at the edge of the stalls, and her spiraling thoughts ground to a halt. "Is that a skating rink?"

Tom followed her pointing finger. "They have free skating every year. Why?"

But Sameera was already hurrying toward the outdoor rink. *Just for a few minutes. A small detour,* she told herself. Something fun, just for her. Tom and Andy followed behind, intrigued.

Sameera loved ice-skating. Her parents had enrolled her in skating lessons at the age of six, after she had announced her intention of becoming a world-famous figure skater following the Winter Olympics. Her figure-skating obsession had lasted three whole years, enough time to convince everyone around her that she would never get anywhere close to the Olympic Village.

She shared this story with Tom and Andy as they stood in line to rent skates. They laughed at her description of her Olympic dreams, and the cruel way they had been dashed by her utter lack of talent. She still loved the sensation of gliding on ice, the feel of the wind through her hair, the elegant moves she'd learned and could (imperfectly) perform. It had been a few years since she had last been on the ice, but the urge to indulge now was overpowering.

"It's just as well. My mom would never have let me wear one of those tiny skating outfits in public," Sameera concluded as they sat on the bench and tied their skates.

The trio got on the ice, and though Tom was the shakiest, Andy wasn't much better. He made jokes about how much his joints were worth, and Sameera skated circles around both men—literally.

"I'm hopeless on the ice," Tom groused after his third tumble. "Just ask my dad."

Sameera's smile vanished. "He was hard on you."

Tom nodded at Andy. "His dad was the same."

Andy was crouched low, trying to maintain his balance, and shrugged when Sameera looked at him. "You know how Brown dads are," he said.

Except she didn't. Naveed had been raised by a strict disciplinarian, sent to boarding school as a child, yet had chosen a different approach with his own children, though her mother sometimes complained that he was willing to let her play bad cop. Sameera was starting to realize that as much as she appreciated her father's gentleness growing up, it had put her mother into the role of forever disciplinarian. A role Tahsin might not always have enjoyed, Sameera realized.

"My dad used to make me write out science and math problems ten times for every single one I got wrong. Sometimes, it would go on for hours," Andy said.

"After my mom died, Rob would ignore me for days. Then all of a sudden, it was like he remembered he had a kid, and then I couldn't do anything right," Tom said.

They both looked at her, and she shrugged, embarrassed. "My dad told me he would always be there for me, but after we had a big fight, he didn't reach out for a long time. If it wasn't for my sister, I'm not sure how long we would have gone without talking."

"I really need to meet Nadiya," Tom said, and Andy perked up at this.

"Will I meet Nadiya, too?" he asked. "You heard your mom. I'm in dire need of a meet-cute."

Sameera shook her head at Andy. After she'd helped Tom up from the ice for the seventh time, he announced he was done. She made a motion to follow him to the bench, but he shook his head.

"You and Andy should finish up your time." Tom shot Sameera a look, as if he was trying to communicate something. "Don't believe anything Andy says," he added, and somehow, she didn't think he was joking.

Andy set the pace, a leisurely skate with stops and starts as he tried to find his rhythm. "I should build an ice rink in my backyard," he remarked as they glided.

"For which house?" she asked. It was a good thing she was a strong skater; it left her mind free to puzzle over Tom's behavior, and wonder how best to bring up the topic of business with Andy. Maybe she should casually mention the case she'd won last spring involving a commercial client whose business was similar to his.

Andy considered her question. "Maybe the one in Switzerland," he said, and she smiled despite her ricocheting thoughts. "We didn't finish our conversation in the kitchen. Also, Tom said you wanted to talk to me about legal representation."

Her heart stuttered. Was this it? She took a deep breath. Now or never. "Tom happened to mention that you're not happy with your current team. I work for Greaves, Hargrave & Bury in Atlanta as a commercial litigator, and we would love to sign on to Team Andy." She winced, but kept going. He seemed to be listening, though he had a strange smile on his face. "I have a few ideas about how you can reestablish your lost market share, and help you rebrand. I have plenty of experience in helping established companies recalibrate and earn back lost revenue, due to competition or real estate issues, anything really," she said smoothly. With any luck, her spiel would whet Andy's appetite to hear more while tiding him over until she could get back to Cooke Place and her pitch deck.

Andy had stopped skating to watch her. There was a calculating look on his face that triggered faint alarm bells. Something was wrong. But what?

"Tom really likes you," he said.

She bit her lip. "I like him, too. He's been a good . . . friend."

Andy barked out a short laugh. "If that's what you want to call it."

She had promised to keep their fake relationship a secret from Rob and Barb, but looking at Andy's sardonic expression, she couldn't keep up their ruse in front of his oldest friend.

"We're not actually dating," Sameera admitted.

"'Situationship,' 'relationship,' whatever you want to call it," Andy said easily. She was about to explain further when he went on. "Do you know what everyone who finds out that Tom is my best friend asks him?"

"For an introduction to you?" she guessed, after he'd paused long enough that she realized he expected an answer. Esa had done the same, she remembered.

"Exactly. They want to pitch me their business plan, or ask me for a loan, or for a donation, or they need ten minutes to ask business advice," Andy confirmed. "Do you know what Tom usually tells them?"

"He shoots them down immediately," she said, again thinking of Esa. Tom hadn't even hesitated with her brother, yet he had offered her a no-strings introduction to his wealthy best friend. The faint alarm bells in her head were growing louder now, and an uncomfortable sensation filled her chest. She had a feeling she wasn't going to like where this conversation was headed.

"But not you," Andy continued in a thoughtful voice. "Tom texted me half a dozen times about meeting with you, Sameera. It made me wonder why he went to so much effort for someone he'd only just met. It made me think you must be important to him."

She felt like a rabbit caught in a cobra's mesmerizing trap, but she felt she had to protest. Even though she desperately needed Andy's help, she wouldn't lie to get ahead, or to save face. Unhappiness and self-loathing lay that way, as she knew all too well. "No, see, I promised to help him film some cooking videos. He wants to grow his social media audience. He's had some television interest, and his agent thinks if he can get his viewership up, they'll offer him a job. He said he would introduce me to you in return, as a favor." She was babbling, and Andy's skeptical expression made her grind to a halt.

"How many videos have you filmed since making this arrangement?" he asked.

She thought. "Two?" Almost in unison, Andy and Sameera looked to the bench near the skate rentals, where Tom sat waiting after changing back into his boots. He stared back, gaze lingering on Sameera, and with a sudden jolt, she recognized the expression on his face.

He's jealous. Of me and Andy, she realized with a rising horror.

"Tom really likes you," Andy repeated now, and the knowing satisfaction in his voice made a prickling sense of unease climb her spine. "I plan to use that."

"What?" she said, sure she had misheard.

"Sameera, you clearly need me to impress your boss at work, or to win a bet, or to save your job, or whatever the hell reason. I truly couldn't care less. All I care about is Cooke Place."

"What?" she repeated. This conversation had set sail for new lands and was disappearing over the horizon, leaving her far behind.

"If you want to be my lawyer, you need to be quicker on the uptake," he said impatiently. "Look, we don't have much time. Tom isn't going to wait around forever, no matter how much he enjoys staring moodily at his girlfriend skating beside his best buddy in the whole world."

"You need something from Tom, and you want me to help you get it," Sameera said slowly, realization finally dawning.

"Bingo, sweetheart," Andy said, grinning, and she had a feeling she was in deep trouble.

Chapter Nineteen

Sameera encouraged Andy and Tom to walk ahead, explaining that she wanted to check out a few gifts for friends in Atlanta from a particular stall. Once the men had disappeared, and she walked around until she found a sliver of cell phone reception, she texted Nadiya.

> Things are getting complicated. I need you, Nads. Please, call me.

She stared at her phone, willing her WhatsApp phone app to ring, but nothing. She checked her watch, and wondered if her sister was sleeping, or out with friends, or working on her dissertation—with Nadiya's random hours, she could never be sure.

Next, she called Bee, but the phone rang several times before voicemail kicked in. She hung up and texted. Then there was nothing to do but find a seat on a bench at the edges of the market and worry about what Andy had explained to her on the ice, about the price he expected her to pay in exchange for working with him.

"Tom and his dad aren't close," Andy had said to her as they skated in slow circles. "I'm sure you've noticed the tension between them. I bet Tom has told you plenty of stories."

Sameera kept quiet, but of course she knew all about the strained relationship between Tom and Rob. Still, admitting as much felt like a betrayal of Tom, especially since she didn't know where Andy was going with this information.

Andy continued, "I love the guy, but Tom has always been hyperfocused on his own goals. That's how he made his catering business a success in a crowded market. He's the best at what he does, no question. I have a different superpower. I always see the bigger picture, which means I can see that Wolf Run, and Cooke Place in particular, is an unexplored gold mine. And I want it."

"You... want it?" Sameera repeated. She felt dizzy and had to stop to take a few deep breaths. "What does that even mean?"

"It means that for the past few years, I've visited Rob and Barb regularly, and done my best to make them like me. I've offered to buy the house several times and pay whatever they like—within reason, of course, but well over what the property is worth. Rob won't even consider an offer, because he thinks Tom will eventually return home and take his rightful place as his heir." Andy rolled his eyes. "You know how parents can be."

Sameera had started to skate backward, away from Andy, almost without realizing what she was doing. He kept pace with her, his skating skills mediocre but up to the job. "I don't understand what you expect me to do about this. I just met Tom. We're not even together, like I told you."

Andy's snort conveyed his disbelief at her words. "If you're not technically together, it's only a matter of time before that state of affairs changes, sweetheart," he said. "I'm not above using every tactic at my disposal. You talk to Tom. Encourage him to tell Rob, in no uncertain terms, that he has no intention of ever moving back to Wolf Run. That he will never again live at Cooke Place. It's the truth, right?"

Sameera tried not to panic. How had this conversation so thoroughly gone off the rails? "I'm not the right person for this mission," she said, trying to keep her voice firm.

Andy's voice turned low and persuasive, threaded with a hint of fear. His dark eyes were intense on her face, and she couldn't look away. "Sameera, I'll level with you: I'm desperate. You're right about my market share. My bubble tea shops haven't recovered after the pandemic, and with inflation, supply issues, and increased competition, I'm not sure they ever will. I have to pivot, and I have to do it quickly. I already have developers lined up. I've been talking with architects; the plan is ready to go. All I need is to secure the property. I plan to turn Wolf Run into a major skiing destination, an eco-resort like nothing ever seen before. Alaska is the perfect spot for it."

Sameera blinked. Wolf Run, a tourist town? She couldn't see it, but then again, her superpower wasn't turning ideas into money, like Andy's was.

"I could use a commercial litigator if I go ahead with this plan," Andy said. "Especially one who has proven their loyalty to my vision. Tom will listen to you. He knows you have no stake in this decision either way. Will you help me?"

Andy's words reverberated in her mind now, and they made her sick. All she had wanted was a chance to pitch him, or, failing that, some peace and quiet to catch up on her billable hours over the holidays. Instead, she was sitting in a tiny village in Alaska because her parents thought she was a liar, and her whale had just revealed himself to be a shark in disguise.

As a litigator, she was trained to quickly and thoroughly consider all options and figure out the best way forward, and she forced herself to do that now. It would be easy to tell Tom what Andy had asked her to do. But would Tom even believe her? They had known each other for about a week. He had known Andy for over a decade. It was highly likely that he would take his best friend's side over hers, especially considering his recent coolness. The other option was to go along with Andy's request. After all, Tom had never given any indication that he wanted to move back to Wolf Run—if anything, he had told her the exact opposite. Except she couldn't deceive Tom in that way; it wouldn't be right. Perhaps she should pretend to go along with Andy's request, tell him she had talked to Tom, let his plans fall apart, and accept her reward? But if Andy was willing to blackmail his best friend's new girlfriend to get what he wanted, he would hardly accept such an easy defeat.

Her head was starting to pound. The only thing she knew for sure was that she needed a vacation from this vacation.

Just then, two familiar figures came through the woods toward the market, and she recognized Esa and Cal. Her brother waved, and something in her heart clenched. At least this trip had brought her closer to him, enough for her to see how much her little brother had grown up, and how deeply she had missed him.

"We hitched a ride into town," Esa said cheerfully. "Cal said I had to try Hilda's doughnuts. What's wrong?" His expression shifted from friendly to alarmed as Sameera's eyes filled with tears.

"Nothing," she said, brushing at her eyes. "Doughnuts sound amazing right now."

Esa looked at Cal, who lifted his chin in acknowledgment before turning around and ambling toward the stalls. Her brother settled next to her on the bench with the air of a martyr—his sacrifice being doughnuts later instead of doughnuts right now.

"Why don't you tell me what's wrong?" he said. "And who I need to punch."

It was strange talking to her brother about her rapidly multiplying problems, but once she started, she found she couldn't stop. The story came spilling out—her fears over her job, meeting Tom at the firm's holiday party, deciding to help each other, Tahsin's interference and the resulting last-minute trip to Alaska, and now Andy's outlandish request. Esa listened without interrupting, smiling only when she spoke about their mother's machinations, with which he was also familiar. She skipped over a few parts, such as her kissing Tom, but otherwise left nothing out.

It was such a relief to tell someone that she immediately felt better. More than that, it felt good to confide in her brother, to feel close enough to him that she could do so. Even a week ago, sharing such confidences would have been impossible. When she finished, Esa looked thoughtful.

"This sounds like the plot from one of those rom-coms you used to watch," he said.

"Which one?" she asked.

"All of them?" he said, then laughed. She punched him lightly on his arm, flinching. Her brother must have started to work out, because his bicep was firm.

"I always believed you when you said you and Tom were faking it," Esa said.

"Really?" she said. This was news to her. At least someone in her family could tell when she was telling the truth.

"Definitely. Tom is way too cool for you." He laughed again, and she made to punch him again but thought better of it and scowled.

"Not helpful."

"You stopped crying, so I disagree." He pointed at himself. "Very helpful."

Her shoulders slumped. "I don't know what to do about Andy."

She had never asked her brother for help before, she realized. They had drifted during the estrangement, and never quite found their way back after her family reconciled. For her part, she had been so busy feeling guilty about not reaching out, she hadn't known how to handle his coldness. But the Esa who sat next to her right now reminded her of the little boy he had once been, the one who used to crawl into bed with her after he'd had a nightmare. Softer, kinder, more like their dad. Impulsively, she put her arms around him in a hug. He seemed surprised but hugged her back.

"Why are almost-billionaires so hopelessly predictable?" Esa asked now. "Andy asking you to help him betray his friend and buy up a small town is the most cartoon villain thing I've ever heard."

"To be fair, I think it's Cooke Place he wants, not Wolf Run," Sameera said.

Esa snorted. "Cooke Place *is* Wolf Run. This town and Rob are totally codependent. And Andy will want everything Rob owns: the stores and businesses, the prestige, all of it. Which would be fine if it was for sale, but it's not. This is just sus."

Sameera agreed that Andy's plan was suspicious and reiterated that she didn't know what to do.

Esa shrugged his shoulders. "The only reason Andy asked you is because he thinks you have some sway over Tom. I think he's right about that. You two give me the ick. In a good way," he hastened to add, noting her frown. "My advice is to find your man and just lay it all out. What's the worst that could happen? It's not like he's really your boyfriend. If he gets pissed and never talks to you again, then at least you warned him."

Sameera stared at her brother, surprised by his insight. He wasn't just a goofball who liked to play pranks—Esa was growing up to be a wise young man, someone who could get to the heart of things. In this case, he was also right. The easy, cowardly way out was to try to work both angles. But in this situation, there was only one way forward, and that was to tell Tom the truth.

"Thanks for listening," Sameera said.

Esa jumped up, his cheerful expression instantly back in place. "Anytime. I can't believe old people have problems, too."

"I'm not that old!" Sameera protested.

Esa looked solemn. "You're almost *thirty*," he said. "One foot in the grave." He danced away before she could pinch him, calling over his shoulder, "Cal got us a dozen doughnuts, but he's already eaten half. Hurry up!"

Grinning, she followed him. They both had a sweet tooth, and she knew that if she didn't hurry, he would eat the other half dozen doughnuts immediately. As she walked, she reflected how good it felt to be close to her younger sibling again. When they returned to Atlanta, maybe they could hang out, on their own or even with their parents.

At the thought of Tahsin and Naveed, Sameera stumbled for a second. As good as it felt to get close to Esa again, she knew that it wasn't enough. She needed to talk to her parents, too. Doing anything else would be a betrayal of the person she was trying desperately hard to become.

The rest of their party had gathered around the food stalls by the time she joined them, and the doughnuts were indeed as delicious as Cal had promised, though as she feared, the boys had claimed the box for themselves. Luckily, Andy ordered another dozen, along with a tray of coffee to distribute. As they ate, Naveed shared that he had bumped into Abu Isra at the market.

"He invited us for dinner tonight at his restaurant," Naveed said. "I accepted, of course. He wouldn't take no for an answer."

While their group shared plans for the rest of the day, Andy bumped against Sameera. She felt him press a folded piece of paper into her palm. While her parents asked Tom for other food stall suggestions, she surreptitiously looked at Andy's note.

He had written an astronomical number, and her eyes widened. Beside the number, he had written: *Starting salary, not including bonuses.*

She shoved the note in her pocket. It felt as if it were burning her hands. That was a lot of money, more than enough for her to pay off all her debts and buy out her mortgage, with some left over for a proper vacation. She wanted to be the sort of person who wasn't tempted by a bunch of zeroes, but . . . She met Andy's gaze, then interrupted her parents' conversation.

"Tom, you promised we could check out that stall you were telling me about," she said. From the corner of her eye, she saw Andy smile to himself. He really was a ruthlessly charming man, and she hated that he always seemed to get what he wanted.

Tom appeared momentarily confused, but then caught on. "Right, of course. Shall we?" He offered her his arm. They all made plans to meet at Abu Isra's restaurant in a few hours for dinner.

"Have fun, you two," Andy said, smiling broadly at Sameera.

"Watch your back, bruh." Esa's comment was bland, but Sameera noticed him narrowing his eyes at Andy. Clearly, he no longer thought of Andy as a friend or mentor. Part of Sameera was relieved. At least her little brother wasn't as easily won over. Then again, Esa still lived at home and hadn't had his heart, and finances, destroyed by a dishonest ex. She hoped he never would be forced to weigh his moral integrity against making his mortgage payments.

They walked back in the direction of Main Street, which by now felt almost as familiar to Sameera as her own neighborhood.

"Couldn't wait to get me alone, huh?" he asked, breaking her reverie. Charming Tom was back, and for a moment, she was distracted from her dark thoughts.

"You know it," she said weakly. "Actually, there's something I wanted to talk to you about."

"You're not leaving me for Andy, are you?" he joked, but there was a thread of worry in his voice. She stared at him, and he continued, "Your mom seems quite keen. I know it would be easier, since Andy is Muslim, or at least he was raised in a Muslim family. He's not observant, either, which might work in your favor, I guess."

She had nearly forgotten about Tom's reaction to them on the ice, too consumed by Andy's outlandish request to betray her fake boyfriend, but she recalled it now. Tom was jealous—and she wanted to laugh. Even if he was right, that Andy was the easier, if not the better choice in her family's eyes, Sameera had zero romantic interest in Andy, and not only because of his complete disregard for his BFF's family legacy, and willingness to throw Tom under the bus. She simply didn't see Andy that way.

Sameera put a hand on Tom's arm and turned to face him. "Your friend has charisma," she said truthfully. "He's rich, and my parents are entirely charmed. But I'm not interested."

Tom rubbed the back of his head and looked sheepish. "I know we're not . . . that you're not . . . I know what we are, I mean. You can like whoever you like. Just . . . watching the two of you skate together,

I guess I felt a certain kind of way. But Andy's a solid guy. I know he wouldn't try anything underhanded. Forget I said anything."

Don't be so sure about that. Sameera wanted to cry, to tell Tom that actually, he should be worried. That his best friend had just asked his fake girlfriend to try to use her wiles to help him get his way. Tom's words had only strengthened her resolve to tell him the truth.

But before she could reveal all, Tom continued, "It's just that lately, things have felt different between me and Andy."

Sameera paused. Tom clearly wanted to talk this out with her, and after Esa had so graciously allowed her to vent, she felt obliged to pay it forward. She also wanted to know what Tom thought was going on before she spoke any further. "That comment you made earlier, about him visiting Alaska without you. It made me wonder," she said now.

"Of course you noticed that," Tom said, smiling down at her. "You never miss a thing. I bet you're hell in the courtroom."

Her heart warmed at his compliment, and she raised her eyebrow, encouraging him to continue.

"Barb told me Andy has visited a few times in the past year or two," he said, shrugging as if it were no big deal. Or that he was convincing himself it wasn't. "I thought it strange he never mentioned it to me."

That was because the reason he had visited was to try to convince Rob to sell Cooke Place, right from under Tom's nose, Sameera thought grimly. Or maybe Tom wouldn't mind?

"That does sound strange," she said, trying to keep her voice impassive. "What did Barb say about it?"

"Just that Andy had been in the state and asked to drop by. He's visited a few times with me over the years, so it's not like he's a complete stranger to the area." Tom's tone was casual, but she could tell that he was willing it to mean nothing while knowing on some level that it did.

Sameera thought quickly. "I thought you were estranged from your dad. That he cut you off when you dropped out of school."

Tom nodded. "He did. We weren't in touch for nearly a year. Gradually, we started talking again, though things weren't the same. Mostly, I find out what's up through Barb. We text, and she calls to invite me home for the holidays. Andy came with me a few times. Rob loves him, of course."

Likely because Andy had gone out of his way to charm Rob. "Does Andy like it here? He made a joke about buying Cooke Place," she said cautiously. She wasn't sure what she was doing.

Tom laughed, shaking his head. "He makes that joke every time he visits. Tells my dad how much he loves the house, the property. Andy falls in love with places, but he soon moves on. That's why he has four houses. Or maybe six."

"You don't think he's serious about buying Cooke Place?" Sameera pressed.

"It wouldn't matter if he was," Tom said. "My dad would never sell."

"Because he wants to pass it on to you. Except you don't want to move back to Alaska. Do you?"

Tom seemed startled at the suggestion. "You know I don't," he said. He seemed troubled by the idea. "Do you think Andy was serious?"

Yes! she wanted to yell. *Your friend is hella sus,* as Esa would say. "What do you think?"

Tom's clouded expression brightened. "Here we are," he said.

Sameera had been so intent on the conversation that she hadn't noticed where they were walking. Tom opened the door to Hilda's Bakery, ushering Sameera inside.

"What are we doing here?" she asked. She wanted to continue their conversation, but Tom seemed content to let the matter drop, for now.

"I asked Hilda if we could make use of her kitchen this afternoon," Tom said, and he sounded almost shy. "To make another video. Would that be okay?"

They could continue their conversation in between filming, she reasoned. Besides, he was adorable when he was trying to tamp down his excitement. "Yes, you dork," she said fondly. "Let's cook."

Chapter Twenty

Hilda set them up in the back, after reminding Tom to tag the bakery's social media account when he posted. "I thought we could make some dessert to take to Abu Isra's place tonight," he said once she'd left them alone. "How about something desi?"

"If you make gulab jamun, my mom will ask Abu Isra to marry us after dinner. She has a gulab jamun addiction," Sameera joked, referring to the golden fried dessert that resembled doughnut holes soaked in rose-and-cardamom-flavored syrup.

"It's bad enough Abu Isra is cooking for us on his day off. I don't want him to officiate a wedding, too," Tom said. "Pie it is."

He gathered flour and butter, then pushed a bag of crisp green apples toward her. "Start peeling, sous-chef."

Mindful of the camera, Sameera asked Tom if he had any pie stories to share. "I bet you've had your share of cream pies to the face," she teased, and he pretended to look affronted.

"What are you implying, Ms. Malik?" he asked.

Sameera shrugged, looking innocently at the camera. "Only that sometimes I think about shoving a pie in your face, too," she said, and squealed when he grabbed her around the waist and lifted her up. His arms were warm and firm around her, and when he put her down, after she'd promised to behave, her cheeks were flushed.

They continued to joke and banter while they worked. Tom had a good vibe for the camera, Sameera thought as she peeled and chopped the apples into small pieces. He was funny and self-deprecating. He also loved to tease her, and judging by the heart and fire emojis as they recorded, their live audience hung on their every word. It was a relief to forget about Andy Shaikh's expectations and her worry about what she would do, at least for a little while.

They stopped the live stream while the pastry dough rested in the fridge. As she stirred the fresh apple filling on the stove, the fragrant smells of cinnamon, nutmeg, cloves, and allspice perfuming the air, Sameera idly asked, "You clearly love to cook. Do you think it's time to rethink your plan to never cook when you're here? Barb told me," she added.

Tom tasted the apple pie filling and added a pinch more salt before he answered, his voice even: "My dad and I had a huge fight about my cooking a few years ago. He called the career I had poured my time, effort, and passion into a 'hobby.'" Sameera winced. "He said it would never amount to anything, that I was wasting my time," Tom added.

Moved by this admission, she put a hand on his arm, and he looked up at her. "That's why you decided to hide from him," she said softly. "The secret dreams and hopes you have. The part that brings you the most joy."

Tom shrugged. "It is what it is."

"I hate that phrase," Sameera said. "What does it even mean?"

"I guess it's a reminder to accept reality, instead of longing for some dream that will never come true. Sort of like you with your parents."

Sameera looked up at him, surprised by this comment. What had he noticed about her? He leaned forward, brushing past her as he reached for the stove and turned the heat off.

"You think I do the same with my family?" she said, and he looked embarrassed.

"We don't really know each other," he started. Then, thinking it over, he nodded. "But, yeah, I do. You were so upset the last time we were at Hilda's because your mom had invited Abu Isra over for dinner. Then a few hours later, you were helping out with cooking and hosting, and you seemed fine. You pushed all that anger and annoyance down, because you knew that it wouldn't do any good, that no change was possible. I admired your ability to do that, to move on."

He must have noticed the effect his words were having on her, because he squeezed her shoulder in reassurance. "I wish I could do the same, Sameera. Though I did wonder one thing." He paused, and she nodded for him to ask. "What really happened between you and your parents? You've alluded to an estrangement a few times now. It's clear you love them a lot. Why didn't you talk to your family for three years?"

Sameera's heart juddered. She didn't really want to get into this. On the other hand, her mother had forced this situation, in large part because of the unresolved issues left over from their long estrangement. Maybe he was owed an explanation. She was also sure Tom wouldn't think differently of her, if he knew the truth; if anything, he might understand.

"My parents, my entire family, are observant Muslims," Sameera started. She had never really shared this story with anyone and wasn't sure how to begin. "And I am . . . not."

"You said your sister used to call you a kafir, an unbeliever," Tom said gently.

She looked out the window of the bakery. In the distance, she could make out a small pond, and she imagined the life that teemed below the frozen surface as she considered her words. Tom was so different from her, on the surface at least. But deep down, they appeared to share more things than seemed possible. They had both been hurt by the people who also loved them the most. They both had trouble with confrontation, and with communicating their needs and identities to their family. They both loved their families deeply but were also frustrated by those relationships.

"I grew up surrounded by faith, fully immersed in the Atlanta Muslim community," she said. "It's still an important part of who I am." This was the part she needed him to understand. Her parents had never made their Islamic belief a hardship, and she had little animosity for the faith itself, or for her family's practice of it. As she mulled over her next words, she realized that part of the reason she never talked about this was because she was always afraid of the listener's reaction. That they would nod in agreement, as if to say, *Of course it's only natural that you would reject Islam and all that it entails. We've seen Muslims in the news. They always seem so angry. They're so different from us. You chose right when you rejected all of that.* Except her Muslim-ness would always be a part of her.

"I didn't grow up religious, but I'm from a small town, and that's sort of similar," Tom said, and his kindness and empathy made her heart clench. He leaned against the counter, thoughtful blue eyes fixed on her. There wasn't an ounce of judgment in his body, and she took a deep breath to continue.

"What I realized as I grew up was that as much as I enjoyed parts of my faith, my mother sometimes used it to try to control my behavior." This was the harder part to talk about, the personal bits that made her feel utterly exposed and vulnerable. "It's not her fault entirely. She was raised the same way, with a lot of black-and-white thinking, and no room for gray. I was either a good Muslim and therefore a good person, or I was a bad Muslim—which was the same as saying I was a bad person, a bad daughter, a disappointment."

"Either you stay in Wolf Run and remain connected, or leave and never look back," Tom said quietly.

Sameera's lips quirked in a rueful smile. "For a long time, I never really questioned the rules my parents had set down for me. I followed the path they expected, like my sister. She made it look so easy."

"But at some point, you couldn't?" Tom asked gently. He had taken her hand while she talked, and he squeezed it now.

"Faith is personal," she said quietly. "It's a thing some people are brought up with, but at some point, you have to take it on for yourself, to make it your own. When I pushed back against a few things, such as why I had to fast every day in Ramadan, or pray five times a day, or why I couldn't date when I felt ready for a relationship, why marriage was always the end goal, or when I questioned the different expectations for men and women, my parents didn't know how to react to my questions. They laid down the law—and in my house, it was my mom who was the disciplinarian, not my dad—and I pushed back. By the time I was in senior year, we were always arguing. I thought about running away from home a few times because I was so unhappy. It wasn't pretty, and it took a toll on me emotionally and physically. I got very sick toward the end of high school. Looking back on it, I think I was depressed."

Tom waited, not pushing her to talk, his body angled toward hers, as if they were inside a cozy world of two.

"After a while, I realized I no longer shared my family's beliefs. I had lost my faith, and that was . . . devastating. It felt like a death." She looked at him, and those feelings came right back—loss, grief, despair. "I cried for days. That's the thing most people don't understand. It would have been easier for me to believe and practice the same way as my family, but I couldn't. Losing that connection wasn't relief or even freedom. It was loss. It felt like a betrayal of my very self."

She huffed out a laugh, but Tom didn't join in, eyes steady on her face. This was serious, and he wouldn't let her minimize the subject. Her heart swelled with gratitude for his concern, at his careful expression full of tenderness and understanding.

"The last straw was when I snuck out of the house to go to my friend's cabin overnight a few weeks before prom. I wasn't allowed to go, so I lied and went anyway."

"Sounds like something I would do," Tom said, and she flashed him a smile.

"Looking back on it, I realize it was pretty standard teenage rebellion, but for my parents, it was the last straw. My mother grounded me for the entire summer," Sameera said grimly. "I was eighteen years old, and I couldn't go anywhere. My dad tried to get her to relent after a couple of weeks, but she said it was the only way I would learn. I couldn't wait to leave for college. I wasn't sure I would ever come back. In some ways, I never did."

Tom reached out and traced the tear that was tracking down her cheek, and she realized she was crying. "It sounds ridiculous, I know," she said, wiping her eyes.

"It sounds like you were a teenager, and you were navigating a tough time. It sounds like you need to be kinder to yourself," he said.

Sameera tipped her head up to look at him, and a sense of wonder entered her heart. Tom really did understand. "Even when I eventually moved back to Atlanta after law school, things weren't great between us. Hunter was in the picture by then, but I didn't tell my parents about him. If I'm honest, he was the latest relationship I had hidden from them, because I didn't want to deal with their disappointment and lectures every time I went out with someone. But an aunty saw us together and told them. When they confronted me about him, I had had enough. We had a huge fight, and afterward, I cut them off. We didn't talk again for three years. I guess I was tired of pretending."

"How did that feel?" Tom asked.

"At first, it felt great, not having to worry about what my parents would think of my choices. I could just . . . be."

"Sounds like heaven," Tom muttered.

"Then things got tough with Hunter. We were fighting all the time. He said I was working too much. Nadiya said his racism was showing, that he had assumed a South Asian woman would be more traditional, whatever that means." She rolled her eyes. "The last year Hunter and I were together, Ramadan rolled around, and even though I wasn't fasting, I still *missed* everything. Those years without my family, it felt like the other half of my heart was missing. It made no sense, because I was the one who had decided not to return their calls. Then again, it wasn't as if my parents tried very hard to get in touch. I'm still angry with my dad, in particular, about that."

Tom was silent at this. "When I'm in Atlanta, I dream about Wolf Run," he admitted quietly. "About my mother, and Cooke Place, and the forest behind the property. About Toboggan Hill. I miss it so badly sometimes, I can't think. Then I get here, and it's like nothing has changed—my dad is still the way he is, and I get itchy and want to leave."

Sameera took a step closer, until her nose was buried in his shoulder. His arm went around her waist automatically, and they stood like that for a long moment, drawing strength and comfort from each other.

"It feels better, with you here," he said, voice muffled against her hair. She looked up at him, and the expression on his face was soft. "Everything feels better with you."

Their kiss was soft, an acknowledgment of their mutual hurt, a gentle reminder that they had survived, and were capable of making peace with their pasts. She took a deep breath and continued.

"After Hunter left, and I realized how much trouble I was in, I was too humiliated to reach out to them. In the end, Nadiya brought us back together. But sometimes . . ." She trailed off. Her fingers played with Tom's, caressing his knuckles, his forearms, and he let her find comfort from his body. "I think we just decided to move on, without having the hard conversation. You know?"

Tom pointed at himself. "You're looking at the king of avoidance."

"And here I thought you were the Prince of Wolf Run," Sameera said, smiling weakly.

"I can be both," he said. "'I contain multitudes.'"

She hugged him again. *Yes, you do,* she thought. "Even though there's still work to be done, and even though we all have our moments, I'm grateful to be in my family's life again," she said.

Tom chuckled softly. "What you're really saying is, I should make samosas for my dad."

"Hey, your samosas are for me. Make Rob something else," Sameera said, smiling.

Tom seemed thoughtful as he started the camera again, filming as he rolled out the chilled pastry dough and greased four round pie tins before stretching out the dough for the crust. Sameera helped spoon the cooled filling into each tin, and even shared a story from when her brother was five years old. Esa had stolen a frozen pie from the freezer without their mother realizing it, and ate the entire thing while watching cartoons. He'd confided in Sameera only because he had a stomachache. Tom laughed heartily. She had forgotten about that story.

They covered each pie with another layer of pastry and crimped the edges into a pretty pattern. He sliced ventilation slits in each crust, then eased the pies into the oven to bake. Their video ended when he filmed her taking the first bite, a scoop of vanilla ice cream on the side, and she moaned her pleasure.

"I want to marry this pie," she said.

"Marry me instead, and I'll make you all the pie you want," he said. It was a joke for the camera, but her heart lurched anyway.

They left a pie for Hilda as a thank-you for the use of her kitchen, and packed two for Abu Isra, which left one half.

"Emily would love this," he said, and after they hugged Hilda goodbye, they made their way back to the Christmas tree farm. His words jolted Sameera. In the excitement and chaos of the past day, she had almost forgotten about Tom's ex-girlfriend (fiancée?), and a pang of jealousy made her swallow hard. She had no right to feel this way, especially when she hadn't yet made up her mind about how she would handle Andy's request to manipulate Tom.

Sameera kept her thoughts to herself as they walked down Main Street toward the tree farm and the attached house where Jan lived, where Emily was staying while she was in town. Thankfully, Jan was nowhere in sight, and they found Emily chatting on her porch, next to a woman dressed in a bright-orange puffer vest and close-cropped hair dyed a bright blue.

"Hey, Emily. Hi, Jean. I didn't know you were back in town, too," Tom said easily, and Sameera noticed that the women were holding hands. "Jean is a pilot with Delta Air, and Emily's girlfriend," he explained.

Sameera had believed Tom when he said that he and Emily were only friends. Mostly. But seeing Emily with her girlfriend made her feel foolish about her initial assumption. She covered quickly. "We flew Delta into Anchorage. Nice . . . planes."

The women were delighted with the half pie, and had already started to dig in when Tom and Sameera took their leave. Abu Isra had invited them to an early dinner, and there was just enough time to walk to his restaurant on the other end of Main Street.

Tom quirked a smile at Sameera once the tree farm was behind them. "For a lawyer, you have a terrible poker face." Sameera spluttered, but he shook his head fondly. "Emily and I were together in high school, but even back then, I think we both knew that we were better as friends. She asked me to pretend we were still together when I went away to college, a favor to an old friend. She needed time to figure things out for herself, and a long-distance, fake boyfriend would stop people from asking too many questions."

"That was . . . nice of you," Sameera said, her mind working quickly.

Tom shrugged. "Jan still isn't happy about Em and Jean, even though they've been together over two years now. I think part of her thinks Emily will grow out of the relationship, as if who she loves is something to overcome, like a bad haircut. But Jean is crazy about her, and they're planning to move to Kodiak Island, maybe fly commercial and freight, with Emily taking care of tourist bookings and other stuff."

Another emotion was eclipsing her embarrassment now, wrapped around a growing realization. "I'm not your first fake relationship," she said.

Tom considered this. "I guess not. But you're definitely my favorite fake girlfriend."

She laughed, but the uneasy feeling was back. She still hadn't told Tom about Andy's bargain, unsure of how she wanted to proceed. She was delaying the conversation instead of ripping off the bandage, one way or another. *Later,* she promised herself.

Chapter Twenty-One

Abu Isra lived with his family above their restaurant, Isra's Mediterranean Cuisine, named after their eldest child. Her parents, Esa, Cal, Andy, and the Cookes were walking up when Sameera and Tom joined them. Andy gave her a significant glance, but she ignored him. She wasn't ready to engage, not until she knew what she wanted to do. When Esa glanced her way, she shook her head.

Hiba must have been looking out for them, because she opened the door and ushered them inside. The restaurant was decorated in bright colors—turquoise blue, sage green, and vibrant yellow. Pictures of framed seascapes hung on the wall, along with Quranic verses Sameera recognized. Tables were grouped in small and large clusters, the kitchen in the back. Though the restaurant was closed, the comforting aroma of garlic, za'atar, sumac, grilled meat, vegetables, and olive oil conjured up the ghosts of countless mouthwatering meals. They followed Hiba up the stairs to a three-bedroom apartment, with a large sitting area, kitchen, and a balcony that overlooked the parking lot at the back.

Abu Isra and Hiba's home was bright and welcoming, with comfortable furniture and soft cushions and blankets. The walls were painted a bright blue with white curtains around the windows. The apartment felt cozy and well loved, putting Sameera instantly at ease, while the tantalizing smells coming from the galley kitchen reminded her of her parents' home in Atlanta. Her mother always made sure her guests had a good time. Even when she was younger, her friends had always commented on how welcome they felt in her family's home. Perhaps she had taken for granted Tahsin's tendency to befriend people wherever she went—it had brought them the unexpected joy of new acquaintances during the holidays, after all.

Hiba bustled into the sitting room with a tray of glasses filled with homemade lemonade flavored with mint. Their host was dressed in a green abaya and a beige hijab that went well with her peaches and cream complexion. She had light-hazel eyes and laugh lines around her generous mouth. Sameera accepted a drink and complimented their home.

"All due to Rob," Abu Isra said, his voice booming from the kitchen. He stuck his head into the sitting room. Rob waved him off modestly, but Abu Isra continued, "I approached him about turning my small takeout into a full-service restaurant a few years ago. And suddenly, the red tape vanished. Thanks to the King of Wolf Run!"

Syrian Santa beamed, and Sameera realized that he wasn't as old as she had initially thought, despite the silver hair.

"We need more businesses opening up in Wolf Run. And you make the best pita and hummus in the state," Rob said, and everyone laughed.

Tom disappeared into the kitchen, his happy place in any home, and Andy sidled next to Sameera. "You heard Rob. Wolf Run needs more business. Did you and Tom have a nice outing? I'm sure you had a lot to talk about."

Sameera smiled faintly. "We ended up filming a food video, baking the pies we brought for dessert."

"Wholesome," Andy said. "Any other developments?"

"Not yet," Sameera said. Looking around to make sure no one was sitting close enough to eavesdrop, she lowered her voice. "Have you tried talking to Tom instead?"

Andy looked at her as if she were crazy. "How would that conversation go, exactly? 'Hey, Tom, can you convince your dad to sell me your family legacy, since you don't seem too interested?'"

"Sounds like a good start to me," Sameera said.

Andy sighed. "If you want to be my lawyer, the first thing you should know is that I am an erratic billionaire used to getting my way."

"You said you're not a billionaire anymore," Sameera said, and Andy laughed good-naturedly. She didn't trust that laugh. He was trying hard to be likable, but he had already revealed his true colors. Maybe she should try another tack. "Why do you want this property? I'm sure there are plenty of options for a man of your significant resources."

"Firstly, thank you for complimenting my significant resources, even if your earlier crack about my reduced circumstances was uncalled for," Andy said. "Secondly, Cooke Place is special. Trust me, I've looked for other properties to snatch up, and they don't exist."

Sameera doubted this. There must be a particular reason Andy was so obsessed with this tiny village. She wondered if it had something to do with his experience visiting with Tom, before he became the Andy Shaikh who had profiles written about him, perpetually surrounded by people looking for favors.

"I expect my lawyers to perform miracles," Andy said. "So, I guess it comes down to how badly you need this."

Andy took a seat beside Rob and Barb on the large couch, leaving her to fume silently. He had seen right through her, had correctly gauged her weakness and desperation to save her job and fix her life. The threat of her meeting with HR in the new year hung over her even now. If she lost her job, it would take months to find a new one. Her finances were so precarious, even spending a month unemployed would be catastrophic, and her consulting contracts didn't pay enough on their own to keep her afloat.

Sameera tried to breathe deeply and will herself calm. It wasn't fair that people like Andy, who had been blessed by fate, had so many resources, while people like Sameera floundered, no matter how hard they worked.

Her phone buzzed with a message, interrupting her panicking spiral, and she was relieved to see it was Bee, though disappointed her sister had yet to respond.

Sorry I missed your call. We drove to Mom's for Christmas. Everything ok?

Sameera moved to a quiet corner before replying: Just thinking about you, and navigating a tricky situation with Andy. I'll fill you in later. Tell your mom I said hi. Miss you.

Her friend replied immediately: "Never trust a billionaire" is my life's motto. Also, waiting on that shirtless Tom pic.

Sameera smothered a smile. Not sure Lorenzo would like that.

Bee's cheeky reply made her snort: He'll consider it motivation. Love you!

Her friend's brief interlude gave her some breathing room, enough to calm her anxious thoughts. She still wasn't sure what to do, so the best course of action was to focus on what was happening right now. Sameera put her phone away just as Hiba brought out several trays of appetizers: hummus topped with aromatic olive oil and decorated with parsley; muhammara, a red pepper, garlic, and walnut dip, slightly sweet and crunchy; freshly fried kibbe, dumplings shaped like miniature footballs made from barley, stuffed with spiced minced meat. When she returned to the living room with another platter piled with freshly baked pita bread and a third with stuffed grape leaves, everyone protested that the family had gone to too much effort.

"We cook for our customers all day long," Hiba said with a smile. "We are happy to share food with friends today. Eat, eat!"

They needed no further encouragement. The adults squeezed around the dining table beside the kitchen and passed around the appetizers, while the children, including Esa and Cal, ate on a sheet spread on the floor of the living room, reclining on cushions. From their peals of laughter, Sameera could tell the younger set were delighted by this arrangement.

Tom helped Abu Isra and Hiba transfer platters of grilled meat, fluffy white rice studded with raisins and sliced almonds, a curry made of eggplant and chunks of beef and tomato, toum garlic dip, a large fattoush salad, and another green salad garnished with olives and crumbling akkawi cheese, drizzled with a tangy dressing and topped with crispy fried pita bread. Everyone ate with enthusiasm, exclaiming over the burst of savory flavors.

While Sameera reached for another pita—the muhammara was truly addictive—she noticed Tom had disappeared into the kitchen. What was he up to? When she peeked inside, she spotted him deep in conversation with Abu Isra, who was putting the finishing touches on another platter of grilled chicken and lamb kabobs.

Back in the sitting room, Hiba was sharing her family's migration story. "We applied as refugees at the start of the civil war. I have an aunt in Texas, and she helped us. We were the lucky ones." Her face clouded with the memory of those she had left behind.

Barb reached out and squeezed Hiba's hand. "It's heartbreaking, what your family went through. I'm so sorry for all you have lost, Hiba, and I hope you can take solace in a new hope for the future of your country."

Hiba's eyes were wet, but she accepted Barb's kindness readily. "Thank you," she said quietly. "We have happy memories, too, and will make more when we return, inshallah. Would you like to hear how Younus and I first met?"

She called to her husband and coaxed him into sharing the story. "I was not a good student when I was younger," he started, with a grin. "Too impatient to make money. I learned soon enough that I would always be considered less than a man with a degree, even though I was smarter!" The party laughed at Abu Isra's bravado.

"I returned to school, to finish what you would call high school, and then I enrolled in the local university in Damascus. I was close to thirty by then, and even my mother had written me off as a hopeless case. All of my other brothers and sisters were married and settled, but not me. My father was more patient with me. He told me I was just like him, a late bloomer, and that when I met my bride, it would feel like fireworks. It had been like this with my mother."

Sameera glanced at Tom, who was reaching for more grilled eggplant. He ate each dish slowly, evaluating and deconstructing every ingredient. He quietly excused himself and returned with salt, which he added to the eggplant curry. She liked the way he unobtrusively took care of those around him, unlike Andy, who turned everything into a big production.

Abu Isra continued his story. "I joined my first-year tutorial for a mandatory literature course, and who do you think was my instructor?"

Hiba smiled. "I had just finished my master's degree when Younus joined my class. I found out later that he was five years older than me, even though he behaved as if he were ten years younger!"

Abu Isra waved off her words. "It was just as my father said. The moment I saw my Hiba, it was over for me."

Sameera met Tom's gaze, serious and intent on her; she knew they were both thinking of their first meeting at the firm's holiday party, the way they had simply clicked.

Hiba picked up the thread; Sameera could tell that they both enjoyed sharing their story, and had told it so often it had become a central part of their family lore. "Of course, I had no idea of his intentions. When he asked me to go for a walk after class, I thought he wanted to beg me for a higher mark on his test. He still wasn't a very good student."

"I'm better at talking than studying," Abu Isra countered, and the table laughed. "I wore her down eventually."

Sameera reached for more fattoush salad. "How did you manage that?" she asked.

"I paid attention," Abu Isra said. "I brought her gifts. I made her favorite tea. When none of that worked, I started to study for her tests."

More laughter greeted this revelation. Sameera recalled the samosas, biryani, chai, and apple pie Tom had made for her and with her. He was constantly feeding her, nourishing her, making sure she was taken care of, comforting her. She met his gaze once more, and hoped her flushed cheeks weren't too obvious.

"I could see he was trying hard to better himself," Hiba confirmed with a fond smile at her husband. "After the class ended, he asked to speak to my father."

"Her father told me I wasn't good enough for his daughter, but by then, it was too late. Hiba would have no one else," Abu Isra declared proudly.

"Actually, my father felt sorry for you, and said I should marry you out of charity because no one else would have you," Hiba teased. "But yes, it is true. I wanted to be only with him."

Sameera glanced from Abu Isra to Hiba. They had met under the most adorable of circumstances, and now lived together an ocean and a continent away from their beloved home. They had built a life here, and were now contemplating returning to their homeland, despite not knowing what they would find. Their bravery and steadfast hope felt like a beacon to her now, a model to emulate. She reached for a kabob instead, and the conversation moved on.

Finally, when there were only pita crumbs left and everyone was groaning and rubbing their full bellies, Rob sighed. "Delicious meal, my friend. Why don't you have that eggplant dish on your regular menu?"

Their host laughed. "We have to keep some things for special nights, yes? In any case, that dish is not my recipe."

"My compliments to Hiba, then," Rob said, nodding her way.

"Actually, your son provided that recipe," Hiba said. "I offered him a job, but he said he has his hands full in Atlanta."

Rob didn't say anything, but Sameera noticed he reached for another helping of the dish. Tom's eyes were on his father's face as he scooped up the curry with his pita, and she watched with a smile as a look of understanding passed between father and son. Perhaps her earlier encouragement had resonated with Tom; perhaps the presence of another broken but healing family had inspired Rob. Whatever the reason, it was clear that something was starting to shift in their relationship. It did Sameera's heart good to see it.

Then she met Andy's frowning glance, and realized that Tom and Rob's improved relationship was not what the irascible former billionaire wanted at all.

For dessert, Hiba had baked basboussa, a dense cake made with semolina and soaked in syrup, topped with crushed pistachios and saffron, and Tom presented their apple pies, to much enthusiasm. There was also cut-up fruit, ice cream, and mint tea to wash it all down. When they finally left Abu Isra and Hiba's home, everyone was stuffed and happy. Sameera climbed into the car with Rob, Tom, and her father for the drive back to Cooke Place.

"That food was amazing. I liked your eggplant dish," Sameera said to him. It was the first time they had spoken all night, and he flashed her a small smile.

"Just a recipe I've been messing around with," he said shyly. "You have to roast the garlic separately."

"I liked it, too," Rob said suddenly. He glanced at Sameera and cleared his throat. "Maybe you could make it for me sometime."

Tom seemed startled at this. "Thanks, Dad," he said. "I'd like that."

Hours later, in her room at the guesthouse, Sameera stared at her phone. Nadiya had ignored her for days now, and she needed her sister. No one else understood her history, her fears, and anxieties in quite the same way.

She lay back in bed and stared at the ceiling. Nadiya used to tease her that she was a chronic overanalyzer. That she couldn't make a decision without listing out all the pros and cons, asking her friends and family for advice, and completing a future forecast. And yet when her mother told her she had bought tickets to Alaska, she had folded almost instantly—which meant that on some level, she wanted to be here. She wanted to spend time with her family. She wanted to watch old holiday classics and argue about whether *Die Hard* was really a Christmas movie. She had enjoyed the Christmas market, and ice-skating, and even making those cooking videos with Tom. It had all felt . . . nice. Like coming home.

There was something about Wolf Run. Coming here had changed her. She felt content, and more relaxed than she had in years. Braver, too. She couldn't remember the last time she had stepped off the treadmill that was her life and simply allowed herself time to be, without judgment, guilt, or blame.

In a strange way, it felt like a callback to those first few weeks after she had severed ties with her family, when she had confused the euphoria of drastic action with happiness. Except this felt better, healthier, cleaner somehow. It felt good to be around her parents and brother, even when she found them annoying. It felt right to confront her feelings of shame and embarrassment, and to talk over the pain of the last few years with Tom.

She might finally be ready to have the hard conversation with her own parents about why she had pushed them away—and ask them why they had let her.

She must have drifted off to sleep, because she woke up to a noise. A dull thud sounded against her window. *Bear* was her alarming first thought. *Tom* was her even more alarming second. Groggy, she staggered to the window and looked into the darkness. Someone stood outside her ground-floor window, grinning at her.

Esa raised his cell phone, and she reached for her own.

I want to show you something, he texted. **I promise it will be fun.** She checked the time—it was nearing midnight. When she looked up, he had disappeared. Shrugging off her exhaustion, she reached for her jacket and slipped outside.

Chapter Twenty-Two

Esa had left a sign outside her window: **SAMEERA AYLA MALIK, WELCOME TO THE NIGHT BEFORE CHRISTMAS!** She stared at the cheap white posterboard, and a flurry of emotions crowded inside her heart: amusement, happiness, and more than that—an overriding relief. Her brother had truly come back to her. He was a teenager, but he still wanted to play with her, even if it was in the middle of the night.

Esa had taken his cue from the most famous Christmas story of all time, Dickens's *A Christmas Carol*. On the back of the posterboard, she found instructions, and Esa had left a flashlight to illuminate the fluorescent stakes he had placed in the ground to mark her path. She followed them into the woods behind the guesthouse, and a few feet into the tree line, a shadowy figure appeared. Another flashlight clicked on and illuminated her brother's face. He was dressed in a long cape and hood, another borrowed costume, no doubt.

"Welcome to your past, Sameera," he intoned.

She grinned. It had been so long since playful Esa had made an appearance in her life. "Thank you, Ghost of Christmas Past," she said seriously. "I'm ready for your vision."

He handed her an object—a carved marble elephant, the body displaying delicate floral designs. "Hathi!" she exclaimed. "Nana gave me this when we went to India. I was sixteen, and you were three years old."

"I'm not sure what you're talking about. I'm the Ghost of Sameera Malik's Past, and therefore timeless," he said in a spooky voice. "But also, yeah, I was about two years old. I don't really remember that trip at all, except that Nana's beard was scratchy, and a lot of old ladies kept kissing me and feeding me milky chai."

"I lost this elephant after we got back home. Where did you find it?" Sameera said. The marble elephant had taken pride of place on her desk, until the day it vanished. She had accused her little brother of taking it, which he had vehemently denied.

"I stole it when I was mad at you. I was six years old, and you refused to play with me. I thought maybe it would make you pay attention," he said. "I didn't even realize it was in my suitcase until I unpacked here."

She tried to hug her little brother, but he put up a hand. "Please keep your hands off the ghost until the end of the show." He handed her another envelope before melting into the woods.

She counted to one hundred, as the instructions asked, then followed the trail he had laid out for her. He was waiting in another clearing, flashlight illuminating his face again, at that same spooky angle.

"I am the Ghost of Christmas Present. Sameera Malik—This. Is. Your. Life!" With a flourish, he sent a collage of pictures to her iPhone. There was a picture of her from her birthday a few years ago, wearing a silly hat and looking at the chocolate cake Tahsin had baked while Naveed and Esa sang. Another picture was one Esa had snapped during a rare visit to her condo. It was messy, her desk piled high with files, with even more files on her couch and dining table, her walls bare. She had kept meaning to decorate, but there was never enough time. Another series of pictures were from their parents' home, with its familiar furniture and decor, the site of so many celebrations, and conflicts, over the years. A picture from Esa's tenth birthday party, the entire family gathered around cake, a pile of gift wrap on the floor. Another from Eid prayers, Nadiya squinting into the camera as Sameera made bunny ears above her head. She missed them. She had missed all of this so much.

The last picture was more recent, from the Eid party last week. Esa must have taken it without her noticing. Sameera was laughing at something Tom had said. For his part, Tom smiled down at her, delight and admiration clear on his face.

When she looked up, her brother had disappeared once more, and she followed the path he'd left near the tree line. They had made a full circuit around the property now. She spotted him near a large shed and walked faster, almost jogging now. It was cold, and she was starting to feel tired. Just then, another "ghost" dressed in a dark jacket popped out from the forested area. What was going on? Everyone knew the next apparition was the Ghost of Christmas Future. Perhaps Esa had recruited Calvin to help?

But when her brother spotted the new ghost, he started to scream. "Begone, jinn!" he yelled, flailing his arms. "I renounce thee!"

The new ghost appeared to glide toward her little brother, and instinct kicked in. With a battle cry, Sameera tackled the interloper, and they both went down hard, snow and pine needles flying as they grappled.

"Oof, get off me!" the interloper said. "What do you think you're doing, Sameera? I expected a warmer welcome after coming all this way!"

Sameera peered down at the apparition in shock. A very annoyed Nadiya stared back. She clambered off her sister and helped her up, a happy grin blooming on her face. Nadiya had surprised her, had surprised her whole family. This was the best Christmas gift ever. Next to them, Esa dropped to his knees, laughing.

"I thought you were a jinn!" he gasped, just as Sameera asked, "What are you doing here?"

Nadiya stared at her sister. "I came to rescue you, obviously. Mom told me where you were staying. I would have been here sooner, but it took forever to convince someone to drive me out to Wolf Run, and it cost a fortune, too. I'll be sending you the receipt, Counselor. Now, are you going to tell me what's *really* going on, or do I have to sit on you like I used to do when we were kids?"

Sameera once more tackled her sister, and they landed on the soft snow, laughing and crying. She knew somehow that everything was going to be okay, now that the three Malik siblings were reunited at last.

They ended up on three Adirondack chairs by the frozen firepit, and Sameera told Nadiya everything. Esa already knew most of it, and he smirked as their sister's expression grew more serious with every word.

"Let me get this straight: This Andy person thinks that because he built a bubble tea empire, he can also build a ski resort, and he's not above manipulating his best friend to do it," Nadiya said, summarizing. "Meanwhile, Tom doesn't want to tell his parents that your relationship is fake because he has no intention of moving back to Alaska. And Mom and Dad are convinced you're lying about everything, which is why you're in Alaska in the first place."

Sameera nodded at the succinct summary. Her sister sat back, thinking.

"I'm still mad at you for not telling me what was really going on," Nadiya said.

"I called and texted, and you left me on read," Sameera threw back.

"Which you totally deserved," Nadiya countered. "Though maybe I should have called you back before I jumped on a plane. I guess we all made a lot of assumptions and unfair judgments." The words were more of an admission than Sameera had ever expected from her stubborn sister.

"I believed Sameera from the start," Esa said smugly. "I just wanted a free vacation to Alaska, and to hang out with Tom Cooke. He's been giving me tips on how to grow my social media following, and they're working. I got nearly five hundred subscribers in just three days."

Nadiya ignored their little brother, focusing on Sameera. "I have one question for you, then. Why are you really here, Sameera?"

"You mean besides Mom's emotional blackmail?" Sameera asked, stalling for time.

"Obvious," Esa piped up. "She's here for us."

Both sisters stared at their little brother. "But Mom came here for me," Sameera said slowly.

"And you're here for us," Esa said, as if he were talking to a very small child. "Get it?"

It did make a strange sort of sense, Sameera thought. Her parents had planned an expensive, last-minute trip to Alaska because they were worried about Sameera. And she had gone along with this mad plan so she could be with them, too.

This was what happened when family didn't talk to each other, Sameera thought. They each behaved in unpredictable, unreasonable ways, because they didn't know how else to say they loved and needed each other in their lives. Which she did. She could accept that now. Her family meant everything to her, and she never wanted to be distanced from them again. Even if that meant flying to Alaska.

Nadiya sighed deeply. "He's right. Not to mention that you are a relentless people pleaser, and it has landed you in more trouble than it's worth. Even now, you're worried we will reject you."

Sameera didn't respond. She didn't have to—they all knew it was true. Nadiya took her sister's mittened hands in her own. "No matter what you do, no matter who you are or whom you love, I will never abandon you," she said.

Tears sprang to Sameera's eyes at these words—she hadn't realized how much she needed to hear them, or how long she had assumed that her family's love for her was conditional. It might have felt that way, but the truth was more complicated, she was starting to realize.

"My love for you does not depend on what you do or who you are," Nadiya continued. "You're my sister, and I'm here for you—always. Even if you do have questionable taste in men."

Sameera's tears were falling freely now, but she laughed at Nadiya's final shot. Esa, clearly uncomfortable with seeing his sister cry, patted her on the shoulder. "What she said," he grumbled. "Also, it's freezing out here. We should go back inside, or . . ." He trailed off, eyes gleaming in the dark.

Sameera looked up, wiping her eyes. "Or?"

Her brother pointed to the large shed, where Tom said a pile of toboggans and sleds were stored. "Or we choose option two."

Freezing-cold wind whipped her face as Sameera careened down the low hill. She whooped and raised her arms, inadvertently letting go of the safety strap on her sled and toppling over into a heap of powdery snow.

She took a picture of herself, collapsed backward in the snow, and sent it to Bee, not expecting a response. To her surprise, her friend was up, and Bee's reply made her laugh: I know what you look like. Give the people what they want! #ShirtlessTom

"Are you alive?" Her brother's voice echoed down the hill, and she lifted a thumbs-up in response before standing up and dusting snow from her legs. Esa's suggestion to make use of Toboggan Hill had been a good one. They had each grabbed a sled, confident the hill was far enough from the guesthouse that they wouldn't have to worry about waking their parents.

After the heaviness of their conversation, and the emotions conjured by her brother's *Christmas Carol* reenactment, they needed to let loose and do something fun. It wasn't lost on Sameera that they never could have done this in Atlanta—not only because of the lack of snow, but because it had been a while since all three of them had been in the same place at the same time. A deep contentment stole over her at the thought.

Her sister was already hurtling down the hill when Sameera started to climb up for another run. Esa took another turn, raising his arms like Sameera had done, as if he were on a roller coaster, but he made it only halfway before tipping off the sled. From the bottom of the hill, Nadiya mocked their lack of sledding know-how, and Esa responded by trying to throw a snowball at his older sister. He missed, which led to more catcalls and trash-talking.

Sameera was starting her third trek back up the hill when a familiar figure in a blue parka materialized out of the trees.

"Can anyone join, or is this a private function?" Tom asked, and her heart melted. It had been doing that more and more lately, whenever she caught sight of her fake boyfriend.

He looked up to the top of the hill, where Esa waved. "Your brother invited me. He said he was outnumbered by girls. I tried to wake up Cal, but he was out cold. Who is that standing beside him?"

"Nadiya flew in to join us," Sameera said. She couldn't see Esa's face in the dark but could imagine his impish delight.

Esa bounced on his feet with excitement when Tom joined them. "What? Tom is my mentor. And technically, this hill belongs to him. For now."

Tom turned to Sameera with a questioning look, but before she could respond, Esa had jumped on his sled and challenged Tom to a race. He had time only to nod a greeting at Nadiya before he was hurtling down the hill after Esa.

Nadiya nudged her sister. "You should tell him what Andy said, and soon. Or you could do as Andy says and save your job. Alternatively, you could play both men against each other, just to see what happens. That's what I would do."

"Thanks for clarifying my options," Sameera said dryly. The sisters watched Tom try to steer his sled into Esa and end up landing in a heap instead. "Thank you for coming here. I don't need rescuing, but I appreciate the backup," Sameera added quietly.

Nadiya shrugged. "Oxford was getting boring anyway." Another pause as they watched their brother and Tom shake powdery snow from their clothes, then trudge up the hill. "You've already made up your mind about what you're going to do," she said.

Sameera nodded. "There's no other option, not really," she said. Beside her, Nadiya was silent.

Later, Sameera completed the proper introductions when the sisters joined Tom at the bottom of the hill. She didn't miss Nadiya's assessing gaze, or Tom's nervous air.

"I thought Sameera had joined a cult when she told me she was flying to Alaska," Nadiya said. "Still not convinced she hasn't. I'll be keeping an eye on you, Tom Cooke. If that is your real name."

Tom visibly swallowed. "Yes, ma'am. Sorry, ma'am."

By the time they'd all enjoyed another few turns down the hill, Nadiya had almost stopped scowling at Tom. For her part, Sameera couldn't remember the last time she'd had this much fun. Her grin was wide as cold wind whipped her face, filling her entire body with a heady sense of exhilaration. Her legs were starting to ache from scampering up and down the hill, and when her sled tipped over again, throwing her onto the soft, fluffy snow at the bottom, she looked up at the night sky and tried to catch her breath.

Andy Shaikh's handsome, smirking face appeared above her. "Having fun without me?" he asked, holding out a hand to pull her up.

She ignored it and clambered to her feet, eyeing him warily. "Believe it or not, we were doing just fine before you turned up, Andy."

"Impossible." He always seemed to show up where he was least wanted. As Sameera took in his meticulously groomed face and hair and clocked his knowing smile, she was yanked out of her pleasant interlude and reminded of her dilemma: stuck between personal betrayal on one side and personal ruin on the other. Which Andy well knew.

She was still dusting the snow from her half-frozen pants when Tom, Esa, and Nadiya joined them, her sister frowning at this latest intruder.

Esa held out his hands. "Don't look at me, I didn't invite him. I don't even have Andy's number. Tom wouldn't give it to me."

"One of my many talents is always knowing where the after-party is," Andy said. His gaze lingered on Nadiya, and he unrolled a slow smile just for her. "You must be the remarkable older sister, about whom I have heard so much. Hello, gorgeous. I have a plane on the other side of those trees, if you want to get out of here."

Nadiya curled her lip in disdain. "Was that your puddle jumper? I didn't know they made them that small."

Esa laughed out loud, and even Tom smiled. Andy blinked before joining in the laughter. "What if I told you I have a bigger plane in Atlanta?"

"I've heard that one before," Nadiya said, a trace of humor in her eyes. "Your reputation precedes you, Mr. Shaikh."

Andy clearly wasn't used to be being trolled to his face, and wasn't sure what to do about it. "You seem too smart to mind a bit of scandal. Can I interest you in a moonlit stroll?" he asked.

"Easy, tiger," Tom said as Sameera laughed quietly. If Andy thought he could charm her sister with a few pretty words, he was in for a swift lesson.

"If I was in the habit of taking late-night strolls, it would hardly be with you," Nadiya said.

"What did you mean earlier, when you said Toboggan Hill belonged to me—for now?" Tom said, turning to Esa. "Has Calvin declared ownership already?" He was smiling, but there was tension behind his words. The Malik siblings exchanged glances.

"I say a lot of things," Esa said lightly. "It's probably best you don't pay any attention."

"An excellent suggestion," Andy agreed. "Esa, Nadiya, how about we take a few more turns with the sled? I'm sure Tom and Sameera have a lot to talk about." He sent Sameera a meaningful glance, which Tom intercepted.

"What's going on?" he asked, and the question had an edge to it. Sameera tried not to panic. This wasn't how she wanted to have this conversation. Luckily, her sister stepped in.

"The truth is, I'm exhausted," Nadiya said. "I'm ready to call it a night, and pick this up in the morning. Or maybe Andy will go ahead and pick it up by himself, like a big boy." The look she shot the man in question was clear, the gauntlet thrown down. "Alternatively, you could get into your toy plane and fly away."

"I never back down from a challenge, gorgeous," Andy said.

"No, you just get other people to accept the challenge on your behalf," Nadiya said with a sneer.

Sameera noticed Tom's confused expression and grasped her sister's elbow. "Let's get you settled at the guesthouse."

"Fancy," Nadiya said, glancing at Tom. "I'm starting to see the appeal."

Tom didn't say anything, evidently still trying to make sense of the conversational currents around him.

"I'll find you in the morning. We'll talk then," she said to him, and his face instantly relaxed into a smile as he looked at her.

"Okay," he said softly.

Arm intertwined with her sister's, they started back to the guesthouse, flanked by Esa, who pulled the sleds behind them.

"Brother, I think I'm in love." Andy's stage whisper drifted to them across the snowy landscape.

Beside her, Nadiya rolled her eyes. Sameera held the door open for her siblings to enter the guesthouse, and she couldn't resist one last glance back toward the hill. She could make out the shadowy form of two men watching them in the dark before she closed the door firmly.

Chapter Twenty-Three

Yawning, Esa went straight to his room, while Nadiya followed Sameera. Her sister had only a small backpack, and she extracted pajamas before disappearing into the bathroom, leaving Sameera to think over the events of the night.

Nadiya's words from earlier that night had spoken directly to her still-fragile heart, reminding her of all she had yet left unresolved: Her long-delayed conversation with her parents, her burgeoning feelings for Tom, even the situation with Andy were all coming into focus, thanks to her sister's sudden appearance, along with Esa's support. Knowing that Nadiya and Esa were here, that they believed her and loved her, made everything possible.

With a detached air, Sameera realized she hadn't thought about work all day. She was still so far behind on her billable hours—and if she were being honest, she had known that catching up over the holidays was unlikely. The damage was already done, as her upcoming meeting with HR in the new year proved. Her only real chance was bringing in Andy as a client, and that chance had gone up in smoke when he had laid out his conditions on the ice. She couldn't pay the price he demanded and live with herself.

She had known, on some level, that she wouldn't be able to go through with deceiving Tom, like Andy wanted. It had taken her sister's arrival and talking with Esa to cement the truth: It was one thing to enter into a fake-dating showmance, quite another to use Tom's growing feelings for her against him.

Because he did have feelings. What they meant or where they would lead was almost irrelevant. She wouldn't use them against him, just as she knew that he wouldn't do the same if their roles were reversed. There was an innate honesty and goodness about Tom that she recognized, one she couldn't bear to betray. He wasn't like Hunter at all.

Of course, sticking to her principles would come with very real consequences: Once Andy realized she wouldn't do his bidding, he would never hire her or her firm. Which meant that she would be out of a job very soon.

Sameera's stomach hollowed at the thought. The drowning helplessness she had felt after she failed the bar exam came back to her now, as did the gut punch of Hunter's betrayal. This felt both worse and better—yes, she was doomed, but at least it was for a good reason. Tom was worth the sacrifice.

She would be okay. She would continue to freelance. Unlike after graduation, when she was scrambling for a job, she knew more people in the industry now. Maybe Bee would have a lead. If necessary, she could sell her belongings and jewelry and, if it came down to it, her condo.

Maybe with some guidance from Tom, she could start making content for social media, too, she thought with a faint smile. She was pretty sure there was a market for an account devoted to lawyer jokes.

It would be hard, but she would figure it out, the way she always had. And if things grew dire, there was always her last resort: asking her parents for a loan.

Any of these options was preferable to manipulating Tom for Andy's benefit. It was clear that Tom knew something was up anyway. Remembering his question to Esa about Cooke Place, and his earlier comments about Andy visiting Alaska, she suspected that on some level he had known all along that his friend was up to something; he just hadn't wanted to admit it to himself.

She knew something about the lies you told yourself, to avoid a painful truth.

Nadiya emerged from the bathroom freshly showered, and Sameera quickly prepared for bed, joining her sister under the blanket. She hadn't shared a bed with Nadiya since they were kids, and she remembered now that her sister was a relentless cover hog. What a relief to have her back.

"I mean, if you *had* to fake date a stranger, I guess this isn't the worst scenario," Nadiya said.

"It helps that he's Alaskan royalty, and lives in a castle," Sameera agreed. They smiled at each other, but Nadiya's smile faded first, and she braced herself for another lecture.

"I'm sort of relieved, actually," Nadiya began, smoothing the duvet. "I was worried you had actual feelings for the guy. But if it's all just an elaborate scheme, I guess I have nothing to worry about."

Sameera turned onto her back. "About that . . ." she started, and her sister hit her with a pillow.

"I knew it—you like him!" Nadiya accused. "You lying liar. It's not fake dating after all!"

Sameera held up her hands in protest. "It was at first, I swear. I mean, I thought he was cute from the very start, but I had no intention of doing anything about it. Really, this is all Mom's fault."

Nadiya settled back into bed, placing the pillow behind her head. "He's a vast improvement over Hunter, I'll give you that. Wanker."

Sameera grinned. She loved when Nadiya used British slang. "The wanker is ancient history. Tom is nothing like him at all." She pulled up the duvet before turning off the bedside lamp, which was shaped like a polar bear, because of course it was.

"What is Tom like?" Nadiya asked in the dark.

"He's sweet. Kind. Gentle. When he kisses me, I feel . . . sparks."

"Yuck," Nadiya muttered. After a pause, she continued, "I was starting to worry about you, Sam. You have so much love to give. I was afraid after what Hunter did, you shut that part of yourself down forever. Even though Tom isn't Muslim . . ." She trailed off.

"Yes?" Sameera said. She knew Nadiya would never become involved with someone outside their faith, and that she didn't entirely understand how Sameera could, either.

"I can see he's been good for you," Nadiya said, and something in Sameera's heart eased at her words. "I'm glad you trust yourself again. I worried you never would."

It was true. Even if things with Tom went nowhere following their sojourn in Alaska, Sameera knew that meeting him, and allowing herself to fall just a little bit in "like"—she wasn't ready to say "love"—with him, made her feel as if she was finally coming back to her true self.

"He's been good to me," Sameera said simply. "I told him about Hunter, about the time I wasn't talking to Mom and Dad, and he listened. He gets it, because he has similar issues with his own father. His mom died when he was ten, and he's had a hard time since."

Nadiya's voice was softer when she answered. "I'm sorry to hear about his mom. And I'm glad you two hit it off. I just worry you're jumping into something without thinking it through. Mom and Dad are so worried about you. They don't want to lose you again."

Sameera turned to face her sister. "Isn't that the problem? They called *you* to share that they were worried about *me*. I'm tired of being judged and convicted without even being able to mount my own defense."

Nadiya's sigh was full of exasperation for every member of their family, but her words surprised Sameera. "You're right. You deserve better, Sameera. I can't defend their behavior, only tell you that their actions are motivated by love, however misguided and reactive."

Sameera stared at the ceiling in silence. She hadn't slept very well in this bed, but with her sister by her side, she could feel her body relaxing. "What was it like, when I wasn't around?" she asked.

Nadiya shifted to face her. "At first, they both thought you would get in touch, and were content to wait. But as the weeks turned to months with no contact, I could see they were starting to unravel. Dad was so sad, and Mom was worried, too. They never thought you would stay away as long as you did. And after enough time had passed, they didn't know how to overcome the issues. It wasn't a good time."

Sameera's heart squeezed. "I'm sorry."

"What was it like for you?" Nadiya asked.

"At first, it was a relief. But that feeling was short-lived. It got lonely, fast. After a while, I started to hear Mom's voice in my head. Just commenting on things. I started to hear Dad's jokes, you know?"

Nadiya nodded, and Sameera felt the movement beside her. She rolled onto her side, to face her sister, lost in remembrance. "I kept wondering what Dad was doing, whether he had finally decided to retire. Then I worried how he would keep busy. I wanted to call Mom and ask if she was still exercising, and to hear stories from her school. I would come across a funny meme and want to send it to Esa. Mostly, I just worried, and I still felt guilty, and then everything with Hunter happened."

"Wanker," Nadiya said again.

"I thought I'd stop feeling guilty and trapped once I cut everyone off. But it didn't work that way." Sameera shifted slightly. "Do you think I'm a bad person because I'm not a practicing Muslim? You used to call me a kafir."

Nadiya huffed out a laugh. "God, I was such a shit. I'm sorry." The simple words were a balm on Sameera's heart. "The more I see of the world, the more I know that the way you live, the faith or belief or whatever you want to call it, that *spark* you hold close to your heart, is completely personal and unique. Even when you're following a religion or philosophy, everyone still makes it their own. And no one—*no one*—should tell someone else how to live. You're my sister, and you're complicated and human and worthy just as you are. I'm sorry if I ever made you feel otherwise."

"You've turned radical in your old age," Sameera teased, and Nadiya pinched her forearm. "Ouch! Uncalled for." Then, after a beat, she said quietly, "You saved me, Nadiya. You kept calling and texting. Weeks would go by, and I thought you'd given up, and then you'd send me a meme about cats, or a picture from wherever you were in the world, and I just . . . I never thanked you for that, for reaching out, even when I stopped returning your calls."

Nadiya pretended to fake snore, and Sameera poked her stomach until she giggled in the dark.

"Is that why you're here?" Nadiya asked, curiosity clear in her voice. "Is this whole trip a convoluted way to work out all your issues with Mom and Dad? Because there are easier ways. Like therapy. Or kidnapping." They both started laughing, and it felt good. "For what it's worth, I think it's time. Tell them how you really feel. Let it all out. Who knows when this opportunity will come back? Unless you plan to lure us all to Antarctica next Christmas."

"It is one of the most isolated places on the planet," Sameera mused. "Nothing to do but talk." Nadiya groaned, and Sameera smiled in the dark.

"They asked about you all the time. They knew I was in touch with you," Nadiya said. "I know they missed you, and while I don't condone this trip to Alaska, in some very twisted way, it is quite the compliment that Mom and Dad would go to so much trouble."

Sameera wondered what her life would have looked like if they had simply had the hard conversation from the start, if they had fought and screamed and railed and then made up. If she had been brave enough to trust that they would still love her, even when she disappointed them. Guilt rose up, but she pushed it down. She could do nothing about the Sameera she had been in the past; all she could do was try not to let her choices be ruled by fear and resentment again.

"What do you think about Andy?" she asked, deliberately changing the subject.

"I don't have to think about him; Andy thinks enough about himself for all of us," Nadiya said tartly. Her sister wasn't going to say more on the subject, and they were both tired. Nadiya soon drifted off to sleep, but Sameera stayed up a little longer, turning the events of the day over in her mind. Exhaustion soon made it all a muddle in her head until she fell into a restless, dreamless sleep.

Sameera jerked awake at 7:00 a.m., disoriented, until she remembered she was in Alaska, and the sun wouldn't rise for hours. Her body was awake, conditioned by too many years spent working sixteen-hour days, the early-morning hours sometimes the only time she had to herself. Her sister was still fast asleep, exhausted from her transatlantic trip. Trying not to make any noise, she fixed herself a cup of coffee in the kitchen and took it outside, along with a blanket against the chill. She would never get used to the lack of morning sun in Alaska, and she was grateful for the coffee, which warmed her hands as she stared into the dark stillness.

She heard movement, the crunching of boots on snow, and then Andy eased into the patio chair beside her, cradling a mug of something warm in a travel thermos. "My favorite type of lawyer is the kind with insomnia," he said conversationally. "They come by their workaholism honestly. Like me."

She tried to ignore him, but Andy was hard to tune out. It wasn't just that he was charming, or that he fairly vibrated with energy; it was more that he had a charisma that was hard to dismiss. Like a crocodile.

"I think your sister put a spell on me," Andy said now. "I can't stop thinking about her. Is she single? It doesn't really matter, but dealing with husbands is such a bore."

Sameera shook her head, incredulous. "Are you serious?"

"Like a third bankruptcy," he said, taking another sip of his coffee and eyeing her over the top of the rim. "Okay, fine, I'll play. Pitch me."

"What?" This conversation was giving her a headache.

"You want to be my counsel, my right-hand woman, the person to whom I confess my deepest, darkest legal sins. Why should I trust you with my business?"

Andy really was unbelievable. "You made it clear that lying to Tom was a condition of any job offer," she said stiffly. Though she had made up her mind last night, she couldn't help a pang at Andy's words.

He shrugged. "I like to be entertained while I drink my caffeine."

Sameera stood, irritated now. "I'm not an app, something to distract you for a minute. And I'm not going to lie to Tom just so you can buy a town."

He shifted to look up at her, unimpressed, and she had a feeling that he was used to people yelling at him. "I bet you made a PowerPoint," he said, meditative. "I hate PowerPoints."

"My slide deck is amazing, but you'll never get to see it now," she snapped. After a moment, she resumed her seat. Andy was aggravating, but she had come out here first. He could leave.

"Tell me why you think I should hire you," Andy pressed. He must be one of those men who only tuned in when faced with opposition.

"I changed my mind. I don't want to work with you," Sameera said tartly. "I'm thinking of pivoting to content creation instead. A channel that's all lawyer jokes, all the time." She was kidding, of course, but she also wanted to mess with Andy.

"I'd subscribe," he said, coaxing a grudging smile. "Come on, Sameera. Since it won't count for anything anyway, don't you want to know what I think of your pitch?"

She did, actually, if only because she had spent so much time preparing it. She tilted her head at an angle, examining him closely. She also knew his type; the only way to really get his attention was to go for the jugular. It might be amusing to watch Andy in the hot seat for a change, especially since they both knew the outcome was inevitable. After everything this spoiled man-child had put her through, she deserved to have some fun.

"You said your assets are closer to six hundred million," she started. "Except I read a profile on you a few years ago that definitely pegged your fortune at the billion mark. That's a substantial loss. Some would even say embarrassing."

Andy's smile dimmed at her words, and he took a sip of coffee. "I liked it better when you were trying to impress me," he said before nodding at her to continue.

"I'm sure you'll blame the pandemic for your fall in fortune, but come on—you're Andy Shaikh, wunderkind. Here's what I think really happened: You've reached a plateau in your expansion, and you've been unable to meet new market demands. When your bubble tea business first burst on the scene, you were called a bold visionary." He smirked, but she continued, relentless. "But lately your business decisions have felt conservative and tired, two things Andy Shaikh is not."

He seemed intrigued by this. "Why do you think my fortunes have fallen? Relatively speaking, of course. I can still buy and sell this town."

She raised an eyebrow in challenge. "Your constant boasts make me wonder if you're compensating for something." She continued while he squawked in outrage, "You're overinvested in retail and underinvested in hard assets, plus the market has become saturated. If you had played your cards right, if you had been a better friend instead of a bully, I could have helped you chase after what you really want."

Andy's gaze held a gleam of interest now. "I want Cooke Place."

She shook her head. This next part was a gamble, but talking with Nadiya last night had reminded her that she could be bold. "I mean, what you *really* want."

"And what is that?" he asked.

Sameera thought about how Tom had described his friend: relentless, ruthless, ambitious, and never satisfied. "A new industry to conquer from the ground up. I think you're feeling restless, unchallenged, and you work best when you're building something."

To her surprise, Andy grinned at her. "You're right. I'm bored. That's why I'm here, trying to buy Cooke Place and build a ski resort on a scale not seen before in this region. Lake Tahoe and Whistler will have nothing on my plans. It's not too late, Sameera. You could work on this project for the rest of your life. Think of how much money you'll make. Think of the job security. Doesn't that sound fun?"

It would have, two weeks ago. Right now, the thought of selling out Tom to work for Andy just made her want to take a shower. And yet there was something cheerfully villainous and inherently likable about Andy. Give him a week, and he'd have them all thanking him for the pleasure of his hostile takeover. Everyone except Nadiya, of course. Her sister would never.

The thought of her sister made her pause. Even Andy deserved a fair warning. "To answer your earlier query—my sister is single, but she would rather eat raw goat brains than go out with you."

Andy shrugged. "I've had goat brains. They're a delicacy in some parts of the world. I'll grow on her."

"Like a fungus," Sameera agreed, and he grinned again.

"You're a lot funnier than my current representation. Better looking, too. Too bad you've discovered principles. Not convenient in a lawyer, Sameera."

"You're trying too hard, Andy," Sameera said. "I'm starting to question your whole persona. I don't buy the whole evil-rich-guy schtick."

Andy shrugged. "Every successful CEO industrialist needs a good mythology. You know my story—second-generation immigrant, working-class parents, put myself through school. I took chances and struck gold, but still attend jumah every Friday with my dad."

"Any of it true?" she asked, remembering what he had said about his father when they were skating.

"Some of it. That bit about jumah was my publicist's idea. I haven't talked to my dad in two decades, and the mosque isn't really my scene."

"Why are you telling me this?" Sameera asked.

"I think we have a lot in common. We're both workaholic insomniacs on the outs with family, and we don't know how to be happy. We both like Tom, even when it feels complicated."

Sameera blinked at Andy's frank assessment. "You're the last person to lecture me on my feelings for Tom. You don't set the standard on friendship," she said.

"Stand down, Malik," he said pleasantly. "You've made your position clear. So, let me make mine crystal: This whole place will belong to me soon enough, one way or another." He winked at her and stood up. "I'll leave you to enjoy your coffee in peace. Oh, and from one lapsed Muslim to another: Merry Christmas."

Chapter Twenty-Four

When she climbed back into bed, Nadiya stirred. "Your feet are cold," her sister grumbled. "Where did you go?"

"I made some coffee, argued with Andy, had an existential crisis. It's been a busy morning."

"I called dibs on fighting with Andy," Nadiya said, her voice sleepy. "Are you okay?"

Sameera considered. She was, surprisingly. "Yes," she said.

"Good. Merry Christmas." Nadiya smiled. "I've never said that before and meant it."

Her parents were already up when the girls emerged from their room, and their happiness at seeing their older daughter was immediate. Thankfully, Nadiya didn't mention any of last night's excitement, saying simply that she had missed her family. As they chatted in the sitting room, Sameera felt a sense of relief steal over her. Her entire family was together again, everyone she loved in one room. Her heart felt full.

"Nadiya, you will like our hosts," Tahsin said. "Tom and his family have been so kind. They have another guest, and you'll never guess who. Andy Shaikh! The one who owns all those bubble tea spots. He's single, too. I've asked for his mother's contact. What do you think?"

The sisters exchanged a look. Their mother was so predictable—but today Tahsin's comment felt amusing, and not annoying like it usually would to Sameera.

"I think you shouldn't WhatsApp a random aunty asking about her son, or she might wonder about your intentions," Nadiya joked.

While Tahsin laughed, Sameera quietly slipped back to her room. If she hurried, she could catch Tom before the rest of her family assembled. Andy's ambush this morning had spurred her to action: It was time to tell Tom what was really going on.

Inside the main house, Tom was at the counter, chopping tomatoes, onions, and red peppers for shakshuka, a breakfast dish with coddled eggs, popular in the Middle East. He smiled sheepishly at Sameera after they'd exchanged Christmas greetings.

"I missed cooking," he admitted. "Also, I took your advice and talked to my dad. Sort of."

Sameera's brow rose. "Did you half talk to him?"

"I told him why I don't cook when I'm here, and then I told him we should talk more, later."

"A 'save the date' type of talk," Sameera said, and Tom nodded, smiling.

"It felt good to tell him. I thought he would get defensive, but he told me Barb has been on him to do better, to be better. He told me he missed me," Tom said shyly. Sameera felt her heart softening. She hated what she was about to reveal about someone else he loved.

"Your sister is terrifying, by the way," Tom added. "Andy is really into it. He left the house early this morning, hoping to run into her." He turned back to his chopping.

"He found me instead," she started.

Tom turned back to her. "I hope he behaved himself," he said, only half kidding.

"I don't think Andy is capable of behaving himself," Sameera said. After a pause, she asked, "Why are you two friends?"

Tom shook his head. "Sometimes I wonder the same thing." Noticing her serious expression, he sobered. "I know he comes across as this ruthless, callous business bro. He can be thoughtless, selfish, single-minded, an egotist—"

"You're really not selling this," Sameera said grimly.

"He's also loyal, caring, and he's been a true friend. I'll never forget the way he had my back in undergrad. He's the reason I launched my business, and he helped me stay afloat during those early years. I owe Andy a lot, and even though we've both changed since college, he's still my brother."

Sameera winced. Would Tom feel the same about his "brother" after she'd told him what Andy had tried to do? Or would he resent her for revealing the truth—or even believe her? How he reacted was out of her hands, she decided. The important thing was that she said something.

"He was also the one who told me I should come back to visit during the holidays this year, after I told him about meeting you and your family," Tom added quietly. "If it wasn't for Andy, none of this would have happened." He smiled shyly at her.

Damn Andy, she thought.

"I was thinking we could film another video," he continued. "The apple pie one has been doing excellent numbers. My agent thinks we might even get an offer for the show in January, if this keeps up."

"That sounds like fun," she said, her voice faint. She took a deep breath and willed herself to stay strong.

Tom stared down at the cutting board, his hand still, as if working himself up to speak. "I know you're heading back to Atlanta tomorrow, and I know we agreed to keep fake dating just over the holidays, but I was thinking . . ." His ears turned red, and he said in a rush, "Can I take you out for New Year's, for real?"

They stared at each other, and Sameera tried to tamp down her feeling of panic. Last night, she had told Nadiya that she had real feelings for Tom. This morning, she wasn't sure if she was ready to leap into a relationship with him, at least not until she had sorted out the rest of her life.

"To a restaurant, or to your kitchen?" she asked, trying for a joke.

"Wherever you like," he said, and his voice was soft. "I'll take whatever you can give me, Sameera. I don't want this to end. Do you?"

Sameera closed her eyes. Before they went any further, before any more promises were made, she needed to tell him about Andy.

"Before we finalize plans, I have to share something first," she said.

Tom wrinkled his brow. "We don't have to go out for dinner. I like breakfast and lunch, too."

"It's not that." She led him to the kitchen table and sat down. Better to get this done all at once, she figured. "Yesterday while we were skating, Andy said he was willing to work with my firm."

A delighted smile suffused Tom's face, and he reached over to give her a hug, but she held her hand out.

"He had one condition," she said.

"Don't tell me he wants you to pretend to be his girlfriend, too," Tom joked. But his smile faded at her serious expression.

"The condition involved you." Better to rip off the Band-Aid. "He said he would sign with my firm if I could convince you to sell Cooke Place to him."

Tom laughed. "It's not mine to sell."

"Rob won't sell until you give up your claim. It's down to you."

Tom stood up, shaking his head. "Funny joke."

"I'm not laughing," Sameera said, and watched as Tom worked through the implications; it was like watching someone's heart break in real time. "I didn't know how to tell you. Tom, I'm so sorry."

"No," Tom said, shaking his head again. "I've known Andy for almost fifteen years. He's my brother. He wouldn't do this. Not when he knows how I feel about . . . you."

Sameera's breath hitched. They would be able to get past this, surely? "I think that's why he wanted me to do the asking."

"I don't believe it." He speared her with a look. "If he asked you this yesterday, why didn't you tell me right away?"

Sameera shrugged helplessly. "We were having a nice time baking pies, and then we were at Abu Isra's, and you were the one who joined us when we went sledding last night. Also, I guess I was hoping he would reconsider."

"That's what Esa was alluding to last night. I suppose your siblings know all about this." His tone was bitter, the expression on his face hard. "Or were you the one who needed time to reconsider? After all, if you were willing to pretend to be my girlfriend in return for an introduction to Andy, if you flew all the way to Alaska just to pitch him, why not do this, too?"

The words stung, because they were tinged with the truth. "I did consider it," she said quietly. "I hate that his offer made me pause. I'd be lying if I said it wasn't tempting. But in the end, it wouldn't feel right. Tom, I like you. A lot. I know you feel the same. I could never betray you."

He wiped his face with his hands. "But you thought about it." She bowed her head, and Tom paced, agitated. "I have to go."

"Where?" she asked, alarmed.

"I don't know. Somewhere I can think. Away from here." He couldn't even look at her.

"I'm sorry, Tom," she started again.

"Stop apologizing," he said shortly. "You've done enough."

He yanked open the patio door and stalked into the snow without his jacket, leaving her to stare after him, stricken.

She ended up back at the guesthouse, because where else could she go? Her conversation with Tom had lasted maybe fifteen minutes, because the rest of her family members were still in their rooms, getting ready for Christmas brunch. Nadiya took one look at her face and led her to the sofa to sit down before filling a glass with water and passing it to her.

"Tom didn't take the news well?" she asked.

Sameera shook her head. "He was devastated. He asked me why I took so long to tell him, and when I admitted I considered Andy's offer for a minute, he left."

Nadiya cursed softly. "Stupid Tom."

"He wasn't wearing a jacket," she said, not sure why this one fact bothered her. "It's freezing outside. He needs his coat."

She felt numb, but when she looked up, she saw that Esa had joined them. Nadiya gave him a look, and he pulled on his own jacket, then grabbed Naveed's parka before heading outside, toward the woods.

Sameera looked down at her hands. She was cold, too. Why was she so cold? She was wearing her warmest sweater. Tom had on only a T-shirt. He had been so angry, and hurt. He blamed her, and with good reason. This was all her fault.

Her sister crouched down until they were at eye level. "Are you done beating yourself up?" Nadiya asked, and her steely tone brought Sameera back to the present, to this house, and to her sister's serious, knowing gaze.

"Wh-what?" Sameera said.

"Would you like to continue wallowing in self-pity and recrimination for another ten minutes?" Nadiya asked.

"I did a bad thing . . ." Sameera started.

"Sameera, I love you, but you need to get over yourself."

This startled a laugh out of Sameera, though what she really felt was shock. What was her sister saying?

"Tom's reaction is not about you," Nadiya said. "He's mad at his friend, the one who actually betrayed him. I'll bet he's mad at his dad, too, because if you think Rob isn't using this whole situation to get what he wants, I have some property on the moon I'd love to tell you about. Maybe he's a bit pissed at you, too, but you're at the very bottom of that list, believe me."

"This isn't . . . You don't understand," Sameera said, holding back her tears. "Tom is mad at me for not being loyal. He *said so.*"

"Maybe he was mad for a second. Because he needed to be mad at someone, and you were right there, telling him what he didn't want to hear about a man he considers his blood. Now he's outside in the cold, feeling angry and sad, but at least he's dealing with his *shit*." Nadiya's voice was unflinching and stark, threaded with compassion. "And, babe, it's time you did the same. It's time for you to have the conversation you've been avoiding for years now."

Nadiya stood up, and Sameera could see Tahsin and Naveed hovering behind, twin expressions of worry and confusion on their faces. Her sister helped Sameera up. "Don't think about Tom. Don't think about Andy. Don't even worry about Christmas brunch," her sister whispered in her ear before giving her a little shove toward their parents.

Sameera took a deep, shuddering breath.

"*Beta*, are you all right?" Naveed asked.

"What has happened to Tom?" Tahsin added. "Is Andy okay?"

Nadiya was right. Nothing else mattered, and this conversation was long past due. She took another breath and, for the first time in a long time, said "Bismillah," or "In the name of God." The expression Muslims spoke before they began anything, from eating to drinking to saying the hard thing to their family.

"Mom, Dad, can we talk?"

Chapter Twenty-Five

Her parents sat on the couch, clearly bracing for something terrible. Sameera had a moment of hysteria as she stood before them, considering her options. *Surprise! I'm not Sameera at all but an AI-powered fembot.* Or *Tom and I are secretly married!* Or even *I've been lying to you for years because I'm afraid you won't love me if you know what I'm really like.*

That last one was the most terrifying.

Yesterday, she had accused Tom of being a serial fake dater after he'd told her about his arrangement with Emily. As she looked at her parents now, their eyes filled with worry and fear, she realized with a jolt that Tom hadn't been her first fake relationship, either.

On some level, she had been pretending for years, lying by omission to the most important people in her life. When that hadn't worked, she'd tried running from them, except her heart hadn't let her run far.

It was time to do the work. She realized Esa should probably hear this, too, but figured she needed to get this out in front of her parents and her sister while the time was right. She took another deep breath and repeated, "Bismillah." From her parents' look of shock, she realized she must have said it louder than she'd thought.

"What is happening, *beta*?" Naveed asked. "Are you hurt? Sick?" He lowered his voice. "Do you need money? I know things have been difficult since that budmash Hunter left. Just say the word."

Her father's kindness made this even harder. "Tom is upset with me. I'll tell you all about it. Brunch will be delayed, which is good, because right now, I want to talk about us," she said, gesturing between them. "I want—I need—to tell you why I cut you out of my life."

People pleaser, Nadiya's voice taunted from yesterday. Sameera was so scared to cause offense, she ran from any hint of a fight. But she wouldn't run now.

"I know I hurt you when I didn't return your calls and stopped visiting for those three years after I moved home to Atlanta," she said. It was hard to look at them. "I hurt myself, too. I missed you all so much. But at that point in my life, for a variety of reasons, it felt easier not to spend time with you."

"*Beta*, that is all in the past," Tahsin broke in. "We don't have to talk about any of this. It will only make us upset all over again."

"We do need to talk about it," Sameera said. "Because it feels like we never discussed any of it—not really. I just popped back into your life, and we decided to pretend I had never been away." Nadiya cleared her throat, and Sameera added, "I mean, when Nadiya forced us to meet, we just had a brief conversation and then never spoke about it again."

"We thought that was what you wanted. We thought it would be easier on you, especially because of all that you were dealing with from that kaminay," Naveed said, referring to Hunter with an Urdu insult. His eyes were already shiny with unshed tears, and for a moment, Sameera thought about backtracking, about accepting this explanation, giving her parents a hug, and then salvaging what she could from this day. Except when she looked over at Nadiya, her sister nodded at her to continue. Her presence gave her courage to say this next bit.

"I think it probably felt easier for you, too, not to talk about this," Sameera said. "But I'm worried we'll end up right where we started if we don't. I'm scared to say this, and I need you both to know that I love you very much."

Now her father was crying, albeit quietly. "We love you too, *beta*."

"Meri jaan, you are my star," Tahsin added quietly.

"For a long time, I felt like your love was conditional," Sameera said. "That if I didn't behave in a way that made you proud, that uplifted our family and community, then I was a failure." Tahsin started to interrupt but was silenced by a look from Naveed. "I was praised for good grades, for memorizing the Quran, and I was punished whenever I asked questions or didn't meet the expectations you had set. I hated when you compared me to Nadiya."

Reaching forward, her sister squeezed her hand, her expression communicating the promise she had made yesterday: *My love for you does not depend on what you do or who you are. I'm here for you. Always.*

"When I started struggling with my identity and my faith, I didn't know what to do with those feelings. I hid them, buried them deep. Except they kept bubbling to the surface. I wanted so badly to be like the other kids around me. I didn't want to live a complicated life full of rules that didn't make any sense to me. I just wanted to *be*. But that meant disappointing you both. For a long time, I lived a double life—behaving one way in front of you, and another way when I was out in the world—because I was afraid of breaking your heart. That's the reason I snuck out during senior year. Why I hid my boyfriends from you in high school and college, and why I never told you about Hunter."

"Wanker," Nadiya said automatically, and Sameera smiled slightly.

"I wish I were different. I tried to *be* different. But this is who I am. Imperfect, and a little bit broken. Muslim in background and culture, but not very Muslim in practice. I love where I came from, but it doesn't define who I am now. I'm still your daughter, and I want to share my life with you, if you will let me. Even if it's not the life you envisioned for me. I'm tired of pretending and hiding, but I can't stand to cut you from my life, either. I hope you can accept me as I am. I want you in my life."

There was silence when she finished, and Sameera felt both a great sense of relief and utter panic. What if her mother said something critical, or cruel? What if her father told her in no uncertain terms that her decisions had been wrong, that she was a disappointment? Her parents had both reacted badly in the past when they'd learned something about her they didn't like. She looked at her sister. Nadiya stared steadily back, her gaze warm and filled with love. Sameera took a deep breath. If the worst happened, she knew she would be okay.

"We always expected great things from our children," Tahsin said slowly. "We expected the same from ourselves, too. It was hard to pick up our lives and move to a new country. We had no choice but to succeed. But we have our own anxieties, our own . . . What do the kids call it, Naveed?"

"Trauma," her father said.

"Yes, that," Tahsin said. "Every parent carries the scars of their own trauma. We try not to inflict them on you, but . . ." She sighed. "A part of me will always wish you had followed in our footsteps when it comes to religious practice, but that will never change the way we feel about you, Sameera."

"We found our own path, and we made our own choices when we moved to the United States," Naveed said. "Though we may not understand every choice you have made, *beta*, we love you, and we will always want to share in your life."

"You are a part of my life. You always will be," Sameera said, and it was a promise. She was crying openly now.

The patio door opened, and Esa slipped back inside. He froze when they all looked at him, a tableau of weeping family. "You're crying *again*?" he said to Sameera. "Who do I have to punch this time?"

They laughed, and hugged, and when her mother pulled her in close, smelling of shower gel and her own particular perfume that always meant *home*, she whispered, "Every dua I make is for your happiness," she said, referring to the Arabic word for prayer.

If nothing else came of this trip, Sameera would always be grateful for this moment, this perfectly imperfect feeling of peace.

"One last thing," Sameera said, and they all looked at her. "I need you to listen and believe me this time: Tom and I aren't together. We never were."

She paused, reconsidering her words. Tom had kissed her; they had spent a lot of time together lately. There was something there. She needed to be honest with her parents, and with herself. "There might be something there, actually, but it's all a bit complicated right now," she amended. Behind her, she saw Esa shoot a knowing glance at Nadiya.

Her parents looked confused. "What is so complicated? He clearly likes you!" Tahsin said. "He made you samosas, and every time Tom looks at you, he smiles. That cannot only be friendship, Sameera. I am surprised he has not yet proposed."

Sameera shook her head, even if her mother's words made her heart sing. "I told you before, we agreed to help each other out. I met him for the first time at my firm's holiday party. About fifteen minutes before you met him on FaceTime, Mom."

Tahsin's eyes grew round with a sudden realization. "Are you saying that if I hadn't hired him to cater the Eid party . . ." She trailed off.

"None of this would have happened." Sameera nodded. "I probably would never have met Tom again. And you could have set me up with one of your friend's sons," she couldn't help but add, feeling mischievous. Her mother face-palmed as her siblings laughed.

It was true—if it hadn't been for Tahsin's incessant meddling and jumping to conclusions, her and Tom's paths might never have crossed again. In such a large city, working in two different industries, he would have remained the cute caterer who brought her cranberry ginger ale. Instead, Tom felt more and more like a necessity in her life. Assuming he didn't hate her now, of course.

"I told you that interfering in our children's lives would backfire one day," Naveed said to his wife, and she shoved him playfully.

"Perhaps you and Tom were not together before we came to Alaska," Tahsin persisted, "but things changed once you got here." She pinned her daughter with a shrewd look. And since Sameera had promised to be more open, to stop hiding who she was from the people she loved the most, she couldn't say no. Because her mother was right, of course. While she couldn't speak for Tom's feelings, especially in light of what had happened just that morning, she knew that for herself, she was halfway to falling in love with Tom.

Instead, she only smiled.

"We also have an update on Andy, too. I'm afraid the WhatsApp aunties will not be impressed," Nadiya said, and her family settled in to hear the news together.

Chapter Twenty-Six

When the Malik family entered the main house for Christmas brunch carrying the presents they had purchased for the family, there was a lightness to their steps, despite the heaviness of the morning. It was the feeling of being on the same page, the clarity that came with a round of truth-telling, and also at having a common enemy: Andy Shaikh.

After Sameera had explained Andy's plan, her parents had reacted in a suitably horrified manner. Then Esa picked up the story.

"Tom wasn't far past Toboggan Hill when I caught up to him. He was kicking at the snow and muttering to himself. He was happy I brought him a coat, though," Esa said.

"What did he say about Andy? Or me?" Sameera asked.

Esa looked at her as if she were foolish. "Not everything is about you, Sameera. He looked a bit grim, thanked me for the jacket, and said he'd be back soon, not to worry. Then I turned around and came here."

"You didn't try to comfort him? Get him to talk? Offer any advice?" Sameera pressed. Tom had been so angry and hurt. She hated to think of him in pain.

Esa shrugged. "He wanted to be left alone, so I let him get on with it. Not everything has to be about sharing your feelings and *crying*." He shuddered, and Nadiya and Sameera exchanged amused glances.

"I owe you an explanation and an apology, too," Sameera said, and Esa looked horrified. "Which I promise to deliver *without* tears." He nodded at her to continue.

"I disappeared from your life for three years. It wasn't about you, but you still suffered. I missed you so much—" Her voice cracked, but she soldiered on. "I want you to know that I thought of you every day, and I hate myself for what I did. I hope you can forgive me, Esa."

Her brother shuffled his feet, clearly uncomfortable with all this emoting. "'S'right," he muttered. "Wish you had been there when I graduated middle school, that's all." He glanced up, a sly smile on his face. "It's not too late to get me a gift for all those missed birthdays, though. You can Venmo me whatever your guilt is worth."

"As long as we're good," Sameera said.

They hugged, and Esa even let her hold him close for ten seconds before wriggling away and announcing that he was starving.

The Maliks trooped inside the main house, where they found Tom stationed once more behind the counter, exactly where he had been when Sameera approached that morning with her unwelcome revelations. The set of his jaw was a tight line, but his hands were a blur as he chopped, diced, and stirred a pot on the stove. He glanced up when the Malik family entered, acknowledging their presence. His gaze softened when he looked at Sameera, and Tahsin nudged her.

"See? He likes you," her mother whispered, and for once Sameera wasn't irritated by the comment.

"As long as you acknowledge that you played matchmaker," she whispered back. Tahsin had the grace to look contrite, and Sameera smiled mischievously. Really, she was relieved that Tom didn't seem to be angry at her anymore.

Nadiya promptly disappeared to give herself a self-guided tour of Cooke Place. When Rob, Barb, and Andy entered the kitchen together, the older man seemed pleased to see Tom at the stove. The morning menu was inspired by their meal last night at Abu Isra's, Tom explained: shakshuka, homemade hummus, akkawi cheese with honey, fresh fruit smoothies, eggs with feta cheese and olives, plus kheer pudding for dessert. "It's a fusion Christmas meal," he said. Sameera noticed he didn't look at Andy once.

House tour complete, Nadiya joined the party in the kitchen and reached for a plate. Andy lined up behind her. "You're still here?" she asked him. "Haven't you caused enough drama already?"

Andy grinned at her. "Just say the word, gorgeous, and we could be sipping cocktails anywhere in the world."

Nadiya was not impressed. "I'm sure the women you usually pursue are eager for any crumb of your attention. Do us all a favor, and go back to them. Your face is putting me off my food."

"I can't say the same," Andy said. "I like your face. Go out with me?"

Nadiya rolled her eyes and helped herself to shakshuka and the sourdough bread Tom had sliced to mop up the tomato curry before finding a seat at the dining table.

"She didn't say no," Andy said to Sameera, grinning. She didn't smile back. She was mad at Andy, and worried about Tom, and also for herself. She had come to terms with the fact that she would be unemployed in the new year. But she had hit rock bottom before and would climb out again.

"My sister is a practicing Muslim woman," Sameera said stiffly to Andy now. "She doesn't date, she doesn't drink cocktails, and she didn't answer you because your question is ridiculous."

Andy turned to Tom. "I will pay you a million dollars if you can convince your girlfriend's sister to go out with me."

Tom's glare was flinty. "I know you're used to throwing money around to get what you want, Andy, so this might come as a shock, but not everything is for sale."

Andy seemed taken aback by this comment, and he glanced quickly from Sameera to his friend's grim face before heading to the table. He sat across from Nadiya, who ignored him. Soon, the kitchen was empty save for Tom and Sameera.

She leaned closer. "If you need a distraction, I can start talking loudly about how bubble tea is basically just falooda," she said, referring to the milky, rose-flavored drink made with basil seeds and vermicelli and topped with nuts, popular among the desi diaspora. "I guarantee that will get my mom riled up for a fight."

Tom flashed her a weary smile. "No need. You already caused a war online with your biryani comment a few days ago. I'm only sorry for the way I reacted this morning. I wasn't mad at you."

Why was her sister always right? "It's okay if you were a little mad at me," Sameera said. "So long as you keep most of that anger for Andy. What he tried to do was terrible. But you were also right. I was scared to tell you—not because I considered his offer for very long, but because I knew it meant that I was saying goodbye to the dream of saving my job. Other than dealing with Blake, I liked working at the Undertakers."

Tom's hand was warm on her arm. "I know, Sam. I'm not just angry at Andy, though believe me, I am. The thought that keeps spinning in a loop through my head is *why* Andy thought my dad would sell Cooke Place. Andy has confidence and bravado for days, but he's not delusional. Not unless . . ." He trailed off, the words causing him physical pain.

"Not unless Rob said something to encourage him," Sameera finished, realization dawning. This was what Nadiya had alluded to earlier. "You're worried your dad is trying to manipulate you into moving back home again. But maybe there's another explanation?" she said hopefully.

Tom shook his head and exhaled. "I can't think about this now. Let's enjoy Christmas brunch, at least. It's better to fight on a full stomach."

"Yes, Chef," Sameera said, and impulsively reached up on her toes to place a gentle kiss on Tom's lips. It felt right, to kiss him. Just like it felt right to allow herself to think about his role in her life when they returned to Atlanta.

He seemed surprised by the gesture, even as his arm went automatically to her waist, pulling her close. They smiled at each other, and the look said *I see you*, and *I'm here for you*, and *I'm glad you're here*.

Everyone was tucking into their meal when they joined the party after loading their plates. Tom's spread had done what good food did best—put everyone at ease and lightened the mood. She took a bite of her eggs, loaded with feta, veggies, and black olives. They were savory and delicious.

Soon, a spirited discussion about the differences between various holidays broke out, with Naveed arguing that though Christmas was a globally recognized celebration, Ramadan was more meaningful.

"Is it a holiday if you have to keep vampire hours for thirty days?" Esa asked. "Eid is a holiday, but Ramadan is a marathon. Fight me." He bared his teeth at his parents, who laughed.

"I'm just saying, the payoff is greater. We work for our joy," Naveed said.

"You've clearly never had to brave Target the week before Christmas," Barb said. "I earned my gingerbread and eggnog just for that!"

Everyone laughed, and Andy added his two cents: "I understand what Naveed Uncle means," he said. "When you don't eat or drink during daylight hours for a month, alongside the rest of your community, there's a communal feeling that's hard to beat. And then at the end of it, you feast—that's what 'Eid' translates to. Last-minute riots at the local mall notwithstanding, Eid al-Fitr is the superior holiday, but only because it follows Ramadan." Sameera had to hand it to Andy, his argument was sound.

"Mistletoe, tinsel, holiday lights, carols, holiday baking . . ." Rob counted off on his fingers.

"Mehndi, samosas, dates, Biscoff-flavored everything, haleem, community," Naveed countered. "We have everything Christmas has, plus more."

"Except the holiday movies," Esa piped up. He had loaded two plates and was polishing off the second one. "Where's our version of *Home Alone*?"

Beside him, Calvin nodded in agreement. "Holiday movies are the best part. I watch *Die Hard* every year." The boys high-fived.

When everyone except Esa and Cal had pushed back from the table and shared their compliments with the chef, Andy tapped on his juice glass and stood up.

"I know we're keeping it halal this year, but I wanted to raise a glass to our hosts, Rob and Barb," he said, waiting for everyone to join him before turning to face the older couple. "I've started to consider Cooke Place, and Wolf Run, too, as more than a second home. In fact, if things go according to plan, I hope we can announce a very special collaboration between Shaikh Enterprises and the Cooke family." He beamed around the table.

Rob chuckled. "There's no reason to talk about that right now, Andy." His glance at Tom was significant. "I have one rule on Christmas Day—focus on family. Who's ready to open presents?"

Esa and Calvin immediately put up their hands, but Andy wouldn't let it go. "Christmas is also the perfect time to announce big plans, Rob. I know we haven't hammered down the details yet, but perhaps it's time. I know Tom would love to hear what you're thinking."

"And here I thought you didn't believe in the direct approach," Nadiya said.

Andy was no fool, Sameera thought. He had realized that Tom knew the truth and wasn't pleased, which was why he was making one last desperate attempt to get what he wanted by pushing Rob. As she watched, his features hardened, the charming, affable guest gone in an instant, replaced by the shrewd businessman she remembered from their conversation that morning.

"I'm sure you're all wondering what beautiful Nadiya means," he said.

"Just Nadiya, thanks," her sister said.

"The truth is, I've been carrying around a dream in my pocket, and I need Cooke Place to make it a reality." Andy paused, surveying the room. Sameera followed his gaze—her parents and siblings hostile, Rob panicked, while Tom looked afraid of what this conversation might reveal about his father. Tom had been happy cooking Christmas brunch that morning, content when he had shyly told her about talking with Rob. From her own difficult conversation with her parents, she knew what a difference making amends could have on a bone-deep level. She couldn't stand to see that taken away from Tom. Not like this.

She stood up. "I love presents!" she announced. Everyone stared at her, and Esa gave her a thumbs-up. "I think we should go open them, *right now.*"

Rob was instantly on his feet and leading the way to the sitting room, where the Christmas tree was set up. Sameera caught Tom's eye, but instead of the relief she expected, he seemed deflated and wouldn't meet her gaze. Had she messed up again?

Andy passed by, leaning close to whisper: "You can't delay the inevitable, Malik. I hope Tom is worth it."

Chapter Twenty-Seven

Sameera needed some air before presents; the stress of the morning was getting to her. Once outside, she recorded a voice note to Bee. Her friend was likely enjoying an ordinary Christmas, unlike her, but she felt the need to unburden.

"I have a few updates," she said into her phone speaker. "Unfortunately, my time at the Undertakers will be coming to an end soon. It's a long story, but basically Andy turned out to be a villain. On the plus side, Tom is the best, even if things remain a bit weird between us. Oh, and I had it out with my parents, and we're cool? It's been a weird trip, Bee, and I miss you."

After she pressed send, she walked as fast as she could to the far lawn, pausing when she got to Andy's propellor plane, which remained cheekily parked on the frozen grass, as if it belonged there. As if it owned everything. Which it *did not*. Rearing back, she kicked the tire on the plane's landing gear.

"Ow! Stupid Andy!" she said, bouncing around on one foot. The pain radiated from her toe, through her thick snow boot. She kicked the snow. "Stupid snow." She kicked the plane again and swore out loud.

"I can grab a crowbar from the garage if it will make you feel better," Tom said, approaching her.

She eyed him warily. "Presents are inside."

"Actually, I'm pretty sure I'm looking at my gift." He took a step closer. "You're all I want for Christmas."

The genuine emotion behind his words made her flush with embarrassment, even as she wanted to hear more. She covered by making a joke, pointing at herself: "The Muslim lawyer you're fake dating for likes?"

Tom's tone was serious as he answered. "No one was more surprised than me when you signed on to my plan. I bet you're regretting my offer to introduce you to Andy, though."

"Be honest—you were trying to offload him onto me, weren't you?" she teased.

He took another step, coming within touching distance. Except he rocked back on his heels instead, hands in his pockets. "Actually, I was afraid you finally had had enough, and were out here YouTubing how to fly a plane."

"YouTube is more my brother's domain. I just needed space." They eyed each other warily. Too much had happened, and neither one was sure what the other was thinking.

"You never answered my question from this morning," he said softly. "Can I take you out for New Year's? Breakfast, lunch, dinner, coffee, chai . . . You decide, Sameera, and I'll be there."

She hadn't believed Andy's whispered taunt. But the expression on Tom's face now cleared any lingering doubts from her mind, and the one on hers must have done the same for him, because suddenly, he was reaching for her.

Their first kiss had surprised them both, and the embraces since had always felt rushed. This kiss was airborne from the start. Teeth clashed, hands grasped, bodies intertwined. She bit down on his lip, hard, and when his knee pushed between her legs, she was filled with want.

He pulled away. "Is that a yes?"

She laughed, nodding, and pulled her back to him. After another minute, he disentangled himself. "They're waiting for us."

"Let them wait. I'm kissing my boyfriend." She paused, heat flooding her cheeks. "Sorry, I meant fake boyfriend."

Tom shook his head, delighted. "No, you didn't. But a guy likes to be taken out for dinner first."

She rolled her eyes as he nuzzled her jaw. "You're obsessed with food."

"I'm obsessed with you," he said.

Sameera smiled; his words made her heart sing. "Don't tell my mom. I have her convinced she caused all of this. She set the ball rolling by hiring you to cater the Eid party. If I'm lucky, she will have learned her lesson and never interfere in my life again."

Their eyes met, and he smirked. "I would never contradict my girlfriend. Even though my plan was to courier you a box of samosas and a six-pack of cranberry ginger ale the day after the firm's holiday party."

"Take a girl out for dinner first," she said back to him.

"It's a date," he said. They stared at each other for another long moment, until Sameera shook her head, trying to center herself on what was happening right now, her family and his waiting for them. Though what she really wanted to do was stay outside with Tom. He made her feel safe, known . . . loved?

"We should head back inside. Andy has probably already claimed squatters' rights by now," she said, and he sighed. "What are you going to do?"

He leaned down and planted a lingering kiss on her lips, then the sensitive spot on her jaw. "Now we can go, beautiful," he said softly. "With you by my side, I can figure out anything."

Inside, there was a clear standoff between Andy and Tom's parents, with Nadiya trying to mediate, as usual.

"Tom isn't here. We should wait for him before talking further," Nadiya was saying, voice tight.

"There's nothing to talk about," Andy said, lazily eating a bowl of fruit. "Rob and I have a verbal agreement."

"Well, I wouldn't go that far," Rob started, more flustered than he had been since they all arrived. "We've talked things over, and I do think a ski resort is a good idea, in theory. But I haven't signed anything yet."

Andy smiled at his host. "Rob, you told me this was what you wanted. That all I had to do was get Tom on board, and I could start building. We both agreed it would benefit Wolf Run, too."

At the door, Tom snorted. "It's not like you to be this slow to understand, Andy. Or maybe you've been so busy trying to manipulate me, you didn't realize what was really going on. My dad has been playing you this whole time." He walked around the table and resumed his seat, Sameera beside him. The uncertainty that had shadowed his eyes and bracketed his mouth was gone now, replaced with a steely determination. Andy noticed the change right away, and his smile faltered.

"You haven't lived here in years. This isn't your home anymore. Why not sell it and make tons of money?" Andy looked around the table, hoping to gather support. Everyone stared back, unimpressed.

"Read the room, dude," Esa said. He glanced at Rob. "Both of you."

Rob cleared his throat, looking from Tom to Andy, then back at Barb and Cal. He knew the time for dissembling was over. "I might have led Andy to believe I was on board with the ski resort," he started, clearly uncomfortable. "It was a good idea. We get serious snowfall here, and Lord knows Wolf Run could use the business. Our town gets smaller every year, with good people leaving and never coming home."

"You mean people like me," Tom said. "Is this your latest tactic to lure me back? Pretend to throw your weight behind a deal with my best friend, hoping to goad me into returning because I was, what? Jealous? You can't honestly think this plan would work."

A faint smile crossed Rob's face. "Brought you home for the holidays, didn't it?"

Tom shook his head. "I came back to visit because I missed you. Not to move back. You pull this every time I return, Dad. You belittle my life in Atlanta, call my business a hobby, and refuse to take any interest in my life outside of Wolf Run. If you want to know why I stayed away for so long, I suggest you look in the mirror."

"Oh snap," Esa said. Beside him, Calvin had his mouth open in shock.

"I never meant to push you away," Rob started.

"Then why do I feel like running every time we're in the same room?" Tom asked. Sameera put a hand on his shoulder; she could feel him trembling with suppressed emotion. He turned to her. "Sameera is the only reason I stayed this time. She's why I felt like I belonged. Sameera and her family have made me feel more comfortable, more accepted in my own home, than you ever did. Dad, if you want to have a relationship with me, you need to start accepting my choices, even if you don't agree with them. Or at the very least, stop trying to control me."

Sameera looked at her mother. Tahsin's guilt over these words, which so closely mirrored Sameera's own, was writ large on her face.

Rob's face crumpled. Naveed stepped toward him, and Barb laid a comforting arm across his shoulder, but he shrugged them both off. "I know I haven't been a good father to you," he said to Tom, and his voice cracked. "After Pam died, I was lost for a long time. I know you suffered. I regret the way I behaved, and I'm trying to be better."

Tom looked pointedly at Andy and raised an eyebrow.

"Being better is an ongoing process," Rob allowed.

For his part, Andy watched this confrontation with a look of confusion. "Wait a minute. Are you going to sell Cooke Place to me, Rob?"

Rob shook his head. "Never going to happen, son."

Andy drew himself up. "Then you'll be hearing from my lawyers for breach of verbal contract. Also because I have a lot of money, and you hurt my feelings." They all stared at him, aghast, and he grinned. "Just kidding. But this was not cool, Rob. Why didn't you just call your son and lay a big guilt trip, the way my mom does? It works a treat, I promise."

"Why did you try to extort Sameera to convince me to sell?" Tom countered, and Andy's grin momentarily dimmed.

"You got me," he acknowledged, turning to Sameera. "No hard feelings?"

"Plenty of them, actually," she said.

Andy nodded. "That's fair." He turned to the assembled group, charm firmly back in place. "Maliks, Cookes, it's been an absolute pleasure. Let's do this again next year."

Tom sighed. "I'll walk you to your plane, Andy."

Andy shrugged. "I'd say you'll live to regret this, but I'm bored playing the Wolf Run villain. I've got an investor meeting tomorrow, and I need to think of some way to hold them off until you all come to your senses." He winked at Nadiya, made a *call me* gesture, and stood to go.

Sameera, Tom, Esa, and Nadiya rose from their seats in an unspoken pact not to let Andy out of their sight until he was out of Wolf Run airspace. Fortunately, he hadn't brought much with him.

"I've learned to pack light during negotiations. My plane can accommodate a second passenger. What do you say, gorgeous?" He waggled his brows at Nadiya.

Her sister invited Andy to commit a solo profane act, but Sameera noticed the ghost of a smile on her face. Nadiya found Andy mildly amusing after all.

"I wouldn't mind a ride," Esa said, but they all ignored him, pulling on boots and jackets and trooping outside.

"You'll never find someone as interesting or as rich as me, you know," Andy said, slowing his long strides to match Nadiya's. "Just think of all the attention and money you'll get if you go on a few dates with me. Endorsement deals, free stuff, it could all be yours."

Esa turned to his sister. "Maybe you should reconsider. I like free stuff!"

Nadiya's voice was dry. "You don't hear 'no' a lot, do you?"

"All the time, actually. I consider it an opening gambit." Andy's cheerful attitude really was irrepressible. Even now, Sameera was having a hard time disliking him. Though she planned to try really, really hard.

Andy chucked his bag inside the plane before turning to face them. "I'll admit this was more fun than I anticipated," he said, rubbing his hands together. "I thought I'd have a quiet Christmas at Wolf Run. Eat turkey. Buy your house. This was way better. Nothing like a challenge to get the blood pumping."

"There is no challenge. You lost, Andy. Let it go," Tom said.

"Never." Andy grinned at his friend. He held his arm out for a hug, but Tom shook his head.

"It's going to take me some time to get over this, Andy. You really tried to screw me over," Tom said.

A flicker of concern and something that looked like regret passed over Andy's face. "Would you believe me if I told you I honestly didn't think you'd care that much?"

Tom stared at him, and Andy ducked his head. "Maybe part of me wanted to have a bit of your magic, a piece of what made you special. I always had to work ten times harder at everything, while you swanned through life. You're even going to get the girl," he said, nodding at Sameera. "If anything, I'm the one who should hate you, but I just can't. I love you, brother."

Tom sighed. "I love you, too. I just need some time to figure out how I can move past this."

Andy looked more somber at these words than Sameera had ever seen him. He turned to her. "Take care of my brother. He's the best guy I know. Don't break his heart, okay?"

He held his arms out to Nadiya for a hug, but she shook her head. He held out a hand instead, and she cautiously shook it. "I knew I'd wear you down eventually. A handshake today, and who knows where we'll end up?"

With a final wink for Esa, Andy climbed aboard his propellor plane. They moved back as he started it up, and watched as he expertly took off. They stood watching for a long time, until the plane was a tiny speck in the clear blue sky.

Beside Sameera, Esa furrowed his brows. "Do you hear what I hear?" he asked. And then they could hear it, too.

Sleigh bells.

Chapter Twenty-Eight

They followed the distinct tinkle of sleigh bells to the front of the house.

"You see Santa, too, right?" Esa asked Sameera. When she nodded, he sighed in relief. "Oh, good. I thought I was hallucinating."

Santa was perched on a red sleigh, dressed in a fur-lined red Santa suit, complete with black boots, a black and gold buckle, and a jaunty red hat. Mrs. Claus was by his side, surrounded by six elves, all arranged on a sled pulled by a train of sled dogs. Atlas joyfully loped up in greeting, as if they were long-lost family.

Abu Isra waved at them from the sled. "Merry Christmas surprise!" he boomed. Dressed in the red suit, his resemblance to Saint Nick was even more striking, and Sameera was grinning so hard, her cheeks hurt.

The rest of the party assembled outside. "Why is Abu Isra dressed in a Santa outfit?" Tahsin asked.

"Because it's fun, Mom," Nadiya said. "Get into the holiday spirit!" Beside Sameera, Esa filmed the whole thing; it would appear on his YouTube channel before the end of the day, she was sure.

"We wanted to prank you back! All the children in town keep asking if I'm Santa. We thought this would be a fun trick," Abu Isra said in his big, booming voice. "We brought you some more baklava and gifts."

Sameera laughed and accepted a pretty green box of the flaky dessert before climbing aboard the sleigh to hug Mrs. Claus, a.k.a. Hiba.

"I don't care what my dad says. This is the best holiday!" Esa said, digging into his box of baklava. Naveed scoffed, but Rob beamed.

Esa continued, "Coming to Alaska helped me get out of my head. It felt good to spend time with my sisters, to hang out with my parents, and to meet new people. Plus, Wolf Run is a special place—it's small and perfect, in its own unique way." His tone was serious now, more than it had been during the entire trip. "To be honest, I've been feeling pretty down lately. My entire family are geniuses. My mom knows how to tame hundreds of teenagers. My dad is a neurosurgeon and a professor, too. My older sister is trying to save the world, and Sameera is the best and only lawyer I know. Meanwhile, what have I accomplished?"

Sameera looked at her sister. Silently, they flanked their little brother, putting their arms around his slim waist. He nodded at them, acknowledging their support, and Sameera was glad to be here, beside her brother, surrounded by everyone she loved best in the world.

Esa turned to Rob. "I think what you tried to do to Tom was a master class in manipulation, but I'm also really glad you weren't serious about selling to Andy. He would have wiped out the soul of this place, and Wolf Run needs to be protected. My time here helped me realize I'm a genius, too, in my own way," Esa said, smiling. "Thanks to Tom's advice, my YouTube channel is starting to take off, and I've finally realized that while I might not be able to save the world, like my sisters, I can make them laugh. So, thank you."

He beamed, and Tahsin and Naveed hugged their son. Sameera felt her heart grow in her chest. She was so proud of Esa, so proud of the man he was becoming. This trip had been magical in so many ways—but getting to know her brother again, as he teetered on the brink between child and adult, might have been the highlight. She nearly choked up again while she hugged him, but stopped herself in time—she had promised Esa no more tears, even if they were happy ones.

The expanded party trooped back into the house, happily chatting, the drama over breakfast not forgotten but set aside for now. Sameera watched as Rob put an arm on Tom's shoulder, and pulled him back to say a few words. They looked so much alike, she thought—they shared the same blond hair and dark brows, the same jawline, but where Rob's features were more severe, there was something boyish and innocent about Tom. He looked up and caught her gaze.

There had been an irresistible attraction between them from the start, but the past four days, spending time together in such an intimate setting, had only deepened that bond. Except she saw something else on his face now—a sadness that made her heart clench. They drifted toward each other while everyone else moved to the sitting room.

"Sameera," Tom started, but she shook her head.

"It's okay," she said. "Whatever you want to do, I understand. We only just met."

Tom's shoulders fell. "I was so invested in my anger and resentment, it was easier to focus on that instead of the reality. Dad and Barb are getting older. I mean, I knew they were, but it's different when you see it, right?"

"In your defense, there's plenty to be angry and resentful about," Sameera said, earning a weak smile from Tom.

"That's not the kind of person I want to be anymore. You made me realize that I could be different," he said, and she felt a flare of something that felt a lot like the first glimmer of love's spark. "I've watched you grapple with your own feelings of anger, love, and hurt with your family, and move through them, reaching for better. You're a wonder, Sameera Ayla Malik."

"Don't blame me for your change of heart," she said, trying not to cry.

Tom gripped her. "My heart is unchanged. You still have me completely enthralled." He took a deep, juddering breath. "Rain check on that dinner?"

Her hand was intertwined with his. "I know you're good for it," she said, trying to smile.

The look of relief on his face made her feel slightly better. "How long do you plan to stay in Wolf Run?" she asked, because that's what Tom was trying to tell her. He wouldn't be leaving for Atlanta in the new year.

Tom shrugged. "Maybe a month, maybe more. I want to spend time with my dad, Barb, and Cal. We need to talk about what we're going to do with the property, without feeling resentful and angry."

There was a new set to his shoulders, now that he had made the hard decision, and if possible, Sameera felt herself falling even harder for Tom. "You're doing the right thing. I know it won't be easy. I'm proud of you, Tom Cooke."

"I should thank Andy for forcing the conversation, really," he said.

"Let's not give him that much credit," she said, laughing.

"Esa is right—if Andy had his way, he would only exploit everything and everyone; he wouldn't be able to help it, not with the type of massive resort he was planning. I'll stay and help them figure out what's next, and the best thing to do with Cooke Place," Tom said. "Maybe Calvin will want to come back after college. But I won't force him. Trying to make me fill his shoes is what nearly destroyed my relationship with Rob. If Cal wants to live here, I'll help. If not, we'll figure something out."

He looked into her eyes, searching for something. "I wish we'd met sooner," he said.

Sameera's throat felt tight. "We met at exactly the right time," she told him. "I've heard good things about Zoom."

Tom laughed. "With the crazy hours we both work, it would have been hard to stay in touch when we lived in the same city. I won't ask you to wait for me."

"You could ask," Sameera said, but Tom shook his head.

"These last four days with the Malik family . . . It's made me realize how much I missed out on that part of my life, on my own family. I want to build something good, with Rob, Barb, and Cal." He pulled her toward him, until Sameera was cradled in his arms, his clean scent enveloping her. "And with you. I'll always be grateful to you for making me realize what I was missing."

"What will you do while you're in Wolf Run?" she asked, her voice muffled against his hard chest.

"I hear Hilda is hiring," Tom said, but her laugh was muted. She was trying hard not to cry. He pulled back to look into her face, searching for something. "I'll work on my recipes. I'll make more videos, though they won't be as good without you."

"What about the TV hosting gig?" she asked.

Tom shrugged. "I know they wanted to start filming in the new year. Either they'll wait for me, or they won't. I'll be fine no matter what. I know that now. The first person I'll call when I'm back in Atlanta will be you."

"I'll pick up that call," she said, and it was a promise. They returned to the sitting room, hand in hand, to make the most of their first, and likely last, Christmas morning together.

Tom's and Sameera's families were waiting for them; it was finally time to exchange presents.

Tahsin volunteered to start—she loved to give gifts, and she watched Barb's face when she opened the parcel she had wrapped carefully last night. Their host's polite smile transformed to one of real delight when she pulled the embroidered shawl from the box.

"I saw the way you admired our Christmas tree, with its vibrant dopatta and Indian jewelry," Tahsin said. "I remembered that I brought another shawl with me. It used to belong to my mother. She bought it when she visited Kashmir."

Barb hugged Tahsin tightly. "I will treasure this. Thank you for brightening our holiday celebration this year."

Naveed gifted Rob a ceramic mug with a large eggplant painted on it. "To remind you of your favorite dish," he said proudly. "The girl at the Christmas market said it was her top seller, though usually women buy it." Esa stifled a laugh, and Sameera nudged him.

Rob gave Esa one of his old cameras, with a few rolls of film and a promise to teach him how to take pictures old-school.

Then Rob presented Tom with a box that contained his mother's old recipe book. "Found it when we were clearing out the attic. I thought you might like to experiment. She would have loved seeing you in the kitchen." Tom was touched, and the men hugged. They were both a bit stiff and awkward, but Sameera knew they would get better with practice.

Esa gave everyone their own novelty pranks, purchased from a shop on Main Street. There was a trick-card pack for Naveed, a splashing flower boutonniere for Tahsin, an animatronic fish for Rob, a can of jelly beans that exploded with springing toy snakes when opened for Tom, and a whoopee cushion for Barb, because you could never go wrong with a classic. For each of his sisters, he had bought silk endless handkerchiefs.

Sameera had bought handcrafted chocolates for their hosts, and an embroidered apron for Tom she had picked up from a specialty store on Main Street. "I didn't have time for anything fancy," she explained when he opened the box. The apron had *Chai King* embroidered across the front, and she showed him her matching one with *Chai Queen*. He was delighted.

He brought his own gift out shyly, handing her a tiny box. Her eyes flew to his.

"It's not a ring," he said with a smile. "But it did belong to my mother."

Sameera opened the box and gasped. Inside was a beautifully handcrafted silver snowflake locket. She traced the crystals along the edge. It was delicate and pretty, and she was instantly in love.

"Something to remember me by," Tom said softly. Around them, their family was quiet, watching the moment unfold.

"You're hard to forget," Sameera said, and she kissed his cheek in thanks. Her parents glanced at each other as Sameera carefully pocketed the jewelry box and started to pick up wrapping paper from the floor.

"See? I told you they weren't faking it," Barb murmured to Rob. Everyone looked at each other and started to laugh.

"Our flight leaves in a few hours. We need to pack," Sameera announced.

The Malik family's brush with Christmas was finally coming to an end.

Chapter Twenty-Nine

Their procession back to the airport was a reversal of their journey to Cooke Place only a few days earlier. Sameera turned around to watch the big house disappear behind her before settling beside Tom. His hand was warm in hers, and he squeezed it, once.

When she checked her phone, she saw that Bee had left several text messages.

What is happening up there?

Girl, are you leaving me on read??

I'll pull some favors at work. We can still salvage this!

Just let me know you're okay.

Sameera texted back that she was fine, and promised a long phone call when she landed. Bee responded with a heart emoji. She settled back in her seat and tried to banish her sadness. Sameera knew that even if she never returned to Wolf Run and never saw Barb, Rob, or Calvin again, she would never forget this trip. She felt fundamentally changed by the journey, with a clearer sense of who she was and what she wanted: a closer, more open relationship with her family; the ability to open her heart to new experiences and possibilities... and Tom. She squeezed his hand back.

"You'll text me when you land?" Tom asked, his voice low and intimate in her ear. "And answer the dozen texts I send every day?"

"I'll respond to one in four," she teased.

"I miss you already," he said quietly.

Their mothers were silent in the driver and passenger seats, but she spotted them exchanging indulgent smiles. *We're not together,* she wanted to remind them. *Long-distance never works. Not for two workaholics like Tom and me.*

Except Barb and Rob had started off long-distance, too, Sameera remembered. But Barb had moved to Wolf Run, which Sameera couldn't do. Her life, her family, her job—for now, at least—were all in Atlanta.

At the airport, the Maliks and the Cookes hugged and exchanged promises to stay in touch. At Tahsin's side, Naveed cleared his throat. "We have a confession of our own to make," he said, glancing at his wife.

Esa gasped. "Your marriage is a sham, too? A long con to inherit a castle in Hyderabad?"

Tahsin tsked at Esa. "Don't be silly, *beta*. Your father and I might have started out that way, but we decided to stay together after year three."

Everyone paused to look at her, and Tom laughed. Sameera followed a beat later—her mother had made a joke, and it was actually funny.

"The truth is, we agreed to come to Alaska with our daughter not simply to help her but also to protect her. We were unsure what she was getting herself into," Tahsin said.

Naveed turned to Rob. "I am sorry to have deceived you all. The truth is, we have never, not once, celebrated Christmas. I'm sure you could not tell, but I wanted to be honest."

Rob cleared his throat and, with a glance at his wife, accepted Naveed's apology. "Quite all right. The chocolate cross might have given you away, delicious though it was."

"Perhaps you can visit us in Atlanta sometime," Tahsin offered. "We celebrate Eid again in the fall."

"The hungry one or the other one?" Tom asked with a smile for Sameera, a callback to their first conversation. Had it really been less than two weeks ago?

"The hungry one," Tahsin answered, confusion on her face. "Eid al-Fitr marks the end of Ramadan. We would love to host you all."

"I'll be sure to bring a chocolate-covered star and crescent," Rob said. And then there was nothing more to do but walk toward the security line. The family group moved ahead of Tom and Sameera, giving them a chance to say a private goodbye.

"You've got everything you need?" Tom asked, his voice gruff. He was playing with the edge of her sweater.

No, she resisted the urge to say. *Because I don't have you. Because you didn't ask me to wait for you.* The moment heated as their eyes locked, but Tom didn't make a move, and she had a flight to catch, a job and a life to return to. Sameera turned to go.

"Wait," Tom said.

"Yes?"

He stared at her as if memorizing every atom on her face. "Have a safe trip."

With a tight nod, she returned to her family. At the security gate, Esa stopped abruptly, brow furrowed. "I forgot something!" he announced.

Sameera tugged on his arm. "It's too late, buddy. We've got a plane to catch."

Esa didn't budge. "I really need to go back for this one thing," he said.

"*Beta*, we will miss our flight," Naveed said gently. "Whatever it is you forgot, we can ask Rob to mail it, okay?"

Esa shook his head, his mouth in a mutinous, stubborn line. "It's not something you can mail. We can drive back and return in time for the flight. You know Mom always lies about the departure time so we're five hours early."

They all looked at Tahsin, who shrugged. "If I told you when our flights really left, we would always be late."

Back at the house, Esa jumped out of the truck and ran inside. Mystified, Sameera and Nadiya hurried to catch up.

Inside, Esa handed the Elf on a Shelf to Calvin, who had stayed home. "This is for you," Esa said. "Keep our Christmas pranking tradition alive, all right?"

Calvin nodded, and the boys solemnly dapped each other.

"This is what you forgot?" Tahsin asked, exasperated, but Esa shook his head.

"Nope. I forgot this," he said, and walked over to Atlas. Reaching down, he hugged the big dog, who only yawned in response, displaying all her teeth. Esa stood up. "Okay, now we can go."

Shaking her head, Tahsin turned to apologize to Rob, only to find him deep in conversation with her husband.

"Actually, Tahsin, maybe we can stay a bit longer," Naveed said, looking at his wife. Sameera recognized the gleam in his eyes. He got the same expression on his face when he unboxed a new Gundam robot. "Rob and I might have a solution to both of our problems."

Sameera, Nadiya, and Tom exchanged baffled glances, but judging from the smug look on Esa's face, he had some inkling of what was going on.

"Spill it, squirt," Sameera said, but her brother only danced away.

"I suggest you all get comfortable. I have a feeling we're not going anywhere today. It's a Christmas miracle!" Esa proclaimed.

"Not our holiday," Nadiya reminded him.

Tahsin and Barb had joined the discussion by now, leaving the younger set to watch their parents, perplexed.

"What could they possibly be talking about *now*?" Sameera asked. Her sister was surprisingly nonchalant about the delay. She plopped down into the armchair Andy had favored and shrugged out of her jacket.

"Dad and Rob were talking on the way to the airport about a business thing," she said. "They were going to talk more over the phone, but I guess now is as good a time as ever."

Sameera traded an exasperated glance with Tom, but he seemed thoughtful. "Coffee?" he suggested, and they retired to the kitchen, where Tom did something complicated with the espresso machine, his back to her.

"If we leave in the next twenty minutes, we should be okay," Sameera started, cutting the tension between them. Her heart started to beat fast, as it tended to do whenever they were alone together. "Don't worry, you won't have to put up with my family—or me—for another night." Her laugh sounded artificial to her own ears, and when Tom turned to look at her, his face was set.

"I want to put up with you," he said, biting off the words as if they were painful. "I could barely manage to say goodbye at the airport. I don't know if I can let you go a second time."

Sameera stared at him. "But you didn't even hug me goodbye!" she protested.

Tom's hands were fists at his sides. Now he crowded her against the kitchen island. He leaned close, eyes dark with hunger. "I didn't want to hug you," he growled. "I knew if I touched you, there was no way you were getting on that plane, Sameera Malik."

This kiss wasn't chaste, or tender, or a friendly brush of his lips against hers. His kiss said *I want you* and *I need you* and *don't go*, all at once, the force of his passion making her lean back against the countertop, until she regained her senses and pushed back.

"You didn't even ask me to *stay*," she said accusingly, one finger poking into his chest. He pulled her roughly to him again.

"You have a life in Atlanta," he gasped when they finally came up for air. "I didn't want to make this harder on you."

A deep sense of contentment filled her, and she nudged him with her hips, still firmly held against his. "I think you're hard enough," she teased.

"I didn't want you to feel obliged, like you owed me anything," he started again. "I can't make any promises because I don't know how long I'll be here. But if—"

"When," Sameera corrected him, kissing him softly once. "*When* you return, and after you make me a batch of samosas, and after you've kissed me senseless."

His chuckle was warm caramel along her spine, and his arms tightened around her waist. "After all that," he agreed. "Then what?"

"Then we figure it out together," Sameera said. "I'm not going anywhere. Are you?"

He shook his head, and they kissed some more before making coffee for everyone. Their parents were still in deep discussion, but her sister quirked an eyebrow at Sameera before indicating that Tom had something on his cheek.

"That shade of pink looks good on you," she joked, and Tom swiped Sameera's lipstick from his face without a trace of embarrassment.

"Get used to it," he said, handing out the coffee.

Naveed waited until everyone had taken a seat before speaking. "Rob and I didn't want to say anything before, until we had a chance to really talk. Esa provided a reason to keep our conversation going."

"Conversation about what?" Sameera asked. Tom sat beside her, and beneath the table, his hand gripped her knee in a familiar gesture, as if it belonged there.

"I've been retired for over two years," Naveed started. "And your mother joined me last year. We've taken cruises and fixed up the house, and I've built a dozen Gundam robots."

Sameera exchanged a baffled glance with Nadiya. They knew all this. What was her father getting at?

"I'm bored," Naveed announced. "I've been bored silly for about six months." He glanced at his wife, and Tahsin nodded. "What we both need is a new adventure. Something different. Something exciting. Something like starting a business, right here in Wolf Run."

Sameera gaped at her father. What was he talking about? It was true Naveed had been at loose ends lately, but this sounded as if he'd been looking for something new.

"Your father and I are going into business together," Rob announced. "Andy had the right idea, you know. Wolf Run needs a shot of new life, but not a massive transformation. Between the two of us, we have the contacts, cash, and interest to turn this place into a ski resort. A small one," he hastened to add.

"Exclusive," Tahsin chimed in. "Aimed at retirees, families, people looking for a bit of skiing in a quaint small town. Wolf Run is perfect."

This time Sameera's confusion was shared by her sister. "But you don't even ski. Are you moving to Alaska?"

Naveed shook his head, then, thinking it over, shrugged. "Not at first, no. But your mother and I will be spending a lot of time here to help get the business up and running." He glanced between Sameera and Tom, who had grown still beside her. "Now you and Tom will both have a reason to return."

Sameera turned to look at Tom, and the happiness she saw in his eyes made her answer easy. "We can't wait," she said.

Epilogue

Ten months later

"This is the hungry one, right?" Tom asked Sameera as they parked their car in her parents' driveway. She shook her head at her fiancé in fond bemusement. After ten months together, he still thought that joke was funny, even after fasting with her a couple of times this past Ramadan. Sameera was still not an observant Muslim, but she found the practice of fasting meditative, and she had decided to participate this year for a few days. It also made her mother happy, which she suspected was Tom's real motivation to "starve himself and not even drink water," as he put it.

Sameera shifted the platter of samosas to her other hand and reached for the pile of Eid gifts. Tom scooped them from her easily.

"Do you think Esa will like what we got him?" he asked, mischief shining in his eyes.

They had bought him a vintage elf doll, in honor of her little brother's successful YouTube show, where he helped young children use their traditions and culture to prank their families. Sameera played the clip of the desi family biting into the samosas turned fortune cookie segment a half dozen times, and still cracked up at the confused expression on the parents' faces when they pulled a curled-up fortune from their South Asian pastries.

"He'll love it, but not as much as Nadiya will love her gift," Sameera said. After much discussion, they had decided to send her sister on a spa vacation—one where she had to stay silent for a week and endure an entire catalog's worth of massages, mud baths, manicures, pedicures, and facials. She would hate every second but come back feeling better. Her sister had been working hard, finishing her thesis and volunteering with various UK charities; she deserved a break.

Rob flung open the door before they got halfway up the driveway. He looked happy, his lined face lighter. Things still weren't perfect between him and Tom, but they were both working on the relationship. It helped that Naveed and Tahsin's enthusiasm for their joint project provided a good distraction, plus a reliably safe topic of conversation.

The parents were clear that they wanted to design and set up their business according to their very specific demographic, though thankfully, they soon realized that building an entire ski resort was too ambitious. Instead, they had settled on a multipronged approach. Step one was to work with the Wolf Run Business Association to set up the town as a holiday destination. The ski run they had envisioned was now a few smaller hills and three bed-and-breakfasts. Each one was already booked for the season, in addition to Cooke Place. At Barb's urging, they had decided to turn the house into an inn. Starting the operation had taken Naveed's full attention; his Gundam robots had been sadly neglected, but Sameera couldn't remember when she had seen her father happier.

Naturally, Tahsin's superior organizational abilities had proven invaluable in this endeavor. In addition to setting up the inn and strategizing for the eventual ski resort, Tahsin had become an expert on local politics, Wolf Run vendettas, rumors, and alliances. It wasn't much different from running a school, she explained to a bemused Tom and Sameera over FaceTime—except schoolchildren were better behaved.

Sameera hefted her tray, which she had refused to relinquish to Tom. She was too protective over its contents, and she couldn't wait to see her family's reaction when they sampled her first *edible* batch of samosas. Traditional fillings only, this time—peas and potatoes in half, the other filled with savory meat.

Rob embraced both Tom and Sameera at the door before leading the way to the kitchen, where her mother stood watch over various pots. Bee and Lorenzo sat at the table, folding linen napkins. Her friend immediately gave her a hug, and Lorenzo and Tom smiled and shook hands. They were on their way to becoming fast friends, as per Bee's and Sameera's instructions.

"Did you invite the entire neighborhood?" Sameera asked, putting her tray down. Tom was already peering inside pots with interest. He had been on the phone with Tahsin every day for the past week, putting together this Eid lunch menu, and he seemed satisfied with the result.

"Don't be silly, Sameera *beta*, this will barely be enough for our family," Tahsin said. Her mother still seemed harried, moving a mile a minute, but she was glowing. Running a business suited her.

Sameera greeted Barb, Esa, and Calvin, who were chatting in the living room, before going in search of her father. She found Naveed in the basement, surrounded by his LEGO bricks and Gundam models and looking a little forlorn.

"Eid Mubarak, Dad," she said as he leaned into the hug.

"Eid Mubarak, *beta*," he said, turning around. "Is Tom here?"

"He's inspecting lunch," she confirmed with a smile. She had been doing a lot of smiling lately. It had been a good year.

When she had returned to work in the new year, it was to surprising news: Andy Shaikh had gotten in touch with her firm to inquire about representation and had insisted on working exclusively with Sameera. The email he sent to her personal account wasn't quite an apology for his behavior, but with the rates he was paying, it didn't have to be. Even Blake had started to treat her with respect, knocking on her office door at least once before barging inside. The senior partners had offered their congratulations, and there was talk of a promotion in her future, though she wasn't sure she would take it. Maybe she'd branch out on her own. Sameera was considering her next move, now that her finances were more settled and her relationship with her family more stable. It felt good to have options.

Life was good. Except her father looked sad, and the glow faded a bit.

"What's wrong, Dad?" she asked. "Did you and Rob get into another argument about the decor? You know, turning the foyer of Cooke Place into a memorial for your favorite Persian poet will only confuse your guests."

Naveed only shook his head, smiling bravely. "It's not that, *beta*. Though I still think having a theme is important. And who doesn't love Hafez?"

Sameera smiled and made a mental note to have some of Hafez's beautiful poetry framed for her father as a gift for his birthday.

"What's the problem?" she asked.

Naveed shook his head, brushing a tear from his eye. "I was thinking about the last Eid party we had. Remember? Things have changed so much."

She took a seat on a stool beside him. Her father had set up a hobby room in this corner of the basement, and though it hadn't been used much in the past six months, it was still decorated with his models, tools, and a tower of board games.

"For the better," she said firmly. Thinking of where she was only a few years ago—broke, brokenhearted, estranged from her family, her obstacles seemingly unsurmountable—now filled her with a strange nostalgia. She didn't want to go backward, but thinking of the past made her appreciate where she was now. There would be challenges in the future, of course. No life was ever stable or peaceful for long. But she was happy for now, surrounded by her favorite people in the world.

Which included Tom. He had stayed back in Wolf Run as promised, and the first few months of their relationship had been long-distance, which had worked surprisingly well. They communicated over phone and text as often as they could, and she didn't feel guilty when she had to work late or on weekends. Similarly, he was able to focus on helping

Rob and Barb clean out the house, make more videos, and tinker with his mother's recipes. After three months, he surprised her with a visit and some news: He was back for good, and his agent was in active negotiations with a few different outlets for a cooking show. Now that the legal contract had been drawn up, with Naveed and Tahsin eager to start on their new joint project with their new Alaskan "family," Rob had told him his presence was no longer required.

"He said he was tired of seeing my sad face, and that I should go back to Atlanta and kiss my girlfriend already," Tom had said, laughing, and proceeded to do just that.

"Is that all I am?" Sameera had teased. She was joking, but Tom got a funny look on his face at her words, and took a step back.

"It's fine, really," she assured him.

Except he was already on one knee.

"Sameera, I know we got started in an unconventional way and that it hasn't been that long since we met. We're so different, but when I look at you, when I hear your voice, when I hold your hand, I know I have never felt more like myself than when I'm with you. I love everything about you—your kindness, generosity, loyalty, and I really love that you're smarter than me."

Sameera choked back a sob-laugh at this.

"If you need time, I'll wait. If you can only give me some of your heart, I'll take it. I'm not going anywhere, ever again. Will you marry me?"

Her resounding "Yes!" had startled an inquisitive squirrel on the porch. Then Sameera had dragged Tom inside her condo to celebrate more thoroughly, and in private.

Her parents were happy for her, though Nadiya had made it clear she thought they were moving too fast. Esa gave her a virtual high five and then decided to do a series on the best way to prank a wedding, which was concerning.

Now she looked at her father with an indulgent smile. "The wedding isn't until the summer," she assured him. "I thought you couldn't wait for us to get married."

"Your mother is the one who wants you all settled," Naveed corrected. "I have been secretly dreading the day." He stood and gave his latest unfinished model a pat on its red robot head.

They walked up the stairs together, where Tom was putting the finishing touches on setting the table. Their family and friends took their seats, plates piled high with every Eid staple: A platter of biryani shared space with three different types of curries, two of them made by Tom, and half a dozen desserts, including sheer khorma, a creamy pudding made with vermicelli and plenty of nuts. Sameera's samosas took pride of place at the center, and she noted that Tom had helped himself to three already. Even Tahsin said they were passable.

A wave of happiness and contentment washed over her as she sat surveying the table. She was surrounded by her people, the ones she had lost and then found, the ones she had stumbled upon and now knew to keep close, the people she loved most in the world.

The doorbell rang. "I thought you said this party was just family," Nadiya said, shooting her mother a suspicious glance.

"It is only family. And maybe someone who might one day become family," Tahsin said innocently. "Why don't you greet your guest, Nadiya, *beta*?"

Her sister jumped up, scowling, and Tom leaned over to his soon-to-be bride.

"Did your mom invite Andy Shaikh to Eid lunch?"

Sameera smiled into his warm blue eyes. "When her first attempt at matchmaking worked out so well, she decided meddling works."

When a scowling Nadiya returned to the table trailed by Andy Shaikh, the table erupted into greetings, arguments, recriminations, and teasing. Sameera caught Tom's glance, and they smiled at each other. She knew what he was thinking: If this was the sort of fireworks he could expect at Eid, he couldn't wait for next Christmas. Neither could she.

Acknowledgments

Bismillah. I truly believe that every book is a work of alchemical magic, made possible through the hard work, brilliance, and sheer will of dozens of people. I'd like to start off by thanking my amazing agent, Laura Gross, for championing this idea from the start. Thanks also to my wonderful and very patient editor, Laura Van Der Veer, for taking a chance on me, as well as Tiffany Martin for helping me realize my vision for this book. Thanks also to Emma Reh for production, Rachel and Valerie for their skillful copyedits, and Bill for his exceptional proofreading and suggestions. Thanks to Kimberly Glyder (cover designer), Rachael Clark (marketing manager), Tree Abraham (art director), and the entire Mindy's Book Studio team. Shout-out to Mindy Kaling for your support and cheerleading!

Thanks also to Nooshin in Atlanta and Nafisah in Toronto for answering all my lawyer questions. And a big thank-you to Yusuf Gad for one very memorable conversation during a Ramadan iftar party a few years ago, which ignited the idea for this story in the first place.

As ever, all the flowers to my entire extended family. I am so very grateful that you have all the quirky warmth of the Maliks but only a fraction of their drama!

Yours for the Season is a bit different from my other books, as it centers on a young woman who grew up Muslim but is no longer observant, despite being part of a practicing family. The tension that can result from differing approaches to faith and spiritual practice was my initial inspiration. As much as this book is a fun and funny rom-com, it also tackles the reality of changing family relationships, which are rarely static. Despite being an observant Muslim all my life, I know many people who have struggled with their faith, or whose relationship with their spirituality has evolved over time. Yet this dynamic is so often displayed in simplistic ways that never felt authentic to me. Faith and spirituality exist on a spectrum; family relationships can be complicated as children grow into adults and forge their own way. Yet despite it all, *Yours for the Season* remains optimistic and hopeful: Sameera and her parents never give up on each other, and their mutual love and care provide the motivation to forge a new, even stronger bond. I hope their journey sparks a few interesting conversations, too!

Finally, as always, thank YOU, dear reader. I hope you enjoyed reading about Sameera and Tom and their respective family and friends as much as I enjoyed writing their story. Until next time!

About the Author

Photo © 2019 Andrea Stenson

Uzma Jalaluddin is the critically acclaimed and internationally bestselling author of *Detective Aunty, Much Ado About Nada, Ayesha at Last,* and *Hana Khan Carries On*. Uzma is a former contributor at the *Toronto Star* and has also written for *The Atlantic*. She lives outside Toronto, Canada, with her husband and children. For more information, visit www.uzmajalaluddin.com.